THE WILDERNESS SINGERS

A SHORT NOVEL AND STORIES

JOHN ZEPF

iUniverse, Inc.
New York   Bloomington

The Wilderness Singers

iUniverse books may be ordered through booksellers or by contacting:

iUniverse
1663 Liberty Drive
Bloomington, IN 47403
www.iuniverse.com
1-800-Authors (1-800-288-4677)

Because of the dynamic nature of the Internet, any Web addresses or links contained in this book may have changed since publication and may no longer be valid. The views expressed in this work are solely those of the author and do not necessarily reflect the views of the publisher, and the publisher hereby disclaims any responsibility for them.

ISBN: 978-1-4401-3337-4 (pbk)
ISBN: 978-1-4401-3354-1 (ebk)

Printed in the United States of America

iUniverse rev. date: 3/24/2009

Contents

LOOKING BACK

Years ago, when I still cared about such things, I attended a creative writers' workshop in rural Maine. It was to last for a week, an immersion experience with an instructor who I knew from the city. Some of the participants I knew slightly from classes, and others I knew not at all. I suppose I thought that if I improved my mechanics slightly, and could learn to write just a little more clearly, I might yet make my entry on the literary scene. In retrospect, I think that the prohibiting factors were not mechanics, or clarity, but more a fundamental difference in values. I had written the stories that I wanted to, but they rarely seemed to ring a bell with editors. I could not convince the cultural establishment that they were important and worthy stories. It's hard to say why, from this vantage. It might have been that my writings had a certain heaviness, a quaintly formal approach, where a light and playful tone was wanted. My writings may have had a noticeable sincerity about them, even over-earnestness, and perhaps these are qualities which cause confusion today. And I think too that from early on, many restless and stray Ideas had somehow crept into my writings, and urged insistently to be heard. Also rather prominent were irony and satire, which in our world today must resemble a couple of underemployed entertainers, who no one can remember seeing around lately.

I knew less about the world then. I didn't understand about the odds of getting original ideas heard, then. I was a younger man in that long-ago summer, and still held on to some ideals. But do you know, even if all you ever experience is rejection by the establishment, you should have no regrets if you created for the right reasons - because you wanted to tell a story that was burned into your heart, so to speak. If you created for the right reasons, and were blessed with a little talent, then it doesn't matter what other people do or say, because you created a world of your own design. And having created a world, with all of the matter and air and space that you can impart to it, certainly it rankles if your work provokes no intelligible response among strangers; but we should not feel any regrets for having tried. It may be that

1

the establishment is only looking for the wrong things, and if so, that is the public's loss.

In that far-off time that I'm writing about, I suppose I thought that I would always want to write. I don't mean that I ever thought it likely, not in any rational moments, that I could earn a living by writing. I already had a career, anyway. But there were stories that I wanted to tell, that were important to me, and that I thought might be interesting to other people. I knew the exhilaration of writing. When the scenes that you imagined were so vivid before you, that you felt you left your surroundings and were living a sort of parallel life, amid the characters and the surroundings of your story - you felt blessed at those times. If you have not experienced this feeling then it is not to be imagined.

I was experiencing, too, the critical rejections that came with trying to reach a public. The one feeling was heaven, the other a hell. Sending out manuscripts felt exactly as if your best efforts were being dropped into a still and silent pond. Or perhaps one feels like the determined radio-astronomer who, in his search for "intelligent life," sends his messages into deep space, and hopes that it is not all gas and rubble out there, as it seems. You got back, usually, a form letter. It has to make you feel somewhat alienated, when something so important to you meets with indifference. And what a degree of nonsense, meanwhile, was being put before the public every day - not only in literature, but in films, music, and so on? The vast majority of it was drivel. To reach a public, one had to negotiate that fetid swamp that is America's popular culture. That is not fun, surely. Ultimately, I would have to concede that continuing to send out manuscripts to the country's editors was just putting more pearls before - well, whatever that expression is.

But I persisted. For awhile, I enjoyed the process - at least, the writing part. Then, for a week during that summer, as I say, I lived at that house above the rocky coast in Maine. We would devote our time to writing and presenting material and offering critiques. And I must say that the experience had a really salutary effect, for it accomplished something that all the previous years of exhilaration and rejection could not. I mean to say that I was cured of my sinister urge.

Since I was a child in school, I found something irresistible about the world of literature. The best stories represented a marvelous place that your mind could go to. Who doesn't need an escape from their reality sometimes? I certainly did. One day I picked up <u>Robinson Crusoe</u> - I was knocked out. <u>Victory</u> - I was speechless. I don't know if kids today could be held in thrall in the same way, by stories of an island castaway or a South Seas romance. The stories probably pale beside the excitement of video games, with their lumbering, not-quite-human heroes who wield guns and swords. You've probably seen the advertisements for these games, if you haven't actually played them. These characters provide distraction, if not moral guidance, for mostly young and dormant minds generally. They constantly punch or chop up or shoot at other living things, for that is the characters' reason for being, their sport and destiny. And a casual viewer might almost feel alarmed at all of the slaughter, until you realize that it is only a game dreamed up by capitalists and computer geeks. Everything comes down to money in the end. These are only games to ameliorate the boredom that man must experience at all ages and times. (If you think about it, there must be a very small percentage of people who are able to alleviate boredom creatively.) Sometimes the super-heroes stop in their tracks, they seem to try, these phantom Frankensteins, to articulate something profound and ineffable - it could be, "Was I given brains and senses only to play at this mayhem?" - but it's only a technical hiccup, and these wily protagonists lumber on to their next adventure.

But I started talking about literature. I know that I'm discursive, but I just can't help it, it's my nature. One of the reasons why I began to limit my reading of contemporary fiction years ago is that the writing was so controlled and narrow, there was no scope for digression, for philosophical asides. Literature is not hermetic, it's the book of life! What we look for is to come face to face with a companionable mind with whose thoughts we can identify. And too often we find a crabbed and narrow outlook, not to mention a parsimonious language - in short, nothing companionable at all. What I was reading breathed no life, there was no air and no space in it. Just that insipid "I-I-I" voice. Whereas, if the art of literature is digression, as I think someone wrote, then it's possible that I produced one or two masterpieces in my own fashion. But who is to know now?

Anyway, if you've ever felt about the great works the way that I did you'll understand the kind of thrill that I was talking about before in discovering the classics. But what is the state of American letters today, and why does it seem to reach a rather small public? It does seem that it is mostly self-appointed "specialists" who care anything about contemporary literature as such. And there is so much junk, frankly, to wade through. Maybe the reading public has changed, or maybe the public has been badly served by the cultural establishment. For that matter, the age cries out for satire, for social criticism that shocks and offends. What else would any real artist do today but howl in protest, in our age which has seen the apotheosis of materialism and creeping conformity? But what do we see instead? Escapism, or pure nonsense, for the most part. The true artist of today doesn't exist, or if he does he is a voice howling in the wilderness.

I used to think that it would be wonderful to have a public forum for ideas of this kind - my ideas, I mean. It would be worthwhile to satirize the cultural establishment itself, for its smugness and meretriciousness. But I know, if you poked a stick at them, what their reaction would be. We are doing our best. It isn't fair to satirize *us*, at all.

But I want to return to the events of that long-ago summer. The workshop grew out of a university seminar that I'd attended. I was casually acquainted with the instructor, and with three of the participants; the rest, four others, I knew not at all. The itinerary was to meet each morning from nine until noon: presenting our stories, or brief extracts from novels, and to receive and dispense that all-important "feedback" which an increasingly bottom-line publishing industry has little inclination to provide anymore. (Unless, I imagine, they think that a ready-made best-seller has fallen into their hands.) The afternoons and evenings belonged to the participants: we could share our work, or take day trips in the area, or, of course, write.

The house that we shared was settled on a bluff about thirty feet above the Maine coastline. Below a large wooden deck, which extended from two sides of the house, was the constant foam and splash of the tide against the rocks. From this deck, and from the expansive living room windows, were views of a picturesque cove, with more rocks and stands of pine trees rising up on a promontory across the bay. A couple of miles beyond, rising out of the water or a spit of land, was the outline of a lighthouse, whose red beacon was sometimes obscured by the heavy fogs that envelop those remote bays and islands.

The steady wind, and constant motion of the water, were heightened by the after-effects of a tropical storm which coincided with our arrival that Saturday. We were not in any physical danger. From the first, it was a setting which seemed to offer much that was peaceful and restorative, to people who, most of us, had been "long in city pent." But, for me, that atmosphere would become roiled - would it be too harsh to say, ruined? - by the presence of my writing-minded housemates. After putting in my time - when I was alone in my car again, retracing those winding lanes and narrow stone bridges that had brought me there in such a different mood - I felt like one who has been released from a prison. But I am, as they say, getting ahead of myself.

What shall I tell you of myself? Like many writers, I was trying to tell a story which was extremely important - to me. I want to be very clear about what I am saying because, looking back, I suppose that excessive irony was one of my limitations as a writer. Every writer's story is important to him, or her. He may even believe the story to be emblematic of what is wrong with society, or of the pain or exaltation of love, or other experience. But does it strike any such chord in the disinterested reader? That is more difficult to say. The sincere artist can only tell his story as best he can. It does not follow that the reader will "get" it, and the fault can be variously attributed, perhaps to the vagaries of current fashion - our shrinking attention spans, for example.

I was writing, at that time, a story of my own wayward youth. Not a story of childhood, *per se*, because I didn't have one, I wasn't allowed to have one. What I remember of childhood is a chronic feeling of worry, of feeling responsible for all of the problems my family was having. Not that I *was* responsible, I just felt that way. I felt that if I could grow up sooner and become a great deal smarter, then maybe I could help to solve some of the family's problems. But I was just a kid, and there really wasn't much I could do, except (and I seemed to grasp this instinctively) by trying not to add to the burdens of the family. You can imagine how I might find an escape in adventure stories. And I had my own adventures, with and away from the family. We lived in the country. During the summertime in particular I remember that I would hitch-hike to the neighboring towns, starting when I was just eight or ten. I would swim in ponds, and fish, and spend hours hiking in woods where I knew where to find streams to drink from and blackberries to eat. Or I would catch crayfish with my fingers in local rivers. The crayfish resembled miniatures of the live lobsters that I always saw in tanks when my mother took me grocery shopping. And I would watch the crayfish for a bit, holding them between my fingers or letting them crawl in the sand, before returning them to the water. So my story was in part these idylls with nature, and part worry over the things that were happening in my family, and I suppose that there was a pathos there - an interesting contrast - if I was able to bring it to life. But it may have been some city-dwelling junior editor, a product of the modern suburbs and Ivy League who, reading of hitch-hiking and streams and blackberries and crayfish, looked up from the page and complained, "No one lives like this!" One did, though - as remote as such a way of living may seem now. Anyway, with just such summary and ill-informed, arbitrary judgments, so are the courses of empires and individuals decided.

If I search my memory I can recall the faces that convened around that battered pine-wood dining table each morning. Mornings that were variously sunny, or rainy, or fog-bound. Just outside the windows, branches of shrubbery stirred in the wind, and you heard the foghorns and the calls of gulls. A pot of strong coffee was always on - made with bottled water, not the iron-inflected well water that came out of the tap on that island.

There was Marge herself, our leader. She was in her sixties, and she had the dry, tanned skin and narrowed eyes of a woman who has been a good deal out of doors. I gathered that the coast of Maine had become a second home to her after New York City, and at the time she was actively looking to buy a house there. (The house in which we would stay that week, she had rented from someone.) I suppose that she viewed herself as a facilitator, and she did try, always, to say something positive about whatever a writer had just presented. I must say that for her. And some of the other participants who had worked with her in the city told me that she would take a personal and not just a business interest in you, provided that you were temperamentally suited and she liked your style of writing. That's what some of them told me, at any rate. She had written a couple of how-to books on the thorny issue of writing. I think that was the extent of her published work.

Next to the head of the table (for we usually took the same places) sat Ellen, a woman in her early thirties. She was from a wealthy family. Someone told us that he'd seen her parents' seaside villa while accompanying her on the drive up. Ellen's heroine was in and out of mental institutions. As she read, you heard a good deal about sedative-filled syringes, and restraining tables and strait-jackets, and even the chilly feel of a new razor blade against the skin. And I must say that this first-person narrative was rather carefully sustained; good writing of its kind, but the language was drab and I began to find it monotonous after awhile. And the gloom was unrelieved. I hoped that they were not her experiences she was describing. While she read I would look outside, and my mind would move in a different direction. I would think, The sun is bright today, this floor feels solid beneath my feet. Most people liked her readings. I remember a conversation with her. Insanity, I said, was inherently tragic, but in the world of art it can be more, it can actually be made to stand for something larger. But I don't think she'd ever thought about her story as anything more than raw experience. At any rate she did not respond to what I was suggesting.

Allan sat next to her, and there were some similarities in the work they presented. He was tall and thin and good-looking, in his late twenties (relatively young for the group), with straight shoulder-length hair. He worked as an editor, or more precisely a fact-checker, for a magazine in the city. His language was certainly more elegant than Ellen's. Allan had also created a pained heroine - not actually off the wall but very strange, very detached. There must be something irresistible about these women who are getting by materially and who are young and beautiful and deeply unhappy. There is a *frisson* to their vague unhappiness, as if in some way it makes them superior to other people.

But when I think about it, all that Ellen and Allan accomplished, in their different ways, was to create narratives of an ironic and stylized detachment. The technique is very much *a la mode*, but seems to be admired more by specialists than any reading public. The genre does not so much tell a coherent story, as render before the reader an extremely flat and vapid emotional life.

It is an affectless style which, for me at least, spells pure monotony. I guess that is just my bias.

I'll mention just a couple of the other writers. Terry was writing a putatively comic novel - I put it that way because Marge absolutely fell down laughing at almost everything that he read. Much of it *was* funny, I'll admit that. But Terry's *schtick* was a kind of run-on language that co-opted some of the rhythms and peculiarities of his characters. Even when he used the third person there was no objectivity, you never felt that you were outside the psyches of his odd characters. And after awhile you did not want to be there anymore. It was that Huck Finn voice run amok. I thought of a kid who lets out a bottle tied to a string in order to test the depths of a quarry. It went on and on, this free-associating, and if you valued economy of language you had to feel you were getting short shrift. It might have been better for him if Marge had once asked him if there was a point to it all, instead of clapping him on the back for being able to let the string out for so long.

And there were others, and I may mention some of them later. But there was one who, from the first, I took to be the most gifted and the most interesting. He was a guy from Jersey named Vincent Feza. He was about my age, among the oldest. We didn't really understand him, and I guess that was our fault. There was something inextinguishably blue-collar about Vincent. An aura of physical labor clung to him. He hadn't gone the usual route of completing a liberal arts degree. And I think that he worked in some sort of manufacturing. These were things that set him apart, for most of us, if we worked, were editors or fund-raisers or worked in advertising.

Vincent was a blunt-faced and crafty-looking guy, and naturally we did not take the noble and high-flown sentiments expressed in his work very seriously. I'm kidding, but not by very much. Vincent disappointed our expectations of the artistic temperament, and for this no one seemed able to forgive him. Genuine talent was rarely so unprepossessing. He had a bluff and Anglo-looking face, despite his Italian-sounding name. You could imagine this face looking back at you in the mirror of a small town taxicab, or perhaps you'd picture him arriving at your house to plaster a ceiling.

That Monday morning was the first time I heard Vincent Feza read. Before he did, Marge announced the forthcoming visit of the man who would later make such a memorable impression on all of us.

"Mason Torgeson is going to be visiting us Friday evening. You'll enjoy meeting him."

I think it was Allan who, after a couple of beats, asked, "Who?" I think he was speaking for all of us.

"Mason Torgeson. Published several novels. You're going to love him."

Quizzical looks passed.

Then Vincent had the floor. In a somewhat phlegmatic voice he read from the beginning of his novel. It was a story of a frustrated lounge pianist, who "played too well for his own good." The man's concert career had taken a nose-dive when he began "hitting mostly fifths." Which is to say that he had a drinking problem, as coded in the sometimes arch language that Vincent had adopted for his story. Those were some of the phrases, as near as I can remember them. Vincent's style here was unclassifiable, you might call it an elegant sort of pulp writing - Mickey Spillane meets Jane Austen. But the group did not seem to pick up on the element of burlesque, and Vincent really was not capable of bringing any kind of inflection to his reading. His words intimated a serious story of thwarted hopes and the possibility of redemption. The pianist may soon be divorced, and he's in debt, and he hasn't yet sworn off drinking. He borrows money from a loan shark, a habitué of the bar where he works. You felt sorry for the character because you knew he was being dragged into an old-fashioned melodrama through no fault of his own, and that the story could only end in tears. Vincent was just properly started in the first chapter, and already you could hear the wailing police sirens and the tired-sounding voice-over of the cop, and the cheap tinny saxophone playing the main title nocturne.

This seemed a strange place to be, and yet it was a compelling story in its way. The language was expressive and atmospheric, and I liked it a lot. Sure, it had a quaint, old-fashioned quality. Nothing about the language said modern, but there was a sturdy elegance about it that was unmistakable. And it really flowed. Ellen's and Allan's pained heroines might have been spun from finer stuff, but this was writing with blood and sinew. I remember an early passage. I can quote it still because I wrote it down afterward in what I used to call my idea book, and it stayed in my mind.

You didn't expect to find this kind of music just anywhere, and you could imagine the owner of the place one day realizing the sound was not commercial, was not contemporary, was not lounge music but was something wholly of the pianist's making, not even songs played end to end, straight through, but scraps of conservatory music and blues and bits of hymn tunes that you could barely recognize before they faded into something different. You thought you heard "There Is A Meeting Here" and sometimes "Blessed Be The Name" and the sound was the bell-like sound of many Southern blues guitarists of the nineteen-twenties.

I thought this and other passages very fine, and I think I said so. I understood perfectly where the genius pianist was taking me musically. But the instructor remarked that the "pace" of the opening was different, and slow. It was an off-hand remark but I think, in retrospect, that it planted a seed of prejudice. Some of the participants picked up on the criticism. I think Vincent was a little nonplussed. But he did respond more positively to the more detailed comments. Possibly he had not presented his work to an audience before. Things that seemed clear to him didn't always get across, which isn't unusual. He seemed to take note of the responses.

A pattern began to form during the week. I don't know what was in the minds of the other participants. Possibly they just considered Vincent's stuff old-fashioned. His readings really did not elicit much excitement. I thought that in his sure-footed way he was moving toward something truly interesting; certain tragedies but also, I hoped, something life-affirming in the end. It was a story that embodied complex and genuine emotions. His characters actually lived, they were not dry sticks of language. Above all it was not an insular kind of story that Vincent told, and for that I must really give him credit. It was a story from the real world. It struck me also that Vincent was trying, usually, to deliver powerhouse emotional scenes. That was very different. He succeeded more often than not.

I know that I offered him some encouragement but not, I suspect, as much as I should have. Vincent was a reserved and difficult guy. None of us got to know him well. When nine strangers are sharing a house you must first of all surrender your privacy. I think Vincent found that more difficult than any of us. He joined us for supper, which was usually cooked at home, and a couple of times I walked with him to lunch in the restaurant down at the cove. It was a simple and unpretentious place with plain square tables, with large windows that were always open to the sun and breeze. There would be small boats along the wooden docks outside, and bicycles leaning here and there in the sand and gravel yard. Gulls would wheel and call.

Vincent could be quite voluble if the crowd was not too large. Over crabmeat sandwiches or fresh lobster rolls and clam cakes, Vincent held forth in his blunt, offhand way about music, about which he seemed knowledgeable, and we talked about favorite authors as well.

"How are you finding this week?" he asked me suddenly. His dark eyes looked large. His expression brought to mind homesickness, the disparate nature of the readings (which were not uniformly interesting, Lord knows), and, I suspected, a growing sense of being distinctly out of place. I think it was Wednesday by then. (We had arrived on Saturday, as I said.) I won't pretend that the group's out-of-class discussions set any standard for erudition or intelligence. I must say the talk was not very distinguished, in fact. Not nearly as interesting as it should have been for such a highly educated group. I could not understand how so much time was spent discussing old television programs, for example - and not, usually, the really landmark dramas and comedies, but the fluff shows that were not even very interesting in their own time, let alone later. When Vincent joined us downstairs, at those times, he didn't say much, and usually he brought a book that he could turn his attention to.

He raised his glass of beer to his lips.

"I'm finding it," I said, "a learning experience."

"Yeah. Right. It isn't a complete pleasure for me, either. What I'm finding is that even though people like to write, it isn't like they have a world of things in common. It could be like having an interest in stamp collecting."

We finished our beers and lunches and went back to the house to contemplate the afternoon.

Next day was a watershed. Vincent read a rather painful scene between his character and the character's wife; their discussion was frequently on the point of open argument, but the musician would try to say something conciliatory. To listen to their discussion, it was pretty obvious that the couple in the story was going to break up.

"Reactions," Marge said.

"It was very real. You felt like you were there," Ellen said.

"What about the main character? How does he make you feel?"

"Frustrated?"

"Yes... He seems very passive in this scene. You think he's going to lose this woman and you feel frustrated. Is that the kind of character you wanted to create, Vincent?"

"It's hard to say. I wouldn't use the same words you used. He's troubled. He acts in the way I wanted him to act, so I guess he's the character I wanted to create, yes."

"M'm. He's also very - deliberate. Like the pace is very deliberate."

There she went with the "pace" again. Vincent shrugged.

"Other comments?"

"I think," Terry said, "this character is a loser. No reader would care about him." Terry was smiling as usual, but I could not fail to notice the hint of malice in his face.

I really thought that Marge was going to take issue with this comment which, for me, definitely crossed over the line of fairness. But her only response was a drawn-out, "Well?"

"What is that supposed to mean," Vincent said.

"I don't think I would put it that way," Marge said. "But he's a very difficult character, his passivity is frustrating to the reader."

"I don't care if he's 'difficult,'" Vincent said.

There was an uneasy silence. I wanted to say something positive. I thought that Vincent was being maligned because he created characters who were more complex than anyone else's. I like to think I would have said something about it. But then Jeffrey spoke up. Jeffrey I have not mentioned. He was a quiet and decent-seeming guy who lived in New York City.

"I think you're all missing the point. This is a complex and troubled character. We've only heard a few extracts, but there are probably good reasons why he acts the way he does. I think you're making value judgments and I didn't think that's what we are about."

More silence. I said, "I agree with what Jeffrey said. Well said, Jeffrey."

Terry was silent. The guy next to him, who had only smirked, was silent. Vincent was stung. I could see that he was controlling his anger. As far as he was concerned the conversation was over. He was not going to get anything useful out of it.

Marge evidently decided, in her own fashion, that the discussion was not salvageable. We moved on. Vincent was tight-lipped the rest of the morning. He did not join in during a subsequent argument. It was about something trivial, but it seemed to reflect a general deterioration in the quality of the group debate.

Someone said, after Allan had finished his reading, "I have a problem with using this word 'purblind.' It means blind. So say it."

"It isn't the same," Allan said, his long hair shaking from side to side.

"It means blind. Say it."

"Will not."

"Class, class," Marge cut in impatiently. "This is not good. Our barge is running aground here and the tide is moving out."

I was startled at this. What other reserves of poetic imagery had Marge been keeping from us?

"Can we continue? Or should we stop here?" We decided to continue.

I've sometimes wondered what error of judgment caused Terry to make that remark. Did he think that he was such an oracle because the instructor praised him so lavishly? Or was it hubris? Or rivalry? Or malice? Or did he think that he was just picking up on a criticism that had already been intimated by the instructor?

I have thought sometimes about that little group, and the dynamics that were at work there, and I'm still not sure that I understand. I felt that there was an antipathy toward Vincent. But what was it about? None of the others seemed capable of appreciating what was to me an original and lively expository style of prose writing. Were they incredulous that someone with a blue collar, workaday background could have developed a fully evolved feeling for language? I felt a disdain for what I took to be their ignorance of many practical matters, for their culture-bound beliefs and unthinking acceptance of whatever is fashionable in the arts, and the subtle prejudice of their class consciousness. I sensed a distrust and discomfort toward this blue-collar worker; as if they felt that no one who lacks the right kind of degree from the right kind of college could possibly be worth listening to, so that Vincent's language, while having some kind of surface eloquence, must be an unaccredited fake.

But for myself, I was hearing a kind of joy in expression that I hadn't heard in years. I had to admit that I didn't hear it, not very often, anyway, in my own writing. It wasn't the parched vocabulary and solipsistic meandering of so much writing that you find today, but a language denser, more inherently joyful, something like – well, to put the thing in musical terms, something like hearing accomplished singers like Ella Fitzgerald or June Christie. Far from just hitting all of the notes, there is a virtuosity in the sound, a sheer joy in singing when the voice itself seems aware of its own limitless capability and freedom. Vincent had this gift. I should say that he had talent in spades, but he had not turned it toward any of the styles that his hearers (many of them, anyway) were able to recognize and to appreciate. And so he had sparked no reaction. What hope was there for me?

I didn't see Vincent after that Thursday morning session. Possibly he was out walking. It was a sunny August afternoon. I felt discontented. I felt like getting in my car and driving, and that's what I did.

The coast of Maine is really a lovely place. I am usually able to visit for only a few days each year, but when I am back in the city the place often returns to my mind as an ideal of order and serenity. There is the natural beauty, and there is something else: I could call it a strong feeling for the past, but that is not adequate. Yes, the people there must save everything. There are more antique stores and flea markets than you are liable to find anywhere else. And bookstores in Maine, except in Portland, are likely to be set in barns, or in old wooden houses where the floors creak, and much of the material there - not only the books but the advertising ephemera, the sheet music, the Saturday Evening Posts, the carefully preserved magazines from as far back as the 'twenties - it all makes you think of the hammock and the corner armchair, of an earlier and less hurried and less harried existence. In such a bookstore I lost myself for a good three hours. The day was warm but fans circulated some air. I felt washed of the strains of that week, of the self-important and often nettlesome company at the house.

I drove further north. I stopped at a roadside stand and on a sunny picnic bench outside I had a fresh lobster roll and a soda. I went as far as Camden. I parked my car and walked around the harbor and the picturesque downtown. The sun was nearly setting, behind the storefronts and the hills with their cover of pines that rose up a half-mile from the harbor. I reflected on what I'd seen during the afternoon - the clean and quiet streets, the orderliness, the neighborly interest of people, the knowing how to behave. "Yankee propriety" may seem stuffy and comical, but it is in fact one kind of higher standard from which, as a society, we seem to constantly and unmistakably degenerate.

We met for the last time the following Friday morning. As I remember I received some positive comments. Certainly I had no reason to feel discouraged. The only other reading that I remember at all is Vincent Feza's.

These morning sessions around the large pine table had begun to wear on me. Even more, the constraint and the limited society of the evenings. Perhaps almost as much as Vincent, I was looking forward to leaving. He prefaced his reading that last day with some remarks which, from the sound of them, I thought he must have gone over several times in his mind. About half of the people had read, when Marge called on him.

"I was wondering," Vincent said, "what I could read today. Because, some of my things provoked comments that I did not find uniformly helpful." (Where is this going? I wondered.) "I was actually offended at the quality of some of the remarks. I don't consider this character a loser. He's a very substantial character and I've given pages of reasons why he is the way he is. He's a troubled character but it's just bad judgment to say that he's a loser. And incidentally, Jeffrey was the only one here who took issue with that remark."

Vincent paused for breath. He really seemed pretty calm. Everyone else was either looking at the table or glancing at Vincent with averted faces.

"Well," Marge said, "I don't know if I heard the word 'loser.' Did anyone else hear that?"

"That was about it, pretty much," one of the women said.

"Yes," I agreed.

"Well. Maybe that wasn't appropriate. It's my fault then. There are no 'losers' here. There are no 'dysfunctional' families. We don't use those words here. That isn't being helpful."

"Anyway," Vincent said, "let me read what I planned." Vincent paused for about five seconds and then read from what sounded like an epilogue. His story had not ended so badly. Actually it sounded rather upbeat. But the brief scene needed to be fleshed out in places. That's what I said when Vincent finished, and Marge said, "Reactions?"

There was only one other comment, a favorable one, even though Marge was trying to elicit comments with some leading questions. Terry and the two guys sitting nearest him just sat there with blank faces.

What jerks, I thought, not for the first time. They would not say anything about Vincent's presentation.

The rest of the meeting dissipated. No one seemed to be going out for lunch, so I took a book and walked down to the restaurant in the cove. Then I walked around a narrow public path that wound and climbed among rocks and shrubbery, treading carefully above the bluffs. Some of the small rocks that I walked over had a strange, silvery luster, and I picked some of them up and studied them. I couldn't swear if I'd ever seen this iridic material before, but the sight seemed to recall something from childhood. It might have been some other trip that was now lost to memory. I fired some of the stones into the ocean below and tried to hear their splash in the water.

We had only to wait for Marge's writer friend to arrive, and have supper with him. I planned an early start the next morning.

The summer day was foreshortened by a passing storm. Sitting by myself on a partially roofed-over area of the deck, I couldn't be sure if it was drops of rain or flecks of the churning tide that bore in upon me. I was happy, at least, that it was not my night to cook. I heard the deck door slide open. It was Vincent. He was wearing a nylon jacket against the strong wind.

"Vincent," I said, gesturing to the chair next to me. "I didn't see you this afternoon."

"I was putting my stuff together. I was going to get started."

"It's too far. Better you should leave in the morning."

He looked drawn. I reflected that as the week passed, Vincent had grown progressively more silent, even during our sessions. If he was hoping to find a fellowship of creative artists here, it certainly did not happen.

"I don't think you should feel discouraged," I said. "It may only be that some of the people lack the experience to appreciate the kinds of characters and situations that you create. I like your stuff, and so did a lot of people. I have a general impression, which is that many people today think it's alright if you don't have anything to say, as long as you express it well."

Vincent appeared to think about my epigram, but he didn't look convinced. I continued, "Some of it may just be the opinion of hacks. Trend-followers. You pay a price in this country if you don't go along with everybody else."

"I don't know. It could represent a majority opinion."

"If it does, it's the world's loss."

"You think the whole world can be wrong?"

"About some things, yes."

"That's confidence. You ought to keep trying, too."

I looked wryly at Vincent. "Think, though," I said. "What a couple of people say doesn't necessarily reflect the group's thinking. People are blasé, they're not even concentrating. They don't speak up, even if they don't agree with what's being said."

"You may be right." Vincent smiled and looked out over the darkening bay. "Thanks for saying it."

"It's what I think." After a moment I said, "I'm looking forward to tomorrow."

"I hear you."

"We just meet this old crony of Marge's." I did not expect much of the meeting. "Get an early start tomorrow."

Vincent didn't have time to respond. It was impossible to hear any of the voices in the house, through the wind and the surf, but we both saw the door open in the lighted entryway, on the other side of the living room. An old man entered. Marge and the others crowded around him. Vincent and I made our way in. It was about six o-clock.

He patted down his thinning white hair, and yanked vigorously on the lapels of his jacket, as if to shake off some raindrops.

"Group," Marge said. "Meet Mason Torgeson."

He bowed slightly. Hands were shaken. Jeffrey, who had met Mason's airport van in the town some fifteen miles away, closed the door after them. The group moved away from the galley kitchen, where supper was being got ready, toward the dining room with its large rectangular table. I stood to the side with a beer. Everyone was giving our guest space. I had a little time to study him.

Mason Torgeson appeared to be in his middle sixties. He was just under six feet, slender and fit-looking. His movements were very deliberate. His glance was arresting, and penetrating: it lingered on people and things, and seemed to reflect a view that the world was filled with both danger and fascinating objects. He had a broad, curling mustache, which like his hair was graying.

Marge left the room momentarily, and Mason asked, rather *sotto voce*, "Are there refreshments?" He rubbed his hands together.

"Gee, I'm not sure," Jeffrey began to say, while he looked at us meaningfully.

Allan said, "Sure there are. Right there in that cabinet, I think there are some things."

Someone handed Mason a glass, which he placed on the counter, and he looked under the cabinet.

"Nice going, Sherlock," Jeffrey muttered to Allan. A couple of us looked at Jeffrey, who rolled his eyes slightly.

Marge returned to the kitchen.

"Ah, yes. Good, good," Mason was saying. He brought a bottle of whiskey out and poured some in the highball glass. He added ice and a splash of bottled water.

"There's nothing like a mild drink to wash down the dust of travel."

"Isn't it raining out?" Marge asked.

Mason took a healthy sip and lowered his glass. "It's just an expression, Marge."

"Oh. I know."

"Is that supper I smell?"

"Meatloaf and potatoes," the night's designated cooks announced.

"I love it. I'm just famished."

"Why don't you sit down, Mason?"

"Thank you, I will." Mason sat in the middle of one of the long sides of the table. Some of us helped to bring out supper. The table began to fill. I was across from Mason. Vincent sat to his right. Mason asked about the "facilities," and Vincent showed him to the first floor bathroom.

When Mason returned he added some more whiskey and ice to his drink. I noticed Jeffrey, who was standing nearby, frown slightly. Mason returned to the table with his glass and we began to eat supper.

"Mason Torgeson," Marge said, "published his first novel in nineteen-fifty-eight, and he has followed that with other novels and books of journalism. He's been my friend for many years and I'm pleased that you are all able to meet him and hopefully learn from him."

If he'd published novels all those years ago, his name must have been pretty totally eclipsed since then. *I'd* never heard of him, and I guessed that his books must have been mostly out of print.

"Pshaw," Mason said. "But at any rate this is a so-delightful supper and I'm pleased to be here. I would like to hear what you are all working on but fortunately - I mean, unfortunately - there isn't much time for that." He took a long sip from his drink and fell to his dinner, which he ate with gusto. In fact as I watched him he made me think of that expression about a person who "did not know where his next meal was coming from." There was not much conversation for awhile.

Later, at Marge's general prompting, Ellen asked him, "What inspired you as a writer?"

"Oh. I guess I just wanted to tell my stories. I didn't know if they would be meaningful to other people, but I thought they were worth telling. As for how or why I stayed at it, I'll tell you a story. When I was still a young man, I had occasion to visit Tiger Wesley's training camp, which was in Jersey. He was one of the great welterweight fighters, and in fact he became champion. I got to spend some time with him because I was doing a profile for one of the men's magazines. Everyone liked this kid. He was a clean fighter, relatively. He was dedicated. And he did things you had to like. For example, he drove a lime-green Cadillac, and if the kids near his training camp recognized him, he'd stop the car and talk with them for a few minutes and give them each a dollar. I visited his camp in Jersey many times. He had style, but it wasn't that I admired so much. It was his dedication. Tiger was like a machine - a fighting machine. Anything that took away from that, he would just avoid it. How many people do you know who really believe in something? He had the same breakfast every morning: black coffee, a boiled egg, two slices of toast. No butter. If he told someone he'd put on weight it might mean he'd gained a pound. He was that serious.

"His workouts were like clockwork. A five mile run, and pushups. Heavy bag, light bag. Sparring. Whenever I thought about what dedication was, I thought of him. More than any writers, or anybody else." Mason paused. "There was a service last year, at Saint Patrick's. I saw a lot of old faces... But I don't know if this interests you very much."

"It's a good story," someone said.

"I didn't know that I'd become a writer until I was twenty-five or so. And I was never able to *just* write, I usually had a job of some kind. When I was in my twenties I worked at a magazine in the city. I edited some of the copy, and I contributed to an unsigned column that appeared every week. It was easy work. Then, kind of casually, I thought of writing that first novel. I wrote out a few scenes to start it. Then for a year, in the evenings after work, I'd look at one of those scenes and I'd revise it. They went through a lot of changes. I wanted the writing to be as simple and direct as possible. When I was satisfied with those few scenes, I went on, and the rest of the book followed pretty directly, because I knew how the sentences should look and sound. I'd prepared, you see."

"You would keep working at just a few scenes?" Allan asked.

I had some trouble understanding this, myself. To spend months revisiting just a few brief scenes? Mason insisted it was the truth, it was not a metaphor.

"That's what I did." With thin, long fingers Mason rubbed his mustache. He looked around the table with a crafty and deliberate expression. He certainly had our attention now.

"How did you manage your time?" I thought to ask him.

"I had the day job, as I said, when I started writing. What I usually did was to have supper when I got home. Then I'd sleep for several hours. Get up at about three in the morning. I'd write for three or four hours and I'd go to work."

"You did that every day?"

"Just about. Yeah, that's how I wrote my first books. You have to find some way to do it. It probably sounds like a crazy schedule. But if you get tired of it - if you get tired of the roadwork, and the pushups, and so forth - then you just stop." He turned his palms upward. "And then it isn't a problem for you anymore."

"Gee," someone said, vaguely, after a general pause.

Mason returned to his supper, helping himself to more meatloaf. He saw that his glass needed re-filling and made to get up.

"What do you need?" Marge asked.

"Oh - would you mind?" He handed her his glass. "And please don't be stingy." He winked, and laughed.

"I read your first book, you know," Vincent said suddenly.

Mason turned, looking surprised. Up to this time he seemed not to have taken notice of any of us as individuals. He looked at Vincent. "Is it true?"

"Yes. Many years ago."

"Did you like it?"

"Very much. Most of it is very straightforward, and spare - I like that. And some of it is like - hallucinations. There aren't many books I've enjoyed more. <u>Children</u> <u>Of</u> <u>Fate</u>, it was."

"Yes. I was never very good with titles. But I am glad that you liked it, really. Was it hard to find?"

"I wasn't really looking, then. Just found it and liked the cover."

"They're all out of print. I buy them myself, when I see one - that's kind of funny."

"It's a shame that they're out of print. Really."

"I'm glad you think so."

"Everybody seemed impressed with that book. The reviews on the back were excellent..."

"Of course they were. I'm no fluke. Marge! Tell these young folks."

"And, I mean, today..."

"I'm not happy about it. After so much work. Of course things could change. A publisher could recognize their quality and reissue those books."

"You don't sound very hopeful."

"Ah. Maybe it doesn't matter very much. What's most important is, I wrote the books that I wanted to. I commend you for your good taste, young man." Mason raised his glass and sipped from it.

Someone asked, "Who do you like to read now?"

"Not much new stuff, I'm afraid. It may be just a bias of mine, but I think I've earned the right not to be bored. I don't have a whole world of time. I guess I find several problems with the new writing. One is that the most celebrated novelists are intellectuals who for the most part can only write about other writers. It might be they lack what is called 'life experience'. Personally, I wouldn't have *dreamed* of making a writer my main character. It's boring! This might be one reason why dime-store novels and cheap romances hold the field today.

"Something happened to literature after the Second World War. It has continued on, of course, but it lacks a certain vitality. When I was starting you had John Cheever, who I knew, and you had some other good writers. You had the Saturday Evening Post that regularly published stories for a wide audience. Some of them were not bad. People read more then. Maybe that seems a quaint sort of entertainment today. Now you have literary quarterlies with maybe five-thousand readers. Why only five-thousand readers? I don't think it's because people are stupid. They just have no interest in what goes on in those magazines - it isn't real to them. And you know, if five thousand academics read a magazine, it won't change the world. I don't think people read enough, and there may be technological reasons why they don't. But, basically, I blame these academics - and the establishment generally, these bottom-line publishers, who are no better than whores - for killing off any interest that remained in literature."

"Well!" Marge said. "That's strong opinion!"

"So be it," Mason said. He was on a roll. His voice had gotten louder by a couple of decibels. He reared back, paused for breath, took another drink - and then set down his highball glass in the middle of a tureen of whipped potatoes. Mason was oblivious, and resumed talking. The glass listed a bit, and then was upheld by the consistency of the honest potatoes.

Vincent, sitting to Mason's right, looked on with a sinking expression that was commensurate. Only the glass, and Mason's movements, held his attention. And I think that what he did next showed Vincent's strength of character in a couple of ways. He waited for his moment, and when Mason seemed quite caught up in his talk, Vincent subtly brought the glass up out of the potatoes. They did not yield the glass without some spillage. Vincent, in the same covert manner, wiped the bottom of the glass with his cloth napkin, and he began to set the glass down out of Mason's reach. With an alertness that surprised me, Mason reached out his hand and nodded toward Vincent, who surrendered the glass to him. Mason continued.

"Thank you. You know, I'll read a novel from that golden era. A Balzac, who I love. But it isn't possible to write in that way anymore. I would not have written such a novel, not in my best years. Societies are different today – you no longer have this subtle and intricate template of how members of *classes* behave. A reader doesn't experience the same surprise, and the entertainment value, in witnessing how a representative of his or her class behaves, which is the essence of those novels. Class is not a predictor of behavior today.

19

So I don't expect to find a Balzac, no, but I want to be entertained, and I want to see something of real life. I know that our attention spans are not what they were – I accept it – but give us something that's sustaining. The work of today feels diminished, literature is contaminated by the age. You read reviews about the next great thing, and you go and read it. You expect something on the order of *Norma,* and instead you find that it's a foolish burlesque of no value."

When supper was finished we began clearing plates from the table. Someone started a pot of coffee.

"I read some of the new novels because I feel obligated to. But almost none of it grabs me. I read one by this new English writer. His father was a pretty good novelist, if I remember. It was supposed to be great stuff, but I read it and it's a smarmy, foolish book. It's a sophomoric prank, misunderstood as high literature when it's nothing of the sort. I could say worse about it but I'm feeling sort of charitable. Then there are these light as air novels, which are amusing for about five minutes. They do no harm, but you know some of the sit-coms do a better job of entertaining, and they do it week after week, and they have skilled actors to bring it to life. In fact this is one of the only things, anywhere, which has actually gotten better in recent years. You know that rubbery-faced comedienne who is on Thursday nights? Delightful. You need to have some enjoyments. Anyway, you do see a lot of this innocuous writing.

"It isn't that no *good* novels are published today. I wouldn't say that. But there is so much worthless stuff published. Formula stuff, and anything that is touched by celebrity. The industry, like so much else in this country, has gotten so bottom-line, so worshipful of the almighty dollar.

"My ex-editor is still around. Or so I hear from time to time. He didn't trust anyone that he suspected of harboring an original idea. Instead he must strive to undermine him if at all possible. But I suppose that his proclivities have served him well in his career as a panderer. As far as I'm concerned, he wouldn't know good writing if he stumbled and fell over it."

His expression had darkened as he thought of these grievances, and Marge remarked, "Mason, your face is an absolute mask of hatred."

"Is it now?"

"You're not so bitter, are you?"

"Oh, I suppose not. Well, maybe I am. A little bit. Do you think so?"

Marge shook her head. "I will always support you."

"Thanks." Mason was silent for some minutes. There was not that much talk without him. He declined the coffee that was offered, but had some cake when it was brought out. The evening had worn on. I was tired but I found Mason very interesting. I could hear rain outside. Mason finished his cake.

"I'm getting dry," he said, and got up to re-fill his glass. We waited for him to return and he began speaking again.

"Few people are reading books of quality. Mass-market tastes have polluted literature, just as they have polluted popular music. The music that you hear on the radio is so common, so lousy. The popular taste is like a sieve that lets nothing of quality through. Nowadays we say that serious orchestral music and all varieties of "pop" music are equally valid. What kind of nonsense is that? Most of the pop music is *inferior* to the classical world - it lacks depth, subtlety, beauty. Let's admit it. Or to return to books - if a child doesn't see any books in the house, isn't he going to regard them as something foreign and unnecessary? I feel sorry for young people today, if they are growing up without books in the house, without serious music. If all you see around you is banality and ugliness, how will you recognize anything else? Are parents instilling any values in children? I wonder. I would guess that in most homes, television is the shrine around which the family gathers. It appears that television and movies are the media for transmitting culture and social norms today. And the people producing this are mostly amoral, juvenile, and meretricious. That's pretty scary.

"But - to return to literature - let me just ask-" Mason seemed to be struggling with indigestion, or perhaps with the whiskey he was drinking. "What are the popular styles now? There are styles that I don't think I would ever want to aspire to. Which they consider successful writing. Some of the stuff I've seen is so damn precious, so over-subtle. In the worst case you have a slightly odd, first-person narrative in which almost nothing happens. If anything *does* happen, it isn't anything that relates to any larger issue. Social or philosophical, I mean. The voice is inarticulate, it's almost catatonic. It's as if the author is trying for particular shades of monotony. This is also boring. Where are the big themes? The humanity? The writing is all self-centered, in which case Art is usually a vice. Why doesn't the age produce any Dreiser's? Does anyone know? Not that *he* was so fabulous. Technically."

The group, when I looked around the table, seemed a little disaffected by what Mason was saying. Some of their expressions seemed to say that the shoe fit - and not well, but painfully.

Mason was still struggling with his indigestion, or whatever it was. But he resumed, more slowly, and in a softer voice. "And the same writers - and many terrible writers - appear time and again. I guess ... because they fit the formula. Or because they still have an established name...

"Well. It's getting late. I think that's my curtain speech for tonight... I'm... It's just some opinions. I hope I haven't stepped on any toes." He looked around the table and smiled placidly.

21

The group did in fact seem sullen, even mutinous, as we sat staring at Mason. He was more than perceptive - he seemed almost psychic. But when we rose from our seats, a moment later, it was not to attack our guest but because of his increasingly erratic movements. He rose from his chair and stood uncertainly on his feet, then turned a hundred and eighty degrees, until he looked in the general direction of the wooden cabinets. "As for myself. I'm really ... quite ... shit-faced." He fell backwards, a reverse swan dive, onto the table, as several hands reached out too late to catch him. He landed with a great clattering of tableware. Marge shrieked.

"Oh, Mase. I could kill you. Help him. Did he hurt his head?"

"I think his head landed on the bread basket," I said, which seemed true from what I could observe.

I went around to the other side of the table where I could be more help. The group had converged around Mason. He was out like a light.

"Oh, take him to his room. Please," Marge said.

We got our hands under Mason and lifted him from the table and started toward the master bedroom on the first floor. I supported his head, which felt quite heavy in my hands. The expression on his face was not pained, but blissful. We turned, a twelve-legged juggernaut, at the short corridor, bumping along the walls as we went. Marge exhorted us to be careful, charging near us like an aroused bluejay.

We marshaled him feet-first and turned him clumsily at the bedroom, when suddenly Mason's arms shot out and gripped the doorframe. I was hard pressed to stop, but it was impossible to go forward. One of the guys in front lost his grip on Mason's leg and sagged to the carpet.

"Wait," I called. Mason's head grew lighter in my hands and soon hovered above my fingertips. He'd revived somewhat. His eyes popped open. Even upside-down, I could see he looked as stern as Ahab. Or like an engraving of an Old Testament prophet.

I shushed everyone, but when Mason spoke it was easy to hear him.

"The wages of literature!" he cried. "Do something useful while you have time!"

We looked at each other. Mason's eyes closed, and his hands released their grip on the doorframe. I felt his head fall back heavily on my hands, and we moved forward again, laying him on the bed. We loosened his clothes, and found that he was breathing normally, and after awhile we left him there, with the door slightly ajar.

I got my early start the next morning. I learned that Mason got up a couple of hours after me, apparently none the worse for wear, and with no recollection of how he'd gotten to bed that previous night. He only complained about what an old blunderbuss he was, for going to sleep with his clothes on.

At this point it occurs to me that I ought to provide an epilogue, describing the different things that happened to some of the others. But I really wouldn't know. In the years that passed there was only one name that I would sometimes think to look for among the pages of the book reviews. I never found it.

After packing that Saturday morning, I remember taking a last look around my room. I felt enormously relieved to be going home. I picked up my idea book, in which I'd recorded many impressions of that singular week. The entries in my idea book had thinned, like my hair, over the years. I closed the elastic strap around it and placed it among my other things for the trip back.

I've never opened it since.

FLAMES, PENGUINS, HOLLYWOOD ARGYLES

Some of the objects that he had loved most in life were set out on little tables, and displayed on threadbare blankets on the asphalt driveway. They were the passions and follies of a one-time minor musical impresario of New Haven, Connecticut. Many of his treasures were here: posters and musical programs for long-ago performances, record albums, and forty-five records. Some of the forty-fives have only paper slipcases over them, others show glossy photos of the recording artists; and some of the record albums feature a studio photo, or maybe the singer is acting out a small pantomime of one or more of the featured songs - watching a telephone, or sitting alongside a bar with a pensive expression. Some sunlight flashes across the driveway as, overhead, fleet clouds are borne along by gusting autumn breezes. A few people are about. Dry leaves of various colors rustle across the drive: brown, red, and yellow.

He could see now that these artifacts, standing for the world of music generally, were in some ways the true and loyal friends that he had always seemed to be seeking in life, and that he had only rarely found among people. The record covers with their faded photographs, and the records themselves, many of them now very worn, with some of the titles on the paper labels barely decipherable – they seemed a metaphor, in a way, for his obscure efforts on behalf of the musical arts, which had met with only mixed success.

There was a souvenir program for a performance by The Five Satins. He had known the group's singers personally. Even if they would not have remembered him, it was nevertheless true that he had met them. But that was a long story. He emceed their performance, or was it a revue, one night in a downtown auditorium. He received no money for his appearance, just carfare, and a plug for his small and struggling recording studio. He was the chubby and slightly sweating guy in front of the too-tall microphone that night. His instructions were to be brief and to say the names of the groups clearly. Which wasn't so hard. The names were easy to pronounce. In those days the groups were called The Orioles, and Ravens – there were even Penguins. The Debonaires. Silhouettes, Solitaires. Each name brought fragments of recollection to his mind – a photograph, or song - sometimes a personal reminiscence.

A sparse show of people looked over the merchandise, searching for bargains. They pawed among his treasures with thick and clumsy fingers. One older couple lifted up a worn forty-five record appraisingly and looked blankly at each other, shrugging.

But they meant so much to me, he thinks. For in his own way he hovered over the scene still, he watched at a certain remove, as in a dream, this tag sale that had been organized by his relatives. Don't pass so quickly, he would have said to the visitors, if he could have.

"It's worn out, I can't read it," someone says.

But that record was pure genius - that one in a thousand record that still provided a thrill whenever he heard it. If he had worked a little harder, if his musical taste had been more discriminating, perhaps he could have managed a group like the Satins. It might even have happened that the forever wonderful "In The Still Of The Night" could have been recorded at his own little studio. If that could have happened, if the record could have been released on his own label – which he had named for his wife, Frances – how different everything might have been. Not for the Satins, who were going to be tremendous in any case. But how his own career would have changed, if only this one thing could have gone differently, could have gone his way. Instead they made their record in the basement of a small church in the downtown, completely unheralded at the time. For the Satins it wouldn't have mattered, they were unstoppable. But his own story would have been entirely different. He'd seen and heard them early on, but he hadn't really heard, he didn't hear the spark of originality, whatever quality it was that created the singers' unique destiny.

In fact there had been few stars in his stable. For tiny Frances records the closest act to a headliner was The Noblemen, a group with a god-awful name that he could not get the leader and lead singer, Vito Gerrone, to change. Vito thought that the name spelled class, and maybe it would have if there had been just one natural tenor in the group, instead of just a bass and three fey-sounding alto's. And the rhythm sections that the impresario assembled for the recording dates, some of them could hardly stay on the beat. In later years when he would play his forty-fives or his reel-to-reel tapes, the sound sometimes reminded him of an old produce cart with uneven wheels moving down a bumpy road. It was nothing that the casual listener would pick up on, but sometimes when he listened critically to these sounds, the experience would bring tears to his eyes.

When he was being honest with himself, he felt that for the most part he had only traded in musical acts that were commonplace and mediocre. He had always wanted to think that he understood talent and could recognize it, but in retrospect he felt that it wasn't so. It was more true to say that he could recognize talent in retrospect, after almost universal acclamation - then he saw it and knew it. But how could this help him, as impresario? Occasionally over the years, someone would speak fondly about some record that he'd released, or an act that he'd managed, and he would smile gratefully. It seemed to him now that bad taste was everywhere in those days, that it was a constant in the lives of people. Given the number of groups and records, how much of the stuff could be truly memorable, anyway? But he felt that he had probably added to the problem. Due to lack of vision, foresight – or the courage to be different, maybe.

Once at a party, someone had played a new forty-five by a Southern blues singer. The record was already anticipating the rock and roll beat, and the singer whooped and moaned while an electric guitar rang out energetically. The singer was rough around the edges, but he had personality in spades. There was a definite style to the record, but it just wasn't *him*, he could never see himself getting behind this music. He could hear in it the sound of the swamp, he could smell the cotton-picking sweat of hard outdoor labor, and he was frankly unsettled by it. Sometimes, when he felt vaguely discontented by all that was bland and formulaic in the musical circles in which he lived, then he would think back to that record, to its unmistakable drive, its spark of originality, perhaps, and he would feel that his musical calling had taken him down a well-traveled road that lacked either surprises or innovation.

He could see it now. He saw so many things differently now, since the great change that had come over him. Since he had "passed over" (that was the phrase that came to him) he existed in a kind of fog, and he could not say how long he'd been here. As far as he knew he had not communicated with anyone. He had the impression that he'd lost his regional accent, which had been a compound of southern New England, and another that suggested New York City, primarily a kind of Brooklyn accent that he'd picked up, probably, from speaking by telephone with New York City-based colleagues, or, sometimes, meeting them face to face. But that accent seemed to have gone, and he sensed that his vocabulary had finally improved, too – at least, he thought so, judging by the many new words that formed in his consciousness. People that he used to know would be surprised to hear him, he felt sure.

Some things in the music business hadn't changed much. Then, as now, it wasn't always the best records that got airplay, but the ones that had some financial backing; artists that someone in the media believed in and who knew how to work the angles. That was what it took: with bad taste fairly endemic at all times, talent was only one part of the equation. He seemed to see so many things more clearly, and not only regarding the music business, that were concealed from him when he was himself in the battle, so to speak. He could hear the music of today, after a fashion, although as if through a haze, and attaching no great importance to it. There was little sense, although a good deal of attitude, and much empty posing, in what he heard. It somehow pained him to hear this music of today, as if to do so was his penance for all those years of pursuing his own misguided musical passion. And if he was active on the music scene today, and lacking the benefit of hindsight, he supposed that he would be sponsoring mediocre products, as before. But if he could not do it better, he would not want to have tried again.

He was aware of many uncertainties. He supposed that the king or queen of creation would at some point weigh his life's deeds in the balance, and probably find some of them wanting in some way. Among all of his follies, and his occasional acts of bravery. But he felt that he was sincere, when he said to himself that he had done his best. And so on balance, the feeling was one of well-being.

He wished, now, that he had done more to promote gospel music during his career, instead of rock and roll. For these songs really spoke to him in his new state. It was late to think about it, though. There was a particular gospel song that he was hearing now and that he liked – it just seemed to be in the air, or was it a mist – that was not like any song that he'd heard before. Or, at least, had paid attention to. Before, back in the days when he flattered himself that he was a shrewd judge of musical talent, he would not have thought twice about this song, whose chorus was, "I Done Got Over." Now he could not hear enough of it. It wasn't even good English, some of it, but that didn't really bother him.

Now as he looked back, he didn't think that his wife had ever really understood his passion for music, either. He used to think that she used every opportunity to clip the wings of his muse. Yes, a little bit. Not that she was ever really cruel about this. She used to tell friends that ever since he started fixing radios and televisions, in the repair shop that he owned, that he knew he wanted to be in the entertainment business. "Go ahead and laugh," he used to say, although he could seldom get angry with her. The repair shop was profitable, for he did much of the work himself. His wife had seemed happy if they could get into the city a few times a year to see a Broadway show, and if they could spend a week at Cape Cod in a rented cottage each summer. They never had any children, although they had wanted them.

A pretty middle-aged woman has picked up "Long And Lonely Nights," but she has trouble making out the title and returns it to the table. "Please," he thinks, "this one is pure genius." It's as if he feels that a part of his soul inhabits this particular circle of vinyl. But the woman, farsighted as she appears, doesn't seem to care about this. She stops squinting and just moves on. The suburban neighborhood is very quiet.

And during this lull, Frank Smaldoni went full-speed down to memory lane. Daydreams and recollections passed before him. It was a sunny day in May and he was driving his car in downtown New Haven. It was some time in the late nineteen-fifties. He had in his shirt pocket a list of vacuum tubes to buy at the electronics distributor, that were needed to fix this or that radio or television. He was hearing that particular song again on the radio. Some local singers had recently made a record of an old Rodgers and Hart tune, and the thing was getting a tremendous amount of airplay.

He could not hear much of Rodgers and Hart in the record, only a small vestige of the melody, as it were. The session producer had added a rock and roll beat, which was rapped out with smart snare drums. And there was some obbligato vocal work behind the main vocal, things like dit-dit-dit-dit, moon-moon-moon-moon, and so forth. This record was either totally bananas, or it represented a late flowering of the mature vocal style of doo-wop – Frank was not sure which, at the time. But either way, you had to be impressed by the sheer baroque inventiveness of the rendition.

"BOMP – BUH – BUH – BOMP." A tear started coming to Frank's eye. But it was not because the lyric moved him so much. He could remember their faces, the dark skin and bright teeth, the unassuming quality of the group members when they visited him at his recording studio. He'd liked them for their manners. He gripped the steering wheel and pulled to the side of the busy street and parked, letting his head loll forward.

"DANG – A - DANG – DANG." A tear rolled down his face. A city bus honked behind him and he was forced to pull away from the bus stop. Gently he slapped at the steering wheel. What song had they sung for him? – *a cappella*, of course. But what did it matter now? They were just another musical act that had gotten away from him. An act that he might have signed. *Could* have signed, he was pretty sure of it. How did he not know?

"DING – A - DONG – DING." He turned the car off of busy Chapel Street, driving slowly. Get a hold of yourself, Frankie. His tears had stopped. What, there are no other decent acts out there? You'll sign other acts, someday you're going to have a hit record, too.

They didn't sing any 'Blue Moon' when they had auditioned for him. He was sure of that. What the hell were they hiding that rendition for, he wondered, it's going to be such a big hit? They just hadn't seemed anything

29

special - although he seemed to be saying that too often lately. Maybe the group wasn't holding out on him. Maybe 'Blue Moon' was just sort of a throwaway idea, something to fill out the recording session, that had clicked somehow. Look at what the record was doing now – it was phenomenal.

He'd managed to calm himself down. Then the group went into the finale in blended falsetto voices, with the steadily rocking string bass and snare drum, and Frank almost went out of his mind again. He brought his hand smartly up to his forehead and muttered something, and, seeing off to the side the entrance to "Count" Lazarov's cozy barroom, he pulled suddenly to the curb. A car honked behind him, but he ignored the driver. He needed a drink, and he was hungry, anyway. He would just have a sandwich, a quick drink, and then resume his errand.

The Count had supposedly been born to a titled Russian family. Whether that was bogus or not, Frank had too much discretion to ask. What was more certain was that he had wrestled professionally in America during the twenties and thirties. There were many studio portraits of him on the walls, and posed or action photos of him with other wrestlers. His tavern, which bore his own name, had been here for as long as Frank could remember. The Count was very often behind the bar, as he was today. He was not a very big man, appearing to be just under six feet. The hair of the one-time "Lion Of The Steppes" had whitened, but there was still a thick mane of it, topping a ruddy, friendly-seeming face.

"Mr. Impresario," the Count said, shaking Frank's hand at the bar. "How is music business?"

"So-so, Count."

"Just so? Record store next door is doing – box-office! Young people can't hear enough of them, it's so?"

"Sure, sure."

"You like this new music?"

"I'm not sure I understand it too well, lately."

"No? You know this record, BOMP – BUH – BUH – BOMP? It just played. They say singers are from around here. Is selling like hot cake!"

"I believe it. They auditioned for me, you know."

"No!"

"I didn't see anything special."

The Count's eyebrows went up. "They sing BOMP—?"

"Of course not. Not *that* one." Frank frowned and took a sip of his beer.

The Count wiped the bar top circumspectly.

"I'm not sure that I do understand the new music. Now you take a Peggy Lee – this I can understand. I can see the talent there."

"Peggy Lee." The Count growled deeply in his chest. "I see, too."

30

"Something like this – well, it's a funny thing. It's just an old song. But add dang-y-dang-dang—"

"BOMP – BUH – BUH – BOMP—"

"Precisely. And it's genius."

The Count looked about to whistle, but no sound came out. "You think?"

The cook came out of the back with a plate. "Ah, here is food. Eat."

Frank fell to his sandwich. In between bites he asked, "How many wrestling matches did you have, Count?" He was sure he'd asked this question before, but he felt like changing the subject.

"Oh, must be thousand. All up and down Eastern sea-port. Phila, Pittsburgh, New York, Providence, Wor-chis-tor, Portland. You think I don't know these city? Summertime, winter, travel alone, come to town, small suitcase. Freezing cold, know no one, check in hotel. Train, car, bus. But you know what?" Leaning in, "Beautiful cities, all. To entertain those people—" He tapped his chest a few times with his fist, and it was another moment before he could speak. "I was blessed."

"Shut me off after one beer today, Count. The day is young and I am on a mission."

"Understand. I will grab you in headlock if necessary."

"That's the spirit. This sandwich is good."

"Only best. You know, in those day we did not have a 'Gorgeous George,' a 'Masked Marvel.' But we r-r-russle! Sometime we r-r-rustle two hour, until one of us fall down and can't get up."

Frank had heard all of this before, but he liked the soothing sound of the Count's voice. Some other customers had come in, and the Count moved down the bar. Frank soon paid up and left.

Frank's basement in those days had a full-length wooden bar, like many homes then. And in another corner was his reel-to-reel tape player and phonograph, and headphones that hung from a peg on the wall. He was not sure whose idea the headphones were (it was his wife's). Many times he would sit there in an upholstered chair with the phones around his head, in what he thought of alternately as his inner sanctum or place of banishment.

During the afternoon he'd completed a couple of repairs at the shop. He considered that a good day. But this evening he was feeling discouraged, not about the shop but about his prospects in the music business generally.

His wife came down the stairs and then she was spinning her fingers next to her ear, in a gesture that meant, he supposed, that she wanted to talk to him.

"What is this" – removing his headphones, and approximating her gesture – "supposed to mean."

"I don't know. You've just, you've always got the headphones on lately when you're home."

"Is anything wrong?"

"No."

"Weren't the headphones your idea? Do you remember? The sound of beautiful music bothers you, doesn't it, dear?"

"What *bella musica?*" she asked. "Where is it?"

"Ah… So now it bothers you if I use headphones, too?"

"It's just, you're in your own world."

"And it's a beautiful world – to me. Just now I'm listening to the newest record of The Noblemen, 'Please Be Mine'."

"Those gavon's?"

"They are not 'gavon's'. They are recording artists. And someday they are going to make it!"

Frank clicked the tape player off. Actually he wasn't enjoying the record very much, anyway.

"There's a word for people like me, Frances."

"Would you like me to guess what it is?"

"No. Because I'll tell you. It's 'self-taught.'"

"That's two words."

"You can laugh. Here's another one: impresario."

"Is that what you are?"

"That's what Count Lazarov calls me."

"That saloon-keeper. He's just pulling your leg."

"He is my best friend."

"Alright."

"An impresario, Francesca. That's what. You can't imagine it, can you? Some of the finest musical acts in New England come and seek me out. Do you know why?"

"I can't imagine."

"Because I am – No, I don't expect *you* to believe it."

"No, tell me. They seek you out why?"

"Never mind. Are you looking for something?"

"Do you have a bottle around here?"

"You know I don't."

"Alright. You know I don't begrudge you your music. I only say, keep your day job."

"'Course I'm gonna keep my day job. Did I say anything different?"

She shook her head and moved closer to him. "Can I hear your record?"

"Come 'ere," Frank said suggestively.

"You … clown."

"Come closer."

"Just play it through the speakers, we both can hear."

He shook his head, growled. She sat on the arm of the chair and Frank reached and cued up the tape and handed her the headphones.

She listened. She looked and acted blasé. Frank pretended to be irritated.

"You don't like it?"

"You're the *queen* behind my *throne*?" she mimicked. "Really."

"What's wrong with it?"

"Well, isn't a little – corny?"

"'Corny'? It was good enough for Shakespeare, wasn't it?" Raising his voice. "Have you read *Macbeth*?"

"Not since high school. Have *you* read Shakespeare lately?"

"Never mind. It's fine as it is."

She didn't say anything, but he could see the doubt in her eyes. "I tell ya it's gonna be a hit! Or my name isn't Francis Smaldoni!"

"Sure, Frank. Whatever you say." She kissed him and he pulled her closer to him.

"Why don't you come upstairs?" she said. "We're not too comfortable here."

"Oh, sure, sure. I'll be up."

But first he had a tape, a demo, to play. He cued it up. This was a new song that had to do with bells. Bells, he had found, always worked in records. Whispering bells, wedding bells. The singers sang about bells, and you worked bells into the arrangements, too, in a subtle way. *Can you hear the bells, my love*? No one ever lost on bells. But Frank had gotten into this particular game late, somehow. His record had bells, but there was nothing bravura, nothing memorable about it. He'd sat in his basement and played this one for many nights running, and he wondered just what was missing. That spark of originality, he supposed. He realized that what he had was just a commodity, a copy of an imitation.

The feeling of discouragement returned. He felt like he was shoveling sand against the tide.

That night he couldn't stop punishing himself further. The new record by the Corvairs, the one that he could have recorded, kept playing in his mind, it wouldn't stop, while he turned and fidgeted in bed. He kept remembering when the group had auditioned for him. Why hadn't he seen it, that special quality?

Why had he said, instead, to the lead singer, Earl, "Earl, I don't think we can do anything right now. But keep practicing. And I'm going to put your name and number in my personal rolodex!"

"In your – what? Oh," Earl had said in his resonant bass voice. "I understand," not really understanding, disappointment flickering in his eyes.

God, had he really said that? His personal rolodex – so important-sounding! What a *gavon*!

He slept fitfully that night. The record kept drifting into his unconscious thoughts. The chorus repeated near the end of the record, with all the singers shifting up into slightly higher keys. Then again, a higher pitch of excitement. In the final chorus these cats sound like rollicking *castrati* singing behind an insane beat. In his dream he is listening indolently, dreamily, as though to some faraway yet hypnotic strain of music.

Higher – higher – improbably higher. More awake than not, he muttered, "Oh, stunad', stunad'." That record was a baroque, freakin' masterpiece, that's all it was.

"Hey, wake up," he heard his wife say.

"What? What for?"

"Because you're keeping *me* awake!"

"'Keeping you awake.' I doubt it."

"You doubt it? You're talking like a madman."

"'Talking like a madman.' How can I be?"

"I mean it. You're talking to yourself again. I think you need help."

"I don't need help. If I'm talking to myself, maybe that's because it's the only time that I have a sympathetic listener that understands me."

"Jeez, you're breaking my heart. Like I don't try to understand?"

He didn't say anything for awhile.

"Frank. You weren't – crying, before?"

"Wha-a-at? 'Course I wasn't crying. I don't think."

"Because if you're worried about money, you could always keep the shop open longer. Couldn't you?"

"'Keep the shop open longer.'"

"I just said that."

"I heard. This is not just about money. You don't understand my artistic needs."

His wife turned over on her side and faced him. "Your – artistic needs."

"M'm," he grunted.

In twenty years of togetherness his wife thought that she had heard everything. Now she felt nonplussed, and said so. "I don't know what to say. It's like you are being eaten up with this – obsession. Can't you forget about the music? What does it get you, when you stop and think about it?"

"It's in here," Frank said, thumping his chest. "Even if it gets me nothing."

She looked at his closed eyes in the early morning light and frowned.

One afternoon Frank auditioned a new group at his little recording studio. They were four young black men. Frank found them exceedingly polite and well-spoken, and they were dressed very sharply, too, in matching business suits of light grey. They did not sing badly, and they had brought a couple of original songs to the audition. One was called "Cherie Lee," and the other, "Wanda." Both were just representative kinds of songs, rather than truly original. But Frank saw some promise. He asked them what they called themselves.

"The Turbans," the young man who took the lead vocals announced.

"Turbans," Frank repeated. "Like the—" And he placed his hands out a few inches from the sides of his head. "That's not bad."

"We usually wear them."

"You mean, on the stage?"

"Sure."

"Oh. I don't know…"

"People dig the hats. They remember us, like."

"I'm trying to picture," Frank said, smiling. He looked at his watch. He said that he would let them know.

When he played the tapes for himself later all he could picture was the turbans. The image distracted him. Some weeks went by, and Frank was astonished to find that the group had a record out, and that it was receiving air play. He asked around and learned that they had a business manager, a rival of Frank's. Frank knew the rival and did not like him particularly. Prior to this, the only accomplishment that Frank's rival was noted for was producing a version of "Stormy Weather" that was sung to a three minute obbligato of driving rain, and which ended in peals of thunder that finally drowned out the vocal. Frank just thought the arrangement was an okay idea that was carried too far.

Then Frank watched as the Turbans' fortunes seemed to rise irresistibly, first locally and then throughout New England. Their names appeared in revues, at first on the bottom of the posters, and then more and more prominently. Soon their photograph, with the signature headgear, was at the very top of the advertising posters. Frank looked on these events with a resentful and sinking feeling that was commensurate with the group's rise.

Trying to find inspiration from disappointment, he began to think that perhaps with the right gimmick, one of his own musical acts might break out of the doldrums. It only took some imagination. He had few stars as yet. The Four Freshmen were huge. Danny And The Juniors, with their varsity sweaters, had recently charted several top-ten hits. Frank had the Three Sophomores, and no one had even heard of them yet. He told them it was only a matter of time, but privately he had his doubts. Or maybe The Noblemen would agree to a name change. He'd always hated their name, anyway. He would broach it to Vito. Now he was thinking about hats and group names. Like The Stetsons – that was too old-fashioned, though. They would look like Southern deacons. The Derbys – too British and zany. Both ridiculous-looking. What about The Berets, he wondered. That could work. Or would they look too French, or too fairy? No, it could work, he told himself. He would stop in a haberdasher's tomorrow.

If only one of the boys could actually sing. Still, it was a hope…

Some of the morning's paraphernalia in the driveway and garage may have been moved around slightly, but most of it seems to remain there in the late afternoon. Few of the impresario's mementos created much of a stir, although a pair of straw-wrapped chianti bottles sold for a dollar.

It would not appear likely that the accomplishments of this minor musical figure will be remembered fondly in any public television documentary, or probably anywhere else, either. Still, no tears should be shed for this toiler among the remote and dimly-lighted byways of the popular arts, where he was guided only by the faulty instrument of his own taste. And if bad taste was endemic in his time, and if he had in his own modest way tended to add to the problem (as he sometimes felt in times of discouragement), perhaps he was only born in the wrong time. Perhaps, in a different era, audiences might have responded more enthusiastically to the songs and the acts that he brought before them. After all, bad taste is known to assume a morbid and monumental character at times. Perhaps if he had lived in our time where, as we see (to paraphrase Balzac), the things of solid worth often sink to the bottom, while light trash floats irresistibly to the surface – then perhaps his enterprises might have fared better, might not have ended in dust and obscurity, and he might have claimed the glittering prizes for his own.

THE WILDERNESS SINGERS:

I

The question had been decided rather suddenly, on the evening of their mother's funeral. After his mother died, it hadn't seemed practical for Richard Marston to stay on in the family house in New England by himself. That was what everyone said, and he was sure they were right, for he had no idea about how to manage a house. His younger brother lived in an apartment in Queens. He told Richard that he could stay with him and see if the place agreed with him.

Now Richard stood in front of his bedroom window getting dressed. To the south, the early morning sky above Brooklyn was piled with purple cotton clouds, which were shot through with sunlight in places; broad and low-hanging clouds, like bellies of fantastic creatures. It was a dramatic sky but it didn't appear to signal turbulence. Richard raised the blind to see more clearly. Sometimes, in response to some nervous spasm, his head would loll on his shoulder and then he would straighten himself and look out again.

For almost a year, with the help of tranquilizers, Richard had been living at home with his mother. Prior to that he had resided at a number of state mental hospitals, and when these had closed down, a series of halfway houses. He had lived at home at intervals, when he felt calm enough. This followed a mysterious "breakdown" that Richard suffered during high school.

His had not been a happy family, by and large. Their father had been confused and disappointed by Richard's condition. As strong and sound as Richard was physically, he'd never actually held a job for any long duration. It was a horrible waste to the old man, who had always lived by his labor in the New England shoe factories. Tension had been a chronic and seemingly unavoidable presence in the house. Sometimes, during family meals, if Richard poured himself a soda, the old man couldn't resist commenting on what a large glass it was. Their mother would defend Richard. There was often this battleground, about things either trivial or serious. Their mother was consumed by battles of this kind, and by grief over the obscure causes of Richard's illness.

Richard pulled a sweater over his head. He was in his middle thirties. He was of just over average height, and broad-shouldered. A shock of straight black hair had been combed into place, but rose ungovernably at the back of his head. Most people would have said that he was handsome. He continued to look out the window. He could see, faintly, the band of blue water below Brooklyn. His eyes went out of focus momentarily, while his hands struck out in front of him; his fingers struck in a rapid fanlike succession against his palm. Then with one hand he pressed on the top of his head, and ran his hand back over his hair as if in a calming motion. He could hear his brother calling him, and he hollered back.

Looking out, he thought that the day might clear; he hoped so. Actually, Richard had been feeling in one of his dark moods. He'd felt it building for several weeks now. He could never explain why. There were days when he felt that he was surrounded by a great circle of light, and then at other times he could see only darkness around him. For one thing, he was thinking more often of his mother, and how he missed her.

His mood may have had to do with his relative inactivity, and his lack, really, of much society. But it wasn't only that. It wasn't just that an everyday observation - it might be the way someone was sitting at a counter and drinking tea in a restaurant - struck him as ineffably sad, and dispiriting; engendered in him a feeling that more than one social worker or doctor had called "depression." Yes, he was sometimes depressed, and that feeling came and it went. But this other feeling that had come over him again was something different, it was something more. It had to do with nothing less than the problem of Evil.

Sometimes he thought his life was a confused and rambling business. He wondered if the tranquilizers robbed him of some of his mental clarity, at the same time that they helped him to function. Sometimes he thought he was living in a dream. Sometimes his sleep was so profound that for several minutes after waking he would feel like he was in a dream state - a waking dream. He remembered some incidents from when he was a child of about ten. The Cuban missile crisis may not have made much of an impression on other children of Richard's age, but he remembered living daily with the fear and uncertainty - the dark and commanding headlines, the mysterious talk of the grown-ups. He since wondered why *he* should have been so affected - why he of all people should have felt that he'd been given a role to play, a principal role, in resolving the crisis. But that was what he had felt, for a brief while.

And it was at that time that reality and irrational fear started to blur in his mind, when dreams and nightmares merged into his waking state. He remembered waking up one afternoon to a strange, crystalline ringing of a telephone, hearing it with dread, and sensing that, somehow, people looked to him to solve the Armageddon that was set in motion. He walked mechanically through his parents' house and pushed at the door to the front hallway - there was only his mother talking with someone on the telephone. But the other visions remained so powerfully in his mind that he had asked his mother: "Is that them?" They were asking for him to intercede - to save this world. She'd stared at him even as she continued to speak into the receiver, but the light and bantering expression on her face flickered away. Only gradually, standing there, did his notion strike him as preposterous, and he turned and walked away in embarrassment and confusion. Later his mother came over to the window where he was standing, near a hissing radiator, his temples now throbbing, and she felt his forehead to see if he might have a fever. Strange, he thought - the worry he must have caused her. It was not just a result of youthful imagination. Even then, the problem had to do with the nature of Evil.

Richard believed that there was a devil. He felt this with almost as much certainty as that there was a God - a benevolent God. The Devil was mixed up in all of the evil and ignorance in the world. Indeed, the world was his domain, almost as much as it was God's. You only had to look around to see it. He couldn't give any shape to this picture of a Devil. Sometimes he thought it existed in another universe, and was using its mysterious powers to control this one. An extraterrestrial force. Or a plasma. A virus. His powers of imagination failed.

Sometimes he thought his notion - of a cosmic battle between Good and Evil - was awfully like some not very good science-fiction movies of the nineteen-fifties. There would be a clean-cut guy at the helm of a space ship. Even the captain's clothing, a solid-color jumpsuit with turtleneck and trim epaulets, spelled purity and determination. The big ship was rocked by dust storms, and by explosions and other tricks conjured up by unseen, malevolent forces. Nothing would deter the captain from trying to right a world gone wrong, and to free the unenlightened people of their hatred and prejudices. This was his code of conduct, it was burned into his heart and was also the credo of his personal captain's log. This vision was like a heroic film that Richard had created within his own mind, and self-created and personal as the vision was, he could never remember speaking with anyone about it.

But he did not doubt the essential truth of his vision. It *was* a serious business. There were many who increased and consolidated the Devil's powers here on earth. There was no getting around this. Others, many people, walked in the light. Richard tried to.

It was this vision of the Devil's immense powers which oppressed Richard. A miasma. He was oppressed with a nightmare vision of history: a dreadful newsreel that never stopped, that never will stop while men live. Here disheveled women, their children taken from them, pleaded silently to the camera. In a besieged city, men fought with starving dogs for the remnants of overturned garbage cans. The Devil played his macabre marches. Worst of all, those films from the concentration camps. They showed them at Richard's Catholic grammar school one day. He hadn't known what to expect. Maybe his teachers, too, were concerned with illustrating the problem of Evil. Perhaps they were not wrong. The Bible taught that there was a Devil. But that atrocity - the inhuman guards, that organized and state-sanctioned evil - how, above all else, could God have allowed this to happen? It could only be that He was not all-powerful. (Although, perhaps, if you were a Catholic like Richard, it was a sin to think so.) God was not all-powerful - and the forces of evil were getting the upper hand. You didn't have to read the newspaper every day to realize this.

The newspapers were filled every day with stories of cruelty and barbarity. He didn't understand any of the rationalizations that people sometimes made for their actions. He would not even venture an opinion about those things. Somehow over the years he had lost that faculty of making judgments, left it behind at the hospitals. And now he did not even like to look at the newspapers, except for the funny pages which sometimes cheered him.

It seemed crazy, now, that Richard himself might have been enlisted in that great battle of Good and Evil. How could he have helped? His thoughts were growing heavier. It was necessary to break free of them somehow, or they would defeat him. And so he had begun thinking if he might be able to get a job of some kind - some sort of day-to-day activity – and he had begun speaking with Paul about it.

There were days when he would like to do nothing so much as climb some quiet hill by himself, and once there to watch the distinct clouds that formed and drifted over the sky. Maybe see a hawk circling. He liked to imagine what a hawk sees: dense forest, outlined highways, a still lake. The small game in open fields.

When he was young he would sometimes climb up a small hill like that, behind a supermarket in his neighborhood. He rarely saw anyone else there, unless - sometimes - he went with one of the neighborhood kids. The top of the hill was level with short grass, without many trees. Richard would lie on his back on a flattened piece of cardboard picked from the supermarket dumpster and look up at the sky, and sometimes the clamor in his mind would ease, whether it was tension associated with school or home, or whether it was about his involvement in that epic battle for the world's soul. Whatever it was that pressed upon his thoughts, he found some release there, thinking to himself, with a transistor radio, or just some tunes that he remembered to accompany him, and the monumental clouds shifting shape and position above; the flight of a bird, the small airplane, sometimes the vapor trail of a jet.

There was no time for it anymore.

You have to move forward, he said to himself. What's past is past.

Today he and his brother Paul were visiting the social services agency. He thought he would like to join a workshop, if that were possible. He used to enjoy that. Paul thought it was a good idea, too; in fact they'd had the same thought. Not that Richard ever earned so much money at the workshops, in fact he thought he spent nearly all that he earned buying coffees and danishes on the morning and afternoon breaks. A fleeting memory of his father came to him: asking him, at the dinner table, how much he had earned that week, and how much did he spend on pastry. He must have known Richard's routine in those days. Richard could tell where the old man's irony was going, and he answered reluctantly and with a nervous smile. Then Richard's mother interjected, "Don't be negative, Dad."

Richard had one of his nervous spasms, looking out the window toward Brooklyn. "Don't be negative, Dad," he said softly, and he worked his jaw to the left and right, and ran his hand straight back over his head in the calming motion. He finished dressing, and in a few minutes he and Paul were walking down the hill toward the subway station. The morning was cold and dry. A question was burning inside Richard. He wondered for a moment if there would be a better opportunity to ask it, decided that there wouldn't be, and spoke.

"You believe in God, don't you, Paul?"

"I guess."

"You guess?"

"Yes. I don't think about it that much."

Richard frowned, his deep-set eyes narrowing as they crossed a street.

"No kidding, you mean you don't even think about it?"

"Not that much, I mean."

"What do you think about?"

"Jesus," Paul pleaded. "Will you give me a break?"

"Oh. Sorry." Richard shifted his jaw.

"I'm sorry. It's as good an explanation as anything," Paul said.

They were near a subway station. "Aren't we going in here?" Richard asked.

"Today we're going to take the elevated for awhile. It's a few more blocks."

Richard shrugged. If he lived in this city another twenty years he still would not know his way around, he thought. But how could Paul not think about religion? Wasn't it the most important thing in the world? What else could anyone rely on but God – certainly not people. That was no place to put your faith. He remembered the darkened, incense-smelling church basement, where the paintings of Christ's martyrdom known as the Stations of the Cross hung on the walls. Not the main church, but the basement. In a yearly observance, the priest would walk slowly with his assistants and pause reverently before each painting. Richard couldn't help feeling thrilled and humbled now, as he had when he sat in one of the pews. He felt small and unworthy before such sacrifice. He remembered the words in the battered old missal, words, supposedly, uttered mockingly by some onlookers: "*Pity your poor dying redeemer...*"

Paul and Richard approached the elevated. Paul bought a newspaper in a variety store. Richard looked at the candies in front of the counter.

"You have gum, don't you?" Paul asked.

Richard studied one of the bright red packages. "Not like this."

"Oh." Paul was about to say: You buy these by the bag, where they are cheaper. That's what his parents would have said. All his life he had thought this way, but he checked himself. "So buy it," he said.

"No kidding - buy it?"

"What the heck. It's not going to break the bank."

"Yeah. 'What the heck,' right?" Richard drew a bill carefully from his wallet and paid the cashier.

They drew up to the blackened steel framework of the elevated and climbed the stairs. When the train arrived they found adjacent seats on one of the benches. It was unusual, and pleasant, to have a view of the passing landscape - you didn't get that on the subway. The train veered gently southward, amid the three- and four-story tenements of Brooklyn. The top stories and the rooftops and gutters were almost flush with the elevated tracks. Many of the buildings alongside the steel elevated tracks were ruined, plywood covered many of the windows. No one seemed to live in many of these apartments anymore. The gutters were supported by ornamented cement struts placed every few feet. Passing through, a rider had a glimpse of the borough's past life. There were projecting spires of churches, some of which were victims of fire or neglect. He saw a looming stucco church with a huge round stained-glass window in the upper wall; but with gaping holes where fitted pieces had fallen or been knocked out. The church's other windows were boarded up. It looked as if even God had left some of these neighborhoods, but

Richard knew that couldn't be so. One saw into back yards and narrow streets where kids now walked with book bags. It was not hard to imagine ice trucks and clusters of people on the stoops listening to the Dodgers on table radios placed on windowsills. But the scene was different now. A wall with nearly faded markings advertised some long-forgotten brand of beer. Maybe Richard's father would have remembered the brand. One saw remnants of the borough's former manufacturing industries: trade names, and business names, represented in paint on the sides of buildings, and on small rooftop parapets or sheds - on almost any surface that could be glimpsed by riders on the el. *SB Krausse Paints Oils Varnishes*. More buildings, more advertisements. *Chains gears sprockets pulleys*. The painted names were faded, and next to them, covering some of the letters, were scrawled graffiti. Why would people spend time doing anything so meaningless? Why did they bother, Richard wondered. Then the train sloped into a tunnel with a breathless rush and remained underground.

The train moved briskly through a darkness that was lit sporadically by banks of incandescent bulbs. Peeling girders were dimly visible, and occasional workmen in insulated clothing, some of them swinging lanterns. As Paul and Richard approached a station the light would grow stronger, and a few cement steps would lead up from the electrified rails, the refuse lying about the tracks, to a yellow magnetized gate and then the level platform where riders waited. The train paused in the semi-darkness.

The crowd of riders standing near the doors shifted at the successive stops. Through the gaps that were created, Richard began to notice a man who was sitting on a bench about twenty feet away. His head was thrown back, and his mouth was ajar. His face looked ravaged, although he was evidently only in his twenties or thirties. And he was not just sleeping, something was wrong about him. One of his arms, which he might have raised to scratch himself, just remained suspended above his head – just pointing, like a limb of some small blighted tree. Richard remembered, from some of the hospitals, people who would remain curled up in a similar way. The man stayed in this posture for as long as Richard could see him through the other riders. He looked a little like one of those music conductors that Richard saw on the television sometimes, with their eyes closed and their attention completely focused on the music. But he looked more like some of the patients that Richard used to see at the hospitals, the ones who were heavily sedated. He looked like he was fast approaching *rigor mortis*. But this must have been caused by some drug that the man took voluntarily, so Richard supposed.

Others found music, and it could mean a great deal to them. Paul once bought a record by a French composer of piano music, that he seemed to play at the family house whenever Richard was staying there, when he wasn't at a hospital or someplace. The music seemed to have no emotional content at all, it seemed rather to describe a crystalline world that was filled with obscure jests, that Richard couldn't understand, and yet the music agreed with him. The sounds were calm and made him feel good.

But it was mostly popular music that Richard enjoyed. The lack of fresh air and natural light in the tunnel-bound train began to feel oppressive, and he closed his eyes and tried to clear his mind, and bid some song from his memory to enter there. This sometimes calmed him. In his mind he heard one of the songs of The Wilderness Singers, who were a favorite gospel-singing group of his. He heard the strumming guitar, and smart snare drum, then the group harmony of the singers - the call and response, the holiness animated by rhythm. *When I was walking in darkness*, they sang, *when my way was dark as night...*

The music that Richard heard caused his feet to tap on the floor, and his hands to light in front of his chest while his fingers struck in a rapid fanlike succession against his palms. His eyes went out of focus and closed, and with one hand he pressed on the top of his head. What was the name of that song? Oh, yes: Since I Laid My Burden Down. A couple of riders looked over at him.

The train jerked forward and stopped. Gradually the next station came into view, and the riders - well-dressed executives, and youths with high-top sneakers, other people wearing clothing that might have come from bins on Fourteenth Street - all lined up with set faces.

"We have to get off the next stop," Paul said.

"Okay." Richard waited a moment, and they both rose and stood by the doors. A large black woman was already waiting there. People jostled and shifted on the platform as the train began to slow down. Why don't they just wait, Richard wondered. There were plenty of seats in the car. Did everyone queue up like this because it was New York and people were just expected to rush forward? Annoyance roiled his stomach and rose to his chest.

He heard Paul say, turning his head back, "When the train stops we are just going to *push out*." Richard nodded. "Stay with me. These people are animals."

"I know," Richard said, but as if by rote, not really responding to Paul's remark.

Outside, a short and slight woman had lined up opposite the black woman. She remained fixed there when the doors opened. The black woman was annoyed. She took a step forward and grabbed the smaller woman by the shoulders, flinging her into the crowd, then walked on with dignity. The smaller woman and the rest of the crowd surged forward before Paul had even stepped from the train. Richard nudged him forward. But Paul seemed to land on someone's foot, he shifted his weight awkwardly, and a woman's voice complained--

"O-w-w, you big horse--"

And Paul lost his balance momentarily, until the surging crowd righted him. The black woman led the way, and she turned her head and nodded to both of them slightly. But what was the need of all this strife, Richard wondered. No one was going to teach these people how to behave civilly anytime soon, that was for sure.

They arrived at a modern office building whose directory showed dozens of city and state and federal agencies. But the interview was disappointing. The social worker seemed distracted, and said there was not much money for the kind of workshop Richard and Paul were asking about. She was sorry. She pulled a looseleaf binder and began ticking off entries on a page.

"You live in Queens, right? M'm. You can fill out an application." She attached a form to a clipboard and, barely looking up, passed it to Richard. It was brief, and he completed it in a couple of minutes.

"I just don't see any openings."

"I need something to do," Richard said.

"Well--" Brusquely at first, then, "I'm sure you do. I wish I could be more helpful."

"That's it?" Richard asked.

"Is there somewhere else we can go?" Paul asked.

She shook her head. "I will make some calls. You left a telephone number?"

They left. "She's not going to call," Richard said.

"Don't be sure. If she doesn't we'll try something else."

They walked along the empty late-morning corridor. When the elevator stopped it was already occupied by a thin and neatly dressed young man. He was smiling strangely and averting his eyes.

He got off the car and Paul and Richard entered. But instead of leaving he re-entered, and held the door and looked up and down the corridor.

"Let's go," Richard said. Paul motioned to him to take it easy. But the guy continued to hold the door, grinning and looking up and down the corridor.

"Let's wait for somebody?" he said.

"Let's not," Paul said.

Richard approached the control panel and said to the guy, "I'm closing the door. Let's not screw around."

At this the guy leaped outside, and looked at the floor and grinned sheepishly. The doors closed on him.

"Screwball," Richard said.

"Don't get upset."

"Probably not even being treated. Probably considered *normal.*"

"Don't worry about it," Paul said.

"Ma was right. She said there are always more crazy people that never *get* any treatment. Considered normal citizens."

"I know."

" 'So don't you feel bad,' she'd say." Richard's voice was calm again. His fingers played over the control panel as the car descended. Suddenly he struck a clear section of wall with the heel of his palm, though not very hard. When the doors opened and he saw the people lined up he took off almost at a run, and paused only when he got outside. Then he remembered himself, and stopped. He was in the middle of a crowded plaza, where the rushing people made a circle around him. He stood in the center of the circle, rocking on his feet, while his hand kept running straight back along his hair in the calming motion. His jaw moved about fractionally to the left and right, and he stared at a space on the cement below. He felt slightly dizzy and wanted to crouch on the ground, but he was afraid that the crowd would trample over him. Instead they just swarmed past him.

"That's what she'd say," he said out loud. "You just gotta persevere."

The song he'd remembered on the train came back into his mind, and looking up he saw that the morning's clouds had parted and the sky was a vivid blue.

His brother stopped some feet away from him, slightly winded. He drew in a deep breath, and then approached and stood just in front of Richard.

"Do you want to get some lunch?"

Richard seemed to have calmed considerably. He drew his coat collar around him against the wind that swept across the plaza.

"I know you're doing your best."

"Sure. Let's get something to eat," Paul said.

"You gotta persevere, you know?"

They walked slowly along the plaza toward the street where there were coffee shops. The crowd continued to stream around them.

II

Richard stood washing his hands at the round communal sink. He stepped on a circular bar and thin jets of water poured down on his hands. In this it was just like the last workshop that he'd been in. There were gray lockers along the wall, and above them the late afternoon sunlight shone faintly through short and grimy windows.

Jamey Delmastro glided noiselessly up to the sink and struck rapidly at the soap release several times. Richard winced at the sudden noise.

"How's it going, Richard?" Jamey asked.

"Alright." Richard went off and stood drying his hands with a paper towel.

Jamey moved toward him with short quick steps. He was a thin man. When he was in motion it seemed as if only his feet moved, underneath baggy, oversized dungarees. His face was pale, with a studied and intense expression.

"You-you-you leaving now?" Jamey asked.

"Sure." Richard himself felt unusually calm today. But Jamey seemed nervous, and Richard wondered what kind of medication he was taking.

"What?" Jamey said.

"Nothing. I'm drying my hands." Richard removed his smock and placed it in his locker.

They left the locker room and passed through the foyer where a guard sat at a desk. They said goodnight and walked down the stairs of the converted school building, out past an iron gate.

Jamey took two small steps to Richard's one, moving quickly and with evident nervousness.

"I'm glad when I can light up," he said, lighting a cigarette. "You want one?"

"No, thanks."

"They tell ya it's bad for ya, but what're ya gonna do? Living every day is bad for ya, too, I'm sure."

Jamey had an odd way of putting things. Unlike Richard, he was a city kid. Richard liked him alright. They walked through the scruffy neighborhood. The sun was setting behind the three and four story brick buildings. There was refuse on the ground. There were a few nondescript grocery stores, that

47

probably would smell of cat urine and have only cold luncheon meats behind the glass, if they had that much. Radios boomed from cars that started up squealing when the light turned. To Richard, this neighborhood in Queens was like a thousand other places in the city.

"I have to go to the city, though," Richard said. He knew that "the city" meant Manhattan to all local people.

"You're going to New York? What for?" Jamey demanded – his voice truculent, seemingly disappointed.

"I have to look for a present for my brother."

"Oh. You have to go to Manhattan for that?"

"Yeah. It's a special record I'm looking for."

"You're always looking for some record, aren't'ya?" After a moment Jamey asked, "How'd you wind up in New York City, kid?"

Richard shrugged, thinking about the question. He remembered his mother telling him, although he couldn't be sure if it was his mother, now - the tranquilizers seemed to rob him of some mental clarity, at the same time that they allowed him to function - how his life was not going to be easy, but that he would have friends, a few good friends, she said. She wasn't really right about the friends, though. This didn't really bother him, it was just the way things were. There were guys like Jamey, guys that you might ride back from the workshop with. Jamey even invited him to his house sometimes for Italian meals that his Mom cooked. But that didn't mean that he was a close friend, in fact no one really knew what made Richard tick. Except his brother, he supposed.

But if there was not a variety of companionship in his life, there had always been music. He heard it in his mind all of the time: the Carter Family, the Mainer Brothers, and Fats Domino and so many others, playing up there all the time.

How had he wound up here? The question was too hard to answer, and Richard only shrugged.

"You live with your brother, right?" Jamey asked him.

"Yes. Like I told you."

"Well, what's he do?"

"Oh, he's an engineer."

Richard felt a kind of pride that he could provide such a straightforward answer. Even if he had only a vague idea of what his brother did for a living, the word had a magisterial sound for him. Jamey's mind, though, was evidently moving in a different direction.

"An engineer, eh? What train does he ride - the BMT?" Jamey's arm went up and he tugged on an imaginary train whistle. He feinted a couple of steps away from Richard, as if expecting a blow for this riposte.

Richard only listened impassively, though, and then said, "Nobody likes a smart-ass, Jamey."

"What?"

"What. Your ideas are two hundred years old, that's what," Richard complained. "Engineers don't just ride on trains anymore."

"I knew that. What're you getting so sore for? Can't I make a joke?" Jamey glided back toward Richard.

Richard looked offended for another moment, shrugged, and then wheeled and nearly caught Jamey's knobby head in a headlock. Jamey yelled and scampered away a few steps, laughing.

They fell in step again as they approached the subway entrance. "I've gotta turn here," Richard said, at the bottom of the steps.

Jamey turned in the other direction and paused. "Hey, Rich. Keep your day job, kid." He flashed the thumbs-up sign.

Richard was getting used to the workshop. He was almost getting used to New York - cold, peculiar city, though. It seemed like you never saw the same person twice, and this did not agree with him. The workshops, of course, never paid very much; he was used to that. It was perplexing to think how the lunch breaks, and the breaks for danishes and coffee that he enjoyed, ate up nearly half of his pay. It was not something you could live on. The other check from the state was supposed to cover his expenses. Paul said that the job was more something to take the edge off his nerves, to give his days a focus. And it did seem to help.

Richard felt tired. He nodded off as he rode on the train. Work was from nine to four every day. He'd worked at a few different stations at the workshop. Waiting for a machine - an automatic lathe, it might be - to finish its run, to collect the pieces in a cardboard box and seal it evenly with tape. Some days he placed plastic bags, which contained eating utensils, in a heat-sealing machine. He didn't mind the work. It was good experience, as he said.

If he was tired it was due partly to the medication, also. That was probably why he went to bed at nine-o'clock most nights. But if he didn't take the medication he'd get - nervous, again. About what? He couldn't say. He pondered what it was - that needless fear - but, on the verge of sleep, his mind supplied no clear picture of it.

Suddenly the door to the forward car swung open, and Richard woke with a start. A young guy entered, wearing shorts although it was only March. He was holding a harmonica, and with his other hand he folded up a paper cup and put it in his back pocket. Was he going to play a song?

The guy paused. Then he began singing, after a fashion. At first it sounded like the guy was howling in pain. The sounds were atonal, the words unarticulated. Gradually a hint of melody and some sense emerged, and Richard recognized the chorus to some popular song that he'd heard on a television commercial. But it never sounded like this. Richard was dumbfounded. The man brought the harmonica to his mouth, and after awhile Richard could make out a gloss upon some totally unrelated tune. Lord, the guy was bad.

Richard looked around the train. There were ten or twelve riders. Were they supposed to pay the guy to stop, or what?

The singer continued, anyway - he seemed to know only choruses, and few of the words, at that - in his painfully wrought falsetto voice. Then he produced the folded paper cup and walked slowly down the center of the train, shaking the cup to either side. Why was he slowing down near Richard?

"You like it?" the guy asked.

Richard turned his head and faced him, considering. "Not very much." he said.

The guy's eyebrows went up sort of incredulously. Actually it was one long eyebrow, that met in the middle. Obviously he was not used to hearing honest opinions. The guy looked like Clarence Guidry, from one of the state hospitals. Clarence didn't sing, though. He used to carry matchbooks with pictures of naked women on the covers, and tried to show them to women who were there on visitor days. The women would usually grin uncomfortably and look to see if there was an attendant around.

Richard shook off his memory of the hospitals, and at the same time the strange thought came to him, not for the first time, that without even looking you could find more oddballs here in this city than you could find at any of those hospitals. That thought always gave him pause.

The guy asked, "Would you like to contribute something?" He was shaking the paper cup. Richard was not surprised that the cup was empty and therefore did not make any sound when the man shook it.

"Well ... I think it's a free country," Richard said.

The guy pulled a long face, shrugged, and continued walking on slowly.

Everyone wanted to be in show business in this town. That's how things seemed to Richard. He felt a bit of annoyance at the guy's forwardness. "You ever hear Nat King Cole?" he asked, when the guy had moved on. He didn't hear, or chose not to turn around. "*That* was singing," Richard said emphatically. He nodded to a middle-aged woman who was sitting nearby, but she only stared straight ahead, with that familiar look of someone who is determined not to be drawn into a disturbance. To heck with her, too. Richard waved his hand dismissively, as much at the impassive woman as at the singing man.

The guy exchanged a few words with a young and tanned-looking woman, who seemed amused by him. Suddenly Richard thought of an old illustration in a book that used to be in his parents' house: Orpheus Charming the Thracian Maidens. Richard nearly laughed, but only shrugged. When the train stopped the guy went on to the next car. Then it was quiet again, except for the motion of the train.

Richard thought that he probably should have told Paul he would be late. But his brother would have suggested meeting him. He might see the present that Richard was planning to buy.

Last week he'd been listening to one of his records when Paul arrived home for supper. The song told the story of the beggar, Lazarus, and how he was left to die. Richard loved the pious lyric, that was nominally about Lazarus but was about Jesus, too. The words always moved him. He loved the way the singers blended harmonies, and the special emphasis placed on some of the words. *Once he was fair...*

"Don't you have another version of that song?" Paul had asked.

"Which?" Richard had to think for a moment. "Oh. I know the one you mean."

"You still have that record?"

Richard shook his head no.

"What happened to it? Was it lost in the move?" "The move," after their mother's death, had accounted for a few lost books and records and some missing clothing.

"No," Richard said. "I just wore that record out."

"I loved that record."

"You did? Did you ever play it?"

"Sometimes. Mostly I remember you playing it."

"Oh." Richard seemed surprised.

Paul must have been thinking of that version recorded by The Wilderness Singers. The recording was at least seventy years old. The vocal quartet was accompanied only by a sweetly droning harmonium, that brought to mind a country church; just that and, what was equally atypical, a kind of large zither that had had a brief vogue in the era when the recording was made, before disappearing from use, and whose dozens of strings, being struck very gently, sounded as ethereal as a heavenly harp.

That was what had started the idea. Richard thought he would see if he could find the record for Paul. One Saturday they had visited Jimmy's Music World, in downtown Manhattan, together, and Richard thought that he could find his way back there without difficulty.

The music had gotten better since the train entered Manhattan. At the Rockefeller Center station, the doors opened to the blind accordionist playing

"Make Believe." He sat on the wooden bench with his face tilted upward, but with his eyes closed, and the opened music case at his feet. Next to him a man with a violin played harmony.

Richard got off the train and began walking east along Chambers Street. It was dusk. A cold wind swept off the Hudson River. The area felt familiar. The World Trade Towers loomed above the smaller commercial buildings. If you stood on the sidewalk and leaned your head back... But better not, he thought. Get dizzy, pass out like that other time, maybe. What had caused that? Some new medication he was taking? No one explained it. The weather felt cold, for March.

New York was nothing like Worcester, Massachusetts, where he'd grown up. Nothing like Worcester with its CHANDLER'S sporting goods store on the main street where he bought the set of York barbells. Loading the box into Pop's trunk. Money from the paper route, or the job at Morath's chicken farm. Dirty job, white coveralls. Didn't last. Chandler's. The Odd Book Store, with its LIFE magazines and girlie magazines. Squeaking floor, damp musty smell like a shower stall. The past. What was so good about it? Another night, buying a pen knife, pearl handle with "Florida," palm trees on it. Pop driving up Route Nine to Shrewsbury - Bigelow's department store. Waiting for Mom and Pop to get back, near the car parked at the edge of the lot. Waiting by the cabless trailers in the field, look up at the stars. Everything the same...

Chambers Street. Stores with cheaply made electronic items and clothing. The whole street a salvage center, a train wreck of spilled and discounted wares. Bins within recessed storefronts, or out on the sidewalk. Socks, colored T-shirts. Porno videos. Richard looks without buying. It's growing dark. Wind swirls some fallen snow against the show window, and, briefly, against his face. Reflexively he pulls at his coat collar, though he feels neither cold nor warm, just now. What was that inner warmth he used to feel most keenly in the winter? A nameless happiness that did not seem to refer to anything specific. Not Dad, or Mother. Or the trips - back and forth, always - to the hospitals. Something instinctive. Rarer now. Maybe the way the snow sloped down the front hospital grounds, down to the stone bus shelter and the streetlamps, and the highway that led to the little town not far away. Saturday morning rummage sales in church basements, seeing for sale some toys that he remembered playing with, old books and record albums, and restaurants with good tasting coffee, better than they served in the hospital cafeteria. Reflection of another outlet store in the window: Meshuganah Mike, the Salvage King. Whatever it meant. Other windows. His face, burning after another visit to Dr. Bailey's in downtown Worcester. Following his parents to the car. Pulling Paul past the display windows at

the old Greyhound bus terminal. Gone now. Visit NEW ORLEANS. A
trumpeter next to a lamp post, wrought-iron tables, balconies, willow trees.

Visit
THE SOUTHWEST!
MONTREAL!

And Worcester. Still there, somehow. The city. Not as he remembered
it, though.

Have to move on, Richard thinks.

Inside the music store he finds that he has just half an hour before
closing. He chides himself, but then he is able to find the record almost
immediately. He doesn't want to leave right away. Standing among the
recordings of country music, he seems to hear mandolins, plunking banjos,
and dry and plangent vocals emerging as if from the dust of past decades. The
store is quiet. In fact you can only hear, faintly, pop music from the other
departments. A song title on a record jacket brings a tune to his mind, and
in a moment he's singing quietly to himself--

Oh Katie dear, go ask your mama
If you can be a bride of mine...

The bridge is always difficult, he thinks - all those high notes. In
excitement he runs a hand straight back along his hair, in the usual calming
motion.

A salesman pauses and stands next to him helpfully, a young guy with
long hair. Richard notices there is just a slight look of concern in the man's
eyes.

"Can I help you?"

Richard recollects himself and tells the salesman he is just looking. His
mood, along with the sounds he was hearing, dissipate. But he feels happy.
The store is nearly empty and he walks toward the cash registers holding his
brother's gift. In this area he can hear show tunes. Suddenly, he recalls a
song his father sometimes sang: "Without a Song" - how the day would never
end. "How true it is!" he remembers his father saying. In Richard's brief
recollection there is no tension in his parents' house. Anyway it was true,
what his father said. Sometimes if there was a favorite song in your mind you
just didn't have to feel nervous at all, for example. Sometimes, anyway. It
could even be that gravelly-voiced singer that Paul liked to listen to. Richard
couldn't think of his name. He couldn't sing worth a shit, really, although

that one song wasn't bad, Diamonds On My Windshield. Richard pays up and walks down the stairs to the street.

After a few blocks he thinks he's back at the same subway station. In the dark it's hard to tell. He looks at some signs and at a map on the wall. He's nervous that there aren't more people around. It was different that earlier time with Paul, that Saturday. He hears a train coming, rushes through the turnstile and down some stairs where the sign had read UPTOWN and DOWNTOWN. A train is slowing down. The markings look familiar, and he's down the stairs and runs onto the train in one continuous motion.

There is one person down at the other end of the car. Richard sits where he has entered. He thinks of looking at the record again but decides that it isn't necessary. The name of the next stop means nothing to him. You had to be constantly on the alert when you rode these trains. Sometimes a train would turn into something different than the one you got on. Or it would turn into a "local" and make all the stops. Or it would turn into an "express" and go right by your stop. Even experienced riders were sometimes confused. Just now the conductor was saying something about Brooklyn, but Richard can't make out the words, which are slightly garbled. But when the train stops at a station whose name is as unfamiliar as the last one, Richard feels a sinking, burning sensation high up in his stomach.

Oh boy.

There is one intact map in the subway car. Someone has scrawled partially over the map with magic marker. Richard studies the map. It's a long time before the next stop. He supposes he's in Brooklyn. He leaves the train and climbs some stairs and walks over to the opposite platform. He needs to reverse direction, that's clear. His mother said you were never lost as long as you had a tongue in your head. But who could you ask around here? There are two young black guys across and down the platform. They seem to be horsing around, their sneakers make squeaking noises on the cement. Brooklyn could give you the creeps, it was so deserted.

A train arrives in about five minutes. Richard is glad to sit down. At least the direction is right - he thinks. He could ask further when he gets to Manhattan. He feels fatigued, closes his eyes against the nervousness in his head and stomach.

When he opens his eyes the guy is standing right in front of him. Had he touched Richard? The guy is holding a knife. It's as if he's waiting for an answer.

"What do you want?" Richard can't take his eyes from the knife, which the guy is holding out in his right hand. He's small and wiry.

"Your money. Now."

Richard wonders if it is possible to run. He can't see anyone else in the car, but he hasn't turned his head. With his eyes on the knife he rises slightly, reaching slowly for his back pocket. For some reason the guy backs off a step.

"What are you - slow?" He's looking at Richard's face. "What's a matter wi'ch'you?"

Richard holds his wallet out with both hands. His back is pressed against the bench. He doesn't know what to answer. The urgency seems to have gone out of the guy's voice. He's playing. The train speeds along.

Richard begins praying. Hail Mary, full of grace...

"Think someone's gonna help you? H'm? What's your problem?" The guy is waving the knife in circles, erratically. What was the matter with him? Suddenly he makes a lunging, slashing movement toward Richard's chest. The train jerks. Reflexively, Richard attempts to ward him off with his left hand, while he jumps to his feet. His hand is bleeding. He feels sick.

"You want money?" he thinks to ask.

He concentrates on the knife, and the guy - both are still. The guy seems transfixed. A smile plays at his mouth. His look shifts from Richard's face to his bleeding hand, and stays there - curious, fascinated - for some moments. Richard throws out his left hand and is able to grasp the guy's knife hand around the wrist. He squeezes, watching surprise register on the guy's face. Richard is standing now. He's aware that the train could lurch at any moment. The guy looks helplessly at his knife hand which Richard has grasped. He's standing flat-footed. Richard sets his feet, and his fist starts from behind his back and comes crashing forward. At the last second the guy moves, but only fleetingly. Richard's fist lands between his eyes. Richard groans as his knuckle pops and pain shoots through his arm. His attacker flies across the car, the plastic bench knocks his feet out, and the back of his head crashes against the thick glass.

There's an inrush of noise from behind the man's head, and sparks, or they might be reflections, from the breaking glass. The guy's face registers shock, and it stays there, his eyes open. He isn't moving. Richard looks past his clenched fists, angry, breathing hard. He doesn't want to look at the guy's face. He takes a step back, and brings his bleeding hand to his mouth. The knife falls out of the guy's hand - somehow he's held onto it - and it clatters loudly onto the subway floor. Richard backs away until a bench presses against the back of his leg, and he starts as if he's been prodded. He sees his wallet on the floor and picks it up, watching his attacker guardedly as if he might still spring up at him. But he's very still. There is blood collecting in a pool on the bench. The train is slowing down. He looks to his right and sees that an old woman with white hair is looking on, horrified, from the end of the car. She sits at the edge of her seat and tries cagily to work the door handle to the next car, but it's locked. She stares at him wildly and clutches at the handle. But hadn't he been defending himself? His heart is pounding. Was that a scream coming from her? No, a sound of brakes...

The train is stopping. Richard turns and looks fixedly through the glass in the doors, sees in passing the faces of a few people standing near the edge of the platform. At the doors near Richard, a small, shabbily-dressed woman darts a few steps in the direction of the slowing train. Screeches of metal. No one has noticed anything. After an instant of rest the doors swing open. Richard hurls himself out of the car, jarring the woman who has centered herself at the doors' opening. "Ay, ay," she complains.

But Richard is bounding up a flight of steps. He reaches the top and runs several yards to a ceiling-high turnstile. He presses his hands against the thick horizontal bars, and begins to push, and the woman's scream echoes up the cavernous subway station. The turnstile releases him. There is no one around. He runs up another flight of stairs to the street.

Slow down. His left hand hurts. He places his handkerchief there and squeezes, puts his hand back in his coat pocket.

He thinks he's in the East Village. There are five- and six-story industrial looking buildings, and closed repair garages, and some uneven paving stones that disturb his footing. The light is poor. It's as if a drum is beating in his head. Cars approach from behind and cause his shadow to run far ahead of him, to lengthen on the pavement and then tower on the grimy brick facades next to him, then to rush toward him and be replaced by new shadows as other cars moved up the street. He looks back to see if any are police cars, and when he looks forward again someone has thrust a paper cup against his chest. Startled, he bats the thing away from him. The derelict who pushed the cup forward grunts something. Richard takes off at a run and doesn't stop for a block. But it looks like there are other derelicts congregating ahead of him. Richard can see lights on the next avenue over. It must be Broadway, he thinks. He runs down the middle of the narrow darkened slip, and reminds himself to slow down as he nears the intersection.

It's better here: students from the universities, clothing stores, fast food. Just a few more blocks to Union Square and he can catch a train. If they're running, he thinks. If everything hasn't stopped because of what happened. Richard's heart races.

But there are only a few people about the entrance. Everything looks normal. There are two cops near the turnstiles. Richard doesn't look at them. Static bursts from their portable radios. He keeps his hands in his pockets, as much as possible - because of the blood, and because if his hands are free he'll start rocking in his nervousness.

He catches a train and in a moment it moves Uptown. His head is pounding. He remembers his medication, extracts a pill and swallows it dry. He wishes he had some aspirin. His mind replays the scene, the outcome. "Bastard," he says automatically, opening his eyes. A middle-aged commuter in a dark suit looks up from his newspaper. Richard looks away.

A scene comes to life behind his closed eyes. A river winds through the center of the picture, and becomes a shallow stream in the foreground. There is a castle in the distance and there are figures conversing alongside the river. In the foreground a shepherd is calling some sheep from the water. Someone who looks like a medieval cleric is sitting on a rock, reading. To the left is a capriccio of ruined architectural forms: a large crumbling portal overgrown with hanging vegetation, and a fragmented colonnade alongside the river. Clouds float in a fair blue sky.

Richard wakes up, disoriented by the scene. For a moment he thought he was sitting in his parents' kitchen. There was a china closet built into one wall, with glass doors. The scene was engraved on a plate of blue china which was displayed there, unmatched to anything else. He used to sit sometimes and watch his mother work in the kitchen, and he would glance at the mysterious scene. It was not like anything on earth, it was more peaceful somehow. Now he felt his heart racing, and the image along with the feelings it engendered faded.

Once when he was about ten years old he was swinging on a tree branch in a park. The branch was about six level feet above the ground. When the branch broke, the loud, sudden snap resounded as he tumbled to the ground. He looked around furtively, taking in the circle of houses around the broad green park. He knew that he'd done something irremediable, and in his alarm he was surprised to find that the aspect of the houses hadn't changed. He might have expected shutters to swing open, or figures to appear in windows or running down walks. He was frightened and lost no time in getting out of there. He went to his room. For an hour or more he felt that the police or the "town" workers would be calling on him at any moment.

But this was worse. It was a lot worse...

The train is having some problems. It waits between stations. Richard prays for it to move - "move before something happens." All he can hear are sporadic exhalations from the train (the brakes?) and the businessman rustling his newspaper. His heart is still racing, he feels as if his system is out of control. There is a five minute wait at the next station. The doors have been closed - as if the train was ready to leave - but then they open again. Richard hears an accordion player, the same one, he supposes, but far off now. He's playing "Street Of Dreams." Playing as if nothing has happened.

His brother has put off supper and waits. Richard has been taking the afternoon train by himself for a couple of weeks. It seemed unnecessary for Paul to continue leaving his own train to meet his brother at the workshop. Now he feels he was too hasty. The city could be such a depraved place.

He turns a light on and looks absently at the food on the stove. He has already called the workshop. There isn't much else he can do. It's after nine o'clock. He hears a clattering of keys outside, and swiftly opens the door.

Richard is brusque. "I bought something," he says. He places the record in his bedroom and returns to the corridor. He's still wearing his coat, in fact his injured hand is still in his pocket.

"Did you get lost?"

"Kind of." Richard starts to take his coat off.

"Your hand is bleeding."

"It's alright. I fell going up some stairs. I'm going to be alright, really." Richard brushes past, heading for the bathroom.

"Yes, wash it," Paul says.

Richard examines his hand at the bathroom sink. The handkerchief sticks to his hand because of the dried blood, and his hand stings as he peels the handkerchief away. He places the handkerchief in his pants pocket. He rinses his hand under the cold water. There is a gash between the thumb and forefinger. But the bleeding has all but stopped. The soap stings. Finally he daubs rubbing alcohol there. When he is finished he rinses the sink thoroughly. He holds a dry clean washcloth in his fist and returns to the kitchen.

Paul reheats some supper, and Richard sits and eats at the kitchen table. He realizes he is starving, and he eats without speaking. His brother stands near the table.

"Let me have a look."

"It's stopped bleeding." After a moment, extending his hand, "You see?"

Before Paul can say more, "I bought you a present. You see the bag there?"

"My birthday? That's swell. This is really nice. Here, do you want some soda?"

"Thanks."

Paul pours some soda into a glass. Richard lifts the glass with two hands, favoring the injured one, and drinks steadily.

He lifts a salt shaker, but it clatters onto his plate and the table. "Sorry."

Paul only looks at the washcloth in Richard's hand. "How is it?"

"It's fine. Don't worry, alright?" He puts his fork down and picks up the shaker with his other hand.

"Okay." Paul begins cleaning the kitchen.

"I was glad to find that record, you know?" Richard says after awhile.

"I am, too." Paul says from the sink. "We'll play it tomorrow. It's late."

"Yes."

"I'm going to go to the living room. Did you take your medication?"

"Yes. I took my medication."

After awhile Richard enters the living room, holding a glass of soda with both hands. He slumps into the armchair nearest the kitchen. "I'm tired, Paul."

"So get some rest. You'll feel alright in the morning."

"Yes." Richard wished him good night.

Near where Paul is sitting, there is a small framed photograph looking down from a shelf. Richard brought this one from home. Paul stands to look at it in the light. It's an out of doors photograph of their mother and Paul and Richard. Richard is standing next to his mother, and Paul, just an infant, is sitting on his mother's lap. She's hunched down and holding him by the waist, and they are both facing the camera. Their mother's face is concealed, deliberately it seems, by Paul's shoulder. You see her eyes clearly - she's smiling - and not much else of her face. There are backs of houses far behind them, a ramshackle eave that covers a porch, tall dried grass that looks like straw, a few bare trees. There is a baby carriage behind and to the left, with its top down. Richard is smiling, too. He is excited about something. His eyes light on some object above and away from the camera. His hands are moving quickly and register as a blur, as if he is reaching for something that is slipping away from him.

ADVENTURES OF LAO HU, A FABLE

Mrs. Lee called him her fierce and protective tiger, and sometimes, the handsomest and most noble character in Sunnyside, Queens. Even if, when a dog on a leash approached them, when they were out walking in the neighborhood, he would usually move to the safe side of Mrs. Lee's trousered legs. If the dog seemed really disagreeable, or threatened to break free of its leash, Lao Hu would sometimes climb a short distance up a tree, and have to be coaxed down afterwards. And while she sometimes called him handsome, when she really paused to look at him – at his massive and battle-scarred head, with ears that flopped this way and that – he seemed as exquisitely homely as some of the stone lions that guarded Chinese temples. Then she would look at him and think, Eee-yah, what a life you must have led!

They would walk throughout the neighborhood together, for Mrs. Lee, nearing eighty, went out nearly every day when the weather allowed. If she visited a public library, Lao Hu would station himself near a tree outside for safety, or if the day was warm, perhaps in the shade of a hedge or evergreen, if there were any, while Mrs. Lee went in and enjoyed the quiet. She could not read English, and the Chinese dailies and weeklies were often taken from the wooden racks. And anyway her eyesight was not what it used to be, so typically she would leaf through the illustrations, and stare numbly at the text and advertisements.

Or they might visit a butcher or fish store, where Mrs. Lee might buy a small quantity of shrimp, one of her specialties. She supposed that the shrimp might be fresher in Chinatown, but it was so much trouble to get on the bus for Flushing now, and anyway she found that she could not tell the difference. Lao Hu could usually tell when she'd brought shrimp home, and he spent the day in a kind of delirium, for fried shrimp Mrs. Lee style was a particular favorite of his. When he heard and smelled the shrimp crackling in a frying pan with oil and garlic, he was almost mad with desire. Most of his meals came direct from Mrs. Lee's hand, and he'd seen enough of the world to understand, in his fashion, that this was an extraordinary bounty. Dried cereals were the rare exception. He would even eat all the grains of white rice when they were imbued with the flavors of the shrimp or fish or pork. He liked almost everything that Mrs. Lee served, in fact, except that he could not get used to vegetable greens.

After the big meal of the day there was usually time for a nap, an evening walk, and later the droning television which Mrs. Lee watched drowsily, and whose darting movements Lao Hu sometimes glanced at with sleepy eyes. It would not be too much of an exaggeration to say that the sounds and images made about equal sense to the two of them. Mostly Mrs. Lee liked to hear the voices, even if she understood little of what was being said. At the moment, the screen showed teams of scantily clad young women, in shorts and low-cut jerseys, running through the jungle. Their exposed skin was subject to insect bites, and this showed in small red welts. Mrs. Lee found the scene risible, and chuckled to herself, for she gathered that the women were in search of bachelors, who might be millionaires, in the manner of the day's reality television programs.

The scene changed to a tavern in the country with leafy trees all around it. Inside, a young man was nonchalantly raising a bottle of beer to his lips. First he raised the bottle and toasted the people around him. Mrs. Lee smiled instinctively, and then chortled out loud, drawing Lao Hu's attention. This must have been the millionaire the young women were chasing. Mrs. Lee supposed that he would be considered handsome, as well as rich. The camaraderie that the young man and his acquaintances appeared to enjoy seemed just, it seemed credible to her, even if she had never experienced a moment like this in her life. Lao Hu stretched his paws up to the couch, and Mrs. Lee was so amused that she didn't worry about him scratching the fabric.

Where is your fortune, Lao Hu? she asked him.

He stared up at her intently, and his mouth opened slightly but without any sound. Her name for him translated to "Tiger," for his coat of grey and black stripes.

Life had not always been so easy for him. Many years ago, he had seemed to be the prized and pampered pet of a young suburban family on Long Island. He watched uneasily, though unaware of the cataclysm that was to follow, as more and more of the family's possessions were placed in cardboard boxes throughout the house. In those days he was known as plain Gulliver, though in his early years he hadn't that much occasion to travel. Then his family moved and, inexplicably, made no provision for him, except for bowls of water and dried cereal on the rear patio, which were soon exhausted. Then the first phase of his wanderings and hardships really began.

He'd remained in that neighborhood for some weeks. His presence there did not excite any great degree of compassion among the remaining neighbors who might have remembered him. And when a new family did move in, the only gestures that any of them made were stamping their feet and shouting, "Scat!" It developed that they already had a cat of their own. Lao Hu had stayed a few more days around this yard or the neighboring ones. Then he'd had a skirmish with the new cat, which was smaller, but emboldened perhaps by some territorial instinct, he'd caught Lao Hu by surprise with an ugly scratch just below his eye. Lao Hu retreated, moved on, and healed as best he could.

For some reason, now when summer had turned to fall, he seemed to migrate daily in the direction of Queens and the city. It might have seemed to him that the glow in the nighttime sky to the west, which was really only the lights of the city, offered some prospect of greater warmth. But life was difficult wherever he went. There were other homeless animals, all competing for survival. The foods that he happened across were, much of the time, too obviously spoiled. In the neighborhoods in which he found himself, the only prospect for rest seemed to be during the day, if he could find some defensible spot that wasn't too cold. The nights were disordered by comparison, and he felt that he needed to be constantly moving. If he was not always on his guard for physical attacks, he was at least nettled by a continuous slamming of doors, of wailing nighttime sirens, and inebriated shouts that echoed harshly over roadways and vacant lots.

When the weather had turned cold he could not even drink from puddles anymore. Sometimes he ate freshly fallen snow. When there was a thaw he might drink the dripping water from a drainpipe. It tasted metallic to him but the water sustained him, and he had little choice.

After those few months on his own he had became more adept at hunting birds. But he was never quite satisfactory at it. His feet were too large, his body too massive, and small birds seemed to recognize his footfalls, or the movement of the air about him. As a result he was hungry most of the time.

One late afternoon in the spring (this was all in the time before he'd first met Mrs. Lee), he'd happened upon some young boys playing in a vacant city lot. He'd been walking all day. Instinctively he shied away from the crowd of boys. The scene in fact summoned a kind of primal fear in him, invoking some cardinal rule of survival that had been passed on to him by his race, that could only be ignored at peril. On the other hand he felt actually weak with hunger, even his step was uncertain, and some of the boys were holding out some dried snack to him. The lot was littered with debris. Lao Hu ventured a few steps forward, as if hypnotized by the bright orange crackers that were held out to him.

When he had drawn a little closer he suddenly felt many hands close about him and hold him fast. A sound of shrieking went up. One of the boys discovered a length of rope on the ground and fashioned a crude noose that was slipped over his head. Lao Hu shook his head savagely but without effect, and when he was thrown to the ground he could only run a few feet before the rope caught about his neck. One of the boys passed the other end of the rope over the branch of a small, stunted tree, and pulled until Lao Hu was hanging in the air. The excited shouts that had burst in his ears began to fade from consciousness, as he was pulled still higher. The flawless blue sky turned dark except for a stream of exploding stars. The pain in his neck was tremendous. Lao Hu may have felt that that blighted tree would be the last object that he would see in this life. But then a boy's face came vaguely into view, the boy who was holding the rope. He pulled further and Lao Hu rose up, spinning slowly, then for a split second he could see the face of his chief tormentor peering at him. Then Lao Hu struck with what little strength that remained to him. His claws caught the flesh of the boy's face, close to one of his eyes, and, startled, the boy cried out in pain and let go of the rope.

Pandemonium had followed as the boys shouted and cursed and stamped their feet in attempts to catch the rope that was still attached to Lao Hu's neck. A foot landed solidly on the rope, and Lao Hu snarled and hissed as he never had in his life. When the boy moved closer Lao Hu leaped from the ground at the exposed flesh of his arm, and his claws ripped into the boy's flesh and he screamed as the other one had.

Lao Hu ran desperately amid those feet that stamped and made a furor like the hands of drummers, and then he heard a gruff and strained shout from near the street, where a person was weaving unsteadily—

"Hey, what you all doin' to that animal—"

All eyes turned in the direction of the voice, which was fierce and commanding in its anger. There was a guitar strapped to the man's body. Lao Hu was able to dart past him and into the street, where he narrowly missed being struck by a car. And he kept on running, the rope trailing behind him, for what seemed miles, with the insane laughter and shouting and the stamping of feet still pounding in his ears. When he paused briefly, no amount of prising or clawing or chewing would loosen the rope.

When he thought he had run far enough he simply came to rest in the space between two evergreens, adjacent to the sidewalk in front of some public building. He lay down, and the length of rope lay on the walk in front of him. He stared at the rope with a puzzled expression, while his tail flicked reflexively. Possibly he could chew through the part of the rope that he could reach, but just to bring his jaws together hurt him tremendously now.

It came to him that he was still very hungry.

But the painful pounding of his heart had eased somewhat, and, as tired as he was, he nodded off for awhile.

It was later that he saw Mrs. Lee approach for the first time. She was short, and wore checked trousers and a jacket. She walked slowly, and he watched her approach for a long while. She, too, looked immensely puzzled to see the rope. But he found that he had no strength to resist, or to run. Something about her face, her eyes, told him that she would not be like the others. She bowed on one knee, and placed a wooden walking stick carefully on the sidewalk. He only flinched slightly when he saw her reach her hand into her jacket pocket and remove a small jack-knife, which she extended. The blade glinted in the afternoon sunlight, and still he didn't move. Then, staring into his eyes all the while, she hooked a finger about the rope and pulled it away from his neck, and sliced methodically at the rope, until she gathered it all up in her hand and closed the knife and returned it to her pocket.

Eee-yah, she said. What has someone done to you?

Her voice had startled him that first time with its unfamiliarity. The tones of her Chinese words rose and fell musically, and seemed to resonate within him. He'd had a fleeting urge to run, once he was free of the rope. He flexed his paws very slightly, to see if they contained any feeling at all after his feverish running. He saw that even this small movement of his feet registered in the woman's narrow eyes, and he blinked and went on staring at her.

She ventured to pet him, though nowhere near his aching neck, and he did not resist. She stood up, and backing off a few steps she brought her hands together in a welcome gesture. She moved off a little further. Lao Hu stood on his legs, stumbling at first, and stepped tentatively after her. When they had walked to the next corner in this fashion, Mrs. Lee dropped the rope into a trash receptacle. She crossed herself, as she had seen Christians do. Then she made her way slowly and carefully over the few more street crossings until she reached her apartment building.

For Lao Hu there had followed a regimen of sympathetic magic of the oldest kind. Mrs. Lee began making a broth that was reduced from chicken necks, and she served it to him every day. Even the necks themselves, Lao Hu chewed on gratefully. In a week's time his strength and his spirit had revived. Mrs. Lee had no doubt that his recovery had hinged on the magical powers of the soup.

Soon he was accompanying her on her walks through the neighborhood. If he happened to be resting somewhere in the apartment when he first heard the clatter of Mrs. Lee's housekeys being lifted from their peg in the hall, his ears would pick up and retract, and the drowsy look on his face would be replaced by something urgent and feral. Then he would dart into the hallway and see her smiling down at him, and his expression would soften while retaining its mood of excitement.

Come, she would say. Come, grandson. We are going out shopping.

And she went to the fish market to buy something for the evening meal. And to the grocers, for a green vegetable that she could set out along with the fish. While she shopped inside Lao Hu would stare through the screen door if there was one, or he would amble to some comfortable spot with a view of the entrance.

Today he was positioned near the curb opposite a sidewalk greengrocer, when he began to feel, and then hear, the grating and caterwauling sound of skateboards being propelled along the sidewalk. The boys who were making the noise turned a right angle at the corner and came straight in Lao Hu's direction. He looked feverishly to the left and right, and short of charging up the aisle of the grocers, which would have meant trouble, or making for a space under the nearest parked car, which had even clearer dangers, Lao Hu could only think to sprint in the direction of the boys and then to leap up a five-foot embankment on which some shrubs were planted, and this is what he did. But the clattering troupe of boys had been so close to him that his heart was pounding, and he leaped to a still higher wall that happened to be someone's empty terrace. He huddled there and attempted to catch his breath, vaguely apprehensive, and was not aware of the time passing.

He may have dozed. He did not hear Mrs. Lee's voice, soft and plaintive at first, calling his name on the street below. She was walking around fruitlessly on the sidewalk, unable to see a trace of him, and was rapidly growing impatient.

"Lao Hu," she almost cried. Then, her voice loud and strident, "Lao Hu! Ni shi zai nar?"

He heard her then, and meowing, he stepped down the slope until, fearful of making the five-foot leap to the sidewalk, he stepped along the wall in parallel with her until there were steps for him to climb down.

Lao Hu remained with Mrs. Lee for a couple of short years. They were his most pleasant years, the idyll of his life really. Then one morning in the Spring the strange thing happened, that would separate them irrevocably. The old woman had picked up her gnarled maple walking stick and jabbed experimentally at the hallway floor, and jingled the door keys in the usual way. Lao Hu came running. They rode down in the small elevator, Lao Hu standing off in a corner.

They had walked through the vestibule to the wide cement entryway, when Lao Hu heard and then saw the walking stick go clattering along the cement. He had been busy peering in all directions for dangers, straight along the walkway and among the recesses of some greenish hedges to the sides. And so he might well have wondered if the walking stick, which he'd seen Mrs. Lee brandish in the air many times during their walks, as some recalcitrant dog struggled against his leash, had now become a missile fired at some threatening beast.

But he saw, crouching low at her side, that Mrs. Lee clutched at her chest, and now fell straightaway to the ground. He approached and saw that she was not moving, and he began to call out just as loudly as he could. Still it was several minutes before anyone came.

During the commotion that followed he was forced to move off several steps. Sometimes he stood on the periphery, at other times a sudden movement or a burst of police-radio static would cause him to hide in the shadows of the hedge. A man picked up her walking stick and looked at it appraisingly, then went back inside the building with it. Voices drifted by—

"Is that her cat?"

"Nice lady."

"I never heard her speak anything but Chinese."

They took her away soon after.

Lao Hu stayed near that entryway through a long afternoon and evening, and for several days to come. When the evening doorman started his shift at six the first day, he left his station in the lobby to come and stamp on the ground and make a running charge of a few steps in Lao Hu's direction. He would do this at least once each evening, but Lao Hu, not greatly concerned, would only retreat a couple of steps, into the deeper shadows of the hedge.

Others showed kindness, at least for awhile, bringing bits of cheese, tin plates filled with water, even canned foods which, while not freshly made, were not unpalatable, either. Some of the people might have been friendly, but Lao Hu would remain safely in the distance until they left their food and moved away several steps. He made no reaction to the clucking sounds that they made, or the gestures of their hands and fingers. Of the people who entered and left the building, he tried to find any who might have matched the few visitors who had come to Mrs. Lee's apartment in these recent years. But there were none that he recognized, nor could he feel quite comfortable with any of the others who approached him.

The old neighborhood of Queens didn't agree with him anymore. With Mrs. Lee gone it had lost its savor, and without her guidance he felt that the cars would prove fatal to him one day. Or that he would perish through some other misadventure that was equally unpleasant, for surely he must have used up several of his nine lives. At liberty again, Lao Hu began to make his way eastward, to the suburbs that had once been his home. As far as he traveled, he could never really find the quiet and safety that he sought.

Seasons passed. No other family took him in, and it was as if he did not expect it to ever happen again, with all that he'd been through. A harsh winter arrived. Some nights it was all he could do to find a lean-to or a garage with an overhang that kept the snow from falling on him, or that offered some protection from the wind. When he saw a mouse walking in a field of snow he would race after it, and sometimes, in sheer desperation, he was able to catch one.

One late afternoon he wandered onto a property with a cluster of old stone buildings. He could hear many of his kind calling, and elsewhere, the barking of dogs. The scene made him uneasy, in fact an inner voice told him that he ought to be extremely mistrustful of this place. On the other hand he was weak with hunger, and parched with thirst. So when a young woman hailed him, seeming friendly, he allowed himself to linger at a distance. And when she came back with bowls of cereal and water and set them down on the ground, he did not hesitate, but walked straight up to her. The woman petted him, and later, as he ate and drank, he did not watch her walk away, and he was just barely aware of the sound of the gate being closed, which began his imprisonment in the shelter. But he was not at all worried at first, for soon he was sated with food and drink, and sheltered from the cold and harsh wind.

Nor was he greatly troubled, at first, by the smallness of his cage, or by the squalling and the sometime smells from the other animals. There was a small window, slightly begrimed, rather high on the wall opposite his cage. Through the bars he could see a patch of sky that was seldom light blue, but more often a soft and liquid gray. Lao Hu hadn't noticed any special quality to the light in the sky, when he'd first approached the area at dusk. If he'd had more experience of the world, he might have noticed that the light that he saw in the window was the same light that is found along beach roads when the ocean lies straight ahead. In fact the shelter was very near the ocean.

All that Lao Hu understood was that the view intrigued him, whether his face was pressed rather close to the metal bars, or whether he was curled on the floor and staring up philosophically. This view became the focus of his days, which really were quite uneventful. He could forget, for moments at a time, all of the other animals crowded around him.

After only about a week in the shelter, there was just one regular ritual there that began to greatly disconcert him. It was when strangers were allowed to pass through, when they paused in front of the cages looking to find a prospective pet to take home with them. Entire young families would pass, and pause, or if a single person, usually it was a young woman. At first Lao Hu was very excited by these visits. He would stand up straight in the middle of his cage. And when the woman, or the group of people, had passed and proceeded up the middle aisle behind his cage, he would be sure to have turned a hundred and eighty degrees, so that they would see him in full again as they passed that way.

He would watch as someone gestured to one of his neighbor cats, and the attendant might prise him from his cage and place him gently in the person's arms. And the cat would sometimes roll his eyes with a hint of alarm, but more often it would start to purr faintly and flex its claws in the air, with a kind of simpering expression on its young face. Some of them would never be returned to their cages. Lao Hu stood for these inspections day after day, but with a growing unease and discouragement. The end of each day found him in the same place.

For the most part the curious faces of visitors barely lit upon his. They seemed to look past him, or through him, regardless of how he presented himself. One day a young woman with gentle eyes and copper-colored skin paused in front of his cage. Their eyes met, but only for the briefest moment before she turned away. Hope drained from Lao Hu's face. It had almost been as if he was invisible, or was no more than an evanescence, a shaft of sunlight falling through the leafy branches of a tree. When she had passed he turned and looked behind him, and he saw that he cast a shadow, from the milky light that came through the opposite high window. His tail twitched on the floor of the cage, and was still. Then he only stared ahead.

Time had not been kind to him. Neither, for that matter, had some of the creatures that he'd encountered. There was a feral look about Lao Hu. The upper part of one ear had a permanent crease that caused it to flap backward. The other ear was split at the top, and from certain angles resembled the top of a pitchfork. He'd lost some of the flesh of one of his lower eyelids. It had happened years ago, when Lao Hu's owners moved, when that cat had surprised him in what used to be Lao Hu's backyard. And so the lower eyelid had a notch, and a rough seam below that, and the eye always appeared to be watering. And it was as if, standing there in his cage at that moment, he understood just what kind of figure that he cut in the world.

In time, that eagerness with which he had first greeted visitors to the shelter was replaced by sullenness and apathy. It was painful when a woman of Mrs. Lee's age, though seldom of her appearance, really, passed him in his cramped cage. Or when a young woman walked past in the same way, to see her eyes settle with interest on some younger and more presentable-looking animal. All of this was galling to him somehow. And yet, whether young or old, all animals were only being true to their natures.

It was as if Lao Hu could feel all of these things, and he could feel something else besides, as a few more weeks passed in this way: it was a premonition, a presentiment of his own doom. For surely life could not continue on indefinitely in this way.

And so he resolved to make his escape. He needed only an opportunity, when the young woman was taking him out for a bath, or for shots, as happened sometimes. Now that the weather was getting warmer, there was usually just the wooden screen door leading to the outside, to grass and forest and, hopefully, freedom. The screen door was within view in front of his cage, and he'd seen people going out with merely a push on the door. He could do the same.

One late morning he saw his opportunity. The young woman approached his cage and said something to him as she worked the handle. The screen door seemed unlocked as usual. She took him in her arms and stepped away from the cage. Looking up, Lao Hu had a view of the pale flesh of her neck. She had never been anything but kind to him. He reached up rather than struck, and one of his claws gently caught under her skin.

His action froze her for just a moment. She stared ahead in fear, not moving, and Lao Hu leaped from her chest to the floor. His shoulder collided with one of the wooden cabinets on landing, and he ran slipping over the smooth tile floor until he could stand and push on the screen door. It yielded enough room for him to pass, though one of his claws caught momentarily and painfully in the screen. He limped into the yard and through an opened gate into a gravel driveway, and then to the fringe of the forest. He turned and saw the young woman approaching slowly and calling to him. But whenever she gained on him he would move further into the deepening forest, and turn and watch. And this continued for awhile until, each time that he looked back, she stood slightly further away from him. Then, at the edge of the woods, she finally turned and walked back.

Within a few days he found himself in a seaside community. There were fewer cars here, and indeed they did not move very swiftly over the dirt and gravel roads. He found that the weeks of rest in the shelter had fortified him, and he did not mind the rigors of living out of doors. Here there were brambles of wild roses, and sandy paths through the sea grass down to the shore. There were unaccustomed species of birds, some large ones, that he watched with interest, lying sometimes just at the edge of the sea grass, the ocean breeze blowing steadily at him, his tail twitching slightly: gulls, herons, the large-headed kingfishers, and small birds that stepped swiftly near the surf. But he did not chase any of them. The dry sand offered very little footing, anyway, but he did not mind. Sometimes a still-edible, sea-salted bit of fish washed up on the shore, or sometimes a fisherman would toss him a morsel of bait that hadn't spoiled.

He found, too, that many of the local people were not unkind. That sometimes, if he would wait very deliberately in the grass-grown path at the door to some little house, the owner might eventually put something out for him. Even if they tried to shoo him away at first greeting, he found that many people would offer some kindness, whether or not they invited him into their homes. It required only persistence on his part, and it was only when a homeowner shooed him away three times or more, that he gave him up as hopeless and moved on. He found also that, compared to what he had endured previously, the winters were not so very extreme here in the bay.

And so he found that life in this place, in short, seemed completely inexhaustible, in terms of sustenance and points of interest. Like few other places that he'd lived, really. This particular morning was of the most pleasant kind. It was the middle of May, and the sun was shining. A briny harbor smell was borne in on the gentle ocean breeze, and mingled with the scent of lilacs in bloom. The small triangular park near the center of town was quiet with benches and well-kept grass and shrubbery. He could see prospects of the ocean between the two-story red-brick buildings of the downtown. Crossing a narrow street, and passing by a brick alley in the old section of town, he was aware of the succulent smell of fresh fish being prepared, and he could almost think himself back in Mrs. Lee's kitchen. An old man, a fisherman by the look of him, with a cap and ruddy complexion, sat on a propped-up board and dozed against a brick wall.

The people that he passed sometimes took notice of him, but in an unassuming way. Some made soft clucking sounds in his direction. Other people, that he'd gotten to know, would pet him if he approached them, and some he trusted sufficiently to let them rub the fur under his chin, while he extended his neck with a feeling of rapture. Lao Hu was still wary of children, as beings of a wholly unpredictable nature. Passing the back of George's Diner, he could tell that the cook was frying sizzling chicken livers and onions in oil. Sometimes, if he waited here, one of the restaurant employees would throw him out a scrap. But even if they didn't, the smells alone were worth pausing for today.

He sat prominently on the scruffy walk outside the service entrance. There, in a rectangle of mild sunshine, he opened and closed his eyes contentedly, staring at the back screen door. There was a gentle breeze at his back. If he could have spoken, he might have given voice to complaints about some of the circumstances of his life. As it was, his expression, his very appearance, seemed to say that life and freedom were enough to be grateful for.

NEMESIS

1

Sunlight poured down on the late afternoon sidewalk in downtown Flushing, Queens. A throng of people moved slowly past small stores and jutting tables of produce sellers. Orientals and Hispanics shared the sidewalk, along with a few white people like George Gessler. He was in his middle forties. His close-cropped hair was graying at the temples. He was of just under average height, and trim, and he moved efficiently and with just a hint of impatience through the slowly moving crowd.

The engineer had finished work There were days when he dressed rather formally - when he needed to make a technical presentation, or meet with visitors come to inquire about a project. Today he was dressed casually in chinos and a short sleeved shirt open at the neck. Pens and pencils stuck out of the shirt pocket.

It was early Autumn. The afternoon was humid and threatened a shower. Gessler passed Chinese restaurants, and small clothing and jewelry boutiques and lottery shops, and greengrocers with fruits and vegetables arranged in wooden bins on the sidewalk. The crowd allowed only slow progress, and he reminded himself to be patient. He glanced in passing at the produce tables, where some of the items were unfamiliar to him. Salsa music pounded from one of the parked cars, while, more musically it seemed to Gessler, the Chinese voices rang out with their distinctive tones that rose or fell. A vendor spoke sharply and incoherently to a customer, a would-be haggler perhaps. The foreign words melded. The common modes of speech here were modulated tones and high-pitched screaming. A problem for the lab, Gessler thought, to try to find any sense in this babel.

Above all of the other noises, a whining police siren cut like a knife. He thought it ought to have been cooler by now, but a viscid late-summer atmosphere lingered stubbornly in the city. He wiped moisture from his forehead with a handkerchief, and then carefully returned the handkerchief to his pocket. The police cruiser sped from the avenue up a side street and was gone. To some robbery or domestic tragedy that he might read about in tomorrow's newspapers, perhaps. Who knew how all of these immigrants lived, and what they lived for? And what sort of desperation there was beneath the surface?

Gessler was on his way to meet a woman for the first time, on what was something of a blind date. The woman was Chinese, and they'd made contact in an unusual way - through a "personal" ad, of all things. In his free time, Gessler studied the Chinese language. One recent evening when he was alone in his apartment he had been looking through a Chinese language newspaper. He was turned to a page of classifieds, and after several seconds he realized that the blocks represented "personal" ads from Chinese women or men. The ads would list the person's age - usually - and a few descriptive comments. Good-looking. Divorced. Single. Children. 25. 40. Gessler had let his mind dwell on the possibilities. He thought he was feeling tired of the single life. His mother, with whom he'd been living for several years, had died recently. He knew that it was not easy to meet new women, and he thought that the "personals" approach was worth a try. He didn't imagine that there was any risk in it. He'd crafted some letters in both Chinese and English, and sent them off to the newspaper and waited.

When she called him Gessler thought that someone had dialed a wrong number. He was about to hang up when he realized that the words were Chinese and that she had spoken his name. They talked for a few minutes, but with difficulty - her English was limited, and Gessler helped her along with his even more limited Mandarin. He arranged to meet Nina - that was her English name - for dinner one night after work.

There had been others, too - three women, in fact. He'd taken them to dinner, or on one occasion just pastry and tea. The first woman he'd met was a divorcee with a daughter in China. The woman told a sad story of meddling in-laws who broke apart her marriage because they wanted a grandson instead of just a granddaughter. She broke down as she told her story. Gessler listened politely. Too troubled, he thought - and on the first date. They did not call each other again.

There was a young woman who worked in a women's nail salon. Gessler liked her shiny black hair, but she seemed naive and unknowing. He didn't mind about the salon - a lack of English limited the kinds of work a person could do here - but she had not been a professional in China, either. Not of my class, he thought.

There was a tall woman in her middle thirties. Her English had probably been the best. She was not only working as a bookkeeper but had almost finished a college degree. When he asked her something she would squint earnestly and answer in a tentative manner. They ate and talked for a couple of hours. Gessler did not have much of a feeling about her. Too blasé, he thought. And if she had any feeling about Gessler then she certainly hid it well.

Now he made his way to the public building where he'd arranged to meet Nina. It seemed to him a strange pass to have come to. After the failure of the first few meetings he was now rather tired of the process. He thought that perhaps he'd made a mistake pure and simple, and that there were no suitable women to be met in this fashion. He would just follow through on this lead, and then step back and take a rest from it.

Maybe there were no short cuts, in fact. Nothing, for someone as reserved as Gessler, that could make the process of meeting people any easier. It was only lately that he'd really begun to think about having a family. He supposed that it was not too late. His life had gotten too solitary, he thought.

For that matter, he had become disenchanted with New York City generally. He was beginning to understand that in his walks through the city it was almost unheard of to make contact with another human being - for him at any rate. And it probably would not be much different in any other city. The women seemed absolutely afraid of contact. When he was younger and more naive he could remember speaking to strange women in parks, only because (for example) they were reading a book that he had liked. Almost invariably the woman would leave without a word or glance - the book closed, put away. It was as though he had committed an unpardonable offense, something absolutely gauche, and she was just speechless. Well, he would not attempt it now. The feeling of anonymity - it was partly his personality, and it was partly just the nature of urban life. You seldom saw the same person twice here. If he spent a thousand days walking around the city it was going to be the same. Weekends ended with the same result, as did the work-week. There were colleagues to talk to, and casual friends, but for the most part he felt cut off from people.

While he waited for her he wondered to himself: What are the odds of meeting someone really fantastic? But it couldn't hurt to try, he thought again. If this is another failure you step back and re-think it all. As for American women, weren't they all basically the same - shallow and materialistic? How much money did you have in the bank, what sort of car did you drive - those were the important things. Were you handsome. Men were blamed for being superficial, but no one was more superficial than women. Listen to them carry on about the latest movie actor, and you couldn't help thinking there was not one of them that did not equate conventional good looks and an expensive haircut with nobility of character, for God's sake.

Gessler did not stop to think to what degree he was generalizing. He also had a notion that all Chinese shared a common value system, and that their concern was rather more with what was inside a person, than outside. But this generalization (if Gessler had thought about it) was based on even narrower experience, namely, his few Chinese friends and acquaintances. The Chinese that he knew were all highly educated, highly cultured, and to some extent Westernized. They had, with acculturation of many years, adopted the American manner of speaking what you feel, without equivocation - and in this, they were hardly Chinese at all.

He waited there on a landing amid the broad steps. He'd sent her a picture of himself, so that she at least would know what he looked like. It seemed that a majority of the women who passed by were Oriental. As he waited a couple of different women seemed to be making directly for him, and his heart would lift, or sink, depending on his impression of the women. But instead they continued past him into the building. As he looked over the sidewalk, a woman detached herself from a clothing vendor there and approached him. They exchanged names, smiling, and shook hands.

Nina was tall, about five-foot-seven, with a willowy figure. And she was good-looking, with clear bright eyes and a long thin face with taut skin. Gessler was impressed. She'd said she was thirty-five, but if anything she looked younger than that.

They began walking along the sidewalk with the crowd. Her Chinese words threw him at first. It was easy for Gessler to articulate a carefully thought-out sentence in Chinese. But he was not prepared to understand her answers: only a few of the words, which she uttered rapid-fire, would register with him. Say again, he would say, and, Say slowly. He described his Chinese studies to her. He asked her if she wanted to have supper and they agreed on a Chinese meal. She led him to a restaurant off of Main Street. By then she had slipped her arm around his.

The restaurant was a large and lavish place which, from the looks of it, could have hosted any wedding banquet. There were large round tables for serving meals family style. It was early evening. Gessler and Nina had a corner of the restaurant to themselves.

"Do you come here often?" he asked. He repeated the question for her.

"No." She shook her head. "I don't like--" She stopped and raised an index finger, and removed a thin case from her purse. When she raised the lid Gessler saw a small screen and a keypad. It was one of the new translating machines that he'd heard about. He supposed that it must have been expensive, at least a few hundred dollars.

"I don't like--" she said again, pushing some buttons and looking at the screen, "um--". She pushed another button, and a metallic sounding but still recognizably female voice said, "Squander." Nina looked searchingly at Gessler to see if the word had registered with him.

"Squander," Nina repeated. "Squander." She pushed a button again and listened.

"Yes," Gessler said. "Squander. Not good." Gessler now took his eyes from her briefly, to consult the prices on the menu. But they did not seem outlandish.

"I bought this today," she said in Chinese, showing Gessler the receipt.

"Nice. It's not cheap. Why did you buy it today?" He also spoke Chinese.

"Yinwei..." She began.

"Because..."

"Be-cause, I'm meeting you. To help us--" Her hands indicated some give-and-take action.

"Communicate," he said for her. She repeated the word.

Nina turned the machine off and turned smiling to Gessler. "You are my first American."

She raised an index finger. Gessler raised an eyebrow. For Nina's eyes had a direct and probing look, that was different - bolder - from any of the Chinese that he knew. She asked him about his family. Gessler explained that he was pretty much alone here. It seemed a little early to go much into his family history.

"What about you?" he asked. "Do you have family here?"

She didn't. She said that she had a young daughter in China. The girl was being brought up by Nina's mother. She hadn't seen either of them in the year she'd been in America. She missed them. Next time she would show Gessler *xiangpiar*. Pictures. That would be nice, Gessler said.

"Ni de zhangfu ma?" What about her husband, he asked.

Nina placed her palms together and tilted her head to the side, and rested her cheek against the back of her hand, in the gesture for sleep. "Ta si-de." Closing her eyes.

Gessler knew the word. Her husband was dead. "I'm very sorry."

"Three years," she said in English. "I don't have boyfriend."

"Yes. It isn't easy."

"Wo ku." She pointed under her eyes. I cry.

Impulsively he reached out and placed his hand on hers, on the table. She did not look up for awhile and so he took the menu in his hands and began looking at that. Nina did, too, in a moment. They ordered.

It wasn't necessarily a problem, he thought, that she already had a child. He would have to take some responsibility, of course - that is, if they became serious. Communicating would be a problem - he could already see that. But if Nina liked him, if she made him happy? Then he thought: slow down a minute. You only just met her.

"You want to have more children?" he asked.

"Sure. Why not?" using her fingers, and with Gessler's assistance, she indicated again that she was thirty-five.

"Yes. It's possible," Gessler smiled.

"Do you like children?"

"Yes. I do. They are very innocent. Life hasn't changed them. They have no preconceptions and no cynicism."

Nina had not understood him, he could tell. "I'll teach you a word," he said in Chinese. He pointed to the translator and Nina picked it up and held it in her hand.

"Spell," she said.

He spelled "innocent." Nina typed the English letters. When she struck the return key a hydra-headed Chinese character bloomed on the tiny screen. He squinted at the image, leaning closer. It was an impossible study, he thought. Interesting, but quite impossible for a Westerner who, like Gessler, was not exactly young. He turned aside this gloomy thought and pointed at the character on the screen, saying, "Children."

"Ah. Yes." Nina nodded in recognition.

"Innocent," she repeated after him, the word sibilant in his ears. She pressed a button and listened to the mechanical voice say, "Innocent. Innocent."

Nina clicked the translator closed and slid it across the tablecloth in case Gessler should want it. "My English - no good!" she complained. "You teach me English?"

"I'll do my best."

"Hao." Good.

They ate for awhile.

"Recently," Gessler said, choosing his Chinese words slowly and carefully, "this year - I feel very different. New York City - I don't much like. I think - I'd like to buy a house on Long Island. But - myself - why should I buy? I think" - here he chose a word that was not precisely what he meant, but close to his meaning - "that's very uninteresting." He meant that he lacked motivation. Enthusiasm. He didn't know how to say these things in Chinese. Nina seemed to get his drift.

"And I think, also," reverting to English, "what good are casual relationships?" He made use of the translator. "What you need is someone who will be there for you. Not just dates with strangers, this going to a movie or something, that usually isn't very good, and not having a lot to talk about after. Feeling like that person across the table has no appreciation for you at all, doesn't know what makes you tick, and is taking you quite for granted..." He saw that Nina looked frankly bewildered by his words, and realized that he'd spoken for rather too long. "I'm sorry," he reassured her. "My words. I will speak plainer." With a gesture of his fingers he tried to indicate words leaving his mouth plainly, like so many arrows. But there was no translating just what he'd wanted to say. Gessler hoped that Nina picked up on some of his meaning, at least. He paused, searching her eyes. "Do you understand?"

"One person," Nina said slowly in Chinese, "not good. You look - one person." With two fingers on the table cloth she showed a person walking. Gessler could not understand all of her words, but he could see the person (or the pair of legs rather) walk and then slow down, and stumble. How poignant it seemed! He could see himself a lonely bachelor, or worse, infirm, with family and friends only a dim memory. He could see it all there in the pantomime of her fingers on the table cloth. That's not what I deserve, he thought, looking up at her face.

"Liang-ge-ren." Two people. Nina sketched another pair of legs catching up with the first, which had stopped. The second pair of legs seemed to offer support to the first. Gessler smiled at the cleverness of her conceit.

"Help each other," she explained in English, although it wasn't really necessary. Her fingers touched his on the table, and Gessler felt something - a spasm of desire for her, and something more. Her fingernails, he noticed, were painted a bright red.

"So - what do you want?" Gessler asked.

"I want" - she looked up searchingly, and back at Gessler - "a happy family. Yes. Most important."

Gessler nodded. Happy family. Why not?

"My luck - has not been good. My husband--" He waited a few seconds for her to continue. "I'm sorry."

"Not at all."

They finished their meal and Gessler said, "I'll see you again soon?"

"I would like to." She wrote a telephone number on a pad and handed the slip of paper to him.

He paid the check and they left the restaurant. He opened the doors and as she passed by him he touched her lightly on the shoulder. The sensation agreed with him.

"It's a clear night," he said. They walked past storefronts. He looked at her face and at the stars above the trees along the sidewalk. "Clear," he said, indicating the sky with his hand.

"Yes. Clear." Nina said.

"And so - you live near here?"

Nina nodded. "Yes. I have apart-ment. Oh - it isn't so nice."

"That's alright. I'll walk you home."

"I wish I can be - how do you say - a host. For you."

"Don't worry about it."

Already, Gessler was getting a very good feeling about Nina. She was young and good-looking; she'd had some tragedy in her life, evidently, and it excited a degree of sympathy in him. She seemed to like him. She wasn't afraid to show some interest, unlike the other women he'd met recently.

81

They stopped in front of her building. Gessler waited, and when Nina extended her hand he took it and held it a few moments before saying goodnight.

"You will call me?" She mimed a receiver next to her ear.

"Sure."

As he walked away he would turn around to look at her. Each time he saw her standing in front of the vestibule, waving to him. He waved again and then turned a corner and continued walking.

As he walked home Gessler thought he felt the happiest that he had in a long time. In fact it had been years since he'd felt this captivated by someone. A new world seemed to be opening up to him again. Nina stayed on his mind, and she would be there when he woke up the next morning.

God must have blessed me, he thought.

2

Gessler's field of specialty was noise. Noise as he understood it was not just a problem of the urban jungle - the execrable muzak, the boom-box, the clashing headphones, which it seemed to him could only please simple and undeveloped minds - but a technical phenomenon that needed to be studied and solved. It was the detritus that clung to the useful information, the low-level jittery stuff that you could view on oscilloscope screens and other electronic instruments. The problem of noise had interested him since college, and he had studied it extensively. That was noise theory and it was no more esoteric than his other engineering studies, which also included imaginary numbers, and variously charged fields in space. Since high school, books and technical journals and the laboratory had been his playground. Experience had confirmed that noise was usually random; it contained everything within it, and was therefore seldom describable mathematically. Therefore not always amenable to solution. Over the years he had successfully treated many particular cases. It was a general solution that was lacking. After years of observation and study, the problem still confounded him. He still hoped that he might find the general solution, either in the lab, or in some innocent looking mathematical expression that he might put to general use. But more often he thought that his brain was probably getting too tired for any fresh assaults on the problem.

He wondered sometimes if his technical studies had made him a bit odd - had carried him somewhat far afield from other people. But it couldn't be the studies. Probably, he thought, you were a little odd to begin with. That must have been it. You had to be a little strange, to study these things, and go on studying them for years. Studying every night instead of going to parties and campus hangouts, working those technical problems all of the time. How could any normal person stay focused on the studies, especially now, when the popular culture told everyone unmistakably that partying and drinking was really "where it was at?" He remembered his classes on circuit theory, how just to do the analysis was a daunting and almost intractable problem. At least it was that in the real world, where you needed what were called integro-differential equations just to describe what was happening electrically. It scared him now just to repeat those expressions. But you learned how to transform the problems into something called the "frequency domain" (which was an imaginary place), as opposed to the "time domain" which was the real world. In this imaginary domain the solutions involved only straightforward multiplication. Then you could transform the result back into the real world, and you had your solution.

How arcane it all seemed. Did they still teach such things? Or had the engineering curriculum become so much more cut-and-dried? Just build up your system from so many modular building blocks.

He spent one semester studying "n-dimensional space." Also a very far out subject. "N" could be just any number you wanted, and all of the mathematics built up from that premise. But why think about n-dimensional space, when three dimensions were enough to describe any point? Why study it, indeed? He supposed it was part of the cultural background that went with engineering, at least at the time when he first studied. If you had the patience for such things you were ready for any real-world problem. Maybe that was the theory. In the working world, the "frequency domain" and n-dimensional space were trips that he'd seldom actually made.

Yes, he thought, you had to be a little strange to begin with, to devote four or more years to studying frequency domains and n-dimensional space.

On his way home from work again, Gessler turned off of the avenue. There was less noise, and more shrubs and trees appeared here. He approached the front of his building via a circular walk. The doorman was there for his after-dinner shift. Gessler entered the foyer and found the elevator waiting. He lived in what was still one of the better buildings in the area. You did not hear, in the halls, the salsa music, or the nagging and monotonous jungle rhythms - not yet, anyway.

He'd often thought that it was time for him to get out of the city - which was changing before his eyes. Neighbors had been mugged, even the doorman had been clubbed over the head one evening and had to be taken to the hospital. Gessler's car had twice been broken into, before he'd been able to find space in a garage which he now rented for something over a hundred dollars a month. His savings would probably allow him to make a down payment on a decent house on Long Island. But he had not pursued this as yet, he supposed, because he lived alone: he could not motivate himself to go looking at houses.

With his mother now gone, these four rooms were his. He put his groceries away in the small kitchen. His mother, who was not a cheerful person by any means, had added some bright yellow and green accents to the kitchen, and the effect was winning. There were snapshots in frames: one, atop a five foot high cabinet, showed Gessler and his mother at a long-ago Thanksgiving dinner. They are sitting at a table and smiling. The picture was taken several years earlier, when his father and Morty were still alive. Morty was Gessler's older brother, dead of a heart attack at forty-six.

In the living room were a fair number of books, not all of them of a technical nature. There were also histories and classic literature. There was a small section of books on the Chinese language, including a scholarly dictionary of Chinese characters translated into English. On a small table was a photo of a neighbor couple with their daughter.

Gessler's family had had a troubled history. His only brother Morty, some eight years older, had suffered a nervous breakdown during high school. He'd stayed at a series of mental hospitals and halfway houses ever since; and sometimes, but rarely, at home - his "nerves" did not allow him to remain for very long. There were weekend visits home, but these were not always satisfactory, either. Morty's nerves were seldom good, as was shown in a myriad of nervous tics; and the problems were exacerbated by their father's impatience, his carping at Morty for forever having the television on, or for eating too much, or drinking too much soda. To Gessler himself they were unimportant things, Morty's idiosyncrasies, although he could remember feeling irritated at times. But the old man seemed to feel a generalized irritation at Morty, for not helping more with household tasks, and for his inability to hold down a job. Family meals became a battleground between their mother, who always defended Morty, and their father.

Gessler did not like to think badly of their father. He'd worked for a maker of electrical fixtures in the city. (The factory had since closed.) He was a hard worker, and when there were layoffs, as sometimes happened, the old man might clerk in a hardware store, or something of the kind. He'd had little education. It had to have been difficult, having a son who while strong physically, had never been able to hold a job for any duration. This had to seem a terrible waste to the old man.

As it happened, Gessler's brother did not outlive either of his parents. The heart attack had been a shock to Gessler. Not long after it happened he visited a specialist in Manhattan. When the tests were complete the doctor told Gessler that he needn't worry: he was going to live to be a hundred. Gessler thanked the doctor, and concluded that half a lifetime of taking sedatives had exacted a toll on Morty's heart; and, perhaps, he had failed to take notice of any warning signs - if there had been any.

His brother's death had been another blow to the family, particularly their mother. It was as if something died in her. Her frequent joylessness of those years now became chronic. And Gessler accepted, but grudgingly, that she was never going to show a good deal of interest in what he was doing with his life. When they were together there seemed little to talk about. After his father died Gessler had lived with her for some four years until her death.

Her physical health had been alright most of the time. But it was a joyless household.

Gessler was reserved but not very introspective by nature. It would not have occurred to him to say that his family's situation had been tragic - although it was that. He knew that experiences shaped your outlook, often in spite of yourself. He didn't like to dwell on the fact, but the realization made him understand that if he was in some ways different from other people, he had his reasons for being so. Knowing this had allowed him to feel a little more accepting of the person he was, but did little to mitigate a feeling of being isolated from other people.

One day, a few years earlier, he announced to his mother that he was going to take up ice skating. Why had he chosen to do this as he was approaching forty? He supposed it was the grace and the mastery of the skaters that he saw on television that had enthralled him somehow. His mother's face had taken on a worried look when he first mentioned the subject. She asked him when he would be skating.

Why, Saturday mornings, he supposed.

But I need you here, she'd complained.

You don't need me every day.

And after a pause she answered, Oh, you'll never be a good skater.

It was a cruel remark and Gessler knew it. He walked out of the room. They never discussed it again. He took up his skating and became reasonably good at it.

But for several months now Gessler had not been to the rink at all. He wondered why, when those Saturday morning visits had become so important to his well-being. Why had he stopped? It could not be a good sign. He had so enjoyed that freedom of movement, the brisk air against his face. And the attentions of a female instructor and even a physical therapist (also a woman, a good-looking, no-nonsense German) who had helped limber him up. That had been expensive, but what was money for? The women were fun. They had trim and limber bodies. They were not really interested in *him* as such; he was really only a customer. At first he'd flattered himself that their interest might be personal. It had taken him a while to realize the truth.

Bu hao, bu hao, he said to himself, recalling a phrase in Chinese.

Not good. Why had he stopped?

Gessler turned on the air-conditioner in the bedroom, and he brought a bowl of cereal in there to eat. He shared a certain kind of bachelor's habit, which was to eat substantially at lunch and very little at dinnertime. It helped him to keep the weight off. Then he thought he would take a nap. The naps had become almost a habit lately. Getting old, he thought to himself. He set the radio alarm for an hour ahead, and fell soundly asleep.

Sometimes he woke from these naps feeling entirely refreshed - wonderful, in fact. He might, for example, have thought of a solution to some technical problem at work. Or he was just filled with a more personal feeling of well-being. But at other times he woke feeling oppressed by obscure worries. He knew that these impressions were caused by the fleeting nature of his dreams. They were the reason - now, for example - he was recalling one of his brother's visits home. It had been an especially awkward visit and, because of Morty's "nerves," had had to end a day earlier than planned. He could remember Morty's barely concealed anger at the old man's carping, and his venturing to say, not too loudly but clearly for the old man's benefit, something about a "brain the size of a pea."

"What's that?" their father had asked. But Gessler managed to intercede at this point - not, he remembered, in any terribly clever way, but it was enough to forestall any open warfare between Morty and the old man. The family had agreed that it would be best for Morty to return to the group home where he was then staying.

Their mother had especially asked Gessler to ride back with the two of them, obviously to prevent further problems. He imagined that he was going to college at that time, in the city.

But what Gessler chiefly remembered about the episode was his brother collecting his toothbrush and few personal things into a paper shopping bag and saying to everyone - not with any evident malice, but as if merely stating a fact - "There's nothing here, anyway."

Recently, thinking back over all the past years, Gessler would think: You are too much by yourself. No wonder he got depressed sometimes.

Sometimes the Chinese studies failed to engage him. He would feel distracted. Sometimes he felt lonely. For some months now he'd been wondering about what it was that gave life meaning. It couldn't be just making money - he had enough to live on. It couldn't just be thinking elevated thoughts, or reading the great books - so much of that was merely to pass the time. He was not going to write one of those great books, either, or write a song that people were going to remember. Sometimes he wondered if these things were possible But what were the odds, for a complete outsider? In his way he thought he'd noticed some things about life that others maybe never even thought of. But it seemed truer to say that his experiences of life had put him on a different wavelength from most people. His outlook was different - singular, even. This difference, with its concomitant of loneliness and isolation, only grew with the years. There was a loneliness you sometimes felt when you were on a wavelength that seemed to be all your own. Sometimes he thought he had never sufficiently tried to bridge that difference. But at other times he thought that his sometime isolation was not so much his fault, but represented a failure of imagination on the part of society at large.

The technical world had offered scope to his abilities, and he had remained faithful to that world. But unless you were creating something that no one else could (and he really did not think of himself and his vocation in this way), or unless you were actually helping people, it was difficult to think of work as something that defined you.

So if it was not in any of these things, perhaps it was family that gave life meaning. Gessler had intelligence, good health - good genes, he thought. It seemed wrong, now, not to have children. He thought that the sometime disorder in his mind might have been depression, but if so he'd never been treated for it. In any case he thought it was mostly a result of the family's circumstances, and was not something organic in his mind.

It is true that there are a thousand more original ways to live a meaningful life than simply having children. But Gessler's mind was not attuned to any of them just now. It was rather the case that the other person's grass seemed greener to him.

He remembered a remark of his mother's not long before she died. She was sitting at the kitchen table. "I wonder if Morty would have had kids by now, if he hadn't gotten sick." She appeared dejected. She was not looking at Gessler. He hadn't felt it necessary to say anything.

It seemed to him that for many years he had been wasting his time in casual relationships with women. The pattern was familiar. He could communicate with them up to a point. Many, though, did not even learn about his family background, even when the relationship should have progressed to that degree. Had the women asked him about his family? He was sure that the fault was his - some morbid sense of privacy on his part. He never felt that he'd found a soulmate. The relationships never seemed to click. If the woman liked him, as sometimes happened, she would want to spend every free day with him, she would press him for assurances. Gessler would begin to back off. Then the pattern would be repeated.

Or there were women he'd started to feel quite serious about, to find that they only wanted to be "friends." That had happened a few times, now that he thought about it. As a "friend" he got to listen to them complain about their boyfriends, who they could not talk with, but who were, incidentally, at least getting laid. Gorillas, probably, he thought - that animal magnetism. They had the fun, Gessler was getting the counseling sessions. But that was a losing game, and he did not go in for it anymore.

A part of Gessler's mind was ambivalent at the thought of sharing his life with a woman – again, it occurred to him, and he thought: Sorry, Mother, but it was not easy. The demanding, domineering type that could rob your life of joy. Was that what he'd been afraid of all these years? It didn't have to be that way. It was not too late to try something new. He could imagine a future with a loving and devoted wife, and children. He allowed his thoughts to run. They had a new focus, now that he'd met Nina.

3

A few nights later, Gessler was on his way to have supper with Nina at her place. The evening was raining. He approached her building, and in the vestibule he pressed her apartment number and waited for her voice on the telephone. She buzzed him in and he walked through a tiled lobby to the elevators. The building seemed pretty old to him, probably built between the wars.

Nina was waiting outside her apartment door. She was dressed casually in jeans and a form-fitting white jersey. She took his hand and led him into the apartment. They had to step past some clutter in the hallway, which was very dimly lighted. He stepped very carefully. The apartment smelled disagreeably of greasy cabbage.

Nina had told him that she lived with roommates. When he reached the dining area he saw that there was another couple eating quietly at the table. There was a dim bare bulb overhead, and it was this light that had reached into the hallway. The man, who looked to be in his fifties, nodded very slightly to him, and Gessler nodded back. Without stopping Nina led them to her room.

The light was better. There were twin beds without frames, just box springs and mattresses on the floor . There were no curtains or blinds over the two windows. Nina brought two sitting chairs opposite each other and gestured to him to sit.

"Are you tired?" she asked, in Chinese.

"A little bit."

With her hand she brushed some hair from Gessler's forehead. "You work - hard," she said in English.

"Dwei." Correct.

She sat down and picked up an orange from the bed table and began peeling it. "Work is okay?"

"Yes." It occurred to him that there was probably not much about his work day that he could talk about with Nina.

"Today - I cook."

"You want to cook dinner?" He repeated the phrase in Chinese, and added, Is it convenient?

It was no problem, she said. Anyway the weather was bad. "One person - cook - I don't like." She frowned. "I cook - for you!" Smiling now.

Very good, he said in Chinese.

"Do you like noodles? Or white rice?" She handed Gessler the orange she'd peeled.

Both good, he said.

She watched him eating the orange. She looked happy.

They talked for a while. Gessler wanted to tell her something about his family. He decided he would be up front about it. She had a right to know, if they were going to become serious about each other.

His mother had not been a very happy woman, Gessler explained. Nina looked quizzical. He told her about his brother. It was difficult to explain. He knew the Chinese word for "sick," and when he said it he touched his temple. Nina frowned sympathetically. Gessler consulted one of the index cards he'd prepared for the occasion, and tried to explain as best he could. "Not dangerous," he said in Chinese. Nina nodded. Gessler was unhappy that this complex subject - his brother's mental illness - was being reduced to broken phrases and hand gestures. But he had not spoken about his family to anyone in a very long time, and Nina seemed sympathetic. Whatever of his speech she was able to understand, anyway, and he was far from clear about how much she did understand.

What he wanted to tell her was that his family was healthy for the most part. That there was a piece of bad luck but no pattern that he knew of, either of mental illness or of heart disease, in the family history. And she seemed to understand this, or at any rate she did not ask much more about it.

"Did you study today?" he asked her.

"Study English? Every day. Certainly."

"Certainly. That's good." Did she have questions?

She didn't have any questions at the moment. "You'll be my - English teacher?" she asked in English.

"Sure."

"Sure," she repeated. Then smiling, "Thank you." It sounded like "Sink you." Gessler smiled indulgently, and then sounded the phrase correctly and asked her to repeat it a couple of times. He finished eating the orange. Nina didn't want any.

She stood up and asked for his hand and led him into the hall and pointed toward the bathroom. She said something in Chinese that he didn't understand, but he knew that she was inviting him to wash his hands. She flipped on the light and pointed to a plastic container with a bar of white soap in it. Then she tapped her fingers possessively against her chest. Her soap? He didn't quite understand. She pulled the door to.

John Zepf

The bathroom needed some repairs. There were missing tiles around the tub, and there was a plastic pail under some leaking plumbing. The window was wide open, without a screen, but all Gessler could see was the red brickwork of some building. He washed his hands with Nina's bar of soap. On the sink there were a few other containers of soap, which must have belonged to other residents. There were no towels, though. He shook the water from his hands, and with his arms held out in front of him he went across the hallway to Nina's room. She grabbed a small towel from the makeshift clothesline that stretched between two walls, and handed the towel to him.

Gessler glanced around the room and in a corner near the door he saw a roll of toilet paper. That explained something else that was missing from the bathroom. The residents must have kept their own supplies of everything. It all seemed very impersonal to him.

Gessler must have been frowning. Nina asked again if he was tired. "No," he said. I'm happy.

She gestured to him to sit down, and brought some hand lotion from the small table and sat opposite him. She squeezed a small amount of the lotion onto the back of his hand and began working it into his skin. She pulled on his fingers, and she kneaded the crevices between his fingers. "You have big hands," she said.

Her hands felt relaxing and stimulating to him at the same time. He never remembered receiving just this kind of attention before.

She massaged his other hand. Later she stood up behind him and she rubbed his neck and his shoulders. They didn't talk for awhile. Here I hardly know this woman, Gessler thought, and she is massaging my neck. That seemed strange. But her hands felt good against his muscles, and he was getting used to the sensation.

"Now," Nina said, pausing. I will make supper, she said in Chinese.

Gessler, rolling his head on his shoulders - the unusual tingling feeling still there - asked if that was still convenient.

Yes. You rest. Nina fluffed the two pillows on her bed and invited him to lie down.

It wasn't necessary, he said. It seemed a little forward to simply go and lie down on her bed.

Please. Be comfortable. She pointed to the nightstand clock, and indicated when dinner would be ready.

He shrugged, and, sitting on the box spring and mattress, rather closer to the floor than he was used to, he removed his shoes and lay down. Nina brought a winter coat from the closet, a long white parka with a fur hood, and lay it over him. He thanked her. From the doorway she smiled at him and switched off the light and closed the door. This, Gessler thought, feels awfully good. He did not mean only the comfortable bed, but the moment, and the feeling of well-being. He meant Nina herself. The fur hood of her coat was against his chin, and from it the smell of her perfume lingered after she left. It was a peaceful feeling, with the lighted buildings and streetlamps casting a faint glow through the uncurtained windows. But he did not actually sleep, at first.

After awhile he put the light on again. Taped to the walls were two studio portraits of Nina. They didn't do her justice, he thought - she looked severe in both of them. He thought he saw coldness - ruthlessness - there, and he stopped looking at the pictures. On the nightstand there was an outdoor snapshot of a girl he took to be her daughter. He would ask Nina about her. There was a postcard-sized image of one of the Chinese deities, a goddess of mercy that he believed was called Guanmin. She had the serene, beatific look. She needed fifty pairs of arms to perform all of her good works. Gessler turned the card over in his hand. It was compliments of a local bank.

He turned the light off again and lay down. He slept fitfully. Once, somewhere between sleep and wakefulness, he imagined he saw the goddess's serene face, then she turned three hundred and sixty degrees and it was Nina that he saw, in the severe aspect of the photographs. He stirred uneasily on the bed. A sword flashed blindingly before his eyes. Alone in the room, Gessler clutched at his stomach as though wounded. He tugged on Nina's coat, pulling the strands of fur away from his face. When he opened his eyes he felt that there was a cold and frightening presence in the room, and the skin of his neck tingled, though not like before. He looked and saw Nina standing framed in the light of the doorway, but he did not recognize her yet. Was this death? Some words escaped from his mouth.

Nina did not understand his words but heard the discomfort in his voice. Without turning on the light she knelt by the bed next to him and touched his forehead soothingly.

"Are you alright? What has happened to you?"

He stared at her face in the darkness. "Just a crazy dream, I guess. Don't worry."

A troubled smile came to Nina's face.

Irrational as it was, the dream had startled him. He tried to shrug it off, thinking of other things.

"You know..." Gessler paused, and ventured a Chinese sentence, speaking with evident seriousness. The words meant: I could not see Nina before, so I was not happy - only that. Gessler kept up a mock-downcast look, and saw that he drew a smile from her.

Let us eat, Nina said. She led him out to the dining area.

It was wonderful to Gessler how these Chinese words conveyed meaning. He knew from his studies that it was so, but seeing their meaning register on another person's face was something different, and delightful.

The table had already been set. There was no one else in the kitchen area now. There was some light from one of the bedrooms whose door was ajar. He could not hear any voices. Nina sat down next to him. There was a whole broiled fish on a tray, and another dish had pieces of what she explained was Peking duck. There was a soup of noodles and tomatoes with a taste of sesame oil. Some slices of cold beef marinated with scallions and a peppery sauce. All of the food was quite good, if a bit spicy. Nina put more food on his plate.

"Do you like?"

It was excellent, Gessler said.

"I can cook for you every night."

"Really."

"You don't like?"

"I will get fat. Pangzi." Nina looked crestfallen at his words. "I'm only joking. It's wonderful." She looked puzzled. "Do you know 'wonderful'?" She shook her head no. "I will teach you a word." He spelled it for her.

Nina punched the letters into the translator, and then looked at the Chinese characters on the screen, saying, "Yes, yes. Won-der-ful."

"Wonderful," Gessler repeated, looking at his plate of food and making his eyes large. He looked at her for a moment, and in a different tone of voice he said, " 'Wonderful' is Nina. Nina is wonderful."

She smiled at him and studied the characters and then clicked the translator shut.

"Thank you," she said. Her "thank you" sounded better to him this time.

Don't be a guest, he told her. Eat now.

After dinner they talked in Nina's room. They sat cross-legged on the bed, with their backs against the wall. Rain drove against the window above and behind them. Gessler did not find the position comfortable but there were few other choices. After awhile he ventured to hold her hand.

Her roommate was out. Nina told him that the roommate had an American boyfriend. He was in his fifties, she said. The roommate and him had met a couple of months ago at a party at some singles club that the roommate belonged to. They were getting married in a couple of months. As she explained, Nina used her fingers to count off the months between the meeting, the engagement, the marriage. Her fingers counted up to four months in all. She nodded her head approvingly.

"Four months?" Gessler repeated. "And they are married?"

"Um-hum." Nodding again.

Gessler looked doubtful. That was quick - too quick. He did not say anything, though.

Nina studied his expression. "Are you very tired?" she asked, looking in his eyes and brushing some hair from his forehead.

"Yi dian," he told her. A little bit. It was after ten.

He stood up to leave. Nina got his overcoat from the closet and helped him on with it. She held up her index finger for him to wait, and went to the kitchen to put some of the dinner in containers for him to take home. Gessler waited outside Nina's room, in the short hallway that led to the common dining room.

The small elderly man he'd seen before, a resident Nina had called the teacher, was doing slow tai-chi movements in the dining area. A television was on, and the man was copying the movements on the screen. He had been a teacher in China, Nina had explained. Here he did whatever he could to make a living. The man paused and looked at Gessler and approached him - kindly, cautiously.

He knew some English. "Be careful," he whispered.

"Yes?"

"It's very dangerous."

Gessler looked at him curiously. "You mean outside?" he ventured. "The storm?" Gessler pointed away, outside. He could not hear the wind or rain just then. He made some fluttering movements with his arms to suggest a gale, but the movements struck him as more birdlike than anything, and he stopped. Something told him the man was not talking about the weather. Gessler wondered if maybe there was something wrong with him.

The man shook his head from side to side. He thumped the middle of his chest with his fist and spoke some words in Chinese. "Inside" was the only word that Gessler understood.

There was a thought in the older man's mind, but he was not able to express it in English. It meant: Sometimes the thing you wanted the most turned out to be ashes in your mouth.

Gessler only looked at him.

But then Nina swept in from the kitchen and took Gessler's hand and pulled him along. He nodded to the other man as he swept past him, feeling more puzzled than enlightened by his words.

"Crazy - old - man," Nina said distinctly.

They said goodbye outside her apartment door. Gessler held her and brought his cheek momentarily against hers before stepping back from her. She stood there smiling, while Gessler smiled and back-pedalled toward the elevator.

4

Gessler had been friends with the Changs for several years. He'd known them since shortly after they moved into a house in the neighborhood. They were one of the reasons he'd begun studying Chinese, and taken an interest in Chinese culture generally. In learning the language, he was in competition with the Changs' eight year old daughter. She went to Chinese school on Sunday mornings. It vexed Gessler to admit it, but the child was making more progress than he was.

He called them from work to see if they had plans for the evening. Laura Chang invited him to stop by the house. Frank was still working at the framing shop that they owned. Their daughter was home.

Laura Chang was now in her early forties. She was small and slim. Her face suggested intelligence and openness. It was not a classically beautiful face, but for Gessler it had a tenacious quality that was winning. He thought that she was an extraordinarily positive person, and he always felt happy to see her.

"Come in," she said, leading him through the living room to the kitchen. She cleared a place at the table and poured him tea from an aluminum kettle on the stove.

"Frank will be home soon."

"How is business?"

"It's alright. We get by. How is your job?"

"The same. Where is Tommy?" Tommy was their other child, a boy of twelve.

"He has hockey practice."

"Hockey. It's so American."

"Yes..."

"It's good, I mean."

"I don't understand it, myself. I wish he worked as hard at Chinese school. 'Why do I have to study Chinese?' he asks me. Can you imagine?" She shook her head as though the question was incomprehensible.

"It isn't easy."

"Thank God they're doing alright."

They heard a high-pitched yell from the basement. "Ma-MA?"

Laura padded over to the opened door and yelled downstairs. "What are you doing? Are you watching TV?"

"I'm working."

Laura grimaced as if impressed. "George is here. Why don't you come say hello."

"Alright." A slightly wearied voice, or as though reluctant to put aside what she was doing. He heard Vivian's tread on the carpeted stairs, and she entered the kitchen. A pretty child, with black bowl-shaped hair.

She was always shy when he first saw her, averting her eyes and twisting her mouth. But she approached Gessler and he kissed her on the cheek.

"How are you, Vivian?"

"Alright. M'm..." She was thinking of something.

"She is writing another book," Laura said.

"Another book? That's wonderful."

"Yes..." Vivian said.

Gessler had seen at least a couple of Vivian's books. She prepared them for school. She wrote her stories in thin blank exercise books. Each page would have a crayon illustration with a line or two of text. There would always be one page with the heading, "About The Author," with a short descriptive paragraph, and the Author's latest studio photograph glued in place.

"You want to show George?"

"It isn't really - complete, yet."

"Oh." Laura's face was playful, encouraging. "She can't show it."

"It's a mystery. Do you like mysteries?" Vivian asked Gessler.

"Oh, yes. Sure."

"It's - pretty scary."

"I want to read it. Is it too scary for me? You think I could sleep after I read it?"

"Well..." She pondered. "You probably could."

He asked her about her Chinese studies. "How many characters do you know now?" She couldn't tell him how many. More than him, he supposed. Vivian's attention flagged. Laura said that her studies were going well. A composition she wrote, in Chinese, was nominated for a school prize.

"Why don't you join Vivian's Chinese school? It's not that expensive, and you could really learn, better than just looking at books."

"Oh, I don't know."

"You feel self-conscious being the only big person?"

"Yes. I think so."

"What is the big deal? You think you would have to sing in the assemblies?"

"That would be pretty funny," Vivian said. "Or dance in the Christmas pageant."

"Yikes."

"That's even better," Laura said. "Seriously, I think you should think about it."

Vivian lingered a few more moments and then asked her mother, "Can I go back to work now?"

"You are writing your book?" Vivian nodded. "Fine. You can go."

"I'll see you later," Gessler said. She went downstairs again.

Laura poured more tea in Gessler's cup. "Frank and I are a couple of squares. *She* writes mysteries. I don't know where she gets it."

"It's a good thing, though. You can be proud. She's doing better in Chinese school, too."

"She's trying harder. I hope we don't put too much pressure on her."

"I don't think you do. She works hard because she's motivated. And because she wants you to be proud of her. It must be very gratifying, yes?"

Laura seemed deep in thought. "Of course. Maybe I don't think of it quite like that."

"Children are so innocent of the world. They haven't seen the bad in people."

"Of course not."

"I love that kid. I'm going to buy her some blank books. So she can write her stories, or whatever."

"She likes you. You do a lot." Laura thought for a moment. "You should have children."

"Yeah? Maybe. I get a kick out of Vivian, I'll tell you. But - I have been thinking about it, actually."

"Really? That's good. Do you have anyone in mind?"

"Possibly."

"That blonde you were seeing, from your job? She's kind of nice-looking. With the big -- well, she was rather attractive, I would say."

"Yes." His friend was right about her - a healthy blonde. "But no. Not her."

"What was wrong?"

Gessler shook his head. "She didn't understand me."

"You always say that. What's so difficult?"

"Me, I guess. I have my moods. I try to keep them under control."

"You don't make it easy for people to know you. I wouldn't worry too much about being under control. Tell people what you are thinking, that's more interesting. It's who you are. But you are like a closed-up shell, George.

No one knows what is inside. Be yourself. Someone out there will appreciate you."

"It's nice to think so. Anyway, I have been taking some steps."

"Tell me about her."

"She's Chinese."

"You mean she's born there?"

"M'm."

"How old?"

"Thirty-five."

"Not bad. And you like her?"

"Oh, yes."

"How is her English?"

"It's not that good. Actually it's not good at all."

"So how do you communicate?"

"Some English. Some Mandarin."

"George, pardon me. Your Mandarin is not that good."

"I know that. But we can talk. A little bit."

"A very little bit, I imagine. Really, do you think this is practical?"

"I know there are some problems."

"I'm glad you realize it. Has she been married before?"

"She's a widow."

"A widow. Tell me there's not a child."

"There is. One. In China."

"George. Think. Is this what you want? Do you want this responsibility?"

"I'm not saying there aren't some problems, Laura. But if she loves me - if she makes me happy - I could accept some financial responsibility."

"You know what I think? I don't think you know anything about her. What do you think of that? Is she a citizen here?"

Gessler hesitated. "A work visa."

"Of course. Don't you see what she wants? She only wants to get established here. Oh, I've seen it before. She wants to bring her family here. These Chinese are so goddamn loving I can't stand them. Do you think she loves *you*?"

"I think she likes me. Look, I know those other things may play a factor. I'm lonely, Laura. I may not get many more chances."

"George - don't rush. That's what I'm saying. Let me ask you one other thing. How did you meet her?"

Here Gessler really hesitated. He decided to come out with it. "I answered a personal ad. In one of the Chinese newspapers."

Gessler had looked away, but now he ventured a look at his friend. She was speechless.

"You look surprised," he said.

"Surprised. I look surprised?" She stood up suddenly and stared at him with an intensity that he had never seen before. "Are you out of your freakin' mind?"

She made as if to cuff Gessler on the back of the head, and he recoiled.

"Hey."

"George. I don't understand you." Laura gestured imploringly with her hands. "All these years you are working hard, you are saving your money. Do you want to give it away?"

"If she loves me I don't mind. I think I can help her."

"What do you mean, help her? Who are you, Jesus Christ? I think you are going crazy!"

"I haven't actually committed to anything."

"Good. Don't. You are an engineer. Think - be logical. At least tell me that you won't rush into anything."

"Alright. Promise."

"You shock me, George."

"Please, Laura. I know you mean well. You've told me."

"I've told you but will you listen." She sat down again. "If you take my advice you'll break this thing off right now. I don't have a good feeling. I know you've talked about having a family. It's possible. But don't do something you'll regret."

Gessler thought for a moment. "If I could go back and live my life again. Back to college, for example, where there were some suitable women. But I mean knowing what I know now, not to go back just for the sake of doing it again. I think I would try to be more sociable. I would worry less, and take things more lightly."

"Sometimes we look back and think, 'Why wasn't I more carefree? I was young, why couldn't I simply enjoy what I had?'"

"Yes, that's what I mean."

"But don't think of the past. It could be like a prison. So you didn't meet the one before. Maybe you were not ready then. Don't look back. Look forward. If you want to have a family it is possible. But don't make a mistake. Can't you meet American women? At least you can talk with them."

"I don't have any prejudices either way."

"I don't think you can force it. Sometimes you meet someone by chance. Just be yourself."

"Maybe that's been my problem."

"No. That's not a problem. Who else are you going to be? Why do you compare yourself to other people? *I* never do. Do you know what you are? You're one in a million."

"Really."

"You are. I appreciate you. You are the scholar type. Hard-working. What is wrong with these American women? If I wasn't already married, I mean, I would consider you very suitable--"

"Did you ever think about us?"

"Having a family? Oh, I was just thinking out loud. Forget I said it."

"We've gotten older together," he said.

"I suppose that things are fated one way, and only one way. When did I meet you? You see it just wasn't possible. I didn't know you then."

"Sometimes I wished I could meet someone like you."

"I'm an old woman. You could probably do better."

"I'm not sure."

"Let's not think about it. You are starting to sound foolish, and I don't want to become foolish, too."

"Thank you for the kind words, anyway."

"Forget that I said it."

"I don't want to."

"Don't then. Remember that someone appreciates you."

"You know. Over the years, I've had my moments with other women. Some of it was fun. But I seldom ever clicked with them somehow."

Laura got up and added more water to the kettle and placed it back on the stove.

"I know, I'm talking a lot of ragtime."

"I don't mind you talking. I never met anyone like you, either. I want you to be happy. You just take a friend's advice and be careful." She looked out the kitchen window. "Frank is home. Maybe we can go out for supper."

Laura's husband was several years older then her. His thinning hair was combed straight back. He entered the kitchen smiling and shook Gessler's hand. Laura worked at the sink.

"How are you?"

"Alright," Gessler said.

Frank said something to Laura in Chinese and moved toward the refrigerator. Gessler understood the words and he spoke.

"I don't need anything to drink, Frank. The tea is fine."

"Oh. Alright." Pausing there. He seemed nonplussed that Gessler had understood his speech.

"George has a new girlfriend," Laura said.

"A new one? That's the way, George. Trade them in. That's what I would do if I could afford to."

"Ha," Laura said. "You want to die in your sleep?"

Her husband thought for a moment. "Laura has become so Americanized," he said.

"So what's your excuse? Funny guy. You want to go out for supper?"

"Why not?" He sat down. "You like to go out, George?"

"Sure," Gessler said.

"Where's Wayne Gretsky?" Frank asked Laura.

"Who?"

"He's still practicing," Gessler said, for both of them.

"It's got to happen, George. Chinese hockey player. Can't all be square-heads with slide-rules. No offense, I mean. I know you're an engineer."

"Hockey player?" Laura said from the sink. "With missing teeth? Looking like Frankenstein? Forget about it." She came over and wiped the table.

"Those hockey players make a fortune. With a little more money we can leave the rat race," Frank continued. "Retire comfortably in Florida."

"There's nothing to do there, anyway," Laura said. "For us, everything is here."

Her husband frowned. He brought a bottle of beer to the kitchen table and sat across from Gessler. "So what about the new girlfriend? Is this the one you're going to get serious about?"

"Oh, it's going pretty well so far. But - it's early to tell."

Frank nodded sagely and sipped from his beer.

5

A woman in a dark trenchcoat and sunglasses walked briskly along one of the sidewalks leading to Main Street in Flushing. It was early in the afternoon, and the day was overcast. The sidewalks were relatively uncrowded. A crow stalked clumsily near Nina as she walked, and she kicked at it. The bird rose a few feet with a complaining noise, and returned to some bags of refuse it was picking at. Nina's face, in the dark sunglasses, was a mask.

She turned onto Main Street. A couple of blocks ahead of her another man was walking by himself. One of his shoes was built up with rubber, and this leg dragged behind him slowly and moved forward in short steps. There was a jangling sound of keys on a metal ring, the sound muffled by the man's overcoat. He made his way along slowly and entered a noodle shop and took a table in the back.

Nina entered moments later. She swept past the maitre-de toward the rear, and approached the table where the man was sitting.

The waiter followed her to the table. With a slight turn of her head she said something in Chinese, refusing the menu. She kept her sunglasses on. Neither she or the man spoke.

Nina looked around the restaurant. No one was seated at any nearby tables. The man was a Chinese of about Nina's age. His clothes suggested a laborer. Hair fell over his forehead. He had a wispy mustache, but with some prominent and unruly hairs that could make a person think of some bottom-dwelling species of fish. His eyes looked empty, and seemed to promise more cunning than intelligence. Nina removed her sunglasses and placed them carefully on the table.

So how is it going? the man asked at last, in Chinese.

Alright.

She looked at him blankly, without smiling. Her face kept this expression.

I've seen you walking with him a couple of times.

Yes? You must not have a lot to do. Why don't you get a job?

Why should *I* have to work? Besides, my English is very bad.

You're very funny. You can be an entertainer at Shang Dynasty.

Maybe I can dance, too.

You get around alright. Stop complaining.

Anyway, Shang Dynasty is too rich for me.

Your English is bad? *No one* around here speaks English. Of course you can get a job. What the hell are you talking about?

Sister.

Don't call me that. If I had a brother like you I would kill myself.

Does that make any sense? Stop criticizing me. When you do your part I will take care of the rest. That's what I am here for. Do you think he will marry you?

Nina looked peevishly around the restaurant.

I don't know. Americans are different. This one. It takes time.

We don't have a lot of time. I think they like the same thing.

You're very common, Pang. I don't know why I didn't see it before.

What is, common?

It means you can't talk intelligently with someone.

That isn't nice. Why don't you come by my place some time?

I just told you.

You are changing, I think.

I'm not interested.

Really. It's been some time--

I told you. I'm not interested.

Nina.

I mean it. When this is over with - I mean, it's just business from now on.

You don't mean that. You are worried? Are you capable--?

Of course I am capable. I am going to have what I want.

Nina's fist clenched slightly on the table.

The man frowned. Let's talk business, then. If that's all you want. Did you tell him about the kid?

Yes.

Was that wise?

He may see her someday.

Yes. What did you tell him about the father?

He's dead.

How sad. Did you cry a lot?

Enough. He is dead to me.

Where is he really?

You don't have to know.

Right. Sorry. Stupid of me to pry.

The waiter brought a tray of noodles and two plates. Pang helped himself, and then Nina took some. Pang lowered his head as if to smell the food, and looked up at Nina and spoke more softly.

You have to see about the insurance. That's very important.

I know that.

So?

You know so much. You think I should have asked him about insurance the first date?

Not so loud. You know what I mean.

I know what I'm doing. You do your part.

They ate without speaking.

Does he have family he would leave money to?

I don't think so. No brothers or sisters.

Good.

Yes. Call me if necessary. Don't come by the place.

The man looked at her darkly before smiling slightly. Coldly.

Nina put her sunglasses back on and stood up. She placed some money on the table for her meal, and left.

6

The thing about love, Gessler thought, it brought you out of yourself. That was the really wonderful thing about it. He supposed that Laura was right, that he really didn't know Nina well. But his feeling for her grew. It grew at an irresistible pace. Just when you were nearly resigned that Fate was never going to bring you face to face with that special someone. Then - bam! - suddenly love hit you like the flu. It hit you like an infectious disease.

Gessler was seeing Nina a few times a week. He was enjoying the time with her. There were trips to Manhattan on the subway. An art museum. Clothes shopping. She was a good-looking woman. When she put on make-up she looked actually glamorous. There had not been any intimacy between them. The neck- and hand-massages were relaxing and just the least bit stimulating. Gessler could be patient. Sometimes when they were alone Nina allowed his hands to touch her. But she didn't seem to respond to his touch. He came to realize that it was some super-added foam material that gave that provocative lift to her chest. It was as if there was a barrier between them, and after awhile the necking wasn't so interesting. For all her responsiveness she could have been wearing a parka or a lead apron.

He hoped she was not one of those old-world women who were passive when it came to sex. He just didn't know. He supposed she would give him some kind of indication - a preview - before they actually thought about marriage. And marriage was beginning to look like a possibility, which was a wonder to the long-time bachelor. He was content to wait.

He enjoyed speaking to her in Chinese, although he was hardly fluent. It was easy to ask someone what kind of food they felt like eating. Things like that were simple. Ideas were more of a problem. States of mind. Sometimes when he was talking with her Gessler looked as if he had seized a concept within his fist; but try as he might, he could not bring forth the meaning in Chinese. This was frustrating. A look of disappointment would cloud his features.

What, he thought, would this be like, day after day? How, returning home, could you express any of the minor frustrations of the workday? Or vent your feelings about what was in the newspaper? Living with a woman like Nina was going to have its pleasures. But communication was going to be a problem. He had not given enough thought to it before.

One thing he had noticed, and liked, was that when he was out with Nina, strange women seemed to look at him with a new respect and interest. When Nina and him were riding on the subway, for example. He could have crossed paths with these other women a thousand times without receiving more than a glance. But now he was with Nina here was one who couldn't keep still, she kept looking at him and almost writhing in her seat, for crying out loud. And she wasn't the only one. Or was he imagining it? Anyway, where were these women before, all of those times when he was alone?

He was visiting Nina again. It was the middle of the week. He noticed that she'd used bedsheets to improvise some curtains for the windows, and he said to her, banteringly, that the place was looking more like a home.

Gessler was sitting in a small chair, Nina on the edge of the bed a few feet from him. She frowned. "Not home," she said. "Home have--"

"Has," he corrected her.

"Has" - she searched for an expression, and then her eyes brightened - "a happy family! Man. Wo-man. Children. Call this fanguan. Apart-ment. No home."

"I didn't mean to say it was," Gessler said. Somehow he'd struck the wrong tone. He drank some tea. Nina served hot tea in glasses, which were difficult to hold. He reminded himself to buy her a couple of nice drinking cups. "Wrong word." He took her hand. "My Chinese - no good!"

"It's not so bad." Nina's frown lifted and she rose and stood behind Gessler, rubbing his neck. "You are tired."

"I think I just always look that way. Maybe, yidian." A little. "I'm going to speak more English so you can learn. Okay?"

"Okay. My English--"

"Yeah, yeah. It will get better. How else can we live together?"

"You think so? Live together?"

"I think it is possible, yes? Anyway - the lesson. Yidian is a little. A little bit. I'm a *little* tired."

He could not see Nina behind him. "Lit-terl. Lit-tle," she said.

"Yes. This is nice, you know?" He pulled Nina to his side, where he could see her.

"Yes? I'm happy." She pulled up the other small chair close to Gessler and looked at him.

"Every day," she said, "when you are working. Every hour, at your desk--" She extended her arms out to her sides and made some callisthenic motions. "You exercise. It's good." She rolled her head from side to side to illustrate another exercise. She closed her eyes and let her head fall to her chest. Her sleek hair fell about her forehead. When she lifted her head again her eyes were still closed. In her appearance there was just a hint of sexual abandon -

something that Gessler glimpsed for the first time. When Nina opened her eyes again he averted his eyes slightly. He was sure that the impression was all in his mind, and not anything that Nina had intended. It was just a glimpse - of a dormant sensuality, he imagined. He was intrigued. He turned his mind back to the subject with an effort.

"What is wrong?"

"Nothing," Gessler smiled. He brushed her cheek with his hand. He noticed again how easily she smiled back at him. It touched him to think about it. "Bu pa," he said. Don't be afraid. "Nothing is wrong."

Nina stood up and brushed some hair from his forehead. He held her there for a while.

"Before," she asked, "you have Chinese girlfriend?"

"Not a girlfriend. No."

"No? So why you like Chinese women?"

"I don't like just Chinese women. But I think they are nice. Sure. And some of them are nice-looking." He reached up from his chair and touched her chin and looked into her eyes. "Nina is good-looking."

"You are - flirt?"

"Me? Maybe a little. Yi dian."

"You are good-looking man. Why you don't marry?"

"It just didn't happen that way."

"Before - you have many girlfriends?"

"There isn't that much to tell. Some. I've had my moments."

Nina looked at him doubtfully. "So why you didn't marry? You didn't love them?"

"Not enough, I guess. Or I did but they didn't love me. It's hard to say. And maybe I like my independence." It was not a conclusive answer but he didn't know how to improve upon it.

"How many girlfriends?" Nina held out the fingers of one hand, then another hand.

Gessler frowned.

"You don't want to talk," she said.

"Nina. You don't really know anything about me. Why do you only ask about old girlfriends? It's very uninteresting."

"I would like to know."

"Do you really care about that?"

"You think I don't care?"

"Why don't you ask me about my family?"

"Your - family? You told me about your family. I understand."

"I guess I am just in a bad mood."

"You are angry of me?"

"Oh…" Gessler shrugged. "It's just that when I try to have an interesting conversation with you, you seem bored. Maybe you just lack the imagination to see how the topic might possibly be interesting, if you would try."

Nina frowned. "I'm sure that is the reason," she said.

But she was perplexed. She thought she might press Gessler about what this 'imagination' was, and just what it entailed. But he seemed tired, and he was already cross with her it seemed.

Gessler saw the hint of sadness in her expression. "No, Nina. I have no reason to be angry at you." He smiled, and stood up.

"You are leaving?"

"I have to."

"You will call me tomorrow?"

"Yes. I will call."

They said goodnight in the corridor. Gessler walked home. He did not feel angry toward Nina. But he started to feel slightly depressed. She seemed to like him. But she did not understand who he was, not by a long shot. And she didn't show much curiosity about him, either - that was the troubling thing. Old girlfriends were really a very innocuous subject. She'd never brought up his family again. Never asked him what he thought was wrong with Morty, for example.

He felt dissatisfied. Maybe, he thought, he'd had stars in his eyes since the first time he saw her.

7

"So we'll do something on the weekend, alright, Nina?"

She and Gessler had been out for supper and were now in Nina's room. The evening was late and Gessler felt like going home.

"Week-end. Yes. I would like. What are you doing tomorrow?"

"Tomorrow." Gessler explained that he might have to work late. That there were some technical and other magazines at home. A book he'd started reading. But his explanations only brought out a sullen look in Nina.

"You don't want to?"

"It isn't that I don't want to. I just have things to do."

"So you are busy."

"Yes. Nina - do you think that you understand me?"

"Why not?"

"I think we hardly know each other. I'm trying to tell you that I have things to do." Gessler said this as gently as he could.

"We don't know each other. So we should - spend time. Yes?"

Gessler looked at her warily. Nina frowned.

"You think I like to stay here?" She indicated her room, and the outer apartment, and with a more expansive gesture the building and the neighborhood. "With these S-ban-ish people? Boom-boom-boom, party?" She covered her ears. "With these black--" She used a Chinese word that he thought meant "ghosts." (Why "ghosts," though? Did that make any sense? Gessler made a mental note to himself to look up the word when he was at home.)

"Look. I can understand. But can't you be patient? Don't be discouraged."

A different look came into Nina's face, the sullenness disappeared. "You are kind," she said.

"Ah, go on. Is that all that's troubling you – the neighborhood? You're not going to be here forever, are you?"

"I don't know." She turned away.

"Try to be reasonable."

"M'm. So you are very busy man." Her face took on a calculating look that he'd seen before.

Gessler frowned. "Do you think we are alike, Nina?"

110

"Alike..." She did not seem certain of the meaning.

"You. Me." Pointing. "Tong-de, butong-de?"

"I think we are alike. Sure. Why not?"

"You don't even know who I am." The thought bothered him. With the little they had communicated, how could they expect to know each other?

"It could take a year," he said.

"One - year?" Nina looked crestfallen. "You think - one year?" He didn't say anything, and when Nina spoke again she tried a more bantering tone.

"I - like - you." She pointed to herself and to Gessler in turn, for emphasis. "But I think you only like me yi-dian-dian." A little. With her thumb and forefinger she measured off something insubstantial.

"That's what you think? I like you only a little?"

She nodded. "It's true?"

Gessler shook his head no. "I need time to get to know you. Maybe it's a cultural difference--"

Nina handed him the translator from the small night table.

"American way," Gessler continued, "is to take your time, get to know someone. Find out if you are compatible." He took the translator from Nina's hand and input the word. He was becoming familiar with the keypad. A couple of Chinese characters that he did not recognize appeared on the small screen, which he turned to Nina. She only glanced at the screen.

"Maybe," she said, "you have other girlfriend?"

"What other girlfriend? Why're you getting so possessive already?" Changing his tone, "Well of course there may be others. Wealthy playboy and man about town that I am. But can I keep it up?" He struck a nonchalant pose, but he saw at a glance that Nina was not amused.

"You are having fun," she said.

"No, I'm not. Don't be that way. I just don't get you sometimes."

"Don't - get?"

"Nina. You're nice. I like you. But how long have we been seeing each other - four weeks now? I feel like you are pressuring me."

"What is pressure?"

Gessler mimed someone warding off blows, and then, more expressively, he brought his hands around his neck as if being strangled.

Nina's eyes widened. "Oh!" She stood up and turned away from him.

"Maybe that was the wrong... I'm sorry."

After a moment she turned and asked, "You want to marry? Have children?"

"Yes, I think so. Why not? But let's not rush."

Nina did not seem convinced. They were just a couple of feet apart, leaning toward each other on the small chairs. He reached and grasped her shoulder, which felt firm and muscular. He slid off of the chair. Kneeling, his bones made a cracking sound. He grasped her waist and kissed her on the mouth. She was wearing a form-fitting jersey and slacks. Gessler did not allow his hands to roam further, except to brush her hair off of her shoulders. Nina's hand was around his neck. She was not very responsive. She inclined her head back. Gessler kissed her neck. After awhile he sat back on his chair, still holding Nina's hands.

"Nina is a good-looking woman," he said. She looked at him, smiling.

"I can see you - not tomorrow, but the day after tomorrow? Is that alright?"

"Mingtian?" Nina asked.

"Not tomorrow. The day after?"

Nina frowned but then nodded. "You call me?"

"Of course." Gessler leaned back in his chair. He was thinking of how few possessions she had here. There was a shallow half-filled closet; the mattress and box spring; her night table with its radio, a few cassettes and snapshots; and a plastic pail by the door that held her bottles of soaps and things. He'd noticed during his visits that the bedrooms could be locked with keys - not that there was so much to steal. Just these things and, he supposed, pocket money that she stashed somewhere. The locks and keys added to that impersonal quality of the place. He thought that perhaps he should be more understanding with her.

"If it is noisy here," he said. "On the weekends, for example--" He put his hands over his ears, grimacing.

"Oh. These - neighbors," Nina said, with a sour expression. "No culture."

"You remember 'culture,'" he said.

"Of course. You taught me."

He felt touched, he felt bad for her in her circumstances. "Well, if it is noisy, you could stay with me one night."

"Stay - with you?"

"In separate beds, I mean." What was the Chinese word for "bed"? He couldn't remember, and he was about to pantomime separate beds. But why the hell was he being so chivalrous, anyway? They were both grown people.

But Nina did not follow up on his idea at all, which surprised him, because clearly she was not happy in this place. He thought that maybe she thought his suggestion too forward.

"You can think about it." He was thinking that it was really time to go, anyway. Still sitting, he touched her knee. "And don't worry about things. I like you. I have fun with you."

Gessler added a Chinese word that suggested both "fun" and "play." Nina repeated the word, and, to his surprise, her face darkened.

"You" - pointing - "only play? You are playboy?" Her voice rising. "Play-boy?"

"Wait." Gessler groaned at this fresh confusion. They were hurled back to their earlier disagreement, and the thought came to him again, how having a passing knowledge of a language could lead to trouble. Nina was looking at him crossly, expecting an answer.

"Nina, what are you talking about?" He allowed himself to wonder for a moment if it could be true. A playboy? It was inconceivable. Not Gessler. Where in the world did she get her ideas?

"No," he assured her. "No. Not a playboy. Let's not fight." He touched her cheek. "Please. I don't think I meant 'play.' Wrong word."

"Alright," she said. "Sor-ry. Do you have to leave?" He'd stood up to go.

"Yes. I will call you tomorrow."

"You are not angry?"

She got both of their coats from the closet.

He was not angry with her, but the truth was that he felt more than a little discouraged.

"Are you coming out with me?" he asked.

"Outside. Yes, I want to. I will not see you."

He put his coat on and paused, looking at her. "We can't always have this argument, Nina. We have to be able to talk reasonably."

"I don't mean to ar-gue," she said, putting her arms around his neck and playing with his hair. "It's because - I care about you." She buttoned his coat, while he looked at her. "You believe me?"

"Sure," he said in a moment. "Sure I do. I'd better go."

They stepped into the corridor, and Nina walked with him to the subway station. They said goodnight near the turnstiles as a train arrived downstairs on the platform.

Gessler had had his doubts about their future before, but now a new and inescapable question was forming in his mind. It seemed a reasonable question in the circumstances, and maybe it was emblematic of any two people in their situation. He knew that Nina had economic reasons for wanting to marry – in order to remain in the country, for one obvious reason. You need to be sure about this thing, he thought. She wants to marry. But was it really him she wanted to marry?

8

Gessler felt a need for some advice. But his friend Laura had already expressed herself plainly about Nina. Laura always did - it was not her way to hold back. What had changed was that Gessler himself now felt some doubts. Serious ones, in fact. But how could Laura have made up her mind so quickly about Nina - without even having met her? That did not seem either fair or reasonable. On balance, he thought it best not to talk to Laura just now. Having expressed herself once, she might only become angry this time.

He called his Chinese professor. He was a personable guy of about Gessler's age, a New Englander. Gessler indicated to him that he wanted a specialist's advice about something. His questions had to do with Chinese culture, and especially the "immigrant culture." That's why he felt that Professor Bartle would have some insight - and so forth. He was as helpful as Gessler could have hoped. He was teaching a Saturday class at the college. Perhaps Gessler would like to stop by his office and discuss the matter in person.

Bartle was of average build, with a full beard and thinning hair. He was given to wearing corduroy and sweaters. He wore wire glasses which he was constantly putting on or off. He had the equanimity of someone who has devoted himself to a specialty and, against odds, is able to make a living at it.

His eyes had a mischievous quality, as though (and frequently in fact) he was on the verge of making some sly and sometimes self-effacing joke. When he spoke of the Chinese and their language he would often employ the wide rolling eyes and the dropped jaw of a comic actor. It was a routine that served him very well when he gave his classes.

"How are your studies going?" he asked Gessler now in his office.

"I stay with it, thanks."

"Are you still reading the book?"

The book was a novel in Chinese, with drawings, that they'd started reading during an intermediate course on the written language. Gessler had wanted to continue formally with the book, but there were not enough students for a follow-on course. This happened a lot. So he studied the book on his own, a page at a time. The author had limited himself to only a few hundred characters; still, reading was slow going, with frequent references to the Chinese dictionary or other texts. It was hard to explain how this kind of sedulous study could also be transporting, and yet it was, for Gessler and other students   You extracted some meaning from the hieroglyphics - it was an exciting and a rewarding thing. He found that he could lose himself in the study. Many times, studying the language cheered him up if he was feeling down.

The study wasn't for everyone, obviously. You needed extraordinary patience as well as a feeling for the culture. The culture and the language were, if not the same thing, at least inextricably bound.

"I read about a page at a time. After I've read several pages I go back and review, but it is tough sledding all over again. I start forgetting. So I think I've only read a quarter of the book."

"It's difficult, when you are not born Chinese. A Chinese kid is just told to begin copying the character when he is five years old. You just sit and copy it a hundred times. That's the Chinese way. We come into the game rather late."

"Yes. I like the book, though."

The book told the story of a bachelor and a beautiful woman who is more spirit than flesh. She was not a ghost, exactly. She was definitely not of this world, though. That was probably going to be the dramatic conflict, in what for the bachelor in the story has become an idyllic scene with her. Probably she tells him one day that she does not belong among mortals, and that she has to leave him. Either that, or she makes a sacrifice, finding a way to stay with him. The story might turn out something like that, if he could ever get through it. There were many stories like this among the folk-tales and the Chinese opera. The book successfully mined that element of romance within the in some ways flinty Chinese character.

Chinese had been a favorite study with him for years. Unquestionably it was more difficult than any Western language, yet it was supremely logical. For example, there was a character for "good" (it showed, incidentally, a woman and child together), but none for "bad." You just used the negative: "not good." And you could use a qualifier and say "very not good." It was a very economical language. You did not have a lot of verb forms to remember, either. Just some suffixes, that you could use with all verbs, to show that the action was just past, or long ago past, or in process.

These were things that compensated in some degree for the complexity of the written Chinese. In the dictionary you had several thousand characters, all grouped under some two hundred different "radicals" (the things that gave meaning to the characters.) So that, under the "tree" radical you would find "table," and other objects commonly made of wood. As a study it was just inexhaustible. It was not true that Chinese characters are "pictures" of things - that was a misconception. But when you learned to recognize the radicals for "fire," "heart," or "water," for example, you began to notice them in characters dealing with things that you cook, or emotional qualities, or things that you drink. So the study was not just about memorizing, it was about forming mental associations. There was really something elevating about it. And in its own, strange way the study could chase away the blues.

Seeing Professor Bartle again reminded him of the many classes he'd enjoyed. Once a semester they would usually visit Chinatown for some field study. There would be a restaurant meal, with Bartle and perhaps ten or twelve students, and as many different dishes which were passed around and sampled. Before eating, though, the students would go off with notebooks in hand and, pausing on the sidewalks, copy characters from the store signs, from display windows and the like. Characters that they recognized, or didn't but thought were interesting. Bartle would sometimes insist that every student transcribe a set number of characters before they ate. Then they would compare notes on the characters in the course of the meal and when they next met in class. The professor could identify almost all of the characters from memory. If he could not - or for the sake of practice - the students would look up the character in the large Chinese dictionary which the professor had urged the students to buy. Gessler's copy now rested on a shelf in his living room.

"I try to study a little every week," Gessler said. "But unless you're a specialist it's hard to find enough time."

"Naturally."

"Lately I have been doing some on the job training."

"Do you mean, friends?" Bartle asked.

"Yes." For it seemed to him that Nina herself was becoming something of a study.

"Ah."

"I met a Chinese woman. We've been seeing each other for several weeks."

"Yes? Where is she from?"

Gessler did not see why that was so important, but he told him. "We get along alright, but she is pressing me for assurances. I think she wants to marry. I don't really know her yet."

"Has she asked you to marry her?"

"No. It's more a feeling I get. We sort of talk around it. I get her drift, let's say."

"You say you've only known her - less than a couple of months?" Gessler nodded. "Do you think she is sincere?"

"I know that she has economic reasons for wanting to marry. I've never dealt with this before I'm not so sure that it's me she wants to marry, if you know what I mean."

"Of course. Does she work?"

"She works at a restaurant."

"I imagine she does want to marry, you know. She's not interested in friendship. If you don't marry her she would say you are wasting her time. She would move on to someone else."

"I think I would marry her. If I am sure. There's something else that bothers me. I told her a little bit about my family history." Gessler recounted some of that history. "I thought she ought to know about it. I would want to know about it. But she's never brought it up again. She has no curiosity. Instead she asks me about old girlfriends." Gessler winced. "Na hen meiyouyisi." That's very uninteresting. "I mean, isn't that an innocuous subject?"

Bartle looked at him with a wry expression. He tapped his fingers together judiciously.

"I hope I'm not being too forward here," Gessler said. "Maybe I'm making you uncomfortable."

"Not at all," Bartle said. "I don't mind at all."

"It's just that I feel like I'm going through some kind of mid-life crisis here. There are some real possibilities for me. A family, maybe."

"Yes, yes. Does she speak English?"

"Not well."

"One thing I would be concerned about is communication. I'm sorry, but this really is a difficult thing. To say nothing of cultural differences. The way you've described things, I don't imagine you are really communicating. Am I wrong?"

Gessler frowned.

"With your Chinese, I don't doubt you can talk about restaurants and the weather. That's not enough. You've said that her English is poor. That's not acceptable."

"She studies every day."

"It's not enough. I'm not just saying this as a teacher. If you are thinking about a life with her, you have to be able to communicate. 'The baby is sick, we need to do something.' Do you see?"

"I know it's a problem."

"The other thing - and by the way, I hope you don't think *I'm* being forward?"

"I want to know what you think," Gessler said.

"The other thing. Does the expression 'airplane ticket' mean anything to you?"

Gessler looked puzzled. "I've never heard it before. You mean - pay for trips back and forth to China? Or bring her family here or--"

"It means a lot more than that. It means getting this woman established here. In total."

"You think she just wants to use me?"

Bartle sighed. *"You* have your doubts. I think you should definitely be on your guard. You really need to take your time. She may be a good person. I don't mean to be overly discouraging. But you should give yourself time, maybe one year."

"A year... What if she doesn't want to wait?"

Bartle shrugged. His fingertips separated. "I have a good friend. He married a Laotian woman. They lived in Washington state. They had a child. One day the woman just vanished, with the baby. I suspect that the woman needed to hear her own language, she needed a support system that my friend couldn't provide. He hasn't been able to find any trace of them. Probably they are in some immigrant community now. He's completely devastated."

"I can imagine," Gessler said gloomily.

"That may be a worst case, however. I suggest you give it some time. Were you introduced by someone?"

"Sort of," Gessler said. It was not true but he did not want to go into the circumstances of how he'd met Nina.

"Can you ask them about her background?"

"They don't know her real well," Gessler said evasively. No one could tell him anything about Nina's background, as far as he knew.

"Have I been helpful?" Bartle asked.

"Yes. I'll be careful. I guess it is not a real good basis of trust, to be starting out on."

Gessler smiled ruefully and they shook hands. When he was outside he thought to himself: Professor, too, is telling me to cool it, in his own way.

9

Gessler was determined not to be discouraged. Nina could be trying sometimes, but the relationship was worth pursuing. He just would not rush - that was the logical thing.

Nina was visiting him at his apartment. She had offered to prepare supper. So together they bought some tofu, and green vegetables, and some prepared dumplings and a kind of oil that Gessler did not usually keep on hand. He brought some pans, which included a wok, from the cupboard.

But there was no rush about dinner. He showed her around his apartment, which Nina hadn't seen before. The living room was growing dark, with some late afternoon sunlight through the two tall windows. The windows were opened slightly, and the place was cool and quiet. He hung up their jackets.

He brought out some tea canisters, and Nina placed some of the loose tea in a ceramic pot. She put water on the stove, and as she did so Gessler put his arms around her waist. She turned on the burner and then turned and twisted out of his grasp. He looked at her questioningly. Why was she so unresponsive? Was it wrong for him to have these feelings about her?

"Your apartment, it's very nice." Nina walked toward the living room and he followed her. She stopped in front of one of the wooden bookcases. "You have much room. It is always this quiet here?"

"Not all the time. But it's decent, I guess."

She seemed to look at the book titles, while Gessler studied her. "Red - And - Black," she said. "I have read this book. I think it was very interesting."

"Do you remember much about it?" He opened the book, which was large and had color illustrations. A soldier, a lady in a ballroom gown.

"It was - long time. Very beautiful," she said, tracing the illustration with her finger. She moved on.

She paused next to one of the windows, where there was another tall bookshelf. Gessler leaned his elbow against the window frame, studying her. She turned and faced him. They were just inches apart.

"Why do you look?"

"You are pretty."

"Yes? You have many books. You have read them?"

"Not as many as I'd like."

"I have books in China."

Gessler had heard similar remarks before - Nina must have had many things in China. Once they were walking past the display window of a women's' lingerie store in a mall. There were some provocative and brightly colored underthings on the mannequins there. Nina had casually said, "I have these in China." It was an interesting bit of information. But Gessler had let the remark pass - stupidly, it seemed to him now.

"Do you read so much?" she asked Gessler.

"I try to."

"You need to have fun, too." She reached out and touched his chest lightly. "Ex-ercise." With her palm she pressed rhythmically on his chest, three times. "It is good for the heart, ex-ercise. You think so?" She looked up at him seductively.

Gessler's voice came out a growl. He could not articulate anything.

"My goodness. What has happen to your voice?"

For answer he held her tighter and kissed her on the mouth. He felt her hands on his shoulders and he pressed against her. He could have made love to her then and there. But her mind seemed to be in a different place. When he released her she looked casually at some of the objects in the room. His arms still held her by the waist.

There was a square of stained glass hanging in the window near them. The piece was a souvenir of one of Gessler's better relationships, bought at a crafts shop somewhere north of the city. The late afternoon sunlight shone through the stained glass and cast a burnished patch of light, a cataract of colored shards, into the room where they stood. He studied the play of the lights across her face. The room now felt as quiet as a chapel.

"I like it here," Nina said, and looked outside. "It is warm in the sun."

"Yes. Are you doing anything special this week?"

"This week. Tomorrow, I - my girlfriend - we go to Connec-ticut."

"Why're you going to Connecticut?"

"M'm..." Nina grasped his wrists. He allowed her to press his arms to his sides. Then she tugged his arms up and down, and he flinched when she made to pinch his chest. She made clicking noises and cash-register sounds. From her pantomime, Gessler began to see the lineaments of a slot machine in a gambling casino.

"You are going to gamble?" he asked her.

"Gam-ble." Nina did not appear to know the word.

Gessler rolled imaginary dice, he dealt some cards into the air.

"Gamble," Nina nodded. "We take a bus. You come with us?"

Gessler was not enthusiastic. "I don't think so, kid. I have to work, for one thing."

"Oh."

The sun was setting. Through the stained glass, the shards of colored lights played over Nina's face, glinting in her dark eyes. Gessler stared at her, seemingly hypnotized.

"Don't you ever gamble?" she asked him.

"I think I always want to know the odds."

" 'The odds' ?"

"You know. Your chances to win. Like that."

"Maybe that is not so interesting, always knowing the odds. Is it?"

"It's just always been my way."

"With women, too?" Nina looked into his eyes.

"Yes. Though maybe I am different since I met Nina." She didn't say anything. "What?" As close as we are, he thought, she always holds herself away from me. Maybe it was him. Yet he wasn't so very old. He felt desire stirring in him when he was this close to her. But it seemed to him that the moment had passed.

"Don't you have to work?" he asked her.

"M'm... I - quit."

"You quit your job? At the restaurant? Why?"

"Nanshuo." It's difficult to explain. "The owner, he is looking at me. Staring." The word sounded like stay-ring.

"That's why you quit? So why don't you tell him to knock it off?"

"I can kill him," Nina said coldly, making a fist. "He said something."

Gessler frowned. "The next time, introduce me to your boss."

"Why?"

"So he'll know you have a boyfriend."

"Oh. Alright. This happens many times. I change jobs."

"You shouldn't have to."

"Men." Clenching her fist again.

"Are you going to look for another job?"

"Yes. Next week." She held his hands and leaned her head against his chest. "You come with us, to gam-ble? Me and my girlfriend?"

"I have to work." Gessler was still feeling annoyed that she'd quit her job. Although perhaps it wasn't her fault, if it happened that way. "I don't think it would interest me very much," he said.

"Why?" Nina turned to him. "You don't like?"

"I'm sorry. Some other day we'll go."

Nina looked at him a long time, touching his jaw. "Sometime. You, me. My girlfriend. Her American boyfriend. We go to karaoke. You know karaoke?"

"I've heard of it. I've never tried it."

"Maybe there is a lot you have never tried. It's fun. You can meet the boyfriend. Talk with him."

"M'm." Gessler was unenthusiastic. "You think he is like me?"

"He is older," Nina said, not understanding the question.

"But is he like me, do you think?"

"Wo bu dong." I don't know. "No. If you are not interested to meet him it is alright."

"I'm sorry."

"Really. It isn't a problem. Maybe you and me can go to karaoke. You need to have some fun. Hao buhao?" Good, not good? Nina, watching his face, said, "You don't want?"

"What kind of figure would I cut as a lounge singer?"

"Why do you worry?"

"I'm a square-head engineer, Nina. It's what I am."

"It isn't important," Nina said.

"No. It is important. It's something you want to do."

"Please." Nina shook her head dismissively.

"Nina has been very kind to me. Maybe I am the wrong type."

"No." Emphatically. "Please - do not worry so much." She patted his shoulder. "You are a good man. I have had bad luck. Until now. Let us try to be happy."

"Of course," Gessler said. They embraced.

"I will make dinner now?" They went into the kitchen.

It was just a few nights later. Gessler and Nina had seen a movie. He'd driven to her neighborhood and parked the car and they went up to her apartment. Nina had seemed sullen. Gessler could not remember when her mood had changed, or if it was a remark of his that had set her off. He wasn't clear about that. This kind of thing was happening too often, though. *Bu hao*, he thought. Not good. Maybe they were not right for each other.

"Nina. What is wrong?"

"Wrong? What do you mean?"

"Everyone but you thought that was a funny movie."

"Maybe I don't understand it."

"Maybe. Are you unhappy about something?"

They were seated at the small table in Nina's bedroom. Nina's arms were crossed over her chest.

"I think - you are taking advantage of me." Her jaw was set in a way that he'd seen before. The old discouragement returned to him. Even when she is like this, he thought, I try to understand. But how long could he go on?

"How, Nina? How am I taking advantage of you?"

"You only play."

Gessler thought for a few moments, and said, "Play? We don't play so much, Nina. If you've noticed. I would be glad to, but I don't think you like it."

"That is all you want. You don't want to marry."

"It's better we should know each other first. When I listen to you I don't think we can get along, anyhow. What are you up to, Nina? I think you are very calculating." Nina was not looking at him. "No decent American wants to marry a woman just like that." Snapping his fingers. "If you don't want to wait maybe you can find an old man who wants a young woman for sex. Is that what you want?"

Nina just went on staring into empty space. Gessler could not help feeling sorry for her, she looked so unhappy.

"Or maybe you don't know what you want," he said.

"You are my first American," Nina said vaguely, reproach in her voice.

"I have a feeling I won't be the last."

"What do you mean?"

"I mean - maybe you will find someone more suitable."

"I don't want someone more suitable. You - you are my first American."

"I've really tried, Nina. But I'm at the end of my rope here. Nothing I do is enough. It is getting tired. If we can't get along let's stop it. We can't always be arguing like this."

Nina stared ahead, a fingernail between her teeth.

"I don't understand you at all," Gessler continued. "I see it now. We haven't invested so much in each other. I'm sure you won't worry about me."

"You are tired of me?"

"Yes. I'm not so desperate. It is easier to be alone. Maybe that is the thing for me." He stood and waited a few moments, and said, "So long, Nina."

She was not looking at him. When the outer door closed after him she got up suddenly and rushed out to the corridor. She could hear his steps down the stairwell and she caught a glimpse of him.

"George..."

But he only stared straight ahead and continued walking.

She spun around angrily and stood there a moment with her arms crossed. In a moment she went back to her room and sat thinking for a while.

10

Without Nina, Gessler returned to his familiar patterns of work and solitude. He was free now, but in the days that followed he felt a gnawing disappointment. He'd gotten used to Nina. The break had come quickly, although when he thought about it, the problems had been building. In spite of all that had happened he missed her. He chided himself for feeling this way – wasn't there something fundamentally unstable about the woman? – but found that he could not improve his mood. You are growing mentally soft, he thought.

On Saturday he visited Manhattan. He generally found the city diverting. He spent some time leafing through magazines at a newsstand - it was a way of taking the pulse of the popular culture. He looked at some short stories in the magazines, but they all struck him as dry and fussy and ineffably boring. They were not characters that he could recognize, at all. Other stories, if that was what they were, looked like academic exercises that had gone awry. Among the books, there were memoirists with tales of their lousy, deprived childhoods. My mother didn't love me, or, My Dad was a drunkard. But who couldn't tell similar stories? He picked up some dime novels, but from their covers they all appeared to be aimed at some demographic that did not include him, and he put them back.

Here among the magazine covers was the woman who had played the lifeguard on the hit television series, with those two tremendous but probably artificial breasts sticking out in front of her. So out of balance! The scientist in Gessler considered logically, and rebelled. But nice, of course, he would certainly like to give her a try.

Here on another magazine cover was a pretty blonde, a female professional "wrestler" so-called. She was more modestly proportioned, more classically balanced. Gessler had seen her a couple of times on the television, too, when he was channel surfing. Mostly, she and her opponent would cavort around the ring in bikinis. But she was nice to look at, tall and statuesque, and who could complain because her so-called wrestling matches were seldom anything Olympian? The woman did not seem like any bimbo, either, rather her face was pert and intelligent. Gessler could easily imagine her as an anthropology professor, or something of that kind. She looked a lot like the woman in his dream, the demure one who sometimes tutored him in quantum physics. At some point she would always remove her severe-looking eyeglasses and loosen her hair and, *voila*, like in the movies, she was transformed into a glamour queen. He didn't suppose that this gorgeous and high-browed woman ever saw herself as a sex symbol – not that he would really know - and she was probably a little incredulous at her role as a wrestling diva. But she was successful at it, she seemed to know exactly how to work the angles, and was probably building a secure financial future for herself, too. Why, he thought sadly, can't it include me?

He read in the article that she was instead dating one of the male wrestlers on the show. That was too much! No doubt he was one of those steroid-enhanced freaks who is all beef and no brain. He certainly looked like it in the picture, primping in front of the camera, with a strained smile that suggested the steroids were going to cause him to flip out at any time. He felt a twinge of sadness for – he couldn't think of her name now – hanging out with such an obvious kook. C'est la vie, though.

Was it the Old Testament prophet Isaiah, Gessler wondered, who said, Unless a man bray like an ass, no woman will take any notice of him?

Whoever, time had proven how oh-so-right he was.

There on another magazine cover was a nice-looking model that he remembered, Breanna-something. Another case in point. She did some acting now, and modeled as a more-or less "full-figured" woman. She still looked very good, though – exquisite, even. Gessler was still pissed off at that ham actor who married her. The rat bastard probably remembered nothing of the past twenty years, having spent most of it in an alcohol- or drug-induced stupor. And you just know that he crammed – well, say that he ravished every part of that woman's body. What did some mothers use to say to daughters? Remember, your body is a temple - not an amusement park! But for the ham, it must have been all amusement park, or should Gessler say trailer park trash! And he supposed that the ham actor had led Breanna down the primrose path of recreational drugs, as well. Gessler was quite sure that if Breanna had been introduced, instead, to great music and the classic literature of Defoe and the Brontes, et. al. – and he would have gladly shaped her nubile mind toward the higher things in life - it would have meant more, in the long run, than cheap sex and designer drugs.

Why was it that these goddesses of the modeling and film world always gravitated to rich, empty-headed lunks from their own demi-mondes? Why, why was it unthinkable that one of them could partner for life with an earnest engineer? So what if Gessler did not have model-material good looks? He would be happy to continue working every day, offering his pitifully small salary toward upkeep of their magnificent house. He wouldn't even become jealous when she spent weeks traveling around the world on location with studly co-stars. But women, it seemed, no matter how much money they had, always must snare a man who had even more money than them. It was just something in women's genes.

To each his own, Gessler supposed. What did women want, though? Greater minds than his had considered the question and come to no definite conclusion. Intelligence itself didn't seem to count for much with women. If it did, there should have been some evidence of an improvement in our species, over all this time. But it simply hadn't happened. It really was something to ponder. No, women went for the happily well-adjusted guys, with just enough brains to get them through life. Maybe a woman wants to be very sure that she is smarter than her mate. But if you had emotional baggage, issues from childhood, well, you must seem a marked man to them.

Looking around, it seemed to Gessler that "they" had stopped making movies and publishing books for people like him. So little of the stuff spoke to him. Sometimes it made him angry to think about it. But was it his problem? He had his own tastes in music, or he could go and read his Stendahl, or whatever, if he wanted. What did it matter what was fashionable? But you had to live in society, you couldn't help noticing things. It was usually the saccharine music that you heard in public places, it was most often the calculated and unamiable books that got all the attention and made all the money. Someone had stacked all the decks, it seemed. But why be disdainful? Everyone, if Gessler thought about it, would produce only masterpieces if they knew how, and if they could make equal money at it.

There was a good deal here in the magazines that was salacious or moronic. He felt vaguely disgusted when he glanced at some of the magazines that were targeted to young people. Was life only about appearances - about hedonism? Or were there such things as sacrifice and commitment to ideals? But his reaction probably meant that he was getting old and out of style. So many of the magazines showed young women in bathing suits. Well, he could appreciate that. A good-looking woman was a work of art, certainly.

But there were other things in life. It was an interesting question, how the cultural establishment had ever gotten to be so low-brow. Why not at least aspire to higher things? Not far away was another magazine cover with a different young woman. He gathered that she was a popular vocalist. This one was staring straight at the audience, and she was flipping everyone the bird, no less! Well, that was pretty ubiquitous nowadays, but still, he thought: Give me a break! It wasn't surprising that a person, particularly a young person, would make a pointlessly vulgar gesture. But why did a meretricious establishment want to aid and abet her in her foolishness? For money, obviously. The almighty dollar.

That about tears it, Gessler thought, metaphorically throwing up his hands. It was just like the lousy media. A person is only looking for a little intellectual solace, and instead they flip him the bird.

Laura used to tell him that it was just his moods that sometimes put the city, or whatever else, in a bad light. Don't make too much of it, he thought.

That evening Gessler played some records by nineteen-fifties singers. The songs were moody ballads for the most part, and they fit his mood. He listened and watched the play of lights over JFK Airport. It's marvelous stuff, he thought. They should include a loaded forty-five caliber pistol with some of these records. If you were in a bad mood, they were enough to make you want to do yourself in.

After awhile he became aware of some hammering noises in the building. Usually Gessler could screen out the sounds. But what sort of infernal racket was this? What sort of morbidity? He listened for a few more moments, and suddenly yelled, "Mrs. Schaum, please stop banging!" Old Mrs. Schaum lived next-door to him. Her mind was going. He felt sorry for her and for her daughter Rosa. He sometimes visited them. He recalled seeing a broken hand-held mirror which the mother refused to part with. The glass was gone, but the object was well adapted for banging on windowsills - tonight, in time with Gessler's music. Rosa must have been out on one of her rare dates. That was why Mrs. Schaum was acting out, obviously.

Things aren't bad enough, Gessler thought, I have to live next door to Mrs. Rochester. And she wasn't the only one. Lunatics had staked out the building, that was clear. But in a few minutes Mrs. Schaum had quieted down, at least.

He collected the day's trash and brought it out to the corridor. On a lark he rang the next-door buzzer, knowing that no one would answer. "Mrs. Schaum?" Silence. He waited and then brought his trash to the chute, opening the creaking closet door. When he closed the door and turned, his heart nearly stopped. Mrs. Schaum was standing there in front of him. Gessler backed up a couple of steps until there was only wall behind him.

She was a small disheveled thing in a dressing gown. There were patches of cold cream under her distended eyes, and she trailed a long security blanket over her shoulder.

"You startled me, Mrs. Schaum." In fact she had nearly scared the shit out of him.

She muttered something incomprehensible. It sounded like, "M'nem?"

"Mrs. Schaum. Please--"

"Moo-sic?" She pronounced "music" with some Eastern European twang.

"Music? You heard? Well, I'm sorry I disturbed you."

"Moo-sic," she said. She lifted the hem of her housedress and essayed a couple of side-steps. But her feet caught in the blanket, and she stumbled a bit. She was dangerously close to the stairwell. He did not want to see her plummet down there.

He touched her shoulder. "Whoa, be careful, now. It's a long way down."

There was no one around to help. "Rosa?" he asked.

"Aow." He took it that Rosa was out.

He began leading Mrs. Schaum back toward her apartment. "Yes. Music. But banging is not music, Mrs. Schaum. Banging is just noise. Yes?" He looked at her sternly. Mrs. Schaum executed a couple of chopping motions with her hand. He was not sure what this meant. He looked distressed and hoped that she got his drift.

The elevator door opened then, and Gessler looked and said, "Ah, here is Rosa now."

"Is everything alright?" the daughter asked. She looked meaningfully at Gessler.

"We're alright," he said.

"She disturbed you again, didn't she?"

"Not hardly."

Rosa shook her head. Before they disappeared inside their apartment she asked Gessler, "Would you like some company?"

Not at all, he said.

She tapped on his door a few minutes later. He invited her to the kitchen and they sat down.

"I can't go out on a date without worrying she's going to hurt herself or disturb somebody," Rosa said.

"I'm sure it isn't easy," Gessler said.

"Oh, I have my hands full."

She was a plain-looking woman in her thirties. Single, or divorced, he wasn't sure which. Sometimes he'd thought about her. If she lost twenty pounds... But a woman needed just a little bit of spark, that she seemed to lack. He had noticed that her eyes seldom even met his.

He asked if she wanted anything and brought her a glass of water. "I've been where you are," he said. "With your mom, I mean. Though not as bad."

"I guess I should look into a nursing home for her."

"So why don't you, Rosa? What kind of a life? For you, I mean?"

"M'm." But she seemed to have exhausted that subject. "I get lonely sometimes." She ventured a look at him. "You should see some of the losers

I meet. You don't know how many oddballs there are out there. Tonight, do you know all that this guy talked about?"

"No," Gessler said. "What?"

"Oh, it isn't that interesting."

"No, I am listening."

"Well, I'm culturally uninformed – because I don't know anything about video games? And because I don't watch the science-fiction channel on television, I mean exclusively? Why doesn't the man grow up, for Chrissakes?"

"You're painting a picture," Gessler said sympathetically.

"Just take my word for it. Weird. Selfish. Those are the ones I meet."

Gessler commiserated. He thought she was done with the subject, until she gritted her teeth and looked at the floor and added, "What flakes!"

A framed snapshot of Nina was there on the table. He glanced at it. I'm not free, he thought to himself. Not yet. That's what he would have to say, if the conversation kept on this way.

"Why're you attracted to that woman?" Rosa asked. Nodding toward the picture.

"I can't explain. I guess it's love."

"Why don't you marry an American woman?"

"I don't have any prejudices. I guess I just haven't clicked with one."

"Haven't - clicked?"

"Yes. Clicked."

"Alright. Well, I haven't seen her around lately."

"We had a little fight," Gessler said.

"But now everything is sugar plums?"

"Well, not really. Not yet."

"M'm."

"Can I get you anything?"

"Nah." A little peevishly.

"Sorry."

"Ah, don't be sorry. I guess I was just looking for sympathy."

"So how am I doing?"

"Not bad, George. Not bad at all. I'd say she's a lucky girl."

Gessler smiled. "Thanks. You know, you're really not bad yourself." Then he heard the telephone ringing and got up to answer it.

"George?" he heard. "It's Nina. Tomorrow - it is very cold. You wear your coat."

"Cold. Yes," Gessler said. She must have practiced just these two sentences. He could tell she had.

"You are alright?" he asked.

"Yes." Rosa passed from the kitchen, and she smiled thinly and waved at him, without stopping. He waved back, and she went out the door.

"You have been studying English?" he asked.

"Yes. I have a good teacher." She meant Gessler.

"I will dress warm. Thank you. I will call you."

"Please. M'm - so - goodnight." Nina's voice trailed off.

Gessler hung up the receiver. Strange. Dress warm - that was it? Obviously she'd been thinking of him. Perhaps he'd misjudged her. He would call her again, maybe in a few days. It was worth trying one more time.

Besides - the thought came to him suddenly, stubbornly - there was nothing here, anyway.

11

Gessler happened to see his friend Laura again, one weekend at the supermarket. They were alone. He was glad to see her. They started walking toward the neighborhood.

"You haven't called lately," she said.

"I was reluctant."

"Why? We are still friends."

"You all but told me I'm an idiot, for seeing that woman."

"I didn't mean that. You don't know women, though."

"No? You're a woman. I know you."

"I'm not like the others."

Gessler did not argue the point.

"I take it you are still seeing her?" Gessler only looked into space, and Laura continued, "I won't take back what I said. That woman is trouble."

"So don't take it back. I know you are a hard-head."

"You are the hard-head. No, because I know I am right."

"Why does it bother you that I am seeing her?"

"I told you. Because I am worried about you. Do you think there is some other reason?"

"No. Forget it."

"Why don't you marry an American woman?"

"I don't find any that are suitable."

"Are you happy?"

"Yes. Most of the time. We have our fights--"

"There, you see? It is starting already."

"Just sometimes."

"I thought she will be afraid to upset the fat goat until after the wedding."

"What in the world do you mean by that? Now I'm a fat goat?"

"It's just an old expression. I don't mean to say you are a goat."

"I never heard it. I think you make up these expressions yourself. Anyway, Laura, sometimes you are impossible."

"Tell me, George - do you imagine she is like me?"

"Like you? No, I don't imagine she is."

"One thing I am sure. She may be younger than me, and prettier--"

"Laura, what the heck are you talking about?"

"She is not as smart as me."

"I don't want to argue about how smart she is. I'm tired of being alone. I think we will be good for each other."

"Well. If you marry her, don't invite me to your wedding."

"Laura." Stopping, pleading with her, "You are my best friend."

"I won't come."

"If that is what you want, then." They had reached her house. "I'm sorry we disagree."

She didn't say any more, but only turned up her walk.

12

One Sunday afternoon Gessler took Nina out for lunch to a restaurant on Long Island. Afterward, he'd led her to think that they were only driving around, but he surprised her with a concert of classical music, which took place in a small Catholic church. The concert featured a choir and orchestra.

When they arrived at the church a smell of ashes, or was it incense, assailed Gessler in the lugubrious entryway. An organ droned within. He saw the small semicircular basins filled with holy water, and wood carvings of a suffering Christ beside the main inner entry.

"You are taking me to church?" Nina whispered. "I didn't think you are Christian."

Before Gessler could say anything an usher approached and brought them to some plush covered seats at the front. The seats were numbered for occasions like this. Theirs were at right angles to the general seating. A central space had been cleared for the performers, in the area he thought was called the apse. Gessler was not a Catholic, but it seemed to him there was a general topography to all of their churches; a name for every area. The place where they sat was called a chancel, he thought.

Nearby were gold gleaming candle sticks almost as tall as a person, and gilt paintings of Christ with a mournful expression. The incense stung Gessler's nostrils.

The choir and orchestra were performing a requiem. Gessler knew it rather well from recordings. But he didn't know if Nina would appreciate this kind of music. He didn't suppose the Chinese had any tradition of requiem works. From Laura Chang he knew that they observed two memorial days during the year, in the Spring and Autumn. Traditionally minded Chinese would visit family gravesites at these times, bringing food for a picnic, and play money. The deceased were understood to share in both the food and the play money in some fashion. Gessler remembered that much. The practice seemed to him a good deal stranger than the Western one of writing and listening to these choral works called requiems.

The chorus entered in a slow procession and stood in rows at the very back of the stage. Then the musicians entered and sat in folding chairs. In a few minutes the orchestra started playing, a soft groundswell of harmonies that relaxed him. There was so much music to discover, Gessler thought -

perhaps he and Nina, together. In his mind, gentle music played over the carpeted living room of their future home. The fireplace crackled away. There would be throbbing Olympian music for when they made love. Nina looked rapt - was she having the same dream? He squeezed her hand. As the orchestra introduced the Dies Irae the conductor jumped in the air and pointed at the singers and their voices surged forward. A split-second in time behind the singers, the horns sounded a percussive echoing theme that was like the windswept wake of a charging vehicle. Hairs stood up on the back of Gessler's neck. Some moments later, the singers began the gentle Lacrimosa. That was perhaps his favorite part. While the music rose into the vaulted marble spaces above, Gessler was in an elysium. As he listened his gaze drifted up there: high up on the walls were tall stained-glass windows which were bordered with sea-blue panels. A cool but vivid light shone through the glass. He turned his head slightly. Nina's head was thrown back, and her mouth was ajar. She was fast asleep.

Gessler turned his head away as if he'd been spying. He looked forward again at the sweating, earnest conductor, and at the placid looking old women who made up most of the audience, with their faintly smiling expressions. Maybe Nina was only tired, he thought. But the tireless horn players should surely startle her into wakefulness. The orchestra swelled, but for Gessler the moment was deflating. Here was a defining masterpiece - the apotheosis of choral writing. Was there anything more sublime? How was it possible to sleep through it?

"Nina, wake up!" he said urgently, tugging on her hand.

She started, and then shrank apologetically on her seat. She mouthed the word, "Sorry," up at him. Gessler, after awhile, became swept up in the music again.

"I was just tired," she said later in the car, in the parking lot.

He brushed at the hair over her forehead. "Would you like something to eat?"

"I'm still full."

"Then I'll take you home." He started the car.

"It was really good," she said. But he wondered if she meant it.

Some light snow had begun falling as they drove off.

"Is it dangerous?" Nina asked.

"No. I'm not going fast. You see?"

Gessler merged with the parkway traffic toward the city. There were not that many cars. There were no buildings along the road. Only an occasional apartment house that would loom above the trees, well back from the road; some darkened factories, glimpsed through the bare trees. The parkway wound and rose at intervals.

It was still early in the evening. Gessler parked the car in the garage, and they went up to his apartment.

"Would you like some tea?" he asked. "Some ice cream?" Nina said yes to both. He got them ready and brought a tray out to the living room. They sat on the couch.

What was the thing about Sunday evenings, he wondered, that made him feel this nostalgia? His mind was really far away now. Was there something about this evening in particular? The solemn music still sounded piously in his ears. But it wasn't only the music. And the moment of dejection he'd felt when he saw Nina asleep during the concert had passed. He felt nostalgic because the evening reminded him of so many other Sunday evenings, when he and his parents would drive Morty back to the state hospital after a weekend at home. Or to one of the halfway houses, whichever. Gessler would often accompany them.

As he recalled, the family would usually not talk much. Morty would say his good-bye's in the car, and they would see him standing at the door of the residence hall while his mother said to his father, at the wheel, "Wait." Then the door to the building would open and Morty would turn and quickly wave. On the ride home his father would sometimes tune in a big-band program on the radio. The music that Gessler heard then still had a particular resonance for him - a sweetness that was tempered with melancholy.

Nina returned his glances when he looked at her. She rested her head against his shoulder. They said little to each other. Through the window he could see some snow falling in the light of a streetlamp. Gessler's memory ranged backward in time. The family was living in a house north of the city then, before his father's work brought them to Queens. It was a time when Gessler and other neighborhood children played games of war and hide-and-seek, when they fished and swam in ponds and explored the life of rivers and creeks, or sledded in wintertime. Most of that would end after the family moved to the city.

Some bare trees in the back yard were alive with the movements of leaping birds. Some flakes of snow fell, the first of the season. Gessler's breath steamed slightly in front of his face. A game of hide-and-seek was underway. None of his playmates were nearby. He peered cautiously into other yards, and scrutinized upper porches and stairs of wooden tenement buildings for signs of activity. The air felt damp, and everything was unusually still. There weren't any grown-ups around. The trees and shrubs, his first choice, now seemed too exposed to hide among. The wooden bulkhead doors that led down to his cellar stood raised and opened invitingly. He did not know if, by the time-honored rules of hide-and-seek, cellars were acceptable hiding places. (A room in a house would clearly not be. A cellar - with the doors open - was probably alright.) He went down the stairs leaving the doors as they were.

It was a cool, dirt-floored cellar. Gessler stood behind a wooden beam and watched what he could see of the back yard. If he saw legs moving there he could retreat further. It was a weekend and although he did not hear any noises upstairs, Gessler supposed that his brother was home.

There was no end of clutter in this place. Except for the cemented walkway through the center there were few cleared areas on the ground. One section was only dirt. There were burlap bags filled with discarded clothing. His father said they would be sold to the ragman, but if there was a ragman in those days Gessler never saw him. Some of the bags had been tied and hoisted onto hooks to become punching bags.

Organizing the cellar was an ongoing weekend project for his father - and for Morty, when the old man could enlist his help. Morty always lost interest, though. Gessler could remember his father complaining about Morty "getting lost" in the middle of these projects. "Where'd you go?" the old man would ask, when they were all back upstairs - sometimes demandingly, but more often humorously, with an ironic look in his eye, which both of the brothers had learned to tell. Evidently Morty could not see the point of the endeavors. In fact the place had resisted all efforts to create order.

Soon Gessler could hear the "Woodchoppers' Ball" playing upstairs. One of Morty's big band records, along with the Charlie Barnets and the Glenn Millers. Worn out over time. A lost era of dance halls and leafy balconies, and voices in the summer night. Lyrics of a romantic yearning. The Glen Island Casino, Meadowbrook Lounge. No one even knew the names of the places anymore. The world was younger then and more innocent somehow.

He was looking out at the empty patch of yard above the bulkhead steps. Closer to him - just above him, in fact - the kitchen floor creaked. A doorknob rattled, he heard the door off the back hallway open. Someone was coming down the stairs.

Gessler retreated several feet, and stepped behind some plywood sheets by a lumber bin as the person reached the bottom of the steps and turned. It was his brother Morty. He really had not expected it to be one of his playmates. Still he remained where he was. His brother - a teenager with a brush haircut - stepped near one of the hanging clothes bags and threw a few punches. The bag moved sluggishly in the cool darkness. The sleeve of a suitcoat, part of a worn floral dress, protruded from the top of the burlap. Panting, Morty threw some hard rights, until the bag was rocking and swinging. He caught the bag and held on to it, bouncing on his toes, and then he ran his hand over the top of his head as though to calm himself down. He stood next to the bag and drew his hands over the burlap, and closed his eyes and tentatively rested his forehead against the rough fabric, drawing his breath noisily. Then he saw Gessler, who had emerged partly from his concealment, watching, and he let his hands fall to his sides.

"What're you doing, squirt?"

"We're playing hide and seek."

"Here? How will anyone find you here?"

"They're not supposed to."

His brother thought for a moment, then waved his hand dismissively. "Ah, that's no fun. You think it's fun?"

"Why not?"

"So how is school? I don't see much of you."

"It's because you are never around."

"I guess not."

"What's it like there? At the hospital."

"It isn't bad. Well, it isn't like there's a lot to *do*. When I get nervous I can talk to someone." His brother paused and lolled his head from side to side, at the same time shifting his jaw sideways, repeatedly. These were nervous tics he'd developed recently. They were new enough to Gessler to seem strange, although he would become used to them later.

"What does it mean? Nervous."

"How can I explain? You're just a kid. What're you now, ten?"

Gessler nodded. "Can't you talk to the folks? When you get like that?"

"It isn't easy. Pop wouldn't understand, and I hate making Mom feel bad. It isn't her fault. It isn't either of their faults. There's something wrong with me."

"You don't seem so different."

"Thanks, kid."

"Some of the kids at school, they say--" The words were out before Gessler had really thought about them.

"They say what?"

"Nothing."

"That your brother's crazy? A nut?"

"No."

"Then what?"

Gessler didn't say anything. His brother was right. They had said that and worse. Once Gessler had gotten in a fight over some of their remarks, when someone compared his brother to some strange-looking actor who was then appearing on the television.

"Look. I had a nervous breakdown. I didn't know what I was doing. If they say anything just tell them it's none of their goddamn business. Alright?"

Gessler nodded. "Why'd you throw Steve in the bushes the other day?"

"He was getting on my nerves. I shouldn't have, though. That wasn't right."

"I think I know what you mean about 'nerves.' He gets on my nerves, too."

"You, too? So why do you hang around with him?"

"He brings the bats."

"Oh."

"Are you going back to school?"

"I don't know, squirt."

"Everybody has to go to school - don't they?"

"You're asking too many questions I can't answer. I think they're calling for you out there. They gave up looking for you."

Gessler stood there uncertainly.

"Go on, kid. Go out and play."

Gessler walked slowly toward the steps leading up to the yard. His brother placed a hand on his shoulder and then turned for the wooden stairs leading up to the hallway. Gessler could hear his footsteps going up, and then he was out in the yard again. He could hear his friends sounding the call – *olly olly oxen free!* - to regroup.

Then the moment passed. It was all so many years ago now.

He remembered Morty complaining to their mother once, about having gotten lost. Probably he'd been walking around the city by himself. As he spoke about it his fingers twitched nervously. He nodded his head emphatically and then ran his hand straight back over his hair in the calming motion. And their mother responded, in a tone that was bright and rather cheerful, "You're never lost, Morty, as long as you have a tongue in your head."

It was an axiom that she'd repeated numerous times, to both Morty and Gessler. But how true was it for Morty? On a deeper level, even if he'd known what questions to ask, who could have helped him out of his illness? For that matter, what more could Gessler himself have done? He never stopped asking himself that.

He imagined, as he looked out of his living room window, that the snow was falling harder now. And the thought came to him, it was some piece of scripture that he couldn't remember where he'd heard: Blessed are the dead which die in the Lord, for they rest from their labors.

Nina was bringing a spoonful of ice cream to his mouth. "Have more," she said. He smiled indulgently and accepted more of the ice cream. "Is it good?"

"It's very good."

"You are very quiet," Nina said.

"You know me by now."

"I think you are drifting far away." She placed the emptied bowl of ice cream on the table in front of them.

"I didn't mean to. I was just thinking of a day many years ago. I was talking with my brother. It all came back to me so clearly, I don't know why. He just started going to the hospitals then."

"Because--"

"You remember, don't you?" Gessler touched his temple with two fingers.

"Yes. You told me. Maybe you shouldn't think of what is past, so much?" She placed a hand on his shoulder.

"I don't try to. Maybe I do think too much of what is past."

After a moment she said, "Thank you for buying the--" Gessler watched her frown, rubbing her fingers and thumb together.

"Tickets," he said. "Piao."

"Piao. Tickets. Thank you. I enjoy very much."

"I like that music."

"I thought - before, when you are quiet - that you were mad of me, because I was asleep."

"Don't be silly. You were just tired, that's all. Right?"

"Of course. I like the music, too." Nina leaned against the back of the couch, facing him. "M'm - what do you talk to your brother about?"

"I think he asked me about school. I was trying to ask him what was bothering him. It wasn't just the words, though. It was the whole situation." He tried to summarize the scene that had just passed through his mind.

"I guess I still have some anger in my heart. Not against any person. God, maybe. Sometimes you wonder if good and bad luck are handed out almost randomly. No, it's probably wrong to think that. And anyway, what's past is past, right?"

Nina nodded. "Certainly."

"I have no regrets for myself. At least I met someone like you. That's lucky for me."

"I am glad you think so."

"But my brother never received much love in this world. Aside from family. He deserved more than that."

"I think that you will never be free from these thoughts."

Gessler looked at her. "Well. This is who I am. I don't want to be anyone else. I guess I can't help feeling that life is unfair."

"What is 'fair?'"

Gessler tried to explain. "It's like when you play a game. There are rules to follow and everyone has a chance to win."

"Not equal chance, maybe."

"I guess that's true."

Morty had been blameless and yet he'd been hurt deeply by life. Gessler understood this much: that his brother's experience of life had influenced his own outlook - had in some fashion burned itself upon his mind and heart. He did not expect to find understanding from other people, did not expect to find others who were on his wavelength. He always hoped to be proven wrong in this, but it had seldom happened. As the years passed he'd found himself increasingly alone. And in his outlook he could decipher, at certain times, an expression of solidarity with his brother - a loyalty. It was not a productive feeling, but it was there, inescapably.

Gessler looked at Nina and noted the look of concern on her features. She seemed a picture of sympathetic understanding. He tried to reassure her. "Nina." He reached and touched her shoulder. "Don't frown. What I'm talking about happened many years ago. Please don't take it too much to heart."

"I am fine," Nina said.

Her fingers played at the back of his hair, and the skin of his neck tingled. "You know, I wouldn't want anyone to take my memories from me."

"Take them from you? Of course not. They are yours. The good and the bad."

"Yes."

"But you must not think of these things too of-ten. You should think of me!" Nina pressed her fingers against his chest, looking at him coquettishly. "I think of *you*," she added.

"I know you do," Gessler said.

Her hand came to rest upon his leg, and Gessler's body began to respond to the gentle pressure. When she moved her hand again she brushed against the swelling against his trousers. Her hand remained there and she began to slowly massage him.

"Do you feel alright now?" Nina asked.

"Oh, yes."

"Good. But your clothes are very tight." Looking into his eyes. Her fingers worked to loosen his belt. Gessler sighed with pleasure. "Please. Allow me."

Nina placed his trousers on a chair and returned to the couch. "Are you more comfortable now?" Her hand reached for him again. "My. I think your pants were going to burst!"

Gessler sighed. "Darling."

He felt the red lacquer tipped fingers of Nina's hand close around him, and he sighed, his heart rate quickened, at the enticing rhythm that Nina made.

Gessler took her in his arms and kissed her, but in a moment he felt her hand pressing against his chest. "Can we make love now?" he murmured.

"Please. I cannot, tonight. Is it alright, like this?"

"Oh. It's fine."

"Good. Isn't it ... relaxing," Nina said casually, in her imprecise English.

"Oh, yes," Gessler said, although "relaxed" was not the way that her touch made him feel.

She paused in her movements, and looked directly into his face with wide eyes. "I don't think that you should feel 'blue.' Do you think?"

"No," Gessler managed to say. "I don't."

"No? Good. You should always try to be" – still holding to him, her arms remained motionless, while her mind seemed to cast for the correct word – "positive. Yes?" Nina took his sighs, and the slight nodding of his head, for agreement. She resumed the steady movement of her hand. She had to give him credit. For an older man he really was very responsive – he was as hard as a stick of rosewood. "Whenever you feel blue, maybe you think of Nina, yes?" She paused again, and he remained firm in her hand.

"Yes, Nina. You are right," Gessler managed to say, his breath coming harder than before.

"Right. Yes, I think that's better. Be positive. Don't worry too much. Good. Good..." Nina murmured.

Afterward he lay back exhausted against the couch. Nina saw that his eyes were tightly closed, and she went on studying his face, smiling slightly to herself.

13

The middle of a weekday afternoon. Nina was at home. Since leaving the restaurant job she had not looked for any new work. She was lying on her bed staring up at the ceiling. The building was quiet for the moment - it must have been that many people were out. She'd struck a casual pose - legs crossed, hands folded behind her head. But she was trying to take stock of her life, and her mind was troubled. There seemed to her reason for gloom and hopefulness in equal measure.

The night before she'd had an awful dream involving her and the engineer. They were both of them dressed in the richly colored jackets and robes of the Chinese opera. She was being carried, alone, in a covered cart. She could see little through the curtained windows, only hear the milling voices outside and frantic bursts of a small orchestra: clashing cymbals, the tick-tock of the wooden blocks, and reedy stentorian blare of the *shang*. Then she and the engineer were alone on the semi-darkened stage. The facial make-up, the slightly skewed lines above his eyebrows gave him a severe and incredulous expression. His arms were around her shoulders, and she saw his face very clearly. Something else was different. He was strangely still.

Then she saw that his eyes were closed.

When she tried to move away from him she found that she was locked in his grasp. The music sounded more frantically, a macabre march. She pushed at him and attempted to back away, but his weight only sagged against her more heavily. It seemed that his hands were locked behind her neck.

It came to her then that he was dead - or did one of his painted eyes open, briefly and reproachfully?

Another moment and they would have collapsed together. That was when she woke up screaming.

She had been trying to put the dream out of her mind. It seemed to her she had never been so impressionable before. Something was seriously wrong with her mind.

Look at you, Nina, she thought. What are you doing here in this country? In this dirty city, surrounded by barbarians. You lie here in idleness. You don't even have a proper job. One factory or restaurant after another. You can't even care for your own child, she grows up without a mother. Don't you have two strong arms, and hands to work - to make a home, to give happiness?

You sit here in idleness with your feet up, with a bachelor's freedom but without enjoyment. This is not fair. But surely it is your own fault. The engineer cares for you - just once, can you be sincere? If anything happened to him his ghost would haunt you forever - that was what the dream meant. How can you connect your destiny to a clod of earth - an insect - like Pang? He is beneath notice. Even <u>Guanmin</u> could not help such a person, would only pass him and sneer and count her money afterwards. Compared to the engineer Pang is a stupid fool. How could his ideas prosper? And how could you build happiness upon evil intentions?

It was not fear of God that she felt. She had no feeling for the concept - as far as she was concerned, this concept of God was just a lot of propaganda. Not much different than what the hypocrite Communists spouted, for their own reasons. She was determined that if she ever saw that God of the lying priests, that God in whose name men killed without any pity or remorse - if she ever saw that God she was going to spit in His face. That was what she thought of Him.

Idiot! she thought. She'd been going about this all wrong. Associating with the likes of Pang - the fool! She didn't need him. Didn't she have any pride in herself? Pressing and pressing the engineer to say he would marry her. No wonder he grew tired. He almost saw through her designs, and no wonder. But maybe it was not too late to do things differently. She did have some feelings for the engineer. Not love, exactly. Perhaps gratitude.

What kind of life? she thought, looking around. What kind of a home? And what kind of - music -- seizing from the whirring tape player one of a few Chinese-music tapes that she listened to to distraction, flinging it violently against the wall where it fell with a clatter. She got up and looked at the broken tape and only felt worse, depositing the pieces in a small wastebasket.

She was so distracted that she didn't hear the entry door open. She didn't see her former roommate, Terry, standing at the door to her room.

"You don't like the music?"

Startled, her heart racing, Nina brought her hand to her mouth.

"I hope it is not one that I bought you."

Terry. You frightened me, Nina said in Chinese.

"I'm sorry. Please calm down."

It is not one that you bought me. But it is lousy. Like the way I feel.

"Why don't we talk English, Nina. Alright?"

"Alright."

"Are you sick?"

"No, it isn't that. I thought you are going to ring the buzzer. You still have your key?"

"I still have it. In case I need it again."

Nina returned to the low bed, sitting up, and motioned to Terry to be seated in the chair. "To return to this place?" she asked. "You are married. Why would you need to?"

"Maybe my husband will get tired of me." Nina looked at her blankly. "No, I'm not serious. I only forgot to return it."

"It is bad luck to say you may return to this place."

"Then I take it back. Since you know so much about luck."

"All bad kind."

"Oh, you make your own luck. You make this place sound something horrible."

"Well? What do you call it?"

"Is it so bad?"

"What do I have here? No pri-vacy. Noise. Boom-boom-boom. I'm surrounded by barbarians."

"Barbarians. Really, Nina. That is old style thinking."

"I live like a bachelor but I am not happy," gesturing with her arms. "I can't raise my daughter. What kind of home? Oh, I am so unhappy!"

"Stop screaming. What happened with your engineer? I thought this man is riding the white horse."

"He is - what?" Not understanding. "I don't let him do anything," she said modestly. "If that is what you think."

"You think I am talking about - sex? Oh, Nina. Really. It is an American expression. It means he is going to rescue you. Aren't you seeing him any more?"

"Seeing him? Oh, yes."

"So what is the problem?"

"It is me. I've been a fool. Putting - what he calls - press - prea-sure--"

"Pressure?" Terry asked helpfully.

Nodding. "--On him. To marry me."

"All women do if they care about someone."

"But I frightened him. I almost--" Nina essayed a Chinese word.

"Broken? Spoiled?"

"Yes - spoiled it."

"Maybe that is understandable. You are not happy."

"I've been a fool."

"Look ahead and not backward. Give him some time if necessary."

"Yes. You are right. I was alone with him, in his apartment the other night--" Nina told her friend about her adventure with Gessler, in a matter-of-fact way that shocked Terry.

"Oh, my. You don't have to tell me everything. Did you enjoy it?"

"Of course I didn't enjoy it. Well - it wasn't bad. But he is different, you see. He doesn't just - climb on top of you, when he is stimulated." Terry's eyes were wide. "I am sorry. I have not known any good man before. It is my fate."

"Maybe it will change."

"There is a problem. Pang - do you remember Pang?"

"I remember." Disapprovingly.

"Yes." She would not tell her about their plan, of course. It was too crazy. Too evil.

"Yes? Tell me about Pang, Nina. Yes, I have seen you together."

"When?" Looking worried.

"Why, just recently."

"Where?"

"Somewhere outside. Main Street. I don't suppose your engineer has seen you together. If you are worried. But - why, Nina? He is not any good."

"Pang is an insect."

With a dismissive sound, "Tell me about it." Terry had used an American expression she'd been hearing lately.

Nina didn't understand. "I *am* telling you about it," she said.

"Of course. I don't need convincing. About Pang. But insects are smarter. I knew that no good could come of that association. But it is useless to talk to you."

"Please, give me a chance."

"It may be that your fate is bad. Maybe only your judgment is bad. Have you thought of that? I am worried for you."

"Please don't say it."

"Do you want to break this off with Pang? Whatever you are doing?"

"Yes, I do."

"Good. Otherwise you can jump in the ocean right now."

"Don't desert me. Please. You are my only friend in the world."

"I'm not the only one, Nina. I am not deserting you. Pang is so stupid that he is dangerous. Don't worry so much - just break it off quickly."

"Thank you. You have made me feel better."

"Shall we go out and eat now? I think you need food."

"Yes."

Nina brought her overcoat from the closet and put it on. She looked in the small wall mirror and patted her face with a hand towel.

"I am crying so much lately, and - I had a very bad dream. But things will be different. I will make it so." She smiled at her friend and followed her out of the room, locking it behind them. She would speak with the engineer. And she would have to speak with Pang.

She saw Gessler first.

She'd called and told him she wanted to see him. She was waiting on the front walk of his building. She ran into his arms.

"It's cold out here," he said. "Why didn't you let me pick you up this evening?"

"Because I can't wait to see you."

"Is everything alright?"

"Yes. Fine."

"At least you can wait in the vestibule." His arm was around her shoulders.

"I will not freeze."

They entered his building and rode up in the elevator, Nina resting her head against his chest.

"I'll make tea," he said when they were inside. Nina followed him to the kitchen. "Don't you want to sit down?" She shook her head, smiling self-effacingly. "Are you sure you're alright?"

"Don't worry about me. I will not break."

She was standing close to him and Gessler took her in his arms. "You feel pretty solid," he said. "Put on a sweater, anyway," he said. He went to a closet and got one of his sweaters for her. Gessler was still wearing a jacket and tie.

"Please."

"Put it on," he ordered. "There's no heat." He helped her on with the sweater.

When the tea was ready they went and sat on the living room couch. "What do you want to say?" he asked her.

Nina did not know where to begin.

"You are a good man," she said.

"You mean you're standing outside in the cold to tell me that?" He sounded irritated. Nina studied his expression to see if he was. She was often unsure of his meaning.

"I'm sorry," he said. "Go on."

"Don't be mad of me."

"I'm not mad of you. *At* you, is correct. Why would I be mad at you?"

"I never thought I can meet someone like you."

"But I feel the same way, Nina."

"Sometimes, there can be an unlucky fate. My husband--"

Gessler waited for her to continue. "Yes?"

But Nina did not want to go on deceiving him. Why say that her husband had been wonderful, as she had told him, when she knew she was well to be rid of him? And the larger deception now seemed abhorrent to her. As well as unnecessary. How did she ever think of pursuing such a scheme? She thought of those times when the engineer had spoken to her from his heart - thinking that she cared. But she did care, in a way. At least, now she did. Maybe it was still possible to make everything right.

"You are a kind person," Nina said. "You deserve someone who is good. Not like me."

"What are you talking about?"

Nina didn't say anything, only pressed her fingers tightly against her mouth.

"I'm not what you think."

"Tell me."

"I can't." She was looking away, deep in thoughts that Gessler could not fathom.

"Nina, you can make me happy."

But she looked away as before. It was as if his words hadn't registered at all. A minute passed. Then she turned to him suddenly. He felt her hands grip his shoulder and hand, and he winced under her pressure.

"Do you think - we can be together?" There was a strange urgency in Nina's eyes.

"How can you ask?" he answered lightly. The look in her eyes did not go away. "Why have we been seeing each other all this time? Nina - you're hurting me," pulling away. He felt her grip relax.

"Together...

"Count on me, Nina. I don't want to live just for myself. I want you."

"Yes? We can - be together?"

"Why not?"

"Oh, yes." When they embraced he was surprised to feel the tears upon her face. She pressed her face convulsively against his shoulder. "Oh, please, please."

"You are not unhappy?"

"No," she assured him.

"Why did you say," he asked a moment later, "'I'm not what you think'?"

"Oh. Can we forget the past?"

"Well, sure. It's alright," he said.

"Yes. It's alright." Smiling, looking at him. "I will be good to you. I promise."

147

He drove her home that evening. He'd suggested walking - it was only about a mile to her building - but Nina said that the weather was not good, Gessler might catch a cold. When he pulled up and put the car into park, Nina reached across the seat, and gripped the back of his head and his jaw, and pressed her lips against the side of his face. Her strength surprised him. He managed to turn to her. He did not know what to make of her behavior. Nina wiped more tears from her cheeks and brushed the hair back from his forehead.

"I will see you tomorrow?" she asked.

"Certainly."

Then she was out of the car, and turned and waved from under the awning of her building. She threw him a kiss, and, smiling, brought her hands together almost as if in prayer.

Gessler waved, too, and drove off, and the image of her there stayed with him. There was no understanding women. If he had made a study of them, like he had noise theory... But no, it wouldn't have made a difference. Any man who said that he understood women, he didn't know what he was talking about. Gessler felt a little confused, but happy.

14

A pair of steps fell in behind Nina's on the sidewalk. A built-up rubber shoe dragged slowly behind. Pang had stepped out from a doorway. With her longer stride Nina was rapidly outstripping him.

Sister, she heard from behind her. She recognized Pang's voice, and at the same moment heard the clatter of the chain of keys attached to his belt. What on earth were they for? she wondered. He sounded like a jailer. Nina turned. He trudged up to her with the keys jangling, dragging his bad leg. Like a ghost from a spooky old opera.

Nina looked circumspectly at the surrounding buildings and at the people that passed.

Come, I'll buy you some tea and cake, he said.

Don't tell me you have earned some money.

You are surprised?

From honest work?

Do you have to ask? Why are you always criticizing me lately?

I don't know, Pang. It doesn't matter to me.

Please. They entered a shop.

I told you, you should call me on the phone. We should not be together.

But the phone is always busy. How many roommates do you have? When I get through they tell me you are not home.

I am out.

With the old man?

Don't call him that. He isn't so old.

I can imagine.

Just watch it.

I can't talk about him?

At least he has a job. He has money.

I'm aware of that.

Show some respect.

You are making progress?

What do you want to know?

Don't be difficult.

Why don't you get a job, Pang? You can get a job like other people.

I'm not used to it. Why do you keep bringing up that unpleasant subject?

What the hell do you mean you are not used to it? What kind of Chinese are you? Didn't your parents teach you anything?

Maybe not.

A waiter came and left a pot of tea and some plain cake. He left and Nina continued.

Are you going to blame old Mao? He's dead. It's the Government's fault?

Please. If I want to hear a lecture I can go to college.

You are not smart enough.

So at least you know what I am. Can we stick to the subject?

What is the subject, Pang?

The old-- Him. And you.

Oh, yes. You want to know if I get hot when I am next to him? How my heart aches when we are apart? You want to know how he likes to do it?

I didn't know he had it in him, to be honest. But I think you can spare me the details. That stuff is always the same, if I can remember.

But I thought you are interested. You are so unromantic.

I don't want to know about that. I asked if you are making progress with him. It is almost three months.

Three months, or six months. What difference does it make?

Pang only looked at her coldly, his right hand fidgeting on the table top.

Why are you interested, anyway? What do you expect to get out of it?

Don't act like we don't have an understanding. Ah - it's come back to you? That's better. Now you don't talk so much. Remember, he can help both of us.

No. Forget about it. I marry him, I'm through with you.

I thought you were going to be sensible. You don't mean that.

I mean it, Pang. This was a mistake. We can't.

Don't burn your bridges yet. Maybe everything is easy right now. It hasn't always been. You remember?

I'll get by.

Remember no one looks out for you. Only me.

If that was true I would really kill myself.

You are talking nonsense again. This isn't so difficult. After you are married he can become lost.

It's a human life.

We always knew that. What is so different now? Well? Don't act like you are better than me. You are just a peasant like me.

Don't tell me what I am.

Have it your way. If you are not going through with this, you are going to leave him?

No. I am going to stay with him.

Stay? No. I don't believe it. You - like him? You can't. What a fool you are!

So I'm a fool. You and I have to separate.

Forever?

Yes.

But - that would leave me with nothing.

Nina only looked at him.

Suddenly Pang's hand shot out and grasped Nina's wrist.

It has to be this way, Nina said. She attempted to pull back her hand. Pang's grasp tightened. Nina refused to flinch, staring at him with hatred. She breathed deeply, remaining motionless, and suddenly wrenched her hand from his. She stood up and her chair clattered backwards. An elderly waiter in a black suit moved forward to assist her. His smile faded as he looked on the scene and quietly resettled the chair.

You, Pang said, still sitting.

Goodbye, Pang. Nina walked briskly from the room.

15

Gessler's friend Tony Nuccio was usually found in one or another locked room in the engineering department. Gessler had visited one room and now stopped at another. He could not remember the push-button combination to the room - it was one of the testing areas - so he rang the bell and waited. One of the technicians let him in. The room was about thirty feet square. Electronic devices sat on rows of metal workbenches, with an aisle separating the rows. Nuccio was in the back.

Gessler approached his friend. He was perhaps five years older than Gessler. He was perched on a high metal chair, but it was possible to see that he was short, about five-foot-six. He was also quite heavy. His broad head, with slightly bulging eyes, set heavily on his neck. He had straight reddish hair with some flecks of white. He was wearing a colorful and threadbare sweater. As Gessler approached Nuccio held a pen in his thick fingers and wrote some numbers onto a sheet. He was testing something. His tongue protruded slightly, in a characteristic way, as he wrote.

When he saw Gessler he put his pen down and turned in his chair to shake his hand.

"George. You don't come down here very often." Nuccio's broad face took on a look of concern. "You're going to have lunch in the cafeteria, aren't you?"

"Sure. I think so. I just wanted to stop down."

"Oh. So that's good." Nuccio smiled broadly. "I always like company."

Gessler asked him what he was examining and Nuccio told him.

"Are they good?"

"Most of them are okay. Listen, George. I understand, I gotta check 'em. But why do I gotta write all this stuff down every time? Why do I gotta fill out a sheet, huh?"

"It's the nature of the beast, Nooch. You gotta keep records."

" 'The nature of the beast.' " Nuccio looked at him severely. "You're a real poet, you know that, George?"

"But that's what they say."

"I don't expect *you* to say it. Anyway, let me ask you something else, George. What do you think about the 'Doppler Effect'? What's your opinion about that?"

Nuccio's face looked heated. His eyes had the slight bulging quality as he looked up earnestly at Gessler.

His friend thought about the question for a moment. It was not the first time that he'd heard it. In fact the two of them had discussed this and other scientific notions before. But it was not where Gessler's mind was at the moment. This was not the reason he'd stopped to see Nuccio.

"Tony," Gessler said, "it's fair to say I don't have any opinion about the Doppler Effect."

Nuccio went on looking at him for some time. His jaw had dropped slightly. It was as if he could not believe what he had heard. Gessler winced - he had not meant to sound quite so flip. Nuccio's face had a forlorn and marooned look, like that of a movie-spaceman who has lost contact with the mother ship. When he spoke it was in a softer voice.

"No opinion," he repeated. "What, you mean you don't even think about it?"

"Maybe if I worked more with radar," Gessler said. But this was only a technical distinction, not really to the point. He searched for a better explanation, something to soothe Nuccio's feelings.

"You mean," Nuccio said exploratively, "you haven't thought about it lately - right?"

"That's what I mean. Not recently." Gessler felt somewhat relieved.

Nuccio considered for some moments, his face a solemn mask. Then he spoke animatedly. "Oh, I don't know, George. I don't know about this. You're an engineer. You got more education than I do. You oughta think about these things."

Gessler's expression was a shrug. It was true that he'd had more of an education than his friend. Nuccio was intelligent and eccentric. He'd had some electronics training when he was in the Army, and Gessler thought that he'd taken some night classes somewhere in the city. But he was mainly self-taught. His learning was driven by his immense curiosity but it was not formally guided.

"What bothers you about the Doppler?" Gessler asked.

Dismissively, "The Doppler! It don't make sense! Here--" Nuccio removed a textbook from the bench drawer and began turning the pages. "Let me show you what it says here. Read this," passing Gessler the opened book.

His friend glanced at the book cover and then he began reading the paragraph that Nuccio had pointed to. He found that his concentration was not good. He was thinking in fact of when he'd first met Nuccio. It was at least ten years earlier. There was a company assembly in the cafeteria, and somehow the two of them started talking. Gessler was sure it was a technical discussion - maybe (who knew?) something about the freaking Doppler. Nuccio followed him back to the enclosed office that Gessler shared with another, older engineer. The other man barely acknowledged Nuccio, but with the dark (and slightly absurd) looks that he gave Gessler he understood that the man regarded Nuccio as a character - someone not worth bothering with. And - as it happened - after Nuccio climbed out of Gessler's guest chair and shuffled off, the senior person asked Gessler, politely, if he would please not invite Nuccio to their office. Gessler did not have to ask why. Nuccio was eccentric. He talked a lot, and he might even have been considered disruptive.

Nuccio and Gessler had a common table in the company cafeteria. The other regulars there included technicians and a department head. Because it was Nuccio's table there was always a small filled bottle of tabasco sauce there at the center. For as long as Gessler had known him he'd had a special relationship with this substance. If there was no bottle Nuccio would go and speak with the cashier and retrieve one from the serving area. Then he would delicately bear one of the tiny red-filled bottles along the central aisle to their table. None of the others used the stuff. Without stinting Nuccio would apply it to meats and vegetables alike, to virtually everything on his plate. For Nuccio the fiery red liquid was the *sine qua non*. It was a restorative, the elixir that, even in the company cafeteria, made all foods palatable.

All of this was going through Gessler's mind as he regarded Nuccio - the earnest pleading look and the slightly bulging eyes - and as he tried to read the paragraph for the third time. What is happening to my mind? A whiff of tabasco struck his nostrils. Gessler scanned the benchtop for one of the small distinctive vessels; the only container anywhere was Nuccio's half-filled coffee mug. Only pens and pencils and some scraps of paper protruded from Nuccio's shirt pocket. It was not one of the bottles that Gessler smelled, but something even more profound: an essence, something alive and gently insistent, that exuded from Nuccio himself. Gessler finished re-reading the paragraph, and he looked at a figure that showed an object moving, and velocities that were indicated with little v's, and so forth. And he thought that he once again grasped the concept. It certainly was not what he'd come to speak with Nuccio about.

"Am I crazy, George?"

"Of course you're not. What don't you like about the idea?" Gessler pursed his lips sagely, looking a bit like a psychiatrist. The hair at his temples was flecked with gray.

"It's - preposterous. It don't explain anything."

"Sometimes" - Gessler paused, reminding himself now of a psychiatrist - "it's only the language that we don't like. You have the phenomena, and then you have the language. Do you see the difference?"

"It isn't only the language," Nuccio insisted. "It's the concept. I'm writing a book about it, you know."

"I know you are."

"It's going to surprise a lot of people."

Gessler had been hearing about the book - or sometimes it was a scholarly paper - for almost as long as he'd known his friend. Some of the most respected minds of the century would be brought under Nuccio's probing analysis. But would the book ever appear? Or would Nuccio even collect his thoughts sufficiently to present Gessler with some scrawled pages at least - enough to hear the tenor of his argument? Gessler thought, on balance, that his friend's mathematical training was insufficient, it was haphazard and informal. How could he marshal his ideas, even assuming that he could write coherently? (And Gessler was not at all sure that he could write.) He'd given Nuccio textbooks, and he had recommended courses to him. He had his doubts whether the book or paper would appear, but for the moment he did not want to show them. Why discourage someone?

"My ideas are going to knock a lot of people on their ass, believe me."

"I know they will," Gessler said automatically.

There may have been something in Gessler's tone that failed to convince Nuccio himself. "Ah," he said, "who am I kidding? I mean what are the chances? Who's gonna listen to a *gavon'* like me?"

"Don't say that, Tony. Don't give up on your dreams. You'll write that book, or that paper."

"You think?" Sounding more cheerful. "I have a lot of ideas. But there's no time. I'm tired, or I can't concentrate."

"I've been told," Gessler said, "a person will create in the most miserable conditions. He will do it in a study, or if there is no peace in his home he'll steal away to his car and work there, or while he is at the laundromat. His clothes are just spinning around in the dryer like everyone else's, but he's thinking his thoughts, or he is writing his book, or his song, although no one else knows or cares. He creates in spite of a hostile world. Or an indifferent world at best. The creative person is always at war with society."

"You've thought about this," Nuccio said. His raised and ragged eyebrows gave his face a look at once inquisitive and nettled.

Gessler himself was not sure where his words were coming from. "The point is, don't let them discourage you or undermine you. You have to keep trying. Even if what they say is true nowadays, that wisdom is sold in the desolate marketplace where none come to buy."

Where had he heard that expression? He couldn't remember.

"You believe that?"

"Sure I do."

"That's heavy." Nuccio's eyes widened. "Did you make it up?"

"I'm not sure. But I believe it."

After a moment Nuccio said, "Thanks, George."

"For what?"

"You know. You're a real thinking man in this push-button world. I can relate to *you*, at least. You're an idol of mine, you know that."

"Bah." Gessler shrugged.

"Did you come down here for something, George?"

"Actually I did."

"It wasn't to talk theories, then. I know I have a big mouth. So why don't you stop me?"

"I want to ask you something. I may be getting married."

"Married? You?" Nuccio paused for breath. "Does my idol have feet of clay?"

"And - so I wanted to know if you'd be my best man."

"Well! Sure I'll be your best man. I'd be honuh'd. Wow, you known her a long time?"

"About five months."

"Man. I took you for a life-long bachelor. It's a good thing, though. Why not? You gonna have a priest? And everything?"

"I'm Jewish, Tony."

"You are?"

"Didn't you know?"

"Well. I guess I knew." Nuccio looked perplexed. "I guess we never much talk about those things, huh, George? So what do we talk about, anyway?"

"Beats the heck out of me. So I'll let you know when?"

"Of course. But what about your fiancee? Is she - Jewish?"

"No. She's a Chinese woman. Very nice."

"That's interesting. Whaddaya know. So it wouldn't be in a church."

"I don't think so."

"Right. What am I saying? Marriage is alright. Maybe have yourselves a couple of kids. I don't see my kids enough. Family functions. The reason I don't see them more is that I usually have to see my ex-wife at the same time." Nuccio's eyes took on a glazed and faraway look. "That *puttana*."

"That - what?" This didn't sound like anything good to Gessler.

"Oh. I don't mean that. She might be a lot of things but I shouldn't call her that. She just destroyed my life, that's all. Anyway I hope it will work out for you. Don't go by me. Of course, I'll be there."

"Thanks."

"I always wondered why the priests had to put their two cents in, anyway. Man and a woman want to get married, they sign a contract. Right? Why the priests have to do their hocus-pocus, huh?"

"I don't know."

"That's right - what am I asking?"

"But I think I feel about the same way."

"Yeah. You know, we ought to do something crazy before you get married."

"Something crazy?"

"Yeah. I know you're not used to it. But go out, have a couple drinks. Just for laughs - while you're still a bachelor. It's a tradition," Nuccio explained.

"Yes, I remember. I don't want to break with tradition."

"We'll do it, then." Nuccio extended his hand to shake. "You and me."

16

A few weeks later Nuccio and Gessler found themselves in a strip club in Queens. Nuccio had picked him up in his car after work. It was the better sort of place - there was a cover charge, which Nuccio insisted on paying. Instead of a bar they sat on stools at a large tile platform, which was empty for the moment. Nuccio's short legs dangled free of the stool. They bought drinks from a waitress who passed, in a kind of showgirl's outfit. Gessler paid for the first round, over his friend's objections.

Nuccio raised his glass. "To Nina. To both of your health's. And the health of your children. And for being a good friend."

"Likewise, Tony."

They glanced around the place. It was mostly dark. There was one other platform, and there was an ordinary bar between them. Instrumental music was throbbing monotonously in the background. No dancers were on, and the music was not loud. The crowd of men seemed mostly professionals. None of them looked like riff-raff.

"Remember, George - we are just going to look."

"That's alright with me. I think they dance in your lap, if you pay them."

"Really?"

"I heard."

"You want that?" Nuccio asked.

"Nah."

"Me, I don't even have a lap. See?" Holding out his arms. "Where's my lap? I'm gonna break my neck."

"So just watch."

"That's the idea. Spoken like a true man of science. So" - Nuccio leaned in and looked up confidentially at Gessler - "you thought any more about what I asked you?" Gessler tried to understand but came up empty. "I'm ... not sure."

"About the Dopp-luh?"

Gessler looked blankly at his friend. Nuccio's expression remained serious, the eyes prominent. Gessler wondered what he could say, and then Nuccio grasped him by the shoulder.

"Kidding."

"Oh." Gessler smiled at last.

"You're kind of a square nut, George."

"I know it."

"It's alright, though. Even a scientist couldn't think about that stuff all the time." Nuccio's short fingers drummed energetically on the tiles, in time to the music.

The ambient light dimmed, their platform brightened. A tall dancer climbed up there. She was wearing a kind of turban-headdress and sequined bikini and high heels. She walked around the perimeter and did some high kicks. The turban was tossed upstage, and a little later some tassels and other things from her exiguous wardrobe. Gessler looked on with a discreet smile. The woman strutted to the other end of the platform, and turned and suddenly drew a bead on Nuccio and came charging toward him. She came sliding knees first. Nuccio lifted his drink from the platform at the last moment, although the precaution wasn't necessary. She shook her upper body in a practiced way. Nuccio looked on greedily. She rose and moved on to other patrons who had come to sit around the tile platform.

Nuccio daubed his forehead with a handkerchief. "We got a ringside seat here, George. You enjoying yourself?"

"Sure."

"Good." Stationary on his stool, Nuccio shifted his shoulders, miming a dance routine. His fists flexed in front of his chest, and his broad head rose and fell on the heavy folds of his neck, in time with the music. He looked a little like a frog who has discovered the happy principle of rhythm.

"You got to strut your stuff a little bit, George."

Was it really necessary, though, Gessler wondered, glancing at his friend. There was no stopping Nuccio. His naturally bulging eyes telescoped further as the long-legged and nearly naked woman pranced toward them like a capering horse. The platform rattled under their drinks with the clack of her high heels. When she was close to Nuccio she crouched and stuck out her tongue suggestively at him. Her tongue played about the corner of her mouth. She seemed to Nuccio to have a good-looking set of teeth, too. This made him think about eating. When she moved on he yawned and asked Gessler if he was hungry. Gessler shook his head no.

She finished her routine. The place grew more quiet again. Nuccio sipped from his drink and said, "This is living, George."

And Gessler half-believed that it was. Except for the cigarette smoke, and the insistently unamiable music, with its vague sleaziness (it seemed as it were innocent of the monotony it engendered) and the yap of inebriated shouts and laughter. The darkness. Certainly the drink was refreshing. He'd enjoyed looking at the woman.

"You have the 'net' at home, George?" Nuccio asked in a moment.

"No. I have it at work. But I don't use it much."

"I was chatting with this woman last night. From Australia."

"That's pretty far away. How does that work - 'chatting'?"

"Well, it's like talking, but you're typing. You should'a seen the sexy messages she sent me. Oh, *maron'.*"

"I'll bet."

"Oh, yeah."

"You know what she looks like?" Gessler asked.

"Sure. She sent me her picture. Wearing a bathing suit. Nice-looking."

"Did you send her a picture, too?"

"Sure I did. Scanned it right in."

Gessler felt puzzled but was trying not to show it.

"Well - not me," Nuccio said. "A picture I cut out of a newspaper. I think the guy's a model or something, young guy about thirty."

"You sent her a picture of someone else?"

"I know - it ain't ethical."

"It's kind of squirrelly, I'd say. You sent her a picture of a guy who's maybe twenty years younger than you?"

"Yeah."

"And maybe a hundred pounds lighter."

"Well, yeah. Why not? So let her think I'm a stud."

"She doesn't know what you look like, maybe you don't know what she looks like."

"So?"

"But what if you meet her sometime?"

"Oh, I'll never meet her. I won't even give her my address. After all she might be a flake."

"*Her?*"

"It's possible. See, this is just for fun."

"You spend much time at this – 'chatting' business?"

"Just a couple hours a night."

"It's nice to know computers are helping people to communicate," Gessler said.

"Are you kidding? It's a great thing, I'm tellin' ya."

"How do you know *her* picture is legit?"

"What do you mean?" Nuccio asked, his interest piqued.

"Well, she could be an older woman. Or how do you know it isn't a guy?"

"A guy," Nuccio repeated, as though he'd never considered the possibility before. "How could it be a-- That's - I don't know - *wei'd.*"

"Well, this whole thing don't sound too healthy, Tony. To me."

"Ah, I'm just foolin around." Nuccio waved a hand dismissively. "Just for fun."

"Okay. Like you said."

"There's another woman that I'm more serious about. I was thinking about getting her address for real and sendin' her a stuffed teddy bear."

"She's your type?"

"'My type.' She's breathin', isn't she."

"Ah. Well, she'd probably like that."

"You know, one of those Toddlin' Teddy Bears. They're tough to find, though."

"That's a special kind?"

Nuccio nodded. He sipped reflectively at his glass of beer. "Very special. Not cheap, either."

"Somewhere they were selling these toy monkeys that talk. Where did I see it now?"

Gessler did not know if he spoke the truth. He remembered seeing something of the kind in a department store. It was more the case that being around Nuccio brought out something antic in him. He fell into a character that he could not escape from.

Nuccio looked at him levelly. "Talking monkeys. That's romantic? I think you're pulling my leg now, George. Since you met this woman you're a little bit unbalanced, you know that."

"I'm just trying to be helpful."

"Sure you are. Seriously, though, you take a woman like that," Nuccio said, gesturing with his thumb toward the now empty stage, "she would kill me."

"You think so?"

"Oh, sure. Maybe not right away. But day in, day out - I'd be a goner."

"You don't look like it would bother you," Gessler said.

"If I made her happy... Ah, young thing like that, it ain't gonna happen, anyway."

Nuccio grew mellow as they awaited the next act. "Life," he said, "has its problems. It's ups and downs if you know what I mean." He grinned suggestively, his thumb flicking to the empty stage again. "But sometimes - seriously - you see a beautiful woman and your eyes just lock. Or maybe not beautiful, but interesting, somehow. And you feel so - *hopeful*. Makes you feel like it's all worthwhile. Doesn't have to be *here*, I mean. Anywhere. You feel that hope, and it just lifts you right up. You know what I mean?"

"Sure," Gessler said. "I know what you mean."

John Zepf

"Yeah. Like I should have to explain it to you. You're getting married, lucky guy."

They sipped their drinks and sat for awhile in silence.

17

Nina kept under her bed a small cardboard box containing some personal mementos. She had decided she would go through these things, although it was true she had few enough possessions in America. She had also obtained some packing boxes from a grocery, for her clothes, mainly, and these stood near her bedroom door. It appeared that she would be able to move out of the apartment before long. She sat on the low bed, a cup of tea on the floor, and brought out the box from under the bed and opened it. It was a late afternoon. In a couple of hours she would have supper with Gessler at his place.

Among the things in the box were some small snapshots of her daughter and copies of her report cards. She studied all of them, and placed them in the pile of things to keep. There were business cards of some stores that she shopped in Flushing or Chinatown. She kept most of them, and placed others in the small plastic wastebasket that she'd placed nearby.

There was a business card from a man she'd met at one of Terry's singles parties. She fingered the card. The man's name was impossible for her to pronounce. He was not Chinese. Nina remembered that he wore eyeglasses. His eyes were large through the glasses and when he talked his eyes stared hungrily and insolently at her. In her minds' eye she imagined a fish swimming toward her in clouded water. Other than this his face was vague. Then his face, eyeglasses and all, seemed to swim into focus, and she found she was no more taken with his appearance now as she was then. In some remote corner of the restaurant he'd pressed up against her. He didn't dare to kiss her on the mouth - she would certainly have struck him. Music was playing loudly, and when he leaned in close to her she thought it was to shout something in her ear. Instead he kissed (or did he lick, rather?) the side of her face. And brought his face, his staring eyes, close to hers, impudently close, and pressed his lower body against hers. She felt against her leg the obdurate pressure of what must have been automobile keys in his pocket. She was not impressed. She was polite but cool toward him. She danced with some other men. Sometime during the evening he'd pressed his business card into her hand. It said that he was the vice president of something at a bank. Impressive. That was probably why she'd kept the card. Later she asked Terry about his title. Terry, Nina felt, already knew so much more than she did about American customs. Terry told her that in fact a single bank could have hundreds of vice presidents. Even the person who cleaned the toilets could be one, according to Terry.

Nina, brought back to the present, fingered the card and glanced at the skein of consonants, mostly, that was the man's name (which, it occurred to her, she would never have to learn to pronounce). Then with a look of mock wistfulness she let the card flutter into the wastebasket.

She remembered another man, a Chinese, from one of these parties, but of him she had no memento - only his personal name, and a recollection of his face. He was remarkably polite and well-spoken. These qualities were not unusual in a Chinese man. But he had something more than this - a quality of gentleness. Calm and conscientiousness seemed to radiate from this man. Here was no gruff masculinity, but something a little ambiguous. She even began to think about his body, something she rarely did. She was almost weak with desire to touch him. She was interested and she wanted him to know. She did not take her eyes from his. Their conversation flagged for a moment and he asked her to dance. When they stood up she saw that she was two inches taller than him. She didn't care - what did it matter? - but she could see his discomfort. But there was nothing to be done for it. She was taller than him and that was that. And when she told him later, in answer to his questions, that she had a child, she saw that his attention to her was now even less. Why should he be responsible for another man's brat? she imagined him thinking. It was a typically Chinese attitude. But some things could not be changed - that was the old Chinese expression. When the song was over he said that it was nice to have met her - as politely as before, but noticeably cooled toward her. She tried to keep the disappointment, the reproach, from her face. She even managed a slight smile then, in the event she was mistaken in what she imagined she saw. Or if he might think better of his coolness, later. But he went off, and he avoided further conversation with her.

Don't think about what might have been, she said to herself.

There was the small image of Guanmin, which she saved. And another small religious card which one of her dates had given her. That had seemed curious. There was a prayer on one side. On the other, a picture of the bearded man with kind and piercing eyes. Looking up to the Heavenly Father. She was going to discard this but then thought that there was no harm in holding on to the card. She added it to the pile to be saved.

Then she heard the tumbling of the front door lock, and voices. It was so typical - there was hardly a moment's privacy in this building. She could not wait for the day she could put this place behind her. For the moment, she stood up and then waited with her fingers holding her bedroom door, listening. It would be rude, but her first thought was to close the door. But who had arrived? She heard the prattling voice of the old woman (she was not so old, really, perhaps sixty), the one who lived with the teacher. There was also a man's voice. The visitors had turned into the short hallway that led to Nina's bedroom. That other voice sounded too familiar. Her heart beat rapidly high in her chest. Nina stood in the open doorway.

Pang was standing there in the hallway. He nodded to her, and exchanged some pleasantries with the old woman. Nina stared at him with hatred and suppressed fear.

Your friend is here, the old woman said. He was standing outside the building.

The woman smiled and made a sort of clucking, ah - ah - ah, sound, while she bowed and looked meekly at Nina. She seemed oblivious, at first, to Nina's cool and defiant look, with its admixture of fear. But as the seconds passed her gaze came to rest rather more on Nina's face than elsewhere, while a perplexed look settled on her own face.

Nina meanwhile had begun to slip her bare feet into some shoes that stood near the door - her best shoes, with the heels. She had done this almost unconsciously. Now she stood at about Pang's height.

What a piece of luck, Pang said, out of the side of his mouth, while looking at Nina. That simpering bumpkin's voice. The oily voice of a procurer.

What do you want, Pang? Nina asked coldly.

At this the smile actually faded from the old woman's face. She looked toward the floor worriedly, now making, oh - oh - oh, sounds.

Can't a friend make a friendly visit?

The old woman interjected a vague worrying sound and looked Nina in the face. Nina, however, did not take her eyes from Pang, even while she spoke:

It's alright, Mrs. Tien. Pang is not staying long.

The old woman went off a few steps, and seemed to remain in the kitchen, from where Nina could hear her movements.

What do you want? she said again.

Can I talk? Pang looked past her into the room.

She allowed him to pass, turning her body with him. Deliberately, she pushed the door open as far as it would go, and turned and looked at him.

I don't think there is anything more to say, she said.

I feel bad about this.

You feel bad for yourself. That is all you think about.

You are probably right.

He took a step toward her and raised his hand slightly.

Nina retreated a half step but was now very close to the wall. Careful, she said.

Pang's hand stayed where it was. He turned his palm up, fingers extended, in what looked like a pacific gesture, and flashed the smile that had become hateful to her. His smile faded as he looked at Nina's implacable face.

He could have helped both of us.

Don't start that talk again. I told you it's over.

So you say.

It is!

Somehow Pang had gotten closer to her, as the seconds had passed. Somehow - the devil! - and now she felt that he was uncomfortably close. Pang looked abject. His hand moved toward her face, the fingers extended and, she could see, shaking. When one finger brushed her throat and chin she arched her neck to draw away from him. He stared into her eyes.

It must be easy for you, he said. An old man like that--

Stop!

Pang seemed to back off then. The slight distance grew between them.

Alright, he said.

Then more swiftly than Nina could have imagined his hand had gripped the back of her head and Pang had spun her against the wall and rammed his body against her. Her head ached. Pang had grabbed her hair and was attempting to ram her head against the wall. She felt his hand come up between her legs, squeezing her flesh. The pain caused a cloud of stars to pass before her eyes. The points of light glittered faintly as the scene grew darker and darker. Somehow Nina roused herself.

Bastard! she screamed. Pimp! Get out!

Pang's forearm pressed against her neck. Her forehead thudded against the wall again and she struggled to remain conscious. Steeling herself, Nina placed the palms of her hands against the wall, and raised her high-heeled foot and brought it down sharply against Pang's leg. Her heel dragged against the skin above his ankle. Pang howled in pain and reached for his leg. As he spun he stepped on a plastic bottle that had fallen from a table, and losing his balance he crashed and fell into the half-filled packing box that stood near the door. Nina reached and removed something that flashed silver from the drawer of the night table and leaped onto Pang.

The point of a kitchen knife pressed against the middle of Pang's throat. He was absolutely still. But when he shifted slightly she saw the small red point of indentation. If he so much as moved-- She had no doubt that she would do it. Only thrust. Only, she thought, I will have to look away at the last minute. A low moan escaped from Pang.

The old woman now stood at the threshold. She wrung her hands. Enough! I'm calling the police!

Nina did not look at her. The same sound continued to come from Pang.

That's not necessary, Nina said without turning. Pang is going to leave. Yes? Holding the knife now with two hands. Pang blinked.

Slowly, Nina rose and backed away from him, the knife still pointed toward Pang. He climbed up from the box and collected himself. Looking at her coldly he said, You would not have used it.

I never want to see you again, Pang.

I am leaving.

He turned abruptly and walked out. The two women followed at a distance until he got on the elevator. He turned and looked at Nina, and it seemed that all the emotion had drained from his face. The doors closed.

18

Tony Nuccio, at the wheel of the Cadillac, looked back and forth at the rearview and side mirrors. Then as if not trusting the mirrors he turned his large head as far as he could and stopped, his eyes bulging. Gessler, sitting next to him, turned and looked and told him that it was alright to back out of the driveway. Nina was in the back seat along with her friend Terry. Nuccio eased into the traffic.

"Today we are driving in style, my friends. Are you comfortable, Terry?" Nuccio asked into the rearview. He hoisted himself in his seat, and still appeared to have difficulty in finding her eyes. Terry's lips were compressed, and her narrow mouth turned down at one corner. Nuccio did not know if this was a common expression with her, or if it was her emotions of the moment. She looked like a small severe Buddha. "I know you," he said at last. "You're Terry and the pirates."

"Of course!" Terry said.

"That was an old comic strip," Nuccio started to explain, but stopped. "Doesn't matter." To Gessler in the front seat he added, "I'm glad she doesn't argue with me, at least. So we're Terry and the pirates," he said absently, and brought the car to a stop at one of the traffic lights on Queens Boulevard.

Nina's face appeared over the front seat, next to Nuccio's shoulder.

"So, where have you been taking my - future husband?" She spoke very clearly - elegantly, even. So it seemed to Gessler. He turned in his seat to look at her. She was lovely. She wore a short white jacket and white slacks. Her trench coat was folded on the seat next to her.

"Me?" Nuccio asked. "Oh, it's a secret. We did some bachelor things. Right, George?"

"What are bachelor things?"

"Alright, we saw a floor show," Nuccio said.

"What is - floor show?"

"Be nice, Tony," Gessler said.

"A leg show."

"Leg show?" Nina repeated.

"Yeah. And not just legs!" Nuccio said slyly.

"So you are looking at women?"

"That was the idea."

"Was it your idea, or George's idea?"

"What're'ya, kidding? I had to drag him there."

"And you just look?"

"What else am I gonna do? George, he hardly even looked. He wasn't interested."

"Really, George? Why not?"

"I looked, too," Gessler said, "a little bit."

"You are nice, Tony," Nina said close to Nuccio's ear. "I'm sure it is very innocent."

"Oh, don't be too sure – about me!" Nuccio gazed into the rear view.

Nina leaned back into the commodious leather seat. Terry asked her something in Chinese and they spoke.

"Terry's talking about me again," Nuccio said, sitting up to find her face in the rearview. "What can I say, George? It's that animal magnetism - women can't resist it." Terry, he saw, was laughing, but he wasn't sure if she got his drift. "Yeah, I passed a woman last week and I heard her say, 'That guy's an animal.' Right, Terry?"

Nuccio parked, and they all walked up the steps of the County Clerk's building. Nuccio was wearing a suit, but unlike the others no overcoat. Nina complimented him on his suit.

"Thanks. It's one that still fits. Sort of." He fidgeted with the belt. The sneakers he was wearing looked new, or at least freshly laundered. "My feet bother me," he said to Terry.

Gessler and Nina moved ahead up the stairs, arm in arm. "I hope I don't get too sentimental," Nuccio said to Terry next to him.

"I have extra handkerchief."

"I may need it."

"You cried at your wedding?"

"No. After."

"After? Oh," frowning, "I can't talk to you. You are crazy. *Crazy.*"

With an effort, Nuccio charged up a few steps to the next landing, and turned and gallantly extended his hand to Terry. "Up, up, and away," he said, as she took his hand and glided up the few steps.

When the ceremony was over they walked across the street to a park. Nuccio snapped some pictures. Now he set a nylon bag he was carrying onto one of the benches.

The weather was raw and only a few people passed. "Let's toast right here," Nuccio said. He reached inside the bag and brought out plastic champagne glasses, and a bottle which he skillfully opened. He filled the glasses and re-capped the bottle.

"To George and Nina. Their happiness."

The honeymoon was a long weekend in Boston. Their hotel room overlooked the Public Gardens. Even in winter it was a beautiful scene below, with walking paths that intertwined under the bare trees, the sinuous and graceful elms and other trees. From their room they could see the sloping lawn and broad walk that led up to Beacon Hill, to the brilliant golden dome of the capitol building. Gessler felt one with the setting. His happiness seemed complete.

They saw a show and sampled the restaurants in Chinatown. They went clothes shopping. They took the train to Cambridge and walked about Harvard Square. In Harvard Yard Nina wanted to feed the eager and inquisitive squirrels, who followed and stood on hind legs, and rubbed their paws together and looked up at them. They visited a few markets before they were able to find a small bag of peanuts. If Nina wanted to feed squirrels he did not mind indulging her. It was a time to act a little crazy. He snapped several pictures of Nina standing there smiling, surrounded by the small group of begging squirrels.

In a little cafe one mid-morning, both of them a little sleepy, sitting by a large window before which the city passed, Nina turned to Gessler and asked, "George, why do we live in New York?"

"Why?" he repeated. She had not said so, but he supposed that she was reacting to the decorum, the relative civility, that they had observed during the course of their visit to Boston. And the city was, at least in some degree, more civil than New York - which was uncouth in some ways.

"I guess because my job is there," he said. "Why do you ask?"

"Well. Isn't it nicer here?"

"In some ways, maybe." He could understand why she asked the question. He wondered if maybe there was a better life elsewhere.

"You have your connections to New York, too, I suppose."

"Why?" she asked. "I don't have family in New York."

"But there is a Chinese community there."

"What does it mean? You are teaching me English - why do I need those Chinese?"

"True. But you want to be able to buy Chinese groceries, for example."

"Who cares? I will eat like an American."

"Whatever you say. We are not bound and chained to New York." Gessler's fingers shaped a manacle around one wrist.

Nina repeated the gesture and asked, "Mei you?" Don't have?

"That's right," Gessler said. "I could work in other places."

"Yes." Nina reached for his hand, across the table. Then he watched as she rose and stood near him, and made to sit on his lap. He did not mind. There was just one other person, sitting far away - and they were on their honeymoon. She put her arms around his shoulders. "We can - think about it?" He nodded. "It was - very good - again, last night," she smiled. "I didn't know it can be so good." She looked around to be sure no one was listening.

"It's been very good," he agreed.

"Why did you say you are not a young man?"

"Did I say that? I don't remember."

"You did. 'Oh, I am losing hair--' "

"Well, that's true. I'm glad I met you before I got too much older. My hair is thinning, I have more aches and pains--"

"You are still a young man," she interrupted him. "If you are any younger I don't think I can get out of bed this morning. I thought I will pass out."

"Are you trying to make me feel good?"

"It's true. If you have any more energy you will destroy me. Where did you learn it?"

"Learn what?"

Nina brushed his hair lightly. "In your hands a woman can glow like heated metal. Who would know?"

He looked at her skeptically, and said, "You're pretty exciting yourself."

She went on brushing at his hair until she caught his look, and pushed his head away roughly.

Then they were driving back to the city. From the interstate he could see the huge tan and gray apartment buildings of the Bronx looming there blankly. The asphalt below, the vacant lots with their choking weeds and scrub trees. A landscape emptied of people, and the towering buildings above. For Gessler it was a familiar first prospect of the city. It had always affected him in the same vaguely unpleasant way - a fluttering in the stomach, like a sudden void. Nina only slept, and he kept his thoughts to himself.

19

Gessler was driving home from work. The late-winter afternoon had been cloudy, and now rain and wet snow began to fall. The leafless trees in his neighborhood swayed under fitful gusts of wind. He approached the garage, and pressing the button of his remote the garage doors folded and rose into the ceiling. He drove through and the door closed swiftly after him. The garage held about fifty cars and it was nearly full. There was no one around. He exited one of the side doors and stepped onto a walk. It was about a block to his apartment building. As he walked the wind whipped at his raincoat, and he shielded his head from the rain with the day's newspaper.

He went up in the elevator and let himself in quietly. He thought Nina might be sleeping, but then he heard a radio and some movement in the kitchen.

"Hello, Nina," he called. He glanced at some of his mail lying on the hall table. Nina came out to the foyer.

She took his hand. "You are wet." She helped him off with his coat and placed it in the hall closet. "Don't you have umbrella?"

"I forgot it," he said, holding her.

"I should remind you. I am not a very good wife."

"Sure you are. I'm fine."

"I'm afraid you will catch cold. Please relax. I am making supper."

Gessler emptied his pockets at the bedroom dresser. He went to the living room and sat down and waited, glancing at the newspaper.

Nina entered the room carrying his slippers. "You like a cold beer?" she asked.

"No, thank you. Unless you are having one."

"I? Don't be silly. Please - take your shoes off." Standing over him.

"Oh, that's alright."

"Please - you will be more comfortable."

She knelt and began untying his shoes. Gessler felt embarrassed and he reached down to help her. "Isn't it better?" she asked.

"Yes. I'm very comfortable." He held out his arms. Nina sat, partly on his lap and partly on one of the chair arms.

"Nina," he said with mock seriousness, "you are going to spoil me."

"*Spoil* you? What does it mean?"

"Wo - huaile." I - broken. It was as close as he could get to his meaning, but it wasn't satisfactory. Nina laughed it off.

"You? Broken? I don't think so. You are getting stronger."

"You are making me stronger."

"Never mind. I am crushing you." She made to get up but Gessler held her there. "Please. If I don't get up you will really be spoiled. I am too heavy. Let me look at supper."

Nina had prepared four different dishes. After they ate Nina pushed him out of the kitchen and he returned to the living room and the couch. He was going to get fat if he kept eating like this, he thought, nearly dozing. Nina joined him again.

"Would you like to go out and see a movie some night?"

"Why?" Nina asked.

"No reason. Just to get out."

"I can't understand what they are saying. It is not clear. Also, I do not see the meaning."

"Oh, there isn't any meaning."

"No? Why do people watch them, then?"

"Oh, to have something to do, I guess. Anyway - you are not bored here?"

"Bored? Of course not! I am happy with you. Don't think such things."

"Yes. Of course. Movies might help you with your English - if you try to understand."

"Maybe. I don't think we should go tonight. I don't want you to catch cold."

"Another night."

"Also - I feel tired."

"You are tired?" She nodded. "Tired how? Weishemma?"

Nina placed her hands next to her cheek. "Yao shui." I want to sleep.

"Only today?"

She shook her head. "Many days."

"Really. Maybe you are - expecting. You know." He looked at her to see if she understood him.

"You may be right. Would it make you happy?"

"Of course it would. Wouldn't that be something... We'll arrange to see a doctor, then. Yes?"

"Yes." Nina smiled and drew closer to him.

Another evening they went out for dinner. He waited in the living room for Nina to get dressed, while she asked him again if he wouldn't rather eat at home.

"We'll have fun," he said. "You are always cooking."

They went outside and walked to the garage. The day was not yet dark, and the air was mild, almost balmy. Gessler paused at the side entrance to the garage, fingering his key. Then he saw that door was opened slightly.

"What is wrong?" Nina asked.

"Someone must have left it open." He pushed at the door and it opened halfway.

"Oh, be careful," Nina said. She threw her arms around him. "Oh, don't go in!"

"Do you want to wait here?"

"No!" Looking around fearfully.

"We'll go together." It must have been her fear that caused him to whisper. They advanced slowly, looking into the spaces between the cars.

"You see, there is no one around," he said.

Suddenly they heard a car's chirping noise. Nina gasped. A small terrier bounded across a front seat and driver and came yapping towards them. Gessler pushed in front of Nina, but she sprinted in the direction of their own car. Mrs. McCready, a silver haired woman in a black overcoat, lumbered out of the driver's seat, calling, "Mindy! Mindy!" She looked apologetically at Gessler and said hello.

"Mindy, must you scare everyone?"

At her voice, the dog left off her barking and ambled past Mrs. McCready and leaped onto the front seat again.

"I'm very sorry." She saw Nina standing off in the distance, her face in her hands, and said, "Oh, my."

"The door was open," Gessler said, pointing. "We were concerned."

"Did I leave that open? Oh, my. But the door sticks, you know. I've told them. Anyone could get in here. But I'll be more careful."

She got back in her car and started up in a few moments.

Nina was standing with her arms folded, the knuckles of one hand pressed against her mouth. Gessler patted her shoulder. "It was nothing," he said.

Nina looked up. "Oh, George. I am so afraid."

"Afraid? Why?"

"Something terrible could happen here. Can't we leave this place?"

"You want to leave the city?"

"I hate it here!"

He touched her face. "Nina, I don't understand you. When did you start feeling this way?"

"Oh, please."

"Where would you like to go?"

"Can't we go to New Eng-u-land? It was nice there."

Mrs. McCready cruised by in a large Oldsmobile. He could barely see her waving behind the frosted glass.

"I think you are just over-excited. Calm down. Are you still up to dinner?"

"Do you want?"

"Yes."

"Alright. If you want."

"I guess I can look into other jobs."

"You will?"

"I will do it, if it's what you want. I don't think you are being sensible, right now. Why do you suddenly have these thoughts?"

Nina was looking away from Gessler, abstractedly, in the space above his shoulder.

"Why?" Gessler repeated.

"I saw the fortune teller last week."

"Nina, I wish you wouldn't go to the fortune teller. It only frightens you needlessly. Don't you see it's just a lot of superstition?" She looked at Gessler, then she looked off as before. Someone else might have surmised that Nina was improvising something. But not Gessler.

"She said - I will never have any peace here. That there is only death for me here."

"That's crazy talk, Nina. Come on, let's go." He opened the car door for her. Nina got in and sat there stonily. She did not respond when, from the driver's seat, he reached to touch her face, and to tug on the woolen beret that covered her head. He started the car.

Nina thought she'd played the scene well. But that was little comfort to her now, hearing as she did, seldom very far away, the mad music of pursuit that threatened every dream of happiness.

20

"You didn't have to bring wine, Tony." They were sitting around the kitchen table in Gessler's apartment.

"It's nothing. Sometime I'll bring my spaghetti sauce. How's that?"

"Good, good," Gessler said. He looked up. "Can't you sit down with us, Nina? Do you need help?"

"I'm fine. Supper is almost ready." Nina took the seat nearest the stove. She was wearing a plain white apron over some casual clothes.

"Here's how," Nuccio said, raising his glass of wine. He and Gessler drank. Nina raised her glass without drinking, held it up to the light, and put it back on the table.

Nuccio studied her. "That's all? Aren't you gonna drink any?"

"I have never drank liquor," she said. "Please. You have it," placing her glass near his. Nina excused herself and tended to some pots on the stove.

"How is the writing going, Tony?"

"Oh. Alright, if I can find the time."

Nina returned and stood near the table. "You are a writer, Tony? I did not know."

"Not the kind of writer you think. I don't write dime-store novels. In fact a lot of the time I don't write much of anything."

Gessler said, "Tony is developing some interesting ideas on scientific subjects."

"Oh," Nina said, although not seeming clear on the point.

"Do you know anything about radar, Nina?" Nuccio asked.

She looked to Gessler for help.

"We don't have to explain them all tonight, Tony," Gessler said.

"Oh. Oh, right."

Nina brought out supper and they began eating. Nuccio had helped himself to more of the main course, which was set out on a large tray, when he paused, finished chewing, and asked, "Say, what is this?" He pointed with his fork to some fried ravioli-sized objects on his plate.

"I'm sorry," Nina said. "It's dao-fu."

"Dao-what?" Nuccio looked intensely curious.

"It's a bean curd," Gessler said, "made from soybeans."

"Oh." Nuccio ventured another small piece.

"Do you like it?" Nina asked.

"It's - different." Nuccio pursed his lips. "It tastes like - Well, it doesn't taste like anything." Nina looked at him anxiously. "But it's good!" he added.

Nina's face lightened and she returned to the stove. Nuccio said in an undertone to Gessler, while he helped himself to more, "I almost put my foot in it that time. I'm good at that."

When they had finished eating Gessler asked, "Did I tell you that I have a job offer out of state? Near Boston?"

"I didn't even know you were looking around. Don't you like it at the company?"

"Oh, sure. They've been good to me. Nina and I feel we'd like to try something different. We have no real ties to the city--"

"Sure you do."

"Except for some friends, of course."

Nina sat down at the table. She rested her chin on her hand and looked at Nuccio.

"But," he said, "what would happen to me?" His eyes widened further. The smile had long left his face. "Who would I have to talk to?"

"You have other friends," Nina said.

He turned to her. "As a matter of fact I don't."

"Your cousins," Gessler said.

"Na. Not like George here," still speaking to Nina. "And my wife moved the kids to Florida. Who do I have?"

Nina appeared to think for a long moment and then said, "So you talk on the telephone. Or you move, too."

"Are you serious? Just like that?" Nuccio looked at both of them. "Man, you kids are impulsive. But, if it came to that - well, who knows?"

He lifted his glass of wine again.

21

Gessler was having his breakfast in the kitchen. Nina, sitting at a right angle, only watched him. She did not understand the appeal of cold milk and cereal, but Gessler seemed to like it. She only drank tea. Gessler drank the coffee she'd made and lingered sitting at the table.

"It's getting late. I wish I didn't have to go to work," he said. Nina's eyes widened a little. "Yes, I never used to say that."

"Is that bad?" Nina asked.

"No. I think it's good." He touched her robe and smiled at her.

"If you don't want to go to work," she said, "what do you want to do?"

"Stay here with you. Go back to bed."

"That's all you want to do? We can't stay there all the time."

"I wish," Gessler said.

"I miss you when you are gone."

"Really? Weishemma? I mean, why?"

"I worry."

"Why? Why do you worry?"

"I wish we don't have to live in the city. I don't like it."

"We don't always have to live here."

"Oh, I wish."

"I know how you feel. I'm doing what I can. Do you think you'd like to retire to Florida some day?"

"Oh, I don't know. We are still young!"

"You're right."

He sighed and stood up. Nina smiled and got up and he pulled her close to him. He kissed her on the mouth and his hands reached around her robe.

"How did I get so lucky, eh?" he asked.

"No - I am lucky."

"I don't know about that."

"I'll go with you," Nina said.

"What. To the car? It isn't necessary. Besides, you're hardly even dressed." He played with the collar of her robe.

"I'll come back for you after lunch," he said. "In time for your doctor's appointment."

"Is it alright? I can take the subway."

"No. I want to go with you. We'll drive."

"Thank you." She made to slip out of his arms, but he resisted.

"Why don't you go back to sleep? You're tired."

"Please - one minute."

Gessler got his coat from the closet. Nina joined him in a moment, putting on some slacks and a white jersey and short coat. They locked the door and took the elevator downstairs. Nina held his arm. Outside, they walked along the street for a block and then reached the garage. The day was not yet light.

"You can go back," he said to Nina, but she remained on his arm. He dug the key from his pocket, and turned the lock, and they stepped in turn through the narrow door. They started walking toward his car.

The gunman appeared from out of nowhere. He had to have been hiding between two of the parked cars. Suddenly he was standing there in front of them. Against odds, perhaps, Gessler had never been mugged before. He tugged roughly on Nina's arm to pull her behind him. The gunman was Chinese.

"You want money?" Gessler asked clearly. He reached carefully for his wallet and held it out in his left hand. The gunman didn't respond. He seemed paralyzed, staring at Nina. She moved to Gessler's right side.

You get out of here, Pang, she said.

I can't do that, Nina. We had a deal, remember.

Gessler understood a little of the gunman's speech. It bewildered him that the man should be addressing Nina, and yet he clearly was. He seemed surprised to see her here.

You were going to see about the insurance.

Gessler thought that he understood the last word. "Nina," he asked, not taking his eyes from the gunman. "Do you know this man?"

"He's going to get out of here," Nina said. You get out of here, she said again, defiantly. You can't do this. I will never see you again.

Pang shook his head very slightly. I can't let you. I have nothing now.

Monster, she said. Get out of here.

They both saw him raise the gun from his side. The gun hand was shaking unpredictably.

Leave him alone, Nina screamed.

Gessler saw that Nina was trying to move in front of him and he put his arm out, moving forward a step and trying to cut off her advance. The gunman yelled something incomprehensible, a panicked look on his face.

The sound of the explosion stunned Gessler. It tore terrifically through the enclosed space of the garage. Nina was blocking him now. But it was as if she had been thrown backward against him. He gripped her around the waist and prepared to push her aside and behind him. But she felt uncharacteristically heavy in his arms. His hand felt warm and damp where he was holding her waist, and he released his arm, carefully, and looked and saw that it was blood on his hand. The gunman was not moving now. Nina was rapidly slipping out of Gessler's grasp, and a moment later she lay sprawled against his legs. No sound came from her.

Gessler had scarcely taken his eyes from the gunman. Pang stood with the gun pointing at the ground, some feet short of Gessler and Nina. For the space of a few moments Gessler considered his options. Make a run at the gunman - or wait and hope that he ran away? Then he would be able, at least, to try and get help for Nina... But her weight against his legs felt inert and lifeless. Hope drained from him. He reached, inexpertly, for her neck, but he found no pulse there. He even imagined her flesh had grown colder.

Fate had dealt him its worst hand - but perhaps fate had one more trick up its sleeve. Gessler looked with hatred at Pang, at the gun which was now pointing nowhere, and he thought: I don't care much about living, but I don't want to die here like a dog.

If all hope was gone why did his heart still beat with fear?

Suddenly he heard Nina groan. The gunman looked startled. Swiftly, Gessler crouched and cradled her head in his hands and lowered her gently to the cement. He stepped in front of Nina. Then he looked deliberately at the gunman and took a step toward him. The gun went up again, unsteadily in Pang's hand. A door clicked open, loud and far away. The gunman's eyes shifted in that direction.

A woman's voice called, "Who is here?"

"Don't come in, Mrs. McCready. It's George. Call for an ambulance. Call the police."

Gessler listened and heard the door slam closed. He took another step forward - the gun now pointing at his chest, the gunman's eyes shifting between him and the exits - and as he did so Pang started retreating backward, and fled.

Gessler returned to where Nina was lying. He removed his coat and folded it and placed it under her head. Then he knelt beside her. Now he could imagine the damage that the bullet had caused. A widening stain of blood had seeped into Nina's light-colored jacket. When he squeezed her hand there was some slight movement of her eyelids. Her arms and her legs were splayed unnaturally on the cement. Gessler straightened them, helplessly, then thought he would run out to summon help.

Nina's eyes opened tentatively. She saw Gessler. Her eyes took in the surroundings, while her head remained still. Then she seemed to recall all of the unexpected chaos of the last two minutes, or maybe it was a spasm of pain that caused her to wince. Her eyes closed for several seconds, and opened again.

"George," she whispered.

"I'm here."

"I am so sorry."

Gessler thought to open her jacket. He placed his handkerchief over what he believed was the wound, and he applied some pressure there. Nina winced.

"We were planning - to kill you. But I told him to stop. I told..."

Gessler began to understand what the gunman's words and actions had already suggested to him.

"It's alright now."

Nina struggled to speak. "I am a terrible person. Please don't leave me."

"I'm here," Gessler said again.

"At least, it is peaceful here now. I thought we would have more time together." Her fingers gripped his, but with little force. "I don't want to die."

"We are getting an ambulance," Gessler told her.

He thought she shook her head from side to side. "It is too late for me."

"Don't say that."

"I thought - I could stop this. Can you forgive me?"

"Yes, yes. Save your strength now." But as he spoke he wondered if it was too late. He became aware of the sirens - the police car, the ambulance - drawing closer it seemed. He touched her chin with the back of his fingers. There was dried blood on his hands. It struck him how little her lips had moved, how soft her voice was. How different her eyes now looked. Death was already come for her, was even now robbing her of the vital force. Nina's eyes closed, and opened. He leaned closer to hear her.

"If there is another life... And I am not - corrupted, like this--" Her eyes shifted and seemed to take in her stained and scuffed clothing where she lay. "Then I would marry you, and make you happy."

With something like a smile her gaze had turned to him, and it now stayed there. After a moment he looked away. He heard one of the garage doors open. Someone called, "Is anyone here?" Gessler tried to speak but no sound came.

"It's alright," he said at last.

Then Mrs. McCready was standing there, along with another neighbor. "My God," she said when she saw them, bringing a hand to her mouth. The man with her glanced nervously around the garage.

"He's gone," Gessler said.

The police arrived moments later.

22

Gessler stood looking out through the glass wall onto the airport runway. It was a gray afternoon. Fuel trucks drove out to the sitting planes. Other planes backed and lumbered along the runway, the red lights on their wings and body flashing in unison. He would hear the big jets rev suddenly, their noses tilting in the air as they became airborne. But the plane carrying Nina's body was long gone by now.

The people at the counter had seemed kind. He'd even told them something of his story, while around him the phones chirped loudly, and computer printers whirred impressively. But for the most part people did not treat him any differently. They didn't understand. At the security gate he'd set off the alarm. He stepped back, he stepped through again, he began emptying his pockets into the plastic tray. But there was always, still, some small piece of metal somewhere on him: a ball-point pen, a candy wrapped in foil. Finally he could walk through without an alarm going off. He submitted to it all patiently. But a part of his mind complained that he must be treated as a person in no special circumstances. It didn't seem fair at all. Unless he were to wear a black armband-- But where did you get them? And how long would you wear it, if he did get one?

It was just yesterday that he'd dealt with the police.

At first there were just two policemen who answered the call. More would arrive later. Gessler was not even aware of them at first. They'd called to the two neighbors and told them to wait outside, they might need them later.

The police entered at either end of the garage. They cops signaled to each other with their guns drawn. They were some time in reaching Gessler, pausing to look into the spaces between the cars on either side, and even crouching to see if anyone was concealed underneath. The lighting inside the garage was poor.

The two officers reached Gessler at about the same time. They were still holding guns. Gessler was kneeling and cradling Nina's head. The arrival of the police seemed to have barely registered with him. Some static and voices burst from one of the cops' portable radios. Without taking his eyes from Gessler, the cop lifted the device and said something tentative into it. Something about a shooting, an approximate whereabouts, and some codewords that Gessler didn't understand. The cop who was closest to him spoke first. He was a big man, at least six-foot-two, with a sallow complexion.

He introduced himself and then his partner, a smaller and darker-complexioned man. But the names did not stay with Gessler. "What's your name?"

Gessler told him.

"Mr. Gessler, what happened here?"

Gessler collected himself and spoke. "A man shot her."

"Do you have a gun, Mr. Gessler?"

"No, I don't have a gun."

"Do you mind if we search you?"

Gessler let go of Nina carefully and raised his arms. Her head rested on his legs. The cops hands pressed here and there against his shirt and about his waist. "That's my coat there," he said, gesturing. "I was using it as a cushion. Check it."

The cop picked up the coat and felt of it and then placed it on the trunk of the nearest car. He crouched on one knee, close to Gessler.

Gently, the cop pressed his fingers against Nina's neck.

"She's gone," Gessler said.

The cop stared hard into Gessler's eyes without moving. He nodded toward the other cop, and looked back at Gessler. "Who is this, Mr. Gessler?"

"She's my wife."

The cop took his hand away and said, "I'm sorry. You said a man shot her?" Gessler nodded. "Can you describe him?"

"A man. Chinese."

"How do you know he was Chinese?"

"He spoke."

"You could tell it was Chinese he was speaking?"

"Yes. I'm sure." The cop stared at Gessler. He could see how the cop's manner could be unnerving. The other one was writing things into a small notebook.

"Why was he speaking Chinese to you?"

"Not to me. To my wife."

The cop studied Nina's face for a moment. "Why was he speaking to her?" Gessler didn't answer. "Was it a robbery?"

"No."

"So--"

"He knew her."

The cop glanced at his partner again. "He knew her. You're sure of that?"

"Yes. I didn't understand much of what they were saying. But she called him Pang."

"Pang. That's his name? P-A-N-G?"

The other cop wrote the name into his notebook.

"Did you know him?"

"No. Never saw him before."

"Why would he want to hurt her?"

"He didn't. He wanted to kill me."

"You."

"But she got in his way."

"She got in his way - deliberately?"

Gessler looked as though he hadn't heard the question. The cop just seemed to be repeating everything that he said. It was unnerving.

"What else can you tell me about him? What was he wearing?"

Gessler told him all that he could remember. The other cop called in the description.

The cop who was doing most of the talking was crouched very close to Gessler. "Do you have any idea why he did it?"

Gessler shrugged.

"Mr. Gessler - George - is it possible that he was a boyfriend? I'm sorry to ask."

"I don't think it was like that. Maybe in the past."

"It's possible, isn't it? In the past, like you say. Maybe he was jealous."

But Gessler didn't say anything more. His eyes looked unfocussed.

One of the doors opened, and a tenant, a young woman, appeared.

"Please stay out," the standing cop shouted.

"But I have to go to work," the woman complained.

The cop nearest Gessler yelled, "This is a police scene. Get the hell out of here!" He took several steps her way and the woman fled back through the door.

He returned to where Gessler was but he seemed to have lost his focus, only looking again at Nina.

"Thank you," Gessler said to him.

"I don't think we have any more questions now," the cop closest to Gessler said. "Will you come to the station later and give a statement?"

"Of course."

He heard one of the cops say, in a quiet voice, impatiently, "Where are they?"

"Who?" Gessler asked.

The cop approached him again, crouching. "Well, the ambulance. There's not much more you can do here. Is there?" Gessler didn't answer, and the cop continued. "And a team to search this place. Before everything is disturbed. Based on your description, and the fact she knew the perpetrator, I'd say there's a very good chance we'll find him."

"Yes. A good chance," Gessler said absently.

"Sir?"

Gessler didn't say anything more. The cop hoisted himself and went off and spoke quietly with his partner.

Gessler had remained with her then for a few more minutes...

A good chance. The words came back to him now as he stood at the airport window, and he spoke them to himself. He felt exhausted.

Professor Bartle joined him, bearing two coffees in his hands.

"What else do you want to do, George?"

"Just the one thing. Call the mother."

"Are you up to that?"

"Let's do it while you're here."

Near where they were standing, a motorized cart whizzed along the concourse, with warning tones whose pitch grew higher with greater speeds. There was a bank of telephones at the other end of the gate area. They walked over there.

Gessler handed him a rumpled slip of paper with numbers written on it. "I forget how the exchanges work."

"It's not a problem," Bartle said, punching numbers. He studied the woman's name, which was written in English. "She knows, correct?"

"Oh, yes."

After Bartle made contact he seemed to utter some consoling words, unprompted. Then he put his hand over the receiver.

"Tell me what you want me to say."

"Did she get the money."

Bartle spoke into the receiver and waited, and said to Gessler, "She says you are very kind."

"Tell her that the plane has left."

Bartle spoke and then listened for some moments. He held the receiver a couple of inches from his ear. "She wants to know how it happened." He paused, and Gessler thought about the question.

"Just say - that she was a victim of violence. Say that."

Bartle spoke for a while longer, evidently adding some consoling words that he improvised. Then the conversation seemed to be winding down.

"Anything else?"

"No. Just... That I'll speak with her again."

"Right." He rung off, and shrugged. "We should go," he said, looking at Gessler.

Gessler nodded. His car was in the parking lot. They walked there in silence.

Professor Bartle said, "You are not going to go over there."

"I don't know any of her family. There wouldn't be any point."

"Perhaps. And the daughter?"

"I'll send what I can for her."

"I'm really sorry - George," Bartle said, after he had driven out of the airport and they were on the parkway.

"I appreciate your help."

"I know you had some doubts. But it seems like it could have been a good thing."

"Yes. It could have been wonderful," Gessler said. "I'm going to visit some neighbors," he said. "For something to eat. You're welcome to come, too."

"Thanks. I have some things to do. You just tell me where to go."

"Of course. Somehow I really don't feel like going home right now."

Soon they were in Laura's neighborhood; a leafy, tree-lined street in Queens, where the sun was now setting. Gessler thought he could see someone on the landing of her front door - Nuccio, speaking with someone inside.

"It's coming up there," Gessler said.

Bartle slowed the car to a stop. "Ah - bad luck," he said vaguely. They shook hands across the front seat.

Gessler paused before getting out. Staring out the windshield, and as if talking to himself, he said, "I didn't really know her well."

Bartle looked at him curiously. He was too surprised to say anything. He went on studying him for some time as Gessler approached the house. Laura and her family and Nuccio stepped out onto the walk. He greeted all of them. Gessler's friends formed a circle around him. The door was opened and he was led inside.

MR. CHARLES BRAINARD LAMENTS THE LATE, GREAT WORLD OF IDEAS

A SATIRE

(*"In America I lived a life of crushing intellectual isolation."*)

Herlihy was a senior editor at a middling publishing house in Manhattan. Many of the firm's recent productions were not, it is fair to say, among the very first ranks of quality. This, however, had not hurt the firm's bottom line. Herlihy was at the moment seated behind a broad cherry-wood desk. Some tall windows offered views of midtown skyscrapers. He was entertaining Mr. Schmenk, a junior editor who worked in his department. In the course of other duties, Mr. Schmenk would offer his best ideas to the senior editor, and forward to him with his comments, the most promising manuscripts that crossed his desk.

Herlihy himself was white-haired but vigorous-looking, only in his fifties, with an alert and often vaguely smarmy expression on his face.

"But none of the things we publish," he was saying, "sell enough copies to satisfy the boss."

Schmenk looked at him artlessly, as though to say: I do what *I* can.

"Schmenk, I always felt that you had a calculating mind--"

"Thanks?"

"Oh, don't be offended. It's what I like about you. But I always thought that you had a little more originality to go along with it."

Schmenk could not remember what he might have done to pique Herlihy to this extent. Or perhaps the senior man was only putting him on again. "Now you're not sure?" Schmenk asked. "Do you remember telling me that a little originality was a dangerous thing to put before the public?"

"I said that? I don't remember."

"Yes, many times. What's wrong? Do you feel bad because we aren't going to do Buffy Bezell's novel?"

Reportedly, the firm had been close to landing that deal, but had missed out somehow.

"Oh…" Herlihy sighed philosophically. "Well, it was a blow, I'll admit."

"I just didn't know that the girl had a book in her."

"Who knew? The girl is twenty years old, she has a hit TV series, Spy Chick, a film and recording contract, she's going to college, *and* she's seen in public dating a different guy every week. When will she even find time to write her novel?"

"Oh, they'll get some schmo to do it for her. You know that."

"We did some of those ourselves, remember, Schmenk?"

Schmenk could remember a couple of commercial successes of ghost-writing along those lines, but he did not remember the experiences at all fondly.

"To tell you the truth," Herlihy continued, "I think I've had enough of celebrity books for awhile, anyway."

"Oh?"

"I don't think I told you, but I was ghost writing Arthur Maximilian's little novel."

"Arthur Maximilian the financier?"

"Yeah."

"Who owns the beachfront mansion in the Hamptons? Always in the society pages?"

"Yeah. That guy."

"H'm. But why wouldn't you tell me about that?" Herlihy shrugged. "Is it any good?"

"Not very. I tried to give it the old 'Hurler' treatment. But there wasn't much to work with. You know, old Max has this reputation as a sort of financial sage. But I don't see it. He inherited a hundred million dollars and he has gone through about three-quarters of it. As far as I can tell, the only astute thing the man ever did was picking those wealthy grandparents of his."

"And we did his book why?"

"The old boy knows his eminence," (Herlihy meant the head of the firm) "and offered to take out some half-page ad's on his own dime – in financial dailies, of all things. He convinced the old man that he had a novel in him. If you ask me it was more of a wet dream. What a randy old coot!"

"Bad, eh?"

"Worse. In chapter one the hero, a white-haired financier who resembles the author somewhat, is carrying on with young women in ways that could get him arrested in several states."

"Under-aged, you mean?"

"Oh, I don't think so. Not in that chapter, anyway." Herlihy seemed nonplussed for a moment.

"H'm. Did he do any of the writing?"

"Not really. I had to spend several excruciatingly boring days on his yacht in the Sound, while he dictated his magnum opus. Oh, what a hack I felt! I told everyone I was on vacation – only my principles were. I don't even get a co-credit, but knowing the end-product and how it will be received, I can't say that I am bothered by that. Though it may sell, at that."

Schmenk frowned sympathetically.

"Oh, the book will have that whiff of celebrity about it, you know," Herlihy continued. "It piques the curiosity of the masses, and it's what we in the media fall back on when we are unable to judge the real merit of the presentation."

"That's kind of harsh," Schmenk ventured.

"Oh, you may be right." Herlihy looked at his colleague, and his features softened. "Bills must be paid, I suppose."

"That is kind of depressing, though. Would you like to go out and drown your sorrows in drink sometime?"

"Oh, that's no solution, my young friend. No, I have cried all the way to the bank, as they say. I think I am over it now."

Herlihy swiveled in his chair, looking up at the framed eight-by-ten of Balzac on the wall behind his desk. The French master looked down scowling and disheveled. Herlihy brought his hands together near his mouth, and closed his eyes as it were contritely.

"I suppose I am only biting the hand that feeds me. I don't mean to sound critical. Really I'm not. But think, Schmenk. The public is going to get tired of this – this pablum, that we put out constantly. I myself am bored."

"Bored?" Schmenk looked perplexed at the idea.

"Oh, just think about it. I always know exactly what kind of books you are going to bring to me. You never surprise me any more."

"Oh, I don't believe it. Sometimes we publish controversial things."

"Such as?"

"Well, how about the woman professor that liked to—"

"A kinky academic. I didn't like her book, frankly. I thought she should keep her weird ideas to herself."

"What about the blue-collar essayist that we almost published?"

"Yes – 'almost.' And he wasn't really blue-collar, either. Do you know where they say he bought his so-called work clothes? Barney's."

"Eh?"

"Oh, doesn't matter. No, I'm afraid that there is no purity of heart in any of the stuff we do. Even the iconoclastic things have something calculated about them. We all seem to be contaminated by this age, where intellectual honesty is a thing as rare as hens' teeth. Tell me, for example, what have you got for me this week?"

"Offhand—"

"Yes. Just offhand. What kind of blazingly original work are you going to recommend to me this week?"

"Marty, I'm not getting you."

"Well, you probably have a memoir that you are going to present."

"As a matter of fact—"

"A celebrity?"

"One, yes." And Schmenk mentioned the name of an actor.

"Oh, he's good. Very underrated. And another by someone who is not famous?"

"Yes, not at all."

"Nobody we would know. Alright, so why do we care about her? Or him."

"Well, she writes rather well."

"Really?"

"And she has been through a lot."

"No doubt. But why do we care?"

"Oh, I think you'll like it. She has only given me a couple of chapters—"

"Oh, I'm not sure. Is it a sensitive coming of age story? Nobody understands me? Why are you not responding, Schmenk?"

"It's some of that. But I mean good, so far."

"H'm."

"You sound blasé."

"Does this memoir contain some awful secret, to create interest. Something weird?"

"Not that I have seen."

"You look discouraged, Schmenk."

"Here I thought I'm doing something creative."

"But of course you are. Do you think that I'm just criticizing you? Not at all. Why don't we talk about the novel instead? The "great big book of life," no?"

"Okay."

"Do you have something really substantial to discuss?"

"Well, there is a novel, too. You're probably not going to like it."

"Schmenk, Schmenk... Why so pessimistic? Don't you want to tell me about the story?"

"You'll freakin' hate it."

"Not necessarily. Tell you what, I'll summarize it for you. There's a young single woman. She lives in New York City. Works at a publishing house, or a glitzy, insipid magazine –'checking facts' – or a fundraising concern. She has several ditzy girlfriends, and there is a string of lousy boyfriends, too. I mean the boyfriends are all kooks, untouchables, they only want to get laid, but they are complete morons. In fact, Schmenk, no one in the story feels like they are especially smart. You read ... And you feel trapped in an unamiable *pastiche*. You feel starved for something of substance to eat, you're marooned, you're drifting away from the mother ship, totally lost."

"Maybe you just don't like the genre anymore."

"Yes, or maybe it's because we publish a novel of this kind every month. They sell their little quota and then are quickly forgotten, most of the time. And the writing? Well, in this popular style, 'big words' are to be avoided, you know. No sense in confusing the low-brows. No, we want a language that's personal, that's first-person, that readers will recognize as speech that is quite ordinary rather than refined or elevated. This common speech is really the province of specialists now, isn't it, Schmenk? 'Oh, what a pretty spell we weave with words.' Is this the type of work that you would like to champion?"

"Don't you think there are any worthwhile novels published any more?"

"Oh, maybe. But do we publish them?"

Schmenk looked from his boss to the parcel, still in its envelope, in his lap, and dumped the package unceremoniously and with a loud thump into the side wastebasket.

"Oh, but there's no need to be dramatic." Mr. Herlihy wheeled his desk chair over the carpet and started to fish the parcel out of the basket. Schmenk came to his senses then and assisted him.

"I'm sorry," he said. "Please," holding his hands out for the package. His boss frowned, but only briefly.

"Why do I say these things?" Mr. Herlihy wheeled in his chair, looked out the window at the Manhattan skyline. With a sage expression, he made the steeple with his fingertips – all gestures that even to him, looked something like those of the ham actor. Schmenk was frowning.

"Indeed, why do I say it, my friend?" Looking out the window again.

Sotto voce and mumbling a bit, "Beats the shit out of me," the under-assistant said.

"Is it to make you feel bad?"

Schmenk arched his eyebrows.

"But of course not. No, here is the point. Of this diet of pablum, as I say, the public is going to tire some day. Then we are going to have a ton of unsold, useless product on our hands. I'm afraid that it is a matter of survival. I am putting the matter in cold-blooded business terms, even though I am speaking here of the late, great world of ideas in America. Certainly, something that you and I, and everyone we know, care very deeply about." He said this solemnly, but a hint of a smirk played about his mouth, which Schmenk, in his simplicity, did not notice.

"The late, great world of ideas, I say. The noble enterprise of literature. Heirs to Balzac, to the Brontes, to--. Where is the next <u>Robinson</u> <u>Crusoe</u> going to come from, my learned friend? It is not a time to be complacent."

"You're killing me, Marty."

"What?"

"Why don't you just tell me what you want?"

"Here is Point One. Like it or not, the public is going to notice that the so-called intelligentsia does not exist any more in America."

"Doesn't exist?"

"No, Schmenk, we are hustlers and pretenders. All players in a charade. The loyal opposition is in tatters, the moneyed classes, and the CEO class, their interests have moved to the fore, and we throughout the media have been complicit in this. Think for a moment about how we continue to export American jobs of quality – oh it's a catchphrase now, the politicians always talk about it, but no one ever does anything. This exporting of jobs has already happened. That battle has already been lost. And, do you know, Schmenk? You and I were not there."

"No, really, it's true," Herlihy started to say, expecting Schmenk to demur, but the junior partner did not protest.

"Nothing," the senior editor continued, "interferes with the master plan. Even the minority political party has hardly a voice any more. They can't utter a single sincere thought. Why? It's as if the entrenched powers that be say, 'We will tolerate you as the voice of the opposition, but in fact we only regard you as powerless whiners. So don't complain *too* much, or we'll squash you.' There is nothing noble about defending the interests of the privileged, Schmenk. But that is what we in the establishment have been doing in recent years."

"Among journalists, there are some who accept secret money from the Government to trumpet Administration-friendly viewpoints. Others fabricate quotes from made-up characters, and their editors are none the wiser for it. Almost all are complicit in the peddling of half-baked ideas that serve the interests of the politically powerful. Have you heard about the presidential advisor who is rumored to have leaked state secrets? If it is true – and what foot-dragging there has been in seeking the truth, by all parties! – then he ought to be pilloried for his misdeeds, and for the general viciousness of his character. But he apparently occupies a position of total trust with our president. If he is ultimately hounded out of the inner circles, he will only move on to more a more lucrative glade within our esteemed media establishment, or in the equally shady world of political consultants. Don't you see? Can't we, just once, take a higher road?"

It was a rhetorical question. Herlihy covered his face in his hands and moved restlessly in his chair. Schmenk stood up and took the wrapped-up manuscript in his hands, as quietly as possible.

"No, leave it," Herlihy said. He uncovered his face, which looked kindly, avuncular. Schmenk only walked out of the room thoughtfully.

One day the following week, Schmenk spoke to his boss again. "I have been thinking about what you said last week."

"What I said?"

"About presenting new ideas and things."

Herlihy made as if to shiver, while a distasteful expression crossed his face. "'New ideas'? You are making me very uncomfortable."

"But you said you wanted to try a new road, or something like that."

"Schmenk, it's dangerous to think that way. Have you told anyone else about this?"

"Can't you be serious?"

"I was probably talking out of my head, Schmenk. Forget about it. It isn't an easy problem to solve. Now, you take me."

Schmenk looked as if he would rather speak himself at that moment. But he surveyed Herlihy's two leather chairs and settled into one nearest the window.

"I think I can say of myself that I'm basically impervious to any new ideas. Oh, I'm not there yet. But I'm close."

"Jeez, you make it sound like that's something to be proud of."

"Well, but it is, isn't it? Why should I trouble my mind further? Isn't it burden enough knowing what the public wants, and what it needs? It is a great responsibility. You know--"

"Yes," Schmenk muttered, as if mostly to himself, "you've been 'in the business' for seventy-five years."

"Schmenk, I can't hear you. How many years?"

"Oh, I'm sure you know best." Feeling utterly deflated now. 'Impervious to new ideas.' Did Herlihy actually say that? What a freaking absurdity! And – good lord! – was Schmenk heading down that primrose path himself?

"But I think there was something on your mind," Herlihy said.

"No."

"You had some … well… ideas. So let's talk about them."

"Well, it was this," Schmenk began tentatively. "There's a novelist who lives in a nursing home nearby. Charles Brainard."

"Oh, sure."

"Do you know him?"

"Ferocious writer, as I remember. Totally uncompromising. His novels are all out of print."

"Well, I know him, slightly. I studied with him many years ago."

"Does he still write?"

"God, no. He's retired. People say that his own brilliance drove him out of his cotton-picking mind!"

"Oh, Schmenk, don't be dramatic."

In a calmer voice, "But that's what I heard about him."

"It sounds like a fishwife's tale. What else do they say about him?"

"Well, there was a woman that he loved. But it never worked out somehow."

"H'm'ff," Herlihy snorted. "Tell me this, if you know. Is his writing as good as I seem to remember?"

"Oh, I think it is. He was a Shakespeare of vernacular language – just rollicking, brilliant. But he was never only colloquial, if you know what I mean. There was real poetry and purpose in the language. A method to his madness, I guess I mean."

"Yes, his books were extremely well received, at the time. You think he can help us somehow?"

"Well, he is bound to have ideas. If we can tap into them somehow. I think you said you would like to restore some luster to, to—"

"Yes, to the late, great world of ideas in America."

"Well, maybe he's our man."

"Do you think he'll remember you?"

"Oh, I doubt it."

"God, he'd be - nearly eighty. But, is the man lucid?"

"I read a short newspaper article about him. He seems to drift in and out. And some days, he's not lucid at all."

"Oh, I don't know, Schmenk. I don't know about this. Can he really help us?"

Schmenk sat looking a little nonplussed, not saying anything. "There might be a book in it. Or maybe just some magazine articles that we could place in one of the magazines we own."

Herlihy watched him and made the steeple with his fingers. "Your idea is, we ingratiate ourselves, and just extract the man's ideas – whatever is usable, I mean – and turn the material to our own advantage?"

"We would credit him, of course."

"I'm not sure we could give him a credit. A by-line."

"But why not?"

"Well, no one remembers him, for one thing. What kind of attention would it get? But if we were to simply borrow from him … to pursue your idea … to use some of his ideas, just as if he were some talented speech writer, or literary paladin… To pull him out of his wretched reveries, whatever they are, and cannibalize what ideas he has remaining, to be improved on by some hacks that we assign to the job. Maybe you, or me… Just take whatever he has to give, then discard him like a half-eaten piece of fruit. Is that your idea?"

"Actually, that is not quite where I was going with it—"

"Schmenk, it's brilliant. You're making a believer of me. We could start by telling him that we want to reissue his early novels."

"Do we? Want to, I mean?"

"Of course not. We're running a business here, not a charitable institution. Why don't you try and go see him. You know what to say. Do you want me to go with you?"

"No, that's not necessary," Schmenk said.

"Waste no time. You're onto something!"

Herlihy was beaming. But Schmenk had his doubts about the senior man's approach. He got up slowly from the chair and seemed about to say something more. But Herlihy had already moved on and was busy.

The object of these mad and feverish speculations was sitting quietly at a window chair at a nursing home in one of the outer boroughs. He was sitting in the main common area of his floor, an area of perhaps thirty feet square. The room was well lighted by windows, and the floor was mostly open except for the sitting chairs which were arranged singly or in banks, and incidental tables and a card table. There was also a small kitchenette without a door, with urns of coffee and hot water on the counters. There was a television, from whose disagreeable droning Brainard habitually sat as far away as possible. He generally preferred to stay in the common area, except at night. He felt at times a dispiriting loneliness in his room, which was less well lighted and which he shared with three other men.

The common room was in this respect something like being in a patio in mild weather, or a small public piazza, where one might see birds flying, or the play of trees in the wind. There was more variety for the eyes, more diversion, than in his private room, even if the passing scene was really very predictable. And from his window seat he could also see something of the world outside. His eyes, even if they were open, often had a vacant and unseeing look when he was thinking back on his earlier life. But he did emerge from time to time, and was capable of speaking with total clarity and force. The retired author had gone through what savings he'd had, including the exiguous royalties from his novels. Like a gathering stream in reverse, those royalties had become a trickle in the course of years. In between he'd had some lucrative work in Hollywood, mainly as a script doctor.

Brainard had first come to Hollywood as script supervisor for a science-fiction television series. The job was in some ways a sinecure position, paid for by the studio which also hoped to use Brainard in a more important role, writing a film script or two. He did not take the job very seriously, at least initially, and neither did any feature films develop. Some weeks he was more script doctor than supervisor, remaining on the set and rewriting long stretches of dialogue to make the scenes less wooden, or more believable, or whatever.

Shooting often went late into the evening, and Brainard would sit off on the periphery of the set, which was several different rooms of a space ship which had been set up in a warehouse-like building. Most important of these rooms was the command and control center. Here on the brig, many of the passions of humans and assorted extra-terrestrials were acted out, and in crew members' cabins, and sometimes on planets that were visited, where the foreign landscapes were rendered in the rudimentary fashion of that time, the seventies.

Many of the extra-terrestrials were hideous. Brainard, who did not create any of these characters, was often at a loss how to give them credible motives and drives and such. Some had antennae on their heads, and other odd appendages, some resembled large woodchucks that stood on two feet. The Alizarian women were different. They were exotic and often pretty, and only the slightly elongated ears and their hyper-intellectual manner showed that they were not earth women. It was never clear to Brainard, and probably to most viewers as well, if these jump-suit-clad women resembled earth women in the full biological sense. They had from time to time seemingly unconsummated romances with male crew members, who were nominally earthlings.

Brainard fell in love with an Alizarean woman, too, or at least with the young and pretty actress who played her. Lisa was his joy and misery during part of Brainard's California years. He lived life acutely then. They were some of his happiest years. It's true that he all but neglected his "art" while helping to fashion what were mainly pedestrian dramas. But his serious writing, his art, had given him, apart from the personal satisfaction, mostly obscurity and poverty, whereas in California he'd been able to purchase a small convertible car, and to live in style in a pleasant little house on the ocean.

In one of his novels, Brainard wrote that in its ordinary course, the three stages of love were fascination, derangement, and disenchantment. But in his own case he had been struck all at once, and fatally.

Those days still seethed in his consciousness, or sometimes they were a balm during the lonely hours at the nursing home, when he often sat in a chair by the window and watched the simple, stripped-down drama of life on a Queens street: the old Chinese lady who walked to the market for vegetables each day, the huffing city busses, the free wandering cats that he learned to recognize by their coats, who scavenged and tip-toed carefully on the sidewalks. But there were days when the past felt more real to him than present surroundings. To the other querulous residents, to the nurses, and whomever, Brainard at these times had simply gone into one of his fugue states. In his own mind, though, was an intensity of feeling that was incommunicable, and not to be guessed at in the old man's vacant eyes, as he withdrew from the hum-drum world around him.

It was with great surprise that he saw, on one of his lucid mornings, dark-suited Schmenk being led toward him by the Haitian day nurse, Marie. Brainard only looked at him critically, a thumb and finger drawn to his mouth. He did not extend his hand when Marie told him that he had a visitor, but only sat in his window chair in a sort of regal attitude, as if a petitioner approached him with some request.

His hair was white but rather full for one his age. Sometimes he wore turtleneck jerseys that covered the sagging skin of his neck. He was, still, a sort of handsome and leonine presence.

"You do want to talk with him, don't you, Charles?"

"Delighted, Marie," he said, politely but without warmth.

Strange, he felt himself zoning out, even as the man opened his mouth to speak. Was he a Jehovah's Witness? Who the hell else ever visited him? But no – a first glance suggested that here was cunning untouched by principle. The Jehovah's at least believed in something.

"I'm one of your students."

Was it possible? Brainard had obtained a few teaching positions at colleges during the lean years, on the strength of having been published before. "Ah, there were so many. And do you still write?" Brainard was curious about the young man, in spite of his mistrust.

"No, I'm afraid not. I'm an editor, now."

"You've gone over to the 'dark side.' " Brainard had been hearing this expression, and if he was unaware of the context, nonetheless he liked the sound of it.

"Oh, I hope not."

"No doubt you are doing all you can to – burnish the intellectual landscape, shall we say."

He sees right through me, Schmenk thought. He thinks I'm a conniver.

"Are you, then?"

"Mr Brainard?"

"Doing – you know."

"I suppose I try."

"No doubt." Brainard glanced out the window. A fat woman entered the variety store. One day he was going to walk over there and ask for a nice cold cut sandwich, of mortadella and provolone, and tomatoes and sliced up pickles and some vinegar dressing. His mouth opened slightly at the thought of this sandwich, and he could almost see himself walking out of the store with it, in a brown paper bag that already showed some slight leaking from the olive oil. In this mental image he appeared younger than he did now.

"Sir, do you keep up with today's literature?"

"'Literature?' Young man, I have earned the right not to be bored shitless. It's a strain for me to read, at my age, and unless the rewards are very great, I just can't waste time. Does this surprise you? I used to think, when you are blessed with a wide-ranging and imaginative mind, what need does a person have for popular entertainments? Oh, it's alright if they are very first-rate. But when there are fascinating dramas that continue to play in your mind, along with flashes of wit, what need does a person have for these preposterous movies and books of today? Why should I waste time on vapid and vaporous novels, or movies that are fitfully entertaining at best? Do you see?"

He could feel himself zoning out again. His visitor's lips were moving, but Brainard could not concentrate on the words. He heard the faraway-sounding trumpet fanfare, that always signaled the beginning of his fugue states, that faintly heraldic-sounding melody that seemed to issue from a deep green forest. Then he always saw himself in his rocket ship, he could hear the chimes and the "standby" signal outside going whoop-whoop-whoop, faintly through the thick cabin window. The ship was taking him up again, far from

Queens, far from home, wherever it was, and it was not so much outer space that he was visiting, as the furthest recesses of his memories.

He was with Lisa again. It was the end of a long day of shooting. Most of the crew members had gone home. In her trailer, he stood and held her in his arms. The brightly-lit makeup mirror was behind them. She wore the purple, form-hugging jumpsuit. The skin of her face and long neck glistened Alizarean green as he embraced her.

"You must be tired," he said.

"Yes, a little. A shower will be nice."

"But don't take everything off, just yet."

"You want me to keep the make-up and things on? Charles, I'm beginning to think you are strange. Do you like me?"

"I like you more every day."

"You are a mess. Do you, really?" She turned and crouched to see herself in the makeup mirror. "I look strange, though."

"You look lovely." Brainard kissed her neck and his hair felt slightly ticklish against her chin.

"But, this is kinky, Charles." She did not want him to stop, though.

"No, it isn't." Brainard's hands roamed greedily over her body.

"No, it's really very kinky." Lisa twisted again to see herself, over Brainard's head. "My skin is green."

"Don't you worry about that."

His hands reached down her back, while he nibbled at those pointed ears that were compounded of flesh and some sort of flavorless wax.

"Charles."

"M'm?"

"Charles. You have to cool off!"

"I'm sorry, baby. You want to go home and shower? Want me to drive you?"

"I have my car. Can we just cool it for awhile?"

"I'm sorry."

She smiled at him. "Don't let me go, though. Tell me why you like me."

"It's ... just something about Alizarean women."

"What, exactly?"

"I think it's their eyes. Sometimes they're cool and tranquil like deep space. Sometimes, it's like a meteor shower passes through them. Either way, I'm just transfixed."

"You'll have to do better than that. Where is the celebrated writer?"

"Forgotten writer, you mean."

Lisa smiled sympathetically and thought to change the subject. She was a pretty woman in her middle-twenties (Brainard was at least ten years older), although with so much make-up it was hard to tell. Her figure was lithe and graceful.

"What else do you like about – those women. I can't pronounce it."

"I think it's their firm but shapely figures."

"You don't say."

She thought for a moment. "Explain to me, Charles. The eggheads, back then, seemed to like your novels. You showed me all of the reviews on the paperback copies. 'He's astonishing!' 'Highly original!'"

"Don't forget 'crazy.'"

"Yes, you told me about that, too. But it was only one episode, right?"

"Well…" Brainard equivocated, shrugging.

"Oh, I'm not judging you, Charles. But your books don't seem to cause any stir these days, do they? How does that happen?"

"Well, they do say that fame is fleeting. I would enlighten you if I could. You would like to know how a star, how a star of the first magnitude, can be so thoroughly eclipsed. They say that there is no accounting for taste. And it might be, there has been a lack of support, from some who once held out a helping hand to me, however grudgingly. It's hard to know – I mean, what people are looking for. But in any case, my work aboard this spaceship convinces me that something is less than jake in the world of American letters."

"Oh, Charles, you are always joking."

"My, but this is a change of subject, though. Suddenly I feel deflated."

"I'm sorry, Charles. But can I ask you, why don't you write me some good lines? I don't want to just stand on the sidelines here."

"Don't you get good lines?"

"Not so many."

"You're not standing on the sidelines, kid. You're very important to the show."

"So are the guys in the paint department. I just look better in tights."

"Don't put yourself down, Lisa. If you knew how I feel about you…"

"I think I know." She smiled. "Just give me something important to say, will you? Don't make me out to be a joke."

"Belnar is not a joke."

"So you say."

"She's probably the smartest person on the bridge."

"So who appreciates her?"

"A lot of people. *I* appreciate her."

"Thanks."

"This isn't often high drama here. But I can try to do something more."

"You won't forget?"

"I won't forget, kid."

"Thank you, darling. Now will you mind very much if I go home and shower now?"

Brainard didn't forget, either. Lisa's character did begin to figure more in the scripts, many of which were written by Brainard himself. And their quality was such that no one minded when the character of the nominal third-in-command, the exquisite-looking explainer of force fields and spaceship capabilities, assumed a more prominent role in the dramas. The reception was enthusiastic. He was not sure that he quite understood Belnar – her "psychology," nor her mental capacity, which seemed immense - and so in order to keep his artist's bearings he tended to present her as essentially a flesh-and-blood woman. Except, that is to say, for the long and pointed ears, and the habit of mental abstraction that was usually evident in her facial expression. A spirit of romantic love ran through the scripts that Brainard contrived. If he was not entirely faithful to notions of Alizarean psychology, this didn't concern him. Nor did the public seem to mind, in fact audiences responded enthusiastically to the episodes.

One drama, stretching over several episodes, Brainard considered the *piece de resistance* of all his Hollywood years. Lisa-Belnar had a prominent role in the drama, of course. In fact he wrote the scenes in a fever dream, her face always before him. One of the federation's planets, out in the Omega 39 galaxy, is in a sort of clandestine revolt. The local authorities are hard pressed to maintain order, and so a fleet of federation spaceships, like a space-age Roman legion, are sent there to restore order.

The charismatic leader of the revolt is a shadowy figure. In fact the authorities cannot identify him, and yet he inspires and inflames the hearts of the populace. He preaches love and freedom, and independence from the tentacle-like reaches of the federation, freedom from the tributes demanded by them; but just as importantly, it seemed, freedom in thought, freedom in the abstract. This man, with the startling name Byron de la Mole, a transplanted earthling among a mixed lot of drones, humans, and assorted extra-terrestrials, was a revolutionary, and in the federation's view a most dangerous one.

Belnar arrives on the troubled planet, and posing as an acolyte in the cause of universal love and freedom, she blends with similarly-minded locals. Brainard presented her as a creature of cunning, a vamp, even. Soon enough she has infiltrated the revolutionary bands and had an audience with de la Mole. She finds him kind and principled. He makes a sexual advance (which she rebuffs), but is not loutish about it, and she feels no resentment. She finds that she admires his principles, but her first duty is to the federation. And so it later happens, in the penultimate scene of the last episode, in fact, that in a public square, amid many of de la Mole's followers and assorted citizenry, Belnar betrays the leader with a Judas kiss.

It's a tender and passionate embrace. Before it is over, the viewer saw the federation soldiers moving in, and the flicker of doubt in Belnar's eyes, and saw de la Mole's followers attempting to leave the square quietly, in light of the federation's overwhelmingly more powerful forces. When the revolutionary leader is led away in chains, and passes before Belnar standing amid a coterie of federation officials, it isn't hatred that is etched on his face. He looks at her resignedly, with something almost like love, and when he reaches out to dry the tear that falls unexpectedly down her face, the federation guards misunderstand his gesture, and restrain and push him along roughly.

Oh, what other grand parables might Brainard have written! Back in the days when his mind was a creative workshop, and not the cluttered attic, filled with mementos, that it more closely resembled now. If he had found the support, from within and without, to persevere! If it had not been for his struggles with drinking, and the periods of depression. If he had enjoyed a supportive publisher, if he had not been rendered unmarketable by the cultural avatars of his time. If, if…

His audience had responded with acclamation to "The Bliss of Byron de la Mole" (that was his title for the drama, and it referred to that moment of embrace with the duplicitous Belnar), and there were so many other stories to be told, if he could have held out, if he'd been stronger. But his further efforts languished, either staying unwritten in his mind, or completed, only to gather dust or lie entombed in manuscript trunks, or become lost altogether…

Something was tugging at Brainard's conscious mind, which turned out to be Schmenk himself. After having stared and called his name for some minutes, he now pushed gently at Brainard's upper chest.

Brainard started and cried out, sorry to have left his dream state. Marie, the day nurse took notice and began walking toward him with long strides. But he gestured with his hands that there was no cause for alarm.

He looked at his visitor craftily. He was unsure how long he'd been out, and his eyes drifted subtly, imperceptibly, to the clock on the wall. It had probably not been more than a quarter hour.

"Do you have any ideas today that you'd like to share with your public?"

"Ideas. *My* public. But I don't have any 'public.'"

"That's not how we feel, Mr. Brainard."

"Do I assume, then, that others at your firm share your maniacal views?"

"Oh, that's rich. Yes, I'm not the only one. There is one even more senior than me."

"But I'm not sure I understand your interest, frankly. In America I lived a life of crushing intellectual isolation for the most part. I still do. The only intellectual solace that I find is within my own imagination, or in the work of creative artists who have been dead for at least thirty years.

"Do you understand that when I retired from what I will grandly call the American cultural scene, such as it was and is, I was shall we say not on the best terms? It is hard to see into minds that are opaque, but I think the establishment regarded me as a sort of curmudgeon, whose books would not sell. Believe me, when I retired, my writings were basically viewed as an unsaleable commodity. Nothing could be more distasteful than this, in the American marketplace of ideas, shall we say. It was only a few counter-cultural types who kept my name from total eclipse. And now they are gone, and so am I, nearly."

"Things may be different today."

"Things are undoubtedly different, but how can they be better, for an outsider like me?"

"Might you have one little thought, that I could take back to the office with me?"

"A thought? Well, let me see. Usually I just share my thoughts with the four walls and with the sparrows that land on the windowsill here. I was thinking the other day, that it's a good thing that the young retain some faith in human nature. Speaking for myself, I have lost much of mine. To live in this world is to become disillusioned with humanity. It seems to me now that mankind's capacity for cruelty, for self-deception, for creating 'mind-forg'd manacles,' is endless and eternal. The few visionaries who stand out in history – Jesus, William Blake, Gandhi – speak a language that is utterly strange, and barely comprehensible. How tragic it is that such voices are nearly attenuated today, while the popular mind is filled with so much noise and rubbish."

"That's awfully good. See, that's the kind of stuff I'm talking about. Would you mind if I wrote it down?" Schmenk brought out a small notebook. "If you could repeat it."

"Certainly. I hardly see what can come from it. But I do admire your good taste." And Brainard repeated his thought, slowly, with approximately the same words, while Schmenk wrote it down animatedly.

"You know," Brainard said, "this little talent that I had, it was a thing that seemed to sprout up like a weed, that no one attended to, and no one else but me tried to nurture. But I worked like the devil to be a good writer. The soil seemed more receptive in those times. And you can scarcely imagine, you could buy my little stories in bus depots and dime stores and city newsstands, with their brightly painted, only slightly lurid covers. I can show you some of them. Now literature seems to be a field by and for specialists. Anyway, I worked in solitude at my craft. I had my French masters to draw inspiration from. Who needed a cheering section? And so I'm truly surprised to see any show of interest now.

"Perhaps you might be interested in some short, satirical columns. But satire is a difficult medium. As people would know, if they tried to practice it anymore. You may be firing on all cylinders, or think you are, but if you don't hit all of your targets squarely, people are going to fault you. But I don't know if I now have the concentration to sustain… I must reflect upon it."

"Yes. Do that. Perhaps I should leave you now." Schmenk got up and bowed formally.

The nurse stopped by a few minutes later. "I'm afraid that man startle you before, Mister Brainard."

"Oh, it isn't his fault. It's my concentration – concentration" he repeated earnestly - "that's lacking. I seem to drift in and out."

"Don't worry about that, Mist' Brainard. You say the word, I won't let him or none of that kind in here. You just tell me." Her voice had a lilting, French-inflected quality.

"I do appreciate that, *cher* Marie. But it isn't necessary. After all I don't receive so many visitors any more."

He was right about that. The nurse could hardly remember anyone coming to see him. She felt his forehead and smiled, and left him sitting at his window chair.

Some days passed, and Schmenk arranged for another visit.

"I have brought my partner in crime, Mr. Brainard. This is Mr. Herlihy, my senior editor."

Brainard extended his hand to both of them. He seemed more animated and cheerful than on the other morning.

"And what does Mr. Herlihy think about your publishing idea? Is he as determined as you are?"

"Which publishing idea?"

"Why, bringing my novels out! Don't tell me you've forgotten."

Schmenk had mentioned this prospect only in passing - as bait - as Herlihy had suggested. Now he had almost forgotten. "Of course not. No, in fact, it was Mr. Herlihy's idea. Right, Ed?"

"Oh, I remember them well, Mr. Brainard."

The smile returned to Brainard's face.

"But isn't it a bold stroke? I mean, a major publisher bringing these old stories before the public again?"

"It is," Mr. Herlihy conceded. "But you know we do like to innovate sometimes." Looking meaningfully at Schmenk, who nodded reflexively in agreement.

"What kind of a new story do you think might sell right here and now, Mr. Brainard?"

"You may both call me Charles, of course. I must say, I have no idea. New literature is not something that I follow much, any more."

Both of his visitors sat staring at him. A look of disappointment crept into their features.

"Well, what I mean is, when I look around at what the American cultural scene produces today, it is just hard for me to fathom. Sometimes I visit the local movie house, for example. And I must say, it isn't often that I feel entertained. I feel, instead, that I am trapped in something rather tedious. Is it only me who feels this way?"

"Probably not," Schmenk said. "Charles, do you mind if we tape our conversation?" He held a small tape recorder in his lap.

"I don't consider myself an oracle. But if it amuses you to use a tape recorder, why, I have no objection, I suppose. Should I say something about the television or the movies? You see, I can't avoid seeing some of it." He nodded toward the television, a talk show that was a-squawk with some hysterical howling.

"Oh, don't get me started. Sit-coms on television aren't funny, and drama shows feel contrived. Some shows are only about real-life personalities, there is no story at all. These shows seem to be an admission that a state of creative exhaustion – a true decline of the West - has been reached. There are "dating" shows, for example, and "dare" shows where ordinary people ingest disgusting things. No, I can't comment on it right now. It is too much. And ordinary people on remote islands, being observed by the camera – to what purpose, it is hard for me to fathom. The shows are a kind of apotheosis of the mass mentality, of a creeping conformity in society, and a sneer of ridicule at real artistry, which has a different genesis, which is usually born of individual suffering. But whatever its causes, this is what the networks offer now. And what can you say about popular music except that is has been demeaned and manipulated by tin-eared executives, and that worthy artists are increasingly marginalized by the system? Literature? Does anyone even read it anymore? Is it anything but gross excess or touchy-feely novels, or academic exercises, or memoir-writers with tales of their deprived childhoods? Who couldn't tell stories? And the run-on, the self-important voice of today, with no vocabulary, no objective style, and no sustaining interest beyond the world of "I," so that it is really impossible to find any intellectual solace in anything that is contemporary. As I think I said during your last visit, Mr. Schmenk."

"Yes, that is awfully good stuff. Isn't it, Ed."

"Very perceptive," Mr. Herlihy agreed.

"But I don't imagine you could turn it into gold," Brainard said calculatingly.

"Oh, I don't know," Herlihy said.

"I'm afraid I am a voice crying in the wilderness."

Brainard's visitors were silent.

"Which book might you bring out first?"

"Which book?" they repeated.

"The first one has got a strong story line." Brainard looked from one man to the other. "Unless you think The Coral Sky has more possibilities? That's a very demanding book, though."

"Well," Herlihy said.

"And there are others. Some I even published using pen names. You might not even know they are mine. Let me show you."

"It's not necessary," Herlihy said.

But Brainard rose from his window chair, saying, "Come to my room for a minute, I'll show you." He raised himself energetically, and with an unusual vigor he walked in his slippers out of the day room and down a corridor, his visitors alongside him. In his room he walked toward a small cabinet atop the dresser next to his bed. Schmenk and Herlihy waited just inside the door. The junior editor felt some vaguely human unease, at these probably vain hopes that he and Herlihy were kindling in the old man.

Brainard paused in front of the dresser and supported himself with one hand on its front corner. Covering the front of the small cabinet that sat atop the dresser was a small bolt of dark fabric, a sort of curtain attached to a rod. Brainard carefully drew aside the curtain to reveal a row of fifteen to twenty books, some hardbound but mostly paperbacks, and of a faded, vintage variety for the most part. "Here, let me show you." He drew out one of the paperbacks, whose cover at a glance bore the still-bright reds and golds of a typical nineteen-fifties scene-painter.

"Well, well," Mr. Herlihy said. The cover showed a brunette in an interesting state of *dishabille*, and views of fire escapes and rooftop chimneys, and a truanty-looking young guy in rolled up shirt-sleeves.

"They do not make them like this anymore, do they," Schmenk said.

"Indeed not," Herlihy said.

They both handed the books back to Brainard, who looked at the covers for a moment before returning them carefully to the cabinet and drawing the curtain again. As he did so, his visitors looked at each other and shrugged. Schmenk frowned briefly.

"I want to go back to my *piazza*," he said. "It's too – confining – otherwise," he gestured as they walked slowly back to the day room.

He sat down in his window chair again. "So, you think about it." His eyes were getting the faraway look. The spaceship theme started playing softly in his inner ear.

"Perhaps you're tired," Herlihy said.

Brainard appeared to smile, slightly and wistfully, without agreeing or disagreeing. His visitors made to leave.

Brainard did not extend his hand. He was already entering his private zone.

In the elevator lobby, Schmenk said, "That's some care that he takes with his books, isn't it?"

"Fascinating."

"Like it was a magic cabinet behind that curtain."

"Well, but it is, to him. That's his own world of wonders in that cabinet."

"I don't know, maybe we shouldn't give him any more false encouragement. I mean, if we're not going to reissue his novels."

"You saw them. How could we publish those musty things?"

"But you don't know what's inside them."

"I'm not really interested, at that."

"Then maybe we shouldn't pursue this."

"How can you say that? The man still has extraordinary ideas, doesn't he? You have them on tape, for God's sake!"

"But no one wants to hear them. As he said, he is a voice howling in the wilderness."

"I am not sure of that. Schmenk, there is a story here someplace. We only have to – extract it!"

"I don't follow."

"Couldn't we take some of his ideas and present them in one of our newspapers or magazines? Make them palatable, of course, and present them anonymously?"

"Why anonymously? Why not credit him?"

"Because it's more mysterious this way. We can create some 'buzz.'"

"Sort of like the masked marvel," Schmenk said dryly.

"That's not bad. No – wait! I have an even better idea. He's the ghost writer for some good-looking male model."

"But I don't understand. Why do we need any go-between at all?"

"First, because people would say, 'Oh, he's just another old-head.' And second, we would have to, let's say, simplify some of his writing."

"No sense straining anyone's vocabulary."

"That's the idea. But you just know he would be difficult about our editing his writing. Creative people are funny about that stuff."

"Do you think the public would accept that these acerbic columns are written by a narcissist who spends three hours a day staring at himself in the mirror?"

"You might have something there, at that. I must think about it."

Schmenk walked into the senior editor's office the following week carrying a folded up newspaper. "I think," he said, "that I saw some of your handiwork in one of the gossip columns this morning."

Herlihy only looked at his colleague with a sly, bemused expression.

"'Who is the swinging shock-jock with a headful of ideas that he can't say on the radio? We hear that his no-holds-barred column will soon be appearing regularly in this newspaper. All Kitty can say is, welcome to the world of print, and godspeed!'"

"Well?" Herlihy was making the steeple with his hands, and looking cagily at his colleague.

"It's got a certain punch. I don't quite understand why you always feel you need a gimmick, that ideas have to be whipped into a *soufflé* for the public."

"Ah, my learned but comparatively inexperienced colleague—"

"I know. You have thirty years in this business."

"Exactly. But as it turns out I have abandoned that idea."

"Really? Why?"

"I finally listened to the man's radio program this week. I know, the corporation has recommended him as the perfect mouthpiece for our ideas – well, not ours, but, you know… God bless him, the man is a total nincompoop! I have never heard such puerile and juvenile 'humor,' so-called. I can honestly say, there was not even a shred of an idea, amid three hours of hokum and ballyhoo. I'm told that the corporation, bless its heart, pays him millions of dollars every year. And he has a coterie of assistants, none of whom seem any brighter than he is. And if there is humor in what any of them say, it is not irony, not a humor of the mind but of bodily functions, rather. Then he has some sycophantic callers-in, whose simplicity is also very shocking. The man's mind must have stopped developing at the age of eleven, to listen to him. It's a shame, in a way. The man is so precisely in touch with the intellectual tenor of our age, and yet - he won't do, Schmenk. Not for our purposes."

"I think I could have told you that, if you'd asked me," Schmenk said modestly.

"No doubt, you can speak with more authority than I about the products of our popular culture. Anyway, I'm afraid that the public is not going to accept this man as the next coming of Ralph Waldo Emerson."

"Eh. Don't feel bad. Maybe we can still give some print space to Mr. B. No gimmicks this time. What if I were to write a personality profile about him, and include some of his comments? I know it has been a while since I tried my hand at a profile, but I could work something up I think. And then he could get some of his ideas out there, as we'd planned."

"But the ideas need a certain buzz. They need a 'spin.'"

"'Buzz.' 'Spin.' I don't get it. Why do we even bother?"

"But you don't think I've given up yet, do you? There is always a solution, my learned friend. Remember, no toss is too great for The Hurler."

"I'll remember that, Mr. H." Schmenk had a kind of sinking feeling in his stomach. The boss was like a bulldog when he got hold of an idea. An ornery old—

"Schmenk! But I've been barking up the wrong tree entirely! Our man is the ghost writer for some beautiful egghead super model!"

"Excuse me?"

"Can't you see it, Schmenk? We present his commentaries as hers. A column – call it, 'From The Top Of My Head,' say. Beauty *and* brains, all in one gorgeous, pouty, cotton-picking package."

There was an ecstatic grin on his face, and Schmenk almost imagined drool coming from Herlihy's mouth.

"The public will just eat it up. This pouty pontificator is going to be big, really big. She is going to make intellect look sexy!"

Schmenk looked at him for a long time, unsure whether the senior editor was sincere or only putting him on. "Boss," he said at last, "I think that maybe you need a vacation."

"Not at all. Just you give me some time to work out the details." Herlihy swiveled in his chair and looked out the window.

Back in the main day-room, meanwhile, on a late morning, Brainard could hear the small trucks lumbering away on the ground below, and he studied the blinking lights of the control panels on the inner screen within his mind. Those vast and intricate controls filled a console before the reinforced forward window of the ship, and he would be primary for working them on the upcoming mission. It seemed a tremendous task for one man. But he was always alone at the beginning of these journeys that were his fugue states. Then his mind would gradually fill with ghosts of the past, with memories that grew vivid once again.

He remembered another evening in Lisa's dressing room, at the end of a long day of shooting. Lisa was uncharacteristically silent this evening. With cleaning pads she had removed the make-up from her face. Then she said to Brainard that she thought she was falling in love with someone else.

"But you love me," Brainard said lightly.

"Oh, you've been good to me, Charles. I know."

"Maybe it's just a passing fancy, yes?"

"I don't think so. There's a certain way that he makes me feel."

"That I don't?"

"I don't want you to feel bad."

"It isn't that ham actor that you sometimes go to the mess hall with?"

She didn't say anything.

"No! It is. Lisa, you can't be in love with that young man."

"Why not?"

"But you can't love him. He's a shaggy puppy, for God's sake!"

"I guess I can't talk with you."

"I'm not judging, I'm just trying to understand. We're living pretty groovy lives here, aren't we? What am I doing wrong? Would you rather that we marry? Settle down, and all?"

"It isn't that. I'm not faulting you at all."

Brainard held a stronger argument in reserve. "But, Lisa, he's a Dremulan."

She loved a Dremulan with pointed ears like her own. But where the higher beings of Alizarea were noted for being supremely rational, the Dremulans were to all purposes pre-rational and pre-verbal. Their kind emitted only bestial grunts, nominally a 'Nyeh,' sound, with variations, that must be modulated to indicate the basic reactions of approval, worry, dislike, and so forth. Like all of his kind, there were deep horizontal furrows in his forehead (Alizareans' were smooth), but they were most definitely not from mental concentration. Brainard couldn't stand to think of him holding Lisa in his arms.

He tried to tell her that the Drem was a beast, he was not worthy of her, not at all a fit intellectual companion for life's journey. The man (was he a man?) was typical of his kind, all Omega 45 galaxy swagger and no substance.

"Don't be prejudiced, Charles. Anyway it's only a role that Chris is playing."

"Lisa, he's no good for you. He'll break your heart."

His hand was reaching out to her, it was as if he was trying to speak her name. But his throat was very dry and no words came out. The day nurse, Marie, came by and offered him a drink of water.

Brainard had forgotten the day, but Herlihy and Schmenk had arranged to come by again that morning, for what Brainard had begun referring to as another recording session. Schmenk would position the small tape recorder on some close-by table, and with the prodding of his two visitors, the old man would give voice to his animadversions on the passing scene. Brainard had felt saddened by the morning's recollections, and so he would have welcomed almost any sort of guests. His mood improved, however. Marie, the day nurse, making her rounds at the backs of his visitors, wore an exaggerated look of mistrust on her face. Brainard started to get out of his chair, but his legs felt stiff. He wanted to refill his mug with coffee, which had tasted especially good to him this morning. Maybe it was only his resurgent spirit that gave the coffee its particular savor. Then Marie and his two guests, all of them at once, offered to get him his coffee from the large urn off in the side room, and Marie went off with his cup. She returned with his coffee and he thanked her.

"What was I saying? Yes, it must now be ingrained in America's popular culture that you do not under any circumstances challenge people to think. Where films, for example, once offered wit, intelligence and irony, today they are for the most part crude, moronic, and completely pandering to the anti-intellectual miasma of our time."

"Too true," Schmenk offered.

Herlihy sat there thoughtfully. Brainard discourse on other topics, and after awhile his eyes closed with mild fatigue. He savored the taste of the coffee in his mouth, and did not go off into any fugue state.

"Maybe you're tired," Herlihy said.

"Not so much. But maybe you have enough material for today. What do you plan to do with these conversations?"

"Well, maybe we could collect them for publication." In fact they had already started to, but Brainard was a selective reader of the tabloids, and had not yet remarked upon the singular fact that a strange woman was voicing his own thoughts publicly.

"And what about my books?"

"Your books," Herlihy said, stalling.

"You do still plan to reissue my novels. Don't you?"

"Well, about that—"

"That's being revisited," Schmenk said.

Brainard's eyebrows went up.

"You can imagine how busy we are," Herlihy said.

"You have no contract to present to me? You have worthier projects in your mind?"

"Well, no, sir. To me, not worthier." Herlihy was flustered, and wondered for a moment if he might have expressed a sincerity, for the feeling was novel to him.

"Well, we can leave it at this, for today," Brainard said. "I don't want to be confrontational. As I have always said, I wrote the books that I wanted to write, I spoke the things that I thought needed saying. If this is really barren soil around us, well, I have tried my best."

"Oh, but don't be discouraged, sir," Herlihy said. "Believe me, Mr. B., I am deeply sorry that the world is such a shallow place."

"Don't blame the world, friend. You make it so," Brainard said impatiently.

He continued, turning in his chair slightly, "I sense about you, Mr. – Schmenk, a taint of idealism."

"Oh, it's possible, sir," Schmenk said artlessly.

"Yes, and if so, let it live." He began closing his eyes again. His guests collected their things and departed, with polite but somewhat embarrassed nods.

Marie stopped by his window chair. "You know," he said to her, "I'm still not sure what those knaves want with me."

They waved from across the room, and Brainard nodded slightly.

Marie seemed to ponder his words. She studied them and said, "I don't like those rascals, Monsieur Brainard."

It probably had nothing to do with Marie's comment, but from that moment Brainard began to feel an active distrust for his two visitors. What was their game, really? he wondered. The imaginary and hypothetical audience that they had offered for his work seemed to recede further as time went on. The morning's visit left him feeling discontented.

He thought of Lisa again. His warnings to her had been so very prescient, although they had gone unheeded by her. Her star had continued to rise, her press was excellent while she remained on the show. Then she had supporting roles in a couple of films. Later, the Dremulan would lead her down the sordid path of recreational drug use. At least, that was what people said. Then followed in short order her flubbed or misremembered lines, the late appearances, the missed work. It was all so sickening to hear about in the press and through the Hollywood grapevine, so sickening and unnecessary. Brainard thought that he himself might have written something really good for her once again. But that wasn't to be.

The public watched her career spiral out of control. The films became increasingly low-budget, increasingly mindless, a succession of poorer and poorer scripts. It broke his heart to hear Lisa mouth the words of the films, in which Lisa herself showed all the spirit of an automaton. From what he could tell of her personal life, it seemed no more rewarding. There were out-of-control public appearances, and even a minor traffic accident that resulted in a DUI charge. Brainard, in the supermarkets in Ventura, California, turned the pages of the penny tabloids with dread fascination. He was pleased when there was no mention of Lisa, even if by then these highly unreliable stories were virtually his only knowledge of her doings. He'd asked her to stop calling him on the telephone, because she was generally either as high as a kite, or maudlin, and her confused ramblings were painful to hear. And she was still with the Drem, for a while longer at least.

Later on, after she had virtually hit rock bottom, Lisa hooked up with a honey-tongued television evangelist. She even made a few guest appearances on his TV ministry which was based in Mobile, Alabama, and then left the public eye. Well, at least she had gotten off the junk. But as far as Brainard was concerned, she could keep her damned false piety to herself. He had not even spoken to her for several years. Still, on these quiet mornings, it was hard for him not to think of her sometimes, as she was then, when they were both out there on the coast together.

Some weeks passed. Paula Pulovna's regular column in <u>The Spy</u> garnered its share of attention. Some astute readers might have wondered if a fashion model, one of a group of people not normally known for having scintillating ideas, could express herself in ways so irreverent, and so wickedly satirical. The illusion may have added to interest in the column, which was not so awfully widespread, really – the preponderance of 'dictionary' words may have limited its popular appeal – but for Herlihy the experiment was a qualified success. Schmenk meanwhile had an actual worry that this was plagiarism, and might have consequences. Brainard, however, was not one of the readers of the column, nor of <u>The Spy</u> or any other tabloid generally.

He was flattered when Schmenk and sometimes Herlihy arrived, when the little tape recorder was brought out and Brainard extemporized on topics of the day. He felt a slight thrill when the other residents paused from their insipid daytime television shows and glanced in his direction while he held forth with his well-dressed visitors.

This particular morning the rocket ship had taken him up on a mission of more than usual urgency. More than usual because the object of his voyage was Lisa herself, marooned on a distant planet and in need of medicines, or basic sustenance, or maybe it was some kind of writ needed to obtain her freedom – he had all of these things and more on the ship, and was moving with all possible speed in her direction. He had a feeling of complete happiness, even as the ship was rocked by a fairly substantial dust storm on the way out. It was a blissful feeling of homecoming that he felt, knowing that he would see her very soon. Brainard remained strapped in and calmly worked the controls. There was a nebula off to his left, reddish in color, which seemed to exert a pull, a gravitational force, on the nimble space vessel. He worked to counteract it, his face tensed in concentration.

The force that he felt was only importunate Schmenk, tugging insistently on his left arm. This was really too much, he thought. He'd been in one of his fugue states, and now viewed his two guests and the ward generally with a suppressed feeling of disappointment.

"Gentlemen," he said.

"Are we disturbing you?" Schmenk asked.

"Oh, not really. But I don't think I feel much like discoursing today. You know, come to think of it, I never see any result. What is the point, really, if you don't plan to publish any of my – witticisms?"

"We are not really sure," Herlihy started.

"What in blazes are you gentlemen really up to?"

They were silent. A cold fury started to well up in the old man. "'You aren't sure'. You seem awfully vague. I sense that there is some perfidious intent behind your interest in me."

"Mr. B., we are admirers," Herlihy said. Schmenk chewed on his lip.

"You are beginning to look like turkey buzzards to me. I offer you these gems of rare gold, this gift of myself. Do you want to bring my books before the public again? You said that you wanted to."

"About that. The board doesn't feel—"

"Oh, screw the board. I don't care anymore."

Marie, the day nurse, was viewing the exchange with some alarm, and now stopped all other activity and looked on anxiously from across the room.

"Maybe you would like us to leave," Herlihy muttered, sure now that the game was up.

"I would like you to leave. Would you like to hear my parting thoughts??"

Herlihy gestured to Schmenk to take up his tape recorder and prepare to exit. They both stood up.

"What is going on here?" Marie demanded.

"These men are leaving, Marie. Fakers!" he shouted after them. "Pharisees!"

They hurried off several steps, and stopped and gestured with apologies. Brainard raised up the coffee mug close to his right ear and prepared to fire but thought better of it. Some of the remaining warm coffee sloshed on his shoulder, and he winced. Marie came over to assist him.

"Mister B., were you going to throw that? What did those men say to upset you so?"

"Oh, it's a very long story, Marie." Herlihy and Schmenk had retreated hurriedly and were nearly exiting the day room.

Marie gently pried the cup from his hand. "My aim couldn't be quite what it used to be anyway," he said.

She wiped some of the spilled coffee from his shirt. "Mister B., you must let me help you. I would not have let them on this ward, if you had told me."

"It's really alright now," Brainard said. "They won't be back."

"I knew those were bad man, Mister Brainard."

"No," Brainard replied, ruminatively. "They're not bad, Marie. Only misguided."

Some light, hushed conversation returned to the room, even as many of the residents continued to stare open-mouthed in his direction. One became aware of the low din of the television again.

NEWS ITEM: (The Spy, January 14, 200-) We understand that a certain supermodel who has recently dazzled our readers with her incisive verbal gems, is about to take a long rest from her creative endeavors. It seems, so her editors tell us, that the strain of being brilliant *and* beautiful, has simply proved too exhausting, and the well of inspiration has gone temporarily dry. Her column, 'From The Top Of My Head' is therefore going, as they say out in television land, into indefinite hiatus.

AUTHOR'S AFTERWORD

A Stroll Through The Cultural Scene

When I look at the reviews of new fiction in the Sunday newspapers, I can feel, among almost all of the book reviewers, a stubborn and fatal ennui. So many of the novels and story collections seem to be formula driven, and in general to lack vitality and relevance. The reviewers frequently offer only tepid praise for these books, yet often wind up recommending them as, presumably, decent enough works of their kind. Strange, when much of what the reviewer has written, or quoted, suggests that the book in question is often self-indulgent and even foolish. One reviewer describes a collection of short stories, where the language seems to aim for a certain manic monotone, from the sound of it, and which you can imagine is exquisitely boring.

Then another novel is described which sounds like an insider's story, with actual authors visiting a nineteen-fifties prep school and making imaginary, avuncular speeches to the tweedy students. It is sort of a different idea, but isn't it sort of effete? Heigh-ho, the world has moved on already! There is a novel which purports to be the narrative of the butler to some industrialist of the twenties (yawn), and, in similar vein, one that is supposed to be the first-person musings of an understudy to the actor John Wilkes Booth! But why this trotting out of historical figures as flesh and blood protagonists of novels? Unless the author have a vaulting artistic imagination, no one really knows what those people felt, not intimately. Don't authors have personal stories to tell anymore, that are burned into their hearts and souls? No wonder interest in serious literature has dried up.

And when you read the letters department, you note that much of the space is taken up by authors complaining because last week they were savaged by a reviewer there – who will then offer a rebuttal, and so on it goes. When really, one go-around with these unamiable characters was more than enough. The book under review didn't sound very interesting in the first place.

Or there are certain dry-as-dust academics writing about their own "kind" (who may be the only kind of people they know), in stories that seem unleavened by either drama or humor. The results are usually worse, though, when academics try to write about the working poor. They usually imagine a scene that is more sordid than it really has to be. The so-called intelligentsia, among novelists, may think that they are a holy minority, but they are parochial in their outlook, they cannot imagine how the working poor really live, and when they choose to write about anyone other than the usual rogue's gallery of academics, artists, and the like, their voices are attenuated, deracinated, and lacking in authenticity.

And here is a novel of the flaccid "beautiful plum" school of literature, with its far-flung similes, and shifting points of view. But, except for some academics, who really cares to read them? Why must so many stories be told in the vapid first-person-colloquial, which today almost always masks a poverty of language? Then there are those novels that are a jumble of first-person voices, that seem to proclaim, "Last chapter I spoke as an old man, but now I'm a seven-year-old girl!" And the language sounds about like it, too.

I know, no one is forcing anyone to read any of these stories - thank God it is a free country - and, who knows, the books may have their reasons for being. Here are stories, at any rate, that seem to crystallize some recent trends in what used to be called the world of ideas, or shall we say, literature.

Here is a review of a new novel written by some hare-brained academic, whose hero had an extraordinarily developed sense of smell. He seemed almost clairvoyant in an olfactory kind of way; he could identify scents with individuals, for example. It did not seem like such a bad premise except that, as the reviewer described the story, this unusual ability got the hero's nose out of joint sometimes - or did he say that it landed him in some bad joints? Whichever, I only skimmed over those examples of how the hero used his gift, and I only remember that it all sounded pretty unsavory. What is very useful in the animal kingdom can just make literary creations look like asses, apparently.

In the same issue was a review of another novel, evidently also of the postmodern, precognitive, academic school of self-indulgent writing. The hero-narrator of that novel was preoccupied with scatological functions, and these were the main burden, the reasoned argument, of his story. And in short he spent, like Prince Albert of old, a lot of time "in the can." But what to others is just so much dross, he spun into the gossamer stuff of literature. Or at least, that is what the author must have thought he was doing.

The perceptive reviewer was not so sure. He seemed to understand that "anything goes" today, that writings about the salacious, the sophomoric, and the just plain revolting are all officially sanctioned by the tastemakers, and in fact are almost de rigueur in what might be called the ruminative work of art today. And so the reviewer seemed genuinely torn. Perhaps he wanted to seem "with it," that is to say, in on the joke. In any case, he concluded his review with a half-hearted endorsement, even if he did not appear to have enjoyed reading the book at all. I'm puzzled by this equivocation, which is so common today. It's as though the reviewer suffers from a kind of aesthetic relativism, or has no clear standard of quality in his or her mind.

I read one further review, of a novel which is narrated from the point of view of a ventriloquist's dummy who is on a spree with his handler in an American city. I am curious about this book, though not enough to go out and actually buy it. The hero has some pretty wild adventures. A mere stick of wood (what the creator of *Pinocchio* might call a *pezzo di legno*), he develops feelings for a rather pretty female mannequin that he sees in a department store display window. But his obtuse handler hurries him on, and romance has no chance to bloom. Saddened, the narrator pines for her, like all romantic heroes until, in a different venue, he meets and begins to click with the woman who interviewed them for a cable television show. I have my doubts, as a prospective reader, if the narrator (or the author) is mining any really promising material here. The reviewer, too, worries if the narrative has just the right "tone." Has the author strained credibility just a bit? His presentation is described as brilliant but flawed, and the narrative as "unconvincing" at times, and, yes, even "wooden." I don't doubt that the writing is all of these things, but to me the entire concept seems double-dutch, and has gone very awry. Or have I just failed to enter into the spirit of this modern whimsy?

Though the writing is not to my taste, these authors have clearly been aided and abetted in their crimes by insiders in academia and the publishing world.

There are also venues for "ethnic" writers who write sensitive coming-of-age stories, which are popular with people who think in tribal terms. And for memoirs that tell of a sordid family drama, and which reveal – hopefully! - some deep and awful secret. No doubt you have seen the reviews for some of these memoirs, called, My Rotten Childhood (I Hope You Care), and the like. Well, who couldn't tell stories? And there is a market for superficial, generally first-person accounts of the travails of twenty-something New Yorkers who toil in white-collar professions, and who are about as interesting, after awhile, as sea-sponges.

Here is another recent story that casts an illuminating light upon our media, and in particular the dicey state of the written word today. It concerns a recently published "memoir" or autobiography – in fact it was completely made up - of a female ex-gang member, drug dealer and general dirtbag, whose no doubt elegant prose is said to have made a deep impression upon New York Times book reviewers. I suppose you cannot blame the reviewers, for that matter, because it is the publishers who presented this material as fact; how would the reviewer know otherwise, not having met the author first-hand? Apparently the story broke down when a family member read an account of the author's supposedly sordid past, and she gave the game away when she complained, "My daughter (sister) was no gang member. She never even joined a sorority!" One would imagine, though, that if the author of the so-called memoir of a gangster girl looked uncannily like a Wall Street lawyer, or let us say if she had the patrician looks and manner of a Gwyneth Paltrow, that the editors might have wondered about the authenticity of her story. When the fraud was discovered, the book was recalled from stores like so much bad beef from a slaughterhouse.

That isn't the only recent case of the so-called autobiography that turns out to be a fraud, with "made up" episodes, or the creation of a wholly fictitious persona. When we learn that another author did not really wake up after thirty-six hours in a drunk tank and begin spontaneously dictating his masterpiece, we feel disappointment that he has embellished and simply "made up" so much. That he is only a lapidary author, whose most serious addiction is to coffee, strikes us as sordid and ineffably disappointing. But why does the so-called "memoir" have so much currency in the book trade, anyway, especially when so many so-called "memoirists" are clearly abusing the hell out of the genre?

Or there are the egregious cases of plagiarism, and not of some stray words, but complete passages. Usually it is some "niche" writer, a literary rock star whose credentials the gullible editor wanted desperately to believe in.

And these are only the known documented cases.

The larger picture in the publishing world is that the editor seeks a "hook" to draw in the prospective reader. The true-life survivor story is one, although it is often found to be bogus. A young author with a built-in "demographic" (typically an "ethnic") is hot, and in some cases the editor is so eager to publish his or her story that he is unable to see the vices of plagiarism or inauthenticity in the manuscript. There exists a slavish fascination with "niche" writers, while on the other hand few seem to aim for any general excellence of presentation and content. It hardly needs to be said that if the modern work of literature today is suspected of harboring an unconventional idea, any outspokenness in a topical vein, it is viewed as the kiss of death by the prospective editor.

Go and visit a modern bookstore, and see if you can escape a certain feeling of ennui at the wares on display. There is a tremendous quantity of imaginative and fictional works, which today includes many science-fiction titles, and many works of fantasy. These "fantasy" writers are clearly an indefatigable lot. You can guess from the covers just about what you would be in for as a reader. The illustration might show a Guinevere type of character astride a horse, perhaps wielding an unusual-looking battleaxe, or maybe just a modern-day, garden variety ray-gun. Something about the background - the flora and fauna or the view of the outer "space," or maybe because the horse is really a unicorn - suggests that we are not on planet earth but some other planet, or possibly some entirely different world, if that can be imagined. But the casual browser is really stunned to see that one of these six-hundred page tomes is just one of a tetralogy or more. That is a lot of fantasy!

God bless the readers who get off on such stuff. If the stories could be made to be sexy in some creative way then I would say, Amen, I am all for fantasy. But I doubt that the stories can claim anything sexy, or for that matter anything of the heroic, which would indeed be kind of refreshing in today's world. No, I suspect that these entrants in the fecund fantasy genre merely plod along like so much other genre writing. And for me, whether the reader delights in police procedurals, or that quaint genre, the "mystery," which extends into increasingly odd and remote venues (like ratiocinating – but hardly scintillating – monks, or literary sleuths whose researches adumbrate the world of some celebrated real-life author), or whether a reader likes the light-as-air novel of romance (which is as subtle as the most banal sort of television movie), in a style perky and colloquial, or it may be crudely sexual; or whether a reader seeks out stories which reflect an outwardly "tribal" or other demographic demi-monde; whatever the reader's preference, I am prepared to think that it is going to be a slog of undistinguished and unchallenging writing, that is written "to spec" and has little to recommend it.

Books of this kind might be recommendable as ballast to counteract the frivolity of video games, of "action" movies of the day, of formula television programs, and all things "video," the sine qua non of the younger generation. One could say more about the glittering world of today's films - but can anyone believe a minute of them? Or consider the excrescences of popular music, which must also reflect, in some way, on the august minds of Amerika's cultural tastemakers. Many young people swear by the movies of Quentin Tarantino. Actually there are any number of film-school grads, who may collectively be called psychotic clowns of the MTV set, for whom the tragedy of human violence is a mere stylistic exercise. And these directors do have their followings. Young people are pretty well versed in the latest videos, hardly at all in the classical world. But, as I try to tell them sometimes, Quentin Tarantino is not Tolstoy. And so if much of the printed media has no wit or elevated language to recommend it, it may keep consumers in the habit of reading, but is essentially no more valuable than the lackluster electronic media of the times.

All rational minds must worry greatly to see this profusion of print which never seems to pause, writing that promises so much yet does not bring humanity any closer to genuine enlightenment. So the modern media generally – it is a leviathan that shuns originality, that drowses and dreams only of money.

I think it is fairly certain, for that matter, that to the extent that the would-be artist is challenging in terms of either style or content, to the extent that he or she subverts dangerous complacency, to just this extent in America today he or she is someone that the popular media does not want to see represented in the marketplace, and increasingly, will manage to silence. When I look around at these things, I can't escape believing that the staleness, the inanity of the cultural scene will one day prove fatal to the nation.

Where was the media, and where was that loyal opposition in the Congress, when so much flawed thinking and deception were being put out by the administration in Washington? You hope that, maybe, slack thinking and biased information will be exposed for what they are. And so you think that you are doing something worthwhile when you devote an hour to reading the newspaper. But what does it amount to, really? While it is obvious that a great deal of muddled and self-serving "thinking," has gone on in Washington in our time, what is not often realized is that the media, too, has been complicit in the peddling of half-baked ideas. So why should one be paying attention to media representatives who are not any smarter or more principled than those who are carrying on the business of Government in our nation's capitol – where it would seem that very few politicians, and politicians turned lobbyists, are not immured in the general contagion of corruption.

One would like to see incisive analysis in the media, but how often does one find it? There is so much fluff. One thinks, most egregiously, of certain Sunday magazine sections, with their lengthy and often soporific features; and "theme" inserts like women's fashion, where you see page after page of unappealing female scarecrows and think, with genuine sadness, that the editors are causing the destruction of healthy growing trees for such fluff. Not to mention encouraging those skinny little pigs in their vacuous self-centeredness.

And so, when a person notices the editorial pages of his newspaper expanding in number, but not, generally, in insightfulness, does he sometimes think, What nonsense! What, do the editors suppose that they have so much wisdom to impart to readers, that two and even three pages are insufficient? Most of these columns and guest columns are nothing but the effluvia of politically and culturally connected hacks. If any one of them espoused anything but the conventional kinds of "wisdom" that continue to get mankind into so much trouble, you can be certain that he would be flagged as unstable, subversive, or simply unpleasant, and be promptly disinvited from the party of insiders.

The World Today

Mankind stands at a crossroads in human history. On the world's stage are economic uncertainties, value systems that are in dynamic conflict, and over all hangs an intellectual miasma and a discouragement as to whether any positive change can occur. One thinks of that swath of developing, third world nations – in truth, some of them seem more retrograde than developing - where there is little rule of law, or where extreme ideologies fester, which are based in part on a hatred of all societies that believe differently than them, and which institutionalize the mistreatment and subjugation of women, for example. There are tribal schisms which trump any notions of a common humanity, and which insure, in some parts of the globe, continued chaos and misery.

It is tempting to think of the ethos of many of these societies as something in essence pre-medieval, but perhaps there is no Western epoch that compares. The enemy is ignorance, as usual, but its instruments today are irrational and extremist beliefs that are inculcated (should we say encoded) in the mind of societies at large, and legitimized by tradition. Hatred coexists with a lack of courage and clarity that is being demonstrated by more moderate individuals. Ignorance is always discouraging, but when people cling to their ignorance as if it was a holy relic, it really begs the question of how any progress is possible. If it were possible to engage these people productively, to urge them further along the scale of human development, I would be all for it. But military force, occupations, in themselves, are not the answer.

In America the scene is not to be compared. But if an observer looks upon the outcroppings of American popular culture, or other aspects of American life, it is also possible to see humankind in his more regressive and atavistic modes. Look at the considerable interest that exists for violent spectator sports, like "extreme fighting," which is surely a debasing and dehumanizing activity for players and spectators alike. Or consider the unsavory, lurid world of professional wrestling, where once-admired athletes are now essentially steroid-addled clowns. A match can be seen to offer many opportunities for brain concussion, even in events that are supposedly stage-managed. But no one seems very concerned about this. Or one will read about staged dogfights in some American backwaters. In these forms of savagery, for some, are man's supreme artistic aspirations. In spite of a humanizing cultural tradition which is long established in the West, if not widely valued today, one sees a multiplicity of instances of what might be called "throwback" behavior, of ignorance being worn as a badge of honor. And I could go on. I have not even mentioned the multi-billion dollar video game industry, with its displays of combat, of thuggery, and so on – these seem the special province of undeveloped minds. Meanwhile the American media seems to portray, and to instill in the minds of some, primarily a spirit of hedonism, of superficiality, a fantasy land of specious celebrity "glamour." I wonder, with so many pernicious influences, if America's young people are not losing any appreciation of the spirit of sacrifice, of the value of hard work and of mental reflection.

Whether one looks abroad, then, or at life in the United States, it seems very certain that unless mankind become a great deal smarter, our inevitable future is doom. He needs to become more truly spiritual, and I do not mean by this more "religious." Religion is such an elastic concept, that in history some of its permutations and practical results are truly ghastly. Whatever of genuine good is done in the name of religion, you will see at many points in history the most inhuman barbarians swear that they are fulfilling a religious destiny. Pardon me for being cynical, but in America much of what is espoused in the name of religious values is an appeal to power politics. Its holy grail is the power and personal enrichment that is enjoyed by the in-crowd. So that in this respect, the American evangelical is not vastly different from the imam of the Middle East. Only his God appears to some of us as a little more benign, and a little more human.

I don't pretend that any lowly scribbler of fiction can or even should always engage such themes as I have been describing. But some effort ought to be made to remain relevant, and the author who does so ought not to be stigmatized on that account. The notion of presenting another "personal" novel, a relationship story, or as I wrote earlier, "the domestic drama that has been done to death," can seem like a terribly self-indulgent process given the state of our world. Perhaps I am missing something, but I find rather insipid the insular family drama, where (perhaps) the teenaged, unmarried daughter becomes pregnant, or spouses become estranged from each other, or sisters have stopped talking to each other, or still more tiresome stories of "academics" and the like. If these are the burdens of the novel of today, I want to say, 'Yecch, reality is bad enough!'" No, what I really prefer to see is adventure, and irony, and topical writing. Reading about Janey Jones's domestic troubles is not going to help me to live my life.

Where will the requisite wisdom come from to re-fashion our world, if not from the literary marketplace, if not from establishment religious spokesmen? Where, indeed, in our age which has seen the apotheosis of mass market tastes, and the American who would attempt to think for himself must feel himself more isolated than a modern day Robinson Crusoe? The media streams its millions of daily messages to a public that seems increasingly receptive to the reach of the Leviathan. Whatever its stated objectives – to inform, to entertain, etc. – the media, including of course, advertising, exists primarily for the ruthless exploitation of the individual. To discover the public's weaknesses and interests, and to profit by them. Yet there are many people who do not understand the forces that are at work, or the role that they play in the process.

Regrettably, our own President has been the exemplar of the nation's shortened attention span, and of favoring simplistic answers, of pointing fingers when confronted with a problem, and of this "impatience toward reasoned argument." In a strange and subtle way, the commander in chief does set a tone for the intellectual life of a country. It has become common to hear the President blame the "other party" for any and all problems. The President's understanding of and prescription for high gasoline prices was that we had to pump more oil. (As I write this, a general economic recession has driven down demand and valuations for all commodities, which is a painful and very unwelcome prescription for reining in prices.) Not to conserve, and not to devote more research to renewable energy sources. And I think that if a President displays slack and lazy thinking, it may well set a tone for Americans generally.

A nation's leaders set a tone for discourse, which is something analogous to the conclusions and prejudices that people draw about life solely based on the example of their parents. (The tremendous importance that children generally attach to parental archetypes is a somewhat murky psychological area whose exegesis ought to have been further developed by now.) But the vapid quality of much of the media, the foolishness of many films which appear to be directed to the intellectual abilities of seven year olds, the hackneyed and formulaic productions of the publishing industry, not all of these ephemera can be traced to the door of the executive branch. That wouldn't be fair.

It's a very difficult thing to meld an entertaining story line with compelling ideas. I have attempted to do this in the stories in this collection (with what success only the reader can judge). I would like to see a novel appear that would show the man of high principle misunderstood and scorned by the people who know him; suffering financial losses, career setbacks, and personal obloquy because he does not think like the herd, with the herd's readiness to sacrifice principle and fair play for a quick buck, and anathema toward challenging ideas. It could be a true story of America today. Such a story might be more than a little subversive. If I had the energy, the drive, and the leisure, I should like to attempt it. But hard as it would be to write, I am sure that it would be even harder to sell the concept to America's mass media – touching, as the story must, on some unfamiliar and off-the-beaten-path ideas that would be uncomfortable to some.

The kind of story that I am alluding to has been handled by Ibsen in <u>An Enemy Of The People</u>, where the advocates of "false profits" to be gained from the town's bogus spa waters clash with one highly principled and stubborn doctor. If the pebbly shoals of America's cultural life could today produce an artist with the social vision of a Dreiser, with Dreiser's absolute conviction that the novel of realism is of compelling importance, and if mass media were at all high-minded and not merely profit-driven, then we might see appear such a story as I described. But this seems very doubtful. Even if such uncompromising work could be accomplished, how probable is it that a principled editor would attempt to bring such an effort before the public?

It is sometimes said that the American public has been "dumbed down." But the concept needs defining. The recent travails of American foreign policy could be attributed to a naïve executive combined with bad advice from experienced Washington insiders. But this is not specific enough. That advice is an outgrowth of the "neo-conservative" line of thinking. (It should be noted that many who are classified with the good name of conservatism are more accurately viewed as dangerous ideologues.) The thinking holds among other things that America must be the one unquestioned and invincible military power in the world, to the extent that we do not require the support or cooperation of any of our sometime allies. Further, the basis for this thinking seems to be that America is the moral exemplar of the world, the shining light of liberty, and so forth. But how to support this belief? Are Americans more discerning than people of other countries? Then how to explain our recent voting in national elections? Why are Americans so easily fooled and manipulated by politicians and by political operatives who work behind the scenes? Think about presidential advisors who haven't a shred of conscience, so far as anyone has been able to tell, and who have yet occupied positions of total trust with the executive because of their cunning, and because their vary lack of a conscience seems to favor their endeavors, in the swampy waters of American politics today.

Or are Americans more moral than other people? Excuse me, but how much of the current worldwide financial calamity originated on Wall Street, in arcane and speculative investment vehicles – in Ponzi-type schemes which, to the layman, are akin to selling the same dubious commodity to three or four different people in succession – which attempted to create money from nothing? No longer content to earn their extra few percent interest on loaned money, the wheeler-dealers found ways to package, sell, and re-sell dubious debt as an "investment vehicle," while federal caretakers seemed to lack the knowledge or the will to exercise any control over their nefarious activities. The motive for these risky behaviors was nothing more complex than an obsessive and unparalleled greed that lies at the heart of corporate America.

So, and excuse me for saying it, the notion that the world at large needs America's moral guidance is a very arguable point. The country's military strength is formidable, and I don't think that any Americans should view that as a bad thing. But the idea that America's leaders, recently, are capable of showing a degree of wisdom and restraint that is at all commensurate with our military strength is also very debatable. Looked at objectively, the idea that America must be both savior and cops of the world is a tarnished ideal, and the attitude is for the most part pure jingoism. The notion that all problems can be resolved with military force is also a tenet that bears scrutiny. The proliferation of military weaponry is part and parcel of the neo-conservative mindset that has come to the fore of American foreign policy in recent years. But the results of the build-up and of military interventions have been less successful than we would have hoped for, as I think most would agree.

About My Aims As A Writer

The stories which I have collected here are a distillation of the work of many years. The stories may seem a curious and hybrid form. At times emotionally nuanced, at other times the subject matter is more topical than one expects fictional writing to be, while at other times the chosen language is satire of (hopefully) an unusually vicious kind. In my life I have always held a variety of interests in a kind of balance. In fact I have spent my working life in the manufacturing world, and on balance I think that this has worked out for the best. If I was unable to share some artistic interests with colleagues, I have at least been able to maintain my independence both intellectually and financially. And I don't suppose, if I had pursued a different career, that I would have found colleagues in academia, or in the media, who would have been more companionable to me.

When I was attending high school I was very interested in the great works of literature, and I was about equally interested in repairing radios and building electronic kits. Engineering has been my vocation, and creative writing, at least in recent years, my avocation. I have always worked in the manufacturing world, in jobs that have interested me and offered me a degree of intellectual scope. The desire for self-expression came later, and a quality, call it perseverance or stubbornness, has allowed me to stay at writing. Having personal stories to tell has helped - stories that are burned into the soul, so to speak - and so my creative side was not quite extinguished over the years, in spite of a total lack of contacts among media people, or much fellowship with other writers. I can't help feeling that my writing ought to have been a door that opened to reveal a world of congenial souls, and a fellowship of creative people. But nothing of that kind has happened so far.

As an outsider, it is probably true that I don't "keep up" enough with trends in contemporary literature. It might only be a matter of my temperament, or of simply not having enough free time. "Fiction" today seems to denote something that is effete and impractical, a craft and technique that is too precious when it is not merely pedestrian. And of course for whatever reason, literature of quality seems to reach fewer and fewer people, if I am not mistaken. There seems to be a good deal of genre or formula writing, or the rather boring and self-referential first person voices who lack vitality (and often, vocabulary), and – of course – whatever flavor of the month is being marketed by media insiders. At least, that is an outsider's impression.

It might be true, for all I know, that the novel had its golden age, and that that age is now past. That the novel of today presents mainly the partial, the oblique view, and not the comprehensive view. And some would say that in our commercially-minded era, imaginative minds should exercise themselves in creating interactive video games, or in workmanlike movies that contain no poetry and display no convictions; rather than to dwell upon the esthetic of Dante, of Swift, or the Brontes, and upon verbal ironies. And they may be right, for all I know, but in my heart I don't believe that. There are many things about contemporary societies that I don't understand – for example, many young peoples' fascination with forms of media, while they seem to give so little thought to actual content – and that I lack the patience to try and understand.

Some of the stories here touch upon personal traumas that happened to my family. Of course, the raw material is transformed in the interests of drama, of conciseness, or whatever. I think that trauma of some kind must be the origin of most worthwhile literature (although I don't doubt there are a number of facile authors who prove the exception). Sometimes I don't attempt to deal at all with those traumas, and yet they probably color much of what I write. In various ways I try come to terms with this family drama that always plays in my mind, but not very often by talking about it, and rarely by forgetting. It is probably writing that has been most helpful to me, in terms of providing psychological reassurance. Because trauma does not lie on the surface of a person's skin, to be read there, as it were; and because mental probity, and a certain admirable spirit of perseverance, and perhaps other positive character traits, are not to be read on the surface, either, it is possible that a person with these hidden depths will fail to arouse much curiosity among others. In fact the introspective person, sorting through some family trauma, might instead be shunned by people. I have even been told that in the course of time he or she might fall into a solitude. For me, writing has proven my main outlet for self-expression, and it has often proven a satisfaction and a means of therapy.

I have found it most comfortable to transform and re-imagine real-life events. So I have never tried memoir-writing. And it is usually with a kind of antic humor that I try to write. Like the spinning-plate artists of old-time television variety programs (for those who can remember), I have tried while writing to balance a complex of serious themes while never forgetting to smile. Or more accurately, to be funny, or at least to try to be. And even if the story that I tell is sometimes a sad one, usually I can still smile when I am working, because in my mind's eye the plates are spinning so beautifully.

I sent a couple of the stories in this collection to magazine editors and such. One thoughtful reader wrote at the top of a page that I should hire an agent, because the writing was *very* good. But why should that be necessary, if the writing has merit? What is the likelihood that one would find a decent and conscientious representative, anyway, now when almost everyone worships the almighty dollar? As gratifying as writing has been for me, efforts to reach out to the media, by and large, proved to be (to quote a song that the late British singer, Sandy Denny, used to sing) a one-way donkey ride. So that while I was writing to my own satisfaction, sporadically, as my imagination and the demands of a full-time career allowed, it did seem that I would forever remain a tuneful Orpheus whose fate was to wander a parched and uninhabited desert, unheard except by a few. And I seem to have passed through many hectares in this fashion, too, when I began to think that I might seek a different way to break through and reach a public.

This is by way of addressing the interesting question, of why a would-be author comes to self-publish in this modern fashion, instead of in the time-honored way of appearing in small magazines or in books published by the mainstream media establishment. I began to think that there is a way for an author to control the content of his or her presentation, to avoid the calculating middle men and instead place his ideas directly before a public; there to let his work, his ideas, sink or swim, as it were, without interference. To have the material out there, at least, for some unknown posterity (if that does not sound pompous), even if the author receives no earthly or temporal gratification. To circumvent the snares of America's media establishment, which is apparently inimical to the original voice and particularly so to the iconoclast.

What, indeed, would be gained by circulating more material among America's media insiders? Probably only rejection slips, form letters that implied: our quota for the next several issues is filled, with the work of hacks, cronies, and assorted academics, who by the way, are probably going to bore the shit out of the few readers that we still have for our magazine...

Not that anyone really talks like that.

There was one story that I sent off with particularly high hopes. But I was surprised to receive, in return, one of those form letters, or to be more accurate, an exiguous slip of paper with a demurral printed on it. But what was really singular about the circumstances, the manuscript was returned to me within about two weeks, and this included mailing time. Was my story even looked at? Or was only the cover letter read, or only the first paragraph? Because how else to explain such promptness? No doubt many unpublished authors are submitting material every day – most often, of course, to have their hopes dashed, shall we say, on the rocky shoals of America's august cultural life. How, then, is it possible, that Amerika's cultural avatars could complete a review of a substantial and subtle piece of literature – a short story of over forty riotous pages – can turn this review around, as I say, in less than a week? (I am deducting the four to seven business days when my good friends at the U.S. Postal Service were faithfully processing my mailing.)

Indeed, it does not seem possible. I have worked in a busy office. I would begin each week with a wish list of projects, many of which would remain open at week's end. And compared to these hypothetical editors, I never received nearly so many submittals, nor cherished hopes to be dashed. No, to respond with such alacrity one must clearly be cutting corners, somehow. What I actually imagine is that some nondescript clerk in the magazine's mail room has instructions to pull manuscripts, to ascertain that the sender is not on any insiders' list of names, and can point to no particular connection to the magazine in his or her cover letter, or no narrow academic credentials in the "literary" way, and for all such senders, our clerk's instruction is to pull the still-warm manuscript out of its envelope, stuff it into the one provided by the sender and return it, and include one of those demurral slips. Maybe he or she is allowed to choose a color, for variety, or some variation in the form of language used for dashing hopes, or pouring cold water on the would-be author's dream.

These writings will probably illustrate an iconoclastic outlook. I have a horror of "received wisdom," of conventional and lazy thinking, which continues to get so many people around the world into trouble. I imagine that my audience might be those people who very seldom hear their thoughts expressed in the mainstream media, and who cannot help feeling alienated at times from so many aspects of American society. People who do not mind that an author is occasionally (frequently) discursive, venturing into the topical and political – which areas, I suspect, to narrowly focused "fiction" specialists, are a kiss of death.

Yet it seems to me that if an author is not politically engaged today, then I'm not sure that he serves any purpose. Editors seem to cling to the form of the insular, the personal story, but I'm not sure there is a place for it in a world that is so seriously troubled. If there is a fictional style *du jour* (I suppose I am referring to a sort of low-brow, colloquial style, in the service of themes that are of no great purpose) then I'm sure that I have not mastered it. But writing by the numbers is work for trained monkeys, not the higher primates. The fact is that I have a career, and fortunately am not starving in any garret. I have always written just the things that I wanted to and that I had to.

I have already commented (and perhaps more often than necessary) on a publishing scene that seems to be the product of will-o-the-wisp marketers. For example, books that cash in on the fame of this or that professional celebrity; while the same editors view with indifference, and must even work to suppress, any true and sincere vision of the world. Or consider journalism that rarely gets at the *malaise* of the international scene; and advertisers who show plainly that they view the consumer as a commodity who is to be exploited ruthlessly in the name of profit. There must be others who see around them a lack of spiritual values, a love of speed for its own sake, and a dedication to materialism; who see a sea-change in political life that seems determined to grind down the middle classes into a state of serfdom, while the rich get unconscionably richer on the backs of laborers, shareholders, and consumers.

But rather than to repeat notions that are probably already better expressed in the preceding works, I will close these remarks with the hope that the writings will resonate with some individuals, and that they afford some entertainment, and touch upon experiences and scenes and concepts that are at least a little bit out of the ordinary.

Some people urged me to, "Please, don't include an afterword." But I thought I had expressed my opinions rather well – what other venue might

I ever have? And certainly no one else is going to speak for me. I suppose the argument against an afterword was that no commentary ought to be necessary, if some or many of the more "creative" pieces hit their marks. Or maybe the feeling was that an afterword clashed with the style of the other works. Or was it only that such an arrangement just "isn't done" normally? But if that is the objection, it is no argument at all. And anyway, now that it's done, I'm glad it is here.